Danica Winters is a multiple-award-winning, bestselling author who writes books that grip readers with their ability to drive emotion through suspense and occasionally a touch of magic. When she's not working, she can be found in the wilds of Montana, testing her patience while she tries to hone her skills at various crafts—quilting, pottery and painting are not her areas of expertise. She believes the cup is neither half full nor half empty, but it had better be filled with wine. Visit her website at danicawinters.net

Justine Davis lives on Puget Sound in Washington State, watching big ships and the occasional submarine go by and sharing the neighbourhood with assorted wildlife, including a pair of bald eagles, deer, a bear or two, and a tailless raccoon. In the few hours when she's not planning, plotting or writing her next book, her favourite things are photography, knitting her way through a huge yarn stash and driving her restored 1967 Corvette roadster—top down, of course. Connect with Justine on her website, justinedavis.com, at Twitter.com/justine_d_davis or at Facebook.com/justinedaredavis

T0337225

MOUNTAIN ABDUCTION

DANICA WINTERS

A COLTON KIDNAPPING

JUSTINE DAVIS

MILLS & BOON

First Published in Great Britain 2024
by Mills & Boon, an imprint of HarperCollins*Publishers* Ltd
1 London Bridge Street, London, SE1 9GF

www.harpercollins.co.uk

HarperCollins*Publishers*
Macken House, 39/40 Mayor Street Upper,
Dublin 1, D01 C9W8, Ireland

Mountain Abduction © 2024 Danica Winters
A Colton Kidnapping © 2024 Harlequin Enterprises ULC

Special thanks and acknowledgement are given to Justine Davis
for her contribution to *The Coltons of Owl Creek* series.

ISBN: 978-0-263-32234-7

0624

MIX
Paper | Supporting
responsible forestry
FSC™ C007454

This book contains FSC™ certified paper and other controlled sources to ensure responsible forest management.

For more information visit: www.harpercollins.co.uk/green

Printed and Bound in the UK using 100% Renewable Electricity at CPI Group (UK) Ltd, Croydon, CR0 4YY

MOUNTAIN ABDUCTION

DANICA WINTERS

To Phyllis,
Mama duck's got you

Chapter One

April's lungs ached and her calves where hot and numb from climbing. Her glutes were burning from the near vertical assent of the last push to the rocky and jagged peak in the heart of Montana. Long ago, she and her group of teenage campers had conquered the zigzag trail that had started just outside Big Sky and led halfway up the mountain—the point where most hikers stopped and turned around.

She tried to control her breathing, not daring to seem wanting for air in front of the bloodthirsty teens, the pubescent sharks who waited to feast on any perceived weakness. One of the girls in her group, Grace, had been kicked out of three high schools for possession of weapons, and while April didn't believe the girl would pull a knife on her up here in the woods, she held no doubts that Grace would be the first to slash at her with her condemning words. The girl was brutal.

A few hundred yards downhill, Grace was breathing hard. Her mouth open as she pushed to follow April's path through the loose, rocky scree mountainside. Her green hair was pulled tight against her head, and she was so sweaty that it looked as though she had just stepped out of the shower. There were beads of sweat dripping from her hairline, leaving behind a green tint on her skin thanks to her cheap dye.

When April had been younger, she and her delinquent friends had used Kool-Aid to color their hair, and the results were much the same. It was a strange comfort to see that some things hadn't changed in the sixteen years since she left high school—*left* might have been a slight exaggeration, as she'd been more or less kicked out after she'd found out she was pregnant.

Her hand drifted down to her abdomen as she thought about the baby that had once been hers. If she could guide other kids through the woods, maybe she, in some simple way, could help them navigate their lives and lead them to realize that no matter what life confronted them with, they had the power to break through and conquer the nearly vertical assents.

"Push past the pain, Grace," she called, trying not to sound placating or cloying in her attempt to encourage the girl.

This was Grace's battle, and only she could find the inner strength to keep going, but April could be there to give her support and celebrate with her for the well-earned and empowering victory that came with conquering the mountain. The mountain was a metaphor for so many things in her life, so many choices, so many mistakes and opportunities that she had failed to grasp.

As much as April wanted to think that she wouldn't continue to fail in her life—that instead this one personal victory would be enough to change her forever and free her of being the imperfect human she'd become—she held no false hopes. There would forever be more mountains to climb. Though she would like to think she could conquer them all, there would be times she failed. It was only when she stopped trying to press her way to the top—when she gave up and let the challenges beat her—that she would truly lose, and she would be losing a part of herself.

Perhaps that was the lesson she wanted Grace and the three other kids who followed behind her on the mountain to realize. Each kid had their own demons and hardships to overcome, but she'd love to think she could give them the tools and fortitude to keep pressing.

Grace had stopped and was looking up at her from down the mountain. "This had better be worth it," the girl growled between breaths. "This is the stupidest thing you've had us do, yet."

"If you wanted something easy, you could have signed up for basket weaving."

"I should have," Grace said, trying to catch her breath. "At least then I wouldn't have had to stare at your ass in my face for the last three miles."

She wanted to be mad at the girl for her rudeness, but something about her fire made April check her laugh. Grace was nothing if not authentic and that had to be appreciated to some degree.

"You know, they make creams for cellulite, now," Grace snarled. "If you're going to wear tight pants, you should probably shell out the money."

Strike that, she thought, *the girl is an authentic ass.*

Any approbation she had been feeling with the girl blew away on the high-mountain wind. To argue with her would be an admission that Grace had hurt her feelings, but to let the comment go without rebuttal was to give Grace the win in letting her rudeness go without consequence. Yet, on this mountain, there were better things than words to use in this clash.

She considered making the girl pick up one of the rocks at her feet and put it in her backpack to carry as some symbolic weight about the pain that could be left by words. This girl was the kind who would never respond to physical punishments, but she also wasn't the kind who would follow the rules.

Maybe Grace was April's real battle, not the hike.

She sidestepped around the loose rock near the top, carefully planting her feet as she moved down the steep hill and reached out for Grace. "Here, take my hand."

The girl sneered at her hand and pushed it away. "I don't need help."

"I know you don't want it, but learning when to accept help when it is provided is a strength in itself." She motioned for her to take her hand.

The other three kids finally came around the corner and into view, looking more tired than even she felt. One of the boys, Andrew, in the back was ruddy faced and he had taken off his jacket and had tied it around his waist.

"I've got this," Grace said quietly, as though she did not want the others to hear.

Grace looked over her shoulder at the group and, instead of taking her hand, she moved farther away and toward an area that was even steeper than where April had chosen to make their final ascent.

With every step Grace took, the rocky crumbling hillside shifted and gave way, the incline too steep to allow for any additional pressure. Grace's face pinched into a tight, resolved scowl as she grabbed at the rocks and moved her body lower toward the ground to move her weight to her advantage.

She gained a few feet before the rocks she had been standing on shifted and gave way, creating a clacking of granite on granite as the cobbles smacked against boulders and scattered downward.

Yesterday, it had rained on the mountain, leaving the ground saturated to the point where a major slide was very possible, but something like that was rare. Though, a decade or so ago, a family had been killed in a situation much like this on this mountain. She didn't want to be a headline or a tragedy others spoke about around campfires and wine circles as some cautionary tale.

"Grace, get over here," she said, trying to sound calm as she watched a rock plummet and explode as it hit a boulder.

The girl didn't look at her. "I said I've got this," she growled through her teeth.

April moved closer, careful to stay where it was less steep. She reached down to her side where she had a rope tied to her in case of emergencies. "Listen," she ordered, trying to sound calm but also clear that she meant business, "you need to move toward me, slowly."

More rocks slipped downhill from Grace's feet. The entire hillside where she stood was unstable. If they didn't move quickly, the girl would undoubtedly find herself at the center of a full, earth-shattering rockslide.

Her mind moved to the phone call she would have to make to Grace's foster mother explaining that her daughter had been killed on April's watch. She couldn't make that phone call, not now and not ever.

"I said—" Grace started.

"I don't care what you think you *can* do. I'm telling you, right now, if you don't come toward me and get out of the center of that unstable rock, you will be the next thing tumbling down that hill."

Grace shot her a look like she was trying to decide which was more important—her pride or her welfare.

The girl started to move toward April.

There were the sounds of clattering stones behind April,

and she turned to see the other three kids moving toward her. "Stay back!" she ordered, louder and sounding more frightened than she had intended.

The kids behind her stopped moving, but there was the same sound of clattering rocks below them that had come with Grace's attempt to climb.

She turned to face the small group. "I want you to start picking your way back to where you came from."

"But, Ms. Twofeather," Andrew argued, motioning toward the top of the mountain, clearly unaware of the situation they seemed to be finding themselves in—one she wasn't about to explain. "I didn't come this far to give up now."

"Just follow my orders," she countered, her heart racing as she watched another rock give way, which caused a little rockslide below her. "Go back. *Now.*"

Andrew frowned, but then motioned for the group to follow him back. She watched as they moved, but she was careful to stay still in an attempt to mollify the groaning and shifting mountain.

There were old tales of miners who were looking for rich deposits of Montana gold and silver who heard the mountain call to them before tragedies would strike. Often, the miners would hear moans and thumping that they called "Tommyknockers," and they had become so well-known that miners would rush to evacuate their shafts.

She turned back to Grace as she attempted to get her heart rate under control.

April wanted to move to the girl, to anchor her with the rope so that they would have their combined strengths in case something happened, but adding more pressure to the crumbling slope was foolish. "Come my way, Grace," she said, speaking softly like to a newborn foal.

There was a moan, but the sound didn't come from Grace or any human. Her body clenched at the ghostly sound. The mountain was warning.

"Hurry!" April said, motioning toward the girl. "We have to get out of here. The whole hillside is going to give way."

Grace looked down the mountain. Her hands searched for her next grip as the rock beneath her started to slip.

"Come!" April stood her ground though she wanted to lunge toward Grace and save her.

Grace sprang from the rock and scrambled toward her as the rocks beneath her started to move like sand, sinking and pulsing with each step and pull.

As Grace got near, April grabbed for her, but as she did, the mountain beneath her crumbled.

Neither was safe.

There was no one coming to their rescue, no one who *could* rescue them. Her feet slipped as she moved to cover Grace with her body.

"Hold on to me. Don't let go," she ordered, pulling Grace into her embrace as the world around them fell to pieces.

Grace cried out with fear. It felt as though they were atop a concrete wave. The world spun. Pain rattled through April's body as she flipped and turned, crashing against the ground. A rock hit her hard in the ribs, making a cracking sound.

The dust created by the granite stones hitting one another, filled with shimmering mica, coated her mouth and skin like wayward glitter.

Falling, Grace's arms tightened around her, her nails digging into her flesh.

They weren't going to make it out of this alive.

The mountain they had come to conquer was now hell-bent to destroy.

Chapter Two

Sean McCormack was attempting to sleep. These days, every moment seemed to be filled with either the needs of his job as a firefighter or those of his group at Big Sky Search and Rescue. They'd had three callouts this week, all lost hikers. In the last seven days, Sean had hiked more than seventy miles.

He was exhausted.

Yet, as he thought about the last call—an elderly couple who'd gotten turned around on a trail and found themselves five miles farther into the backcountry than they had intended—he found it nearly impossible to sleep. He pinched his eyes closed, trying.

On his last shift at the firehouse, he'd been up for so many hours that he wasn't sure he hadn't seen an Oompa Loompa skipping around in their kitchen—then again, that could have been his buddy Steve who loved acting a fool when they had downtime. The lucky bastard.

Sometimes it felt like he still lived in a frat house, albeit this time there were both men and women. Everything was always moving no matter the time, things were in a constant state of needing repair, there were unidentifiable smells and everyone was always hungry. The biggest difference was the lack of kegs. Many of the younger guys made up for this on their off time, though, and one even prided himself on brewing his own craft IPAs like he was Hank Schrader from *Breaking Bad*—complete with a few bottles blowing up in his garage and pissing his wife off in the process.

Yep, I'm never going to sleep.

His phone buzzed on the bedside table. He sat up and rubbed his face. The bed creaked under his weight, a victim of too many sleepless nights.

He clicked on the notification on his phone. There was a missing woman and girl, known victims of a rockslide on the back side of Lone Mountain, just outside the ski resort's boundaries. The peak was more than eleven thousand feet above sea level, and it was a hell of a backbreaker. Most people didn't make it to the top, as the easiest route up was nearly vertical and so high that the peak was well above the tree line.

He let the SAR group know that he was available and would take the callout.

They'd meet at the trailhead where they'd be briefed about the situation, and each given their assignments.

Do we have an ID on the vics? he texted Cindy Des-Champs, the head of SAR.

She was a good chick and super great as their leader. She took no crap and was a positive influence on the team. She could bring people together and diffuse problems like no one else he'd ever met.

There was a pause and then the distinctive dots as she started to type her response.

Her texted popped up: Looks like it was a woman and a girl from the Sulfur Springs At-Risk Youth Group. Girl is sixteen, Grace Bunchen. The counselor is April Twofeather.

His stomach sank. April Twofeather, seriously? He'd gone to high school with April. Then again, who didn't he go to high school with within his age bracket? In this small town, everyone knew everyone and *everything*. Though he and April had shared a few classes, he hadn't been on good terms with her, especially when everyone in the school had found out she had gotten pregnant.

Not long after, she had disappeared from the school. Rumor had it that she was too embarrassed to show her face. She'd been dating Cameron Blakely. The thought of the guy and his tragic death made Sean's stomach clench. The day Cameron had died had been one of the worst days of Sean's life.

Some people swore the baby wasn't Cameron's, but Sean had known better. After Cameron died, April had been rubbing elbows with a lot of college-aged guys who came over to Big Sky to ski for a week—but who hadn't? From November to March, there was a constant flow of ski bums from surrounding areas and abroad. Locals had their pick. There was always a line of fresh gossip.

Then again, if gossip was to be believed, Sean had also bedded more than his fair share of ski bunnies and, according to one juicy story he'd heard about himself, he'd even shared a bed with two at the same time. If only his life was that interesting. Though, if he had a chance in real life, he wasn't sure he'd take it—that sounded like something he could fail at, and failure in that department wasn't an option. He'd take one good woman over many any day.

His phone buzzed again, pulling him from his thoughts of the past.

The SAR team would meet on Lone Mountain. From his house, it wasn't too far a drive, but the dirt roads leading to there were notoriously rutted and, after yesterday's rain, would be like driving in Silly Putty.

He grabbed his go bag and hit the road, listening to the

radio chatter between the SAR team members as he headed in their direction. It sounded like Cindy and her boyfriend were already at the trailhead and there would be four two-member teams to look for the missing females.

He had been right about the Silly Putty, and as he hit the logging road leading to their access point, he had to put his vehicle in four-wheel drive to keep from sliding around. April was probably as used to these kinds of roads as he was if she had felt comfortable in taking on the behemoth of a mountain.

With this level of ground saturation, it was no wonder that they had found themselves at the epicenter of a rockslide. On this mountain, rockslides weren't a normal occurrence, but not unheard of—they were like lightning.

He wanted to mentally condemn April for choosing this hike in these kinds of conditions, but he would be hard-pressed to say that he would have done anything different. Yet, it was that very "it won't happen to me" mentality that often kept him and his teammates both at SAR and the fire department busy.

Cindy was waiting beside her pickup when he arrived. She was dressed in layers and was going through her hiking backpack. She looked up and gave him a smile and a wave as he slogged up to the little parking area at the bottom of the trail.

Mud caked the outside of his pickup, and as he got out and slammed the door a chunk dropped from behind his tire. "How's it going, Cindy?"

She gave him a little nod. "So far, our two teams are a go. The two other teams are going to start at the next trailhead over. I want us to work the possible edges of the rockslide without having to cross over any potentially questionable conditions."

She was right. The last thing they needed to do was to cause another slide.

"Has anyone seen or heard from the missing females? Any cell phone pings?" he asked.

Chad, Cindy's boyfriend, stood up on the other side of the pickup. "We had Detective Leo West run a pinpoint on April's phone. We have a general idea of where her phone was last picked up by the towers, but as you know it isn't exact. Plus, given the conditions, the phone may not be with her if she had been carrying it in a backpack—or it could be buried."

Thank you, Captain Obvious. As much as he liked Cindy, he wasn't as much of a fan of Chad.

The guy had pushed his way onto their team, and though he definitely had the chops to be a member, it gnawed at Sean that Chad was an automatic walk-on when everyone else had to go through a heavy vetting process. There were few things more irritating than an out-of-stater expecting to get what they wanted without so much as a written test, and it going in their favor.

He sighed, reminding himself not to be too salty. A good addition to the team was a good addition, regardless of the methods in which they had taken to get there.

Besides, sometimes the best teams were made up of people who weren't necessarily best friends. It created an environment where everyone still wanted to prove their value-add and be at their best physical levels. Since Chad had joined his team, Sean had made sure to add twenty-reps when he lifted.

"How many other kids were with the females?" Sean asked.

Cindy stood up after closing her bag. "There were five in total. The other three, two boys and a girl, are at the local hospital getting checked for any injuries. They said they had rushed out after the rockslide, but they were all hit with falling debris from the slide. One of the boys had a pretty good shiner." She touched the area under her left eye.

"I hope they're all okay," he said, as another truck rolled up with Steve, who was assigned to his team today.

It didn't take them long to hit the mountainside, but the climb was brutal. He could almost imagine the whining and moaning the high school kids must have been dishing out on their nearly vertical assent. He was huffing by the time they hit their fifth switchback on the trail and the altitude started to take its toll.

Cindy paused for a minute on a larger area in the switchback where they could all catch up and hear one another. Steve was still smiling, which irked him. This guy didn't appear to be in any better shape than him. Thankfully, Chad was pulling up the rear and his face was red, he was winded and beads of sweat were pouring down from his temples.

"We are going to split up here," Cindy said, motioning toward the continuing switchbacks. "I want you and Steve to work the rockslide from here, up. According to the kids, this is where the slide kind of played out."

He nodded, trying not to speak to hide the fact that he was struggling to catch his breath and get his heart rate under control.

"Let's touch base every hour or so," Cindy continued. "We will hike up another couple hundred yards and work the edge so we don't kick things loose, but we can cover more area. I want you to work the left half of the main slide. The other teams will be doing the same on the other side."

"Got it," he clipped.

"Good luck, guys," Cindy said, turning toward the trail but giving them one look back over her shoulder. "And make sure you watch for any falling rocks. As we all know, this is an unstable environment. While we need to work fast, we also need to make sure we work safely."

"Let's find these ladies alive," Steve added, like it was their call to arms.

Steve was one hell of a guy and, not for the first time, Sean was glad to have him on his side.

He and Steve carefully picked a lateral line on the mountain and steadily moved to the north. Coming around the top of the ridge, the slide came into view. It was massive. Tons upon tons of loose rock had poured down the mountain and even though it had happened more than four hours ago, there was still a strange taste of dust in the air.

There was no way these women were still alive.

Given the conditions, he didn't want to call out to April and Grace if it were to cause more of the mountain to break loose. But before they found themselves victims of the slide, this was the time. They wouldn't get another opportunity.

Steve looked over at him as he came to a stop. "What's up?"

"You think we should give a shout?"

"If these two are alive, I want them to know we're looking for them. Or if they're sitting on the edge of this slide or injured somewhere... Well, *you know*. But what if you trigger another slide?" he countered.

Sean pinched his lips. "We have to hope that I won't, but I know for a fact that we are the first ones on scene. We need to make a choice."

Steve sucked in a long breath and scanned the rockslide like they were looking at a field of grave markers. "Do it."

"April! Grace!" He held for a second. "April Twofeather, this is Sean McCormack with Big Sky Search and Rescue! Call out if you can!"

He waited for the telltale sound of falling rocks but was instead met with the feeble sounds of a woman's cry. She sounded like a hurt animal, and the sound tore at his soul.

"April?"

She gave a warbled call. The sound came from above them on the hill, and he rushed toward it with Steve close on his heels.

Picking through the edge of the fall, weaving between boulders, he came over a small knob. Sitting on a rock, bloodied and battered, was April Twofeather.

"April," he said, relief filling his voice, "we're gonna get you out of here."

She looked up at him, her right eye was nearly swollen shut and black and purple. Her arm was hanging at a weird angle and blood streaked down the legs of her pants. Tears poured down her cheeks. "I'm... I'm sorry," she said between ragged breaths, which made him question whether she was suffering from some broken ribs as well.

"You have nothing to be sorry for." He moved to her and dropped to his knees. He wanted to ask her if she knew where the girl was, but from the state she was in, he doubted she'd be able to answer. He gently put his hand on her leg as he looked up at her. "Don't worry. I've got you. I'll get the helo in here and get you airlifted out."

"What... Where..." she said, wheezing.

"Don't worry, we will. You can trust me." He smiled, trying to bring her comfort. "Steve, you wanna call in Casper and have the air crew roll in? Make sure they steer clear of any unstable areas."

Steve nodded. "Already on it," he said, tapping on his phone. "Cindy said they spotted Grace above. They aren't to her yet, but she is alive."

April started to sob.

Sean rubbed her shoulder gently, and she softened under his touch. "We've got you guys...you're safe."

And, thankfully, still alive.

Chapter Three

There was a man. He'd appeared in a halo of dust in the evening sun. She had to squint to focus, but even squinting it was like she was looking through water. He couldn't be real. Not with those blue eyes. They were the same color as the headwaters when they came out of the mountains. Maybe she had died, and this was some kind of afterlife that pooled her perfect location and her ideal man.

She glanced around, looking for more familiar faces, but he was the only person she could see. This had to be real, this moment. Yet, what was he doing here?

A warm drip moved down from her temple. Reaching up, she touched the liquid and brought it down. Her fingertips were covered in blood. *Her blood.*

"April…" the familiar man said, but his voice was muddled and heavy, like it was coming from an antique gramophone. "You're going to be okay."

She tried to recall how she had gotten here. She was sitting on a rock.

Rockslide.

The world collapsing around her.

Pain. So much pain.

"Grace! Where's Grace?" she cried. She tried to stand up, but her body was wracked with pain…it hurt *everywhere*.

Her head spun, making her close her eyes, and she plopped down.

"Grace is up the hill. She didn't fall as far as you." The man was touching her shoulder. His fingers were cool against her feverish skin. "She said you covered her with your body."

She remembered moving toward Grace and pulling her into her. Then the darkness.

Kids? What…about the others? she tried to ask, but there was a sharp pain in her chest as she tried to breathe.

A wave of nausea washed over her as the stabbing from her ribs broke through the adrenaline-induced anesthesia.

"Sick… I'm going to be sick," she said, her deep breaths only compounding the agony.

The man said something, but he sounded like he was far away and moving farther. He couldn't leave her. She needed him. She needed help.

He said something about getting her on a board and moving her to a safe place for the helicopter. As she looked up at him, the world started to disappear around his halo like some monster was trying to devour him and her world. The darkness moved fast, and the beast swallowed them whole.

THE NEXT MORNING Sean sat in the corner of April's room in the ER after he'd made sure Grace was squared away in the pediatric ward. Grace had a sprained wrist and was doing well, but they wanted to keep her overnight for observation. It was amazing how much better she had fared than April.

The doctors had given April a heavy dose of pain meds to keep her comfortable. From what they had told him, they were waiting to get her into CT to get a scan—it was possible, given her fall, that she could be suffering from some kind of head or neck injury.

The Bozeman hospital had been the closest, and they were a good Level III trauma center, but they were limited thanks to a large car accident on I-90 and patients had stacked up. Maybe he'd made a mistake in having Casper and his team fly her here instead of a larger hospital like one in Seattle or Salt Lake City.

He hoped beyond all hope that she would only be dealing with what they had already found—so far, a concussion, a dark bruise on her face, cracked ribs and her right arm had been broken in several places.

The nurse in charge of her care walked in with a new bag of IV fluids. "How's our girl doing?" she asked, like it was just any other day in the ER, and he hadn't pulled this woman off the mountain after a catastrophic slide yesterday.

"She hasn't moved," he said, trying not to laugh at the inanity of his statement. Of course she hadn't budged, but he wasn't really sure what else the nurse could have expected him to say. "Did you manage to get in touch with one of her emergency contacts?"

The nurse shook her head as she hung up the bag and set about her work with the lines. "I called the man she had on file. It was her father. Unfortunately, it sounds like he has passed. I asked the woman who answered if there was anyone there who was related to April or knew her, but it sounded like she was on her own. I've given the search over to social work to see if they can make more headway. It always bothers me when patients are here alone—many don't recover, or their recovery is greatly slowed when they don't have support."

Just like him, April was alone in the world. It made an odd, hollow sensation build within his chest.

The nurse gave him a grateful smile. "You know, she is lucky to have you."

If she had been lucky, I would have never been called to her rescue, he thought as he rubbed at the back of his neck. *My being here only proves how unlucky she really is.*

"I don't know about that," he said, brushing off the nurse's well-intended but naive compliment.

He glanced over at April; her blond hair was dirty and matted with blood and dust, and her eye had gotten impossibly darker. He had never noticed how pretty she was when they had been growing up, but then again he couldn't say that he had ever really looked at her before.

It felt strange looking at her like this and thinking her beautiful. Or maybe it wasn't. It was a helluva thing to be at a person's worst and still be good-looking. When she made it through this, which she *had to*, he would have liked to see how she presented herself to the world.

"We are going to be taking her down for her CT in five minutes," the nurse said. "You are welcome to wait here until she gets back."

He looked down at his clothes. He was covered in blood—*her blood.*

"I'm going to run to Peds and check on Grace, then I'll go home and clean up. I'll come back to check on her in a few hours," he said, but as he did there was a pull inside of him. It could have been partly what the nurse said about dismal recovery rates when abandoned, but he didn't want to leave April's bedside.

He tried to tell himself that his being there didn't matter—and that the nurse was just trying to get him to stay. April didn't even know he was here, and if by some reason she did know, she wouldn't recognize him. When someone went through an event like hers, oftentimes they forgot the immediate aftermath—it was as if the brain protected itself from the trauma of major incidents by wiping the slate clean…well, mostly.

He knew from personal experience how some forgotten horrors came back—normally in the middle of the night. He always feared when life was going too well, as it seemed to be in those moments of relative peace and calm, that the horrors would come to life.

The memories were part of the reason he'd gone into firefighting—through his work, he had learned to control his fear and keep the nightmares mostly at bay.

"Sean?" the nurse asked, pulling him back to reality and away from the blood that was splattered over the legs of his pants from when he'd helped get April on the board and into the helo.

"Yeah, sorry. What?" he asked.

The nurse frowned. "You probably need to get some sleep." She started to adjust April's bed as she readied it to wheel down to Imaging.

"Yeah," he said, his exhaustion hitting him as he stood up from the pink vinyl chair he'd been sitting in. He hated those damned chairs.

"Make sure you drive home safely… Better yet, you should get a ride." The nurse clicked down the bed's side rail.

He walked toward the door, trying to cover a yawn. As he reached the door, he turned back to face the nurse and April. He looked over at the dark-haired woman from his past. "If I'm not back in time to talk to the doctor, please give me a call if there are any changes. Okay?"

The woman gave him a sweet smile. "You got it, Sean."

He tipped his head and moved toward the Peds Unit. His hiking boots still had dirt in them, and there was a click on the tile as he walked like there was a pebble stuck in the treads. It was strange how such a little thing could be so annoying.

It was, however, a welcome change of thought from April and all the things he could have done differently and more effectively in her and Grace's rescue. Though they had gotten to them rather quickly, he wondered if he could have shaved off time. Maybe they should have called in the helo before they even arrived on scene.

All through the night, he had questioned every move they'd made—if they'd only arrived a few minutes earlier, maybe it would have made a difference if April was dealing with head trauma. If their lag had led to some sort of brain damage, he wouldn't be able to look himself in the mirror.

No. I have to stop, he told himself for the hundredth time. *We did the best we could. We were fast. Yes, we could have been faster, but we did well.*

He wasn't really paying attention to the world around him as he walked on autopilot thanks to his exhaustive self-flagellation. He turned the corner toward Grace's room. A nurse came hurrying out, rushing toward their station.

He was pulled back to reality.

"What's going on?" he asked but the nurse ignored him, and he rushed toward Grace's room. Her bed was ruffled, but empty. He hurried toward the station, hoping to get the nurse's attention. "Hello? What happened to her? Where's Grace?" he asked, his stomach clenching with panic.

The nurse turned to look at him. "Who are you?"

"Where is she?" he countered, not wanting to play the stupid song and dance. "Is she okay?"

The nurse looked him over, her gaze stopping at the dried blood on his pants. "Grace…" She looked up at him and there was a panic in her eyes. "Grace is *missing*."

Chapter Four

When April woke up, it took her a minute to make sense of
her surroundings. Pink vinyl chair. A window that looked
out onto a brick wall. Why would anyone put a window
against a wall?

It was like some cruel joke—a teasing, speck of sun only
to be captured and entrapped.

It had been two days of lying in her hospital bed, and she
felt more trapped with each passing minute. If there was a
hell, this was it. If it hadn't been for the monotonous beeps
of IV pumps and occasional blaring of machines, she was
almost sure that she would have been able to hear the *tick*,
tick, *tick* of the clock on the wall, and it would have driven
her to madness.

She picked up her phone, checking her emails. Everyone
from Sulphur Springs had been surprisingly quiet. The kids
from the trip had sent her get-well texts, but no one had
texted in the last day and a half. She'd sent out a few messages to the other counselor at the camp, Kimberly, but the
only response she'd gotten was: "Don't worry. We've got
everything handled."

Maybe they were all trying to let her rest. In the last day
and a half, most of her time had been spent sleeping. Her
nurses had told her that a man involved in getting her off

the mountain had popped in. She was almost relieved he hadn't woken her up. She wasn't sure how she was supposed to adequately thank a person who was responsible for saving her life. A simple "Thank you" would never do, but the next best thing she could come up with was a fist bump and thanks to her bruised hands, even that was out of the question.

It felt like there wasn't a single location on or within her body that didn't hurt. She'd like to hope that every inch of her would start to get less tender and sore, but any time she tried to move she was reminded about all the hidden bruises.

There was a knock on the door. "Yes?" she called.

"I'm here to take you dancing," a man said. His voice was familiar, but she couldn't quite place him. "That is, if you are decent. You dressed?"

She pulled the dusty-rose-colored blanket up around her chin, the waffled texture imprinting on her skin as she held it tightly. "It's hard to say I'm dressed. I saw what all these gowns cover—or *don't*—in the mirror earlier. However, you are welcome to come in."

The man walked in and the sight of him made her jaw drop. "Heya, April." He sent her a smile that made her more aware than ever that she wasn't wearing any underwear. She pulled the blanket tighter against her body as she tried to control her embarrassment at feeling so vulnerable and exposed.

"I didn't think you were real," she said, nearly stumbling over her words like they were two left feet.

He pressed his hands to his chest and felt around his body in a way that made her want to do the same. "Last time I checked I was a real boy."

There is that damned stunning grin, again.

She had to look away so no more color would rise into

her cheeks. She stared at the blank brick wall outside like it was the Mona Lisa.

"Wait," the man continued, "you aren't seeing anyone else in the room, are you? Ghosts or something?"

She jerked back to face him, but she was met with that damned grin again. "No. No ghosts." She ran her hand over her hair and decided to fight fire with fire, and she sent him the best and most seductive grin she could muster in her battered state.

"So, no hallucinations that I should be concerned about?" he teased.

Unless he counted the one in which he'd had a halo...

"Only the one where you think you will be taking me dancing," she said, smiling up at him and hating to admit that she was enjoying his charm. "You know, I was thinking if you sprung me from this joint, that we could do something...*bigger*."

He quirked his brow. "Bigger? Than dancing? Impossible."

She gave a little jerk of her head, teen-like. "Oh...heck yes. I was thinking we take to the sky—take a leap of faith and skydive."

He tilted his head back with a laugh. "I like your style," he said between laughs. "However, I'm not one for leaps of faith...or skydiving for that matter."

"That's strange," she said, her smile widening.

"What is?" he asked, leaning against the window frame and crossing his arms over his chest.

"Well, you are asking me to commit to a leap when you wouldn't do the same."

"How's that?" he asked, frowning.

She didn't like when his smile disappeared, the loss made her room seem substantially colder. "Well, you walked into my room here, you make jokes, and yet, I have no idea who you are."

The warmth returned. "Oh, I see…"

"Yes, for all I know you are here to kill me. Some kind of murder-for-hire plot. I mean look at me," she said, finally letting the blanket fall from her hands as she waved over her body, "I've never been more vulnerable. The only real question would be what kind of weapon you'd use to do the job."

"Do you have a lot of people who want you dead?" He sounded genuinely concerned, bringing her back to the reality of her current situation.

"I was joking around," she said, avoiding her fears and trying to keep things from getting too dark. "You still haven't told me your name."

"Yeah, man, sorry. I'm Sean McCormack. I'm the one who found you."

"Oh…" She covered her mouth with her hand, embarrassed that she hadn't recognized the man she had been fearing to see.

He shrugged. "Don't feel bad. You were under stress and then the mind plays tricks on you to help you keep from reliving the trauma of the event." He looked away from her, and she wasn't sure, but she could have almost sworn he'd looked let down. "Actually, the science behind trauma is incredibly interesting." He kept yammering on about psychology, like he was feeling as awkward as she was.

"I'm familiar with a few of those points," she said, trying to win back his favor and possibly his friendship. He had saved her life. "I'm sure you know, but I work with kids—"

"At Sulphur Springs. Yep," he said, finishing her sentence. "You know, though, we actually went to high school together as well."

She tried to recall him from those days, but all she could

think about of her time in high school were the tough decisions she had been forced to make and the baby she had given up for adoption when none of the family wanted to step up and help. For the second time in as many minutes, she found herself at a loss and embarrassed by her poor memory.

"Don't worry about it," he offered, clearly sensing her discomfort. "I'm actually kind of glad you don't remember me. Those adolescent years weren't some of my best."

"Mine, either," she said.

His face pinched, and she knew that her reputation from those years had preceded her.

Damn it. She took a breath. *There goes the rest of my chances in making him fall for me.*

He shifted against the window and his feet pointed toward the door. The poor man was right in wanting to run. Before he could, she needed to say her piece.

"Sean, no thank you is enough for what you did for me and the kids I was with. If there's anything I can do to repay you or your unit, please let me know."

His look of discomfort deepened as he seemed to shrink in upon himself. "Actually, there was something I was hoping to talk to you about, something you might be able to help me with."

"Anything." She pressed down the edge of her blanket and smoothed the fabric like she could brush away all the strange edges of this moment.

"Has anyone talked to you about Grace?"

She looked up at him, and some of the blood receded from her face. "Is she okay? The last thing I heard was that she was doing well. Did something change?" She asked her questions in a single, frenzied breath.

"Unfortunately, she has gone missing." He straightened

slightly. "I talked to the local police, and they say they're doing everything they can, but given her age and her checkered past, they don't seem to be doing much to find her."

"But she's missing!" How dare they not go after Grace just because she had made mistakes in her life. Especially considering how horribly life had treated her up to this point—she'd been bouncing between low-level foster homes, given up by parents who she had helped care for while they dealt with the ravages of fentanyl addiction, and in high school…well, the teachers and her peers could sense the girl's weakness. Now even the police were letting her down.

They were making a villain of a victim.

Her blood pressure spiked on the monitor by her bedside.

"That's why I'm here." He moved closer to her and put his arm on her shoulder. "I needed to find out if you knew where she might have gone or who she might have run away with."

"You don't think she was kidnapped?" she countered, upset that Grace was automatically at fault.

He raised a brow like he was questioning whether someone would actually want to spend time with such a difficult teen. "Right now, they don't even know how she made it out of the hospital without being seen."

April sat up straighter. "This place must be covered in cameras. There has to be something to tell us about what happened to Grace."

"She didn't show up on any of their recordings. They started looking this morning, but…" He trailed off as he looked out at the brick wall. "I'm worried about her. I just need to know she's okay. Do you know her foster parents?"

Grace hadn't been overly chatty with April about her family situation, which was true to form about most of the kids she had worked with at the camp. "These kids aren't the type who are born with silver spoons in their mouths. Most of them are wards of the state or struggling through the foster system."

He nodded. "We tried to contact her foster family, but they haven't been answering their phone. My buddy at the sheriff's department said they drove out there, but no one was around."

"Did they talk to other kids who might have been in her foster home? Her friends from the camp?" She moved gingerly to the side of her bed, swinging her legs over the side. The sudden movement made her ribs ache, and she had to pause to catch her breath.

"What are you doing?" he asked. "Can I help you get something?"

"Yeah, you can help me get the hell out of here. There's no way I'm going to sit in Club Med here while Grace is still missing. I can't let the world give up on her, and no matter what happened to her, she needs help."

Chapter Five

Sean didn't agree with her leaving the hospital. April was there for a reason, and though he had teased her about springing her from the joint, it hadn't really been his plan. She needed to heal and get better, or she did no one any good and had the potential to be more of a liability than an asset. Though he had gently tried to explain all of that to her when she had stepped behind the curtain and gotten dressed, it hadn't stopped her from going AMA—or, against medical advice.

They'd slipped out of the room and down the hall without a nurse even taking notice.

"Don't you think we should just wait until you are officially discharged?" he asked.

"I let the nurse know I was leaving. They said they had to wait for the paperwork from the doctor, but I don't care."

He slowed down, looking back at the nurses' station. No one was around, and there were beeps coming from one of the rooms where the staff must be. "Are you sure?"

She nodded and walked ahead. "All they are doing is giving me NSAIDs at this point. I'll be fine. CT came back clean."

As they walked down the stairs and made their way outside and into the parking lot, it had struck him how and why

Grace had been able to disappear so easily—the nurses were overworked and understaffed; they could only do so much, and babysitting wasn't on their list of duties. He felt bad that they were the ones who had been questioned at length about Grace's disappearance. No doubt, her nurse had taken a stern talking-to as a minor had gone missing. Hopefully, she hadn't lost her job when so much was out of her hands.

April got into his pickup and stared out the window. Her face was expressionless, but he could tell she was struggling with Grace's disappearance. He didn't want to scare her with all the possibilities, or how little they could really do to help the girl. "How's your arm feeling? Did you get some pain meds this morning or do we need to stop and grab you some?"

April glanced over at him. She lifted her pink-casted arm slightly, as if reminding herself that she had a broken wing. "It's fine. I have a bit of a headache, but that can happen after a concussion."

"You should have stayed—"

She put up her good hand, waving him quiet. "I would have been getting out today anyway. I'm going to be fine. The only thing I'm worried about is finding Grace. Her foster family trusted me with her care. The last thing I could do was sit around and wait for her to be found."

He couldn't argue. He wasn't the kind to sit around and wait, either.

"When was she last seen?" April asked, looking over at him.

"She disappeared almost as soon as she was moved up to the pediatric floor."

"So, two nights ago?" She ran her hand over her face in exasperation. "She could be just about anywhere by now. Why didn't you tell me before? Why didn't *anyone*?"

"I was out looking for her, coordinating with law enforcement. They did their best, but their hands are tied."

"Wait…" She paused, staring at him. "You're not a cop?"

He shook his head.

"Then what are you doing here?"

"I told you. I want to make sure she is safe."

"Why? She's not your kid," she countered, but as soon as she spoke her hand flew over her mouth in embarrassment. "That didn't come out right. I… I just mean…"

"I know it's not conventional for a firefighter to be out here working the beat for a missing kid, but I'm also part of a search and rescue team, and this is a small town and I feel like I can make a difference. I also knew how much Grace going missing was going to bother you. Last night, when you were pretty heavily medicated, you were saying her name in your sleep."

She opened her mouth like she was going to say something, but then snapped it shut.

"If you don't want me helping to search for Grace, I can bow out, but like you… I just can't stand sitting idly by when there is something I can be doing."

He was tempted to tell her more, but he didn't want to do April any more harm. She already had enough to deal with without him dumping on her.

"SAR is part of this search, still?" she asked, cocking her head to one side.

She was making him want to tell her the truth, but he wasn't ready. Yet, he didn't need to come off like some kind of over-reaching psycho, either. He shook his head. "No. I'm working this while I'm off. I have the next couple of days before I have my next shift at the fire station."

"Oh," she said, nodding slightly like his being a first responder helped make sense of why he was acting so altruistic. "Is that why you are so ready and willing to go out of your way to find her? You are always a hero?"

He threw his head back with a laugh. "Not hardly. Everyone in Big Sky is keeping an eye out for this girl."

"Okay," she said, shooting him a smile. "But why?" she pressed. "What's in this search for *you*?"

She wasn't letting it go, and it was *killing* him. He pulled out onto the road leading back to Big Sky. "Do you always think the worst of people? Or is this just because you don't like me, or something?"

"What?" she asked, sounding surprised. "I never said I didn't like you."

"Then why would you imply that I have some ulterior motive for looking for Grace?"

She sighed. "I didn't mean to cause a fight. I just…"

"You *just* don't trust *me*."

She leaned her head back against the truck's headrest. "I don't trust *anyone*."

He wasn't sure how to respond to that kind of blanket statement. He didn't wholeheartedly agree with her sentiment, but he could understand how and why she could come to feel that way. "Not all people are bad."

April nodded. "I don't think people ever want to be *bad*. At least, not usually. I think that people, in general, only do things when there is some kind of personal gain. No one does anything completely unselfishly."

He tried not to be offended as he thought about the thousands of hours he had spent in meetings, in training and actively volunteering to find those—like her—who needed help the most. "What about you? Why do you work with these kids? Are you saying that you are selfishly motivated in taking them out on activities?"

"First, I get paid," she said, putting up a finger like she

was going to make a long list in her argument against not only him but herself as well. "Second, I enjoy them. And third, I like to think I can make a difference."

"How is enjoying your job selfish?"

"I love helping them. *I do.*"

He tapped on the steering wheel. "Fair, but why?"

She tilted her head as though she was thinking, and her subtle little look of concentration made him want to stare. He had thought her naturally pretty before, but now all he could think about was how stunning she truly was in the way her blue eyes sparkled in the sun. There was a scratch on her chin that he had been staring at since he'd first found her on the mountain. Like the bruise around her eye, it appeared to be in the healing process, and it would likely be gone within a few days.

It was strange, but he would miss that little mark. He'd come to see the slight imperfection as much a part of her as the color of her eyes.

"I live just down there," she said, after they'd been driving for a bit. She pointed at the next road to their right. "If you want to swing by, I could use clean clothes and some gear."

"You got it," he said, pulling down the road.

He parked in the lot of the apartment complex next to a nineties-model, burgundy Chevy Caprice. The back window of the car was covered in a black plastic trash bag and secured with tape.

The place was made up of what looked like small units; parked in front of most were beat-up cars. Big Sky was made up of three types of people, the few and far between locals, the poor ski bums who worked hard in the summer to save up so they could ski all winter, and those with second homes who lived off trust funds and bonds. Just like him, April was definitely not a member of the latter.

"It's not much," she said, her face taking on a look of shame.

"Hey, you have a place to call your own," he said, trying to make her feel better. "You know as well as I do that around here a lot of people live in their cars."

She nodded, perking up slightly. "Did you hear that many business owners are complaining they can't find workers who will stay?" She guffawed. "I mean, how can they? No one can afford to live here on the wages most places are paying."

The thought made him think of Grace. What if she was out there, sleeping in one of the cars or campers that were parked in the woods and at every little pullout along the side of the road? What if someone was keeping her hostage?

"You can wait here," she said, stepping out of his pickup and closing the door before he had time to argue.

He wished he could tell her that she had nothing to be embarrassed about, truly. He didn't judge someone based on where they lived in this community. He judged people on their actions and the character they exhibited. Criminals and saints existed in every income bracket.

She rushed up to the first-floor apartment and slipped inside. It didn't take her long to come out carrying a small canvas bag that had had "Hike or Die" emblazoned on its side—he tried not to think about the irony.

His phone pinged with a message from his buddy, Jim Hagen, the fire marshal at the department. He clicked on it. Looks like we have a possible arson at the south end of town. All units are being called.

Do you have enough guys? he responded, watching as April came rushing toward his truck.

He had today and tomorrow off but he couldn't just leave her now, not with Grace still missing. If he bagged, she would never forgive him even if it was to go to work. Sure, she would tell him she knew that he had a job to do and a life outside what was happening in hers, but in the back of her mind she would feel abandoned. If he wanted to remain her friend—if that's what they even were—there would be no coming back from that kind of disappointment and hurt.

Yep, we're all set, Jim answered.

He put his phone face down on the console. April hopped into the pickup next to him and clicked her belt into place. "I think we should start looking for Grace at her best friend's house. Summer and a couple of her friends have an apartment not even that far from here." She took out her phone and opened Snapchat to see if Summer had a public account. "Yeah, according to this, Summer is a few blocks away. We can probably catch her."

He couldn't stand how invasive social media was in teens' lives without them even realizing the anonymity and freedoms they were giving up being a part of the "in crowd." As a kid, his parents had rarely known where he'd actually been, but in that ability to get lost to the world, he'd found who he truly was and had had the freedom to make choices that helped shape him into the man he was today.

Or maybe he was just old and stuck in the recursive and muddled loop of nostalgia.

When had thirty-two meant someone was old?

Then again, when he was running up the stairs and carrying hose in their training tower, he definitely felt his age.

"Yeah?" April asked, pulling him out of his negative self-talk.

"Good a spot as any to start," he said. "Did Grace have a boyfriend?"

She shrugged. "She had been hanging out with Andrew, but she and I didn't have the kind of relationship where she would have opened up about that kind of thing with me." She paused. "I wish we would have. That's what most of these kids need—a safe place and a mentor to help them navigate life—but it takes an event to form a bond."

He pulled out of the parking lot and drove in the direction she pointed.

Big Sky was a charming little town, tucked into the bottom of the ski hill. As they came to a stop at the sign at the end of the block, he spotted Mr. Crowly from the grocery store chatting with Sean's ex-girlfriend Persephone Samson. Mr. Crowly waved, but Persephone did her best impression of being blind. He couldn't blame her, especially after everything between them had ended so badly—and with too many fireworks.

April waved at Mr. Crowly. Thankfully, April didn't mention his most recent ex, but he didn't know if it was because she didn't know about his former relationship, or if she was kind enough not to mention it. Then again, she seemed to barely remember him from high school.

He pressed on the gas, only too happy to leave part of his past in the rearview mirror.

While he didn't know everyone in this town, he could confidently say that he knew everyone through one degree of separation. With that kind of accessibility and social media, it was like living in a fishbowl. The insularity made it almost impressive that Grace could have disappeared—he doubted she could have done it without some kind of help, but no one had stepped forward with any knowledge as to the girl's whereabouts.

The deputy in charge of her case had dotted all the *i*'s and crossed all the *t*'s in looking for her—and it didn't sound like they had found anything to make them think criminal or nefarious activities had taken place. From the coffee talk, the deputy seemed to be leaning toward thinking Grace had merely skipped town.

He wouldn't have blamed her if she had.

But he wished she *had* given someone some insights into why and where she was going.

Even in this small town, human trafficking was a concern. Several girls had snuck away and caught flights in Bozeman and headed toward the big cities, only to be later found on degenerate websites selling their bodies. One had even been murdered in the underground tunnels of Las Vegas.

"So…" April started. "Do you want to tell me why that woman back there with Mr. Crowly acted so weird?"

He sighed. "You noticed, huh?" He wished she hadn't.

"I think that any adult woman would have noticed the cold shoulder you just received. Did you hit it and quit it, or never give her a chance?" She sent him a cute, understanding smile.

He returned her smile, but he could feel the pain in his. "Boy, you just shoot from the hip, don't you?"

"Straight for the heart." She reached over with her casted arm and took hold of his hand, which rested on the console next to his phone. He moved his fingers up, wrapping her fingers with his. The action was so unexpected, that it made his heart sputter.

"I'm sorry," she continued.

"It's cliché, but everything happens for a reason." He glanced down at their hands and then gave her a squeeze.

She smiled. "Right now, I'm more thankful than ever in knowing that's true."

Chapter Six

April hadn't meant to slip her hand into his, but now she was glad she had taken the risk. Part of her problem was that she'd always allowed her mouth to get her in trouble— though her parents would have argued it wasn't just her mouth. She'd always been strong-willed and a Hell-yes girl, and that hadn't changed as she'd grown older.

Her impulsiveness had been a gift as much as it had been a burden, and thankfully this time it had worked in her favor. She could have stared at Sean forever. He was so handsome, and she'd be lying if she didn't have a thing for men in uniforms. Add the fact that he'd saved her *and* was a fireman…well, her personal restraint never stood a chance.

Unfortunately, this moment couldn't last. On Snapchat, Summer's blonde Bitmoji was quickly approaching. April pulled her fingers from his as she clicked on her phone. Sean then clasped his hands, making her wonder if he was questioning their brief touch.

As they neared, she spotted the teenager sitting out on the porch of her rental, vaping. She was standing with five other newly minted adults, none of whom looked overly happy about their arrival.

Sean parked across the street, and as they approached, she spotted the telltale movements of kids hiding beers.

Lucky for them, she wasn't there to be a voice of reason or run interference.

"Hey, Summer," she said, giving the girl a slight wave. "How's it going?"

Summer looked at the boy who was standing closest to her, like he was in control of her responding or not. April remembered those days when she'd ran second to a boy, but far from fondly.

The kid gave her a small nod and the girl turned back. "We're doin' okay, April. Who's the guy?"

"He's a friend," she said, not feeling the need to give the girl any real room for judgment until she could get a better feel for what she was walking into. "Did you hear about what happened up there on the hill?"

"Yeah," Summer said, a furious expression peppering her features. "I heard you screwed up and nearly got my best friend killed."

Anger pooled in April's belly, but she reminded herself that she was the reason they had been on the mountain in the first place. In so many ways, what had happened up there had been her fault and her responsibility.

"I am sorrier than you know about what happened," she said, lifting her cast slightly so they could see the evidence that she, too, hadn't come away unscathed, though her black eye had probably already done the trick.

Summer sniffed. The kids who'd been standing with her turned and escaped the storm as they headed inside. The only one remaining was the boy whom she'd been looking to for permission.

April stepped up onto the porch, Sean tailing her. "Did you happen to see or hear from Grace since it happened?"

"That's exactly what the cops asked the other day."

"And?"

"I told them exactly what I'm gonna tell you. Grace ain't been here."

April nodded. *So, we're going to play the twenty-questions game. So be it.*

"You know Grace and I had been hanging out for the last six months or so, pretty solid," April started, giving Sean a look like there was some secret that they shared.

Sean nodded, playing along.

"And?" Summer asked, taking a long drag off the vape pen. "She told me something about you… Things I bet you wouldn't want your little boy toy there hearing about—you know *exactly* who I'm talking about." She smirked.

"Whatever." She hated how much she sounded like a teenager as she thought about her ex, Damon.

"Funny thing, I guess Grace was right," she said. "You do seem to get more men than the average woman." She nudged her chin in the direction of Sean, but she clearly was also talking about Damon.

"Do you really think you should be shaming anyone?" April looked at the boy beside the girl and at the door where the rest of her squad had disappeared. "From what I see here, you have your choice of guys. You're having fun, and I don't begrudge you for it for a second. Have fun while you can."

The girl opened her mouth like she wanted to snark back but couldn't run with anything as there was no real condemnation.

"Look, *lady*," the guy standing beside Summer said, "you don't need to be coming here and starting a fight. The girl you're looking for ain't here. If what you're sayin' is true and she's been running with you for months, then she better be thinking twice before coming around, too."

"I wasn't trying to start anything. I just needed to know that she wasn't here, for sure."

Summer rolled her eyes. "You can't think you would get me to roll over when it comes to Grace."

"Oh?" April quirked a brow.

"Well, Grace is more than just a friend to me. She's almost a sister," Summer said.

Sean stepped up beside April. "If she's more like a sister, then we all know damned well that she has called you at the very least." He leaned against the post. "Grace isn't in any kind of trouble. We just need to know that she is okay and accounted for. So, if you've spoken to her…at least tell us and we can stop looking for her."

"We just need to know she's safe," April added.

There was a long pause, and Summer took another drag off her pink vape pen. She exhaled, and the air around April filled with the strange scent of cotton candy. If the girl was trying to come off as hard-edged, smoking something that smelled like sugar wasn't her best choice.

"Here's the deal," Summer started. "I ain't one to rat on my friend."

"So, you have spoken to her?"

"Last I heard, there was something going on with her foster parents. That was before your little hike. Since then, I ain't heard from her." Summer took another pull off the pen.

April stared at the girl, weighing her expression to tell if Summer was lying or telling the truth. Grace had offhandedly mentioned something to her about her foster family, something about them going on vacation.

"What do you mean, *something going on*?" Sean asked. "What was happening with her family?"

Summer's watchdog snarled at Sean's attempt to speak to her. "Look, man—"

The girl put a hand up, silencing her pet. "First, to call those adults *her family* is one hell of a stretch. They give her a roof over her head, and sometimes that is even hit or miss. Before she went to the Springs, she was spending a lot of nights over here with us. I even had to ask her to start chipping in on rent, but she decided to sign up with your camp instead."

"Bunch of good that did her," the watchdog snapped.

"Listen up, bucko…" Sean snarled back. "We are trying to help your friend here, and if you were as smart as you think you are, you'd be bending over backward to help us— that is, if Grace really was your friend, at all."

In the blink of an eye, the watchdog's fist was flying through the air. April let out a yelp as the kid's fist nearly connected with Sean's jaw. Instead, Sean grabbed his wrist and deftly maneuvered it behind the kid's back in an arm bar hold. He flipped his wrist back and the kid bent over in pain.

"What in the hell were you thinking, bucko?" Sean growled. "You may be able to take some fifteen-year-old idiot behind the football bleachers, but you're out of depths with me."

"Sean, stop." April shook her head. "Let's go, before someone calls the cops."

He turned back to the young guy he'd pinned. "You going to try something, again?"

The kid shook his head, tears in his eyes.

"Let him go," April ordered.

Sean dropped his arm. "I hope you learned something here, today. Don't mess with the old guy, kid, experience always wins."

Chapter Seven

Sean hadn't intended on things going as they had back at the adolescent tenement. At least he hadn't let the guy get the drop on him or he would have never let himself live it down. Ever since they'd left, April had been silent, and the tension rested between them like a boulder.

"So, you think we should head over to Grace's foster home?" he asked, knowing full well the police had already been there and there wasn't a chance in hell that Grace would go there to seek solace.

"Maybe you should take me back to my apartment," she said, pointing in the direction from which they'd come.

He chewed at the inside of his lip. "Look, I'm sorry about what happened. I didn't mean for things to go sideways like that. The kid was just—"

"Being a kid," she said, stopping him from saying what he really thought about the arrogant snotbag. "You need to realize that he and Summer are very much like the kids I work with at Sulphur Springs. They all have a chip on their shoulder. Your putting them in holds and getting in fistfights doesn't help in my attempts to prove to them that the world, and the adults in it, aren't their enemies."

"You are being idealistic," he countered, not meaning to start a fight, but unable to hold his tongue. "The world isn't filled with butterflies and rainbows. These kids know that better than anyone. Unfortunately, they are the ones who've had struggle to raise themselves, were indoctrinated into the underbelly of this society from an early age. You can fake it all you want, but people can't be trusted."

She jerked and turned to face him from the passenger's seat of his pickup. "Did you forget who you are talking to? Where I've come from? I thought you knew all about me. All about the girl I was in high school. I thought that's why you pitied me."

He scowled. "First, I don't pity you. Second, we talked about our high school years—they're not a time in either of our lives that we have to dig into. I know you had a hard time back then, but you aren't the only one with a past."

"Oh, really? Did your first love *die*? Did you have to give birth to the baby the two of you created all alone? Hand the little girl off to a stranger? Did you have to give away a part of yourself and the person you loved?"

He slowed down the pickup and pulled over to the side of the road near a small restaurant. It had a Closed sign in the window, which had faded with sun and age. He stared at its chipped edges as he tried to find the right words. For years, he had been carrying his secret...a secret that would have more of an impact on her than he'd realized, until now.

She sat back in her seat, sinking into it slightly. "I had to say goodbye to the two people I loved the most in this world all in the same year—Cameron and my baby, Ann. Ann was his mother's name," she said slowly.

It was a story he hadn't known and it was breaking his heart.

He wasn't ready to open up, to tell her his truth...not now.

"You don't know how sorry I am that you have gone through all that." He pulled back onto the road. "I hate the

fact that anyone should have to face such a thing alone…
That's why I wanted to be a first responder. First, as a fire-fighter and second, as a volunteer for SAR."

"You are an anomaly. Everyone says they want to help, but then when it comes right down to it, no one shows up when you need them the most."

Her words drove into him, cutting him to pieces. He couldn't tell her all the reasons he'd been called to public service. If he did, it was likely that she would never speak to him again. There was no doubt in his mind that she would hate him, at the very least.

"Grace's home…it's just a few blocks down here," April said, pointing south. "Her foster parents rent a place."

"What do they do for a living?" Sean asked.

"Grace never really spoke about it, but from what I managed to glean, they both worked for the Spanish Peaks Restaurant. He as a chef, and she as a waitress. They don't seem to keep jobs for long, though."

"They're unreliable?" He felt stupid asking, but any number of things could have impacted their inability to maintain employment.

"I think that in this case, they aren't the best caregivers, or employees. However, I don't know them well enough at a personal level to say anything."

In the distance, a tendril of smoke rose into the sky. The site made his breath catch in his throat. This time of year, it was legal to burn slash outside town, but there was too much of the black billowing smoke to make him think that this was some little camp-or brushfire. Trying to keep his eyes on the road, he took out his phone. He pulled up his text messages, and he sent a quick one off to his buddy for the address of their active callout.

He pressed the gas pedal down harder as something in

his gut made him wonder if the fire was somehow related to the missing girl.

Sirens were piercing the air as he approached a small duplex. Flames licked up the side of the building. The original color of the place looked to be beige, but now was mostly charred. Black, tarry smoke billowed out from the second-floor windows. At the far side of the building, red and orange flames were pouring out of the top of the window and meeting the fire crackling on the outside the structure.

The place had to have been burning for at least an hour as it was totally engulfed. Hopefully, if there had been people or animals inside, they had safely made it out.

Jim stood beside engine #406 talking on his phone. He waved at him as they rolled up to a stop on the other side of the street. There were people standing all over, rubbernecking and talking. Three different sheriff's deputies were patrolling the area, talking to what looked like several of the neighbors as well as managing crowd control.

"Is this Grace's foster family's place?" he asked.

"I think so, but..." April picked up her phone and tapped for a few seconds. "Yeah...it is." She sounded breathless.

His stomach roiled. "You don't think that Grace was in there, do you?"

She shook her head. "I hope with every part of my soul that she wasn't—Grace has and will continue to be a survivor."

APRIL'S HAIR FELL around her face and stuck at her temples. The fire was in a full roar now, even though the firefighters had been throwing water at it for an hour or more. Sean was safely away from the fire and was manning a hose from the second firetruck, and his T-shirt was sticking to his back, dark with pools of perspiration.

She had no idea how long they had been here, but since she'd arrived and from what she'd overheard, none of the firefighters had been able to venture back inside thanks to the intense heat and instability of the structure. However, the team who'd gone in earlier was now standing behind the first firetruck talking.

She didn't want to bother them and ask more questions, as they all looked exhausted and were drenched with sweat thanks to the heat of the fire and the seventy-degree weather. The man nearest to her was dark-haired and built like a muscle magazine cover model, and for a moment she could totally understand why most women found firefighters the sexiest thing on this planet.

There were two women across the street, both likely in their midthirties, who were tittering and giggling as they stared at the firemen. The women could have any one of them they wanted. That was, until the brunette pointed in the direction of Sean, who was moving the spray of water toward the second-floor window at the center of the building.

Her anger flared like a fire's hotspot. No. He was out of bounds.

As much as she wanted to march her butt across the street and tell the women to get back into their houses and quit objectifying what was hers, she restrained herself and simply made her way over to the resting firemen. Though she would have rather gone over to Sean and marked her territory, this would work as a close second in her attempts to let the women know that she was the one in the power position.

As she approached them, she realized how stupid she was being. First of all, she didn't want any of these men—Sean included. *I mean, it's not like holding hands meant we have anything beyond a friendship. Friends hold hands all the time—don't they?*

Second of all, she shouldn't have been thinking about the hot or not qualities of the cover-model-esque and sweaty men surrounding her. She needed to quell the lizard part of her brain that was sending her into the primal way of thinking, which involved chest pounding and clubs.

There were so many other things she should have been thinking about. Thankfully, no one had mentioned finding any signs that anyone had been in the house at the time of the fire.

"What's up?" Another fireman by the engine turned to her and sent her a sweltering smile that had nothing to do with the heat.

"Do you guys need anything?" she asked, doing her best not to send the women across the street a suck-on-that look as much as her ego wanted.

The blond smiled. "We're good. Sean said you're the woman he found on the mountain the other day. How's your arm doing?" he asked, motioning toward her cast.

She wasn't trying, but damn if his concern didn't make her thoughts move to Sean. Hopefully he wasn't watching and seeing she was talking to these ridiculously good-looking men. Then again, would he even realize how handsome they were? Or, for that matter, that she thought they were sexy?

Gah… I am a hot mess. She tried to keep her thoughts from being read upon her features, but she could feel her cheeks warm. *I can think other men are sexy. I'm not in a relationship. I'm not spoken for. Besides, they didn't hold a candle to Sean. And damn it, I'm not dead.*

Dead. The word echoed through her.

"My arm's fine. A little sore, but I'm sure that's nothing in comparison to what you guys are feeling. I bet you're exhausted."

He sent her a sexy smile that made her step back.

Why did her best attempt to talk to these men sound like she was trying to hit on them? *All I'm missing is the hair flip and the vapors, and they would think I was vying for a husband. Maybe Summer and Grace are right... I have a problem when it comes to men.*

Stop being awkward, she told herself. *Stop. Being. Awkward.*

"Are you okay?" Blondie asked, frowning at her like he was concerned she was having some kind of stroke in front of him.

Come on, really? This couldn't have been the first time you've had a woman go full spastic in front of you, she wanted to say. Instead, she smiled. "I'm fine, sorry. I'm just really concerned. One of my campers from Sulphur Springs was supposed to be living in this duplex. Her name is Grace. She's sixteen."

The man's playful demeanor disappeared and was replaced with a look of gravity. "Sean told us a bit about the girl. We didn't see any evidence people were in the building when we went in, but that's not to say we couldn't have missed someone. Until the fire is contained and we can get back inside, I'm afraid I can't say anything for sure."

What if Grace had been inside? What if she had *caused the fire*? "How long do you think it will take to get inside and look for possible remains?"

The blond man looked at his friend and then over at Sean, as though he wished she had put any one of the other men on the spot besides him. "You will have to talk to Sean, but I would say it will be at least a day or so."

"You won't know if someone died in this fire for at least a day? What about finding out the cause of the fire? Will that take a month?" she growled, trying and failing at not losing her temper. All she wanted to know was if the girl they were looking for was alive or dead at this point, and yet…*nothing*.

The man frowned and ran his hand over the back of his neck. The men he'd been standing with seemed to take a step back and the farthest from her actually turned away and made a show of going to the side of the engine and starting to work with a section of hose.

She was blaming the wrong person, but she couldn't help how desperate and powerless she felt. "I'm sorry, I didn't mean to come off like a jerk. I just…"

The blond man motioned for Sean, who was glancing over at them. "I'll go grab him for you. He can answer your questions better than I can." Before she could say anything else to try to make up for her rudeness, he nearly started jogging to get away from her. The women watching were probably eating up the men's retreat from her.

The blond took over the hose, relieving Sean, whose shoulder muscles were pulled tight against his shirt. As the man spoke to him, he glanced back over at her and there was a look of concern on his face. Sean was probably three steps ahead of her and thinking about Grace and her potential for being somehow linked to this fire—or, and she hoped not, how Grace was dead inside.

He wiped the back of his hand over his forehead and said something with a nod to the blond, then he made his way over. He walked slowly and deliberately toward her. Even from here, it was clear that there was something he didn't want to tell her.

"Is she dead?" she asked, terrified.

If Grace was gone, she'd never be able to forgive herself. April was supposed to be this girl's mentor and not only had she gotten her involved in a rockslide, but then she'd been unavailable in the hospital and now…

She grew nauseous.

Sean rubbed his left wrist, a sign that he was nervous. "Since we arrived, the deputies have been out here taking statements from the neighbors, as well as any other potential witnesses. Have any of them made their way over and chatted with you yet?"

The wave of nausea grew within, forcing her to try to swallow it down. "No. Why? What do they think happened?"

He took her by the hand. "Let's go sit in my pickup for a minute, so we can have some privacy while we talk."

She couldn't move her feet. "If there's something you know, something about Grace…you have to tell me right now. I can't… I *need* to know if you think she's dead."

As though he could tell that she was fighting within herself to remain in check, he gripped her hand tighter. "It's okay—I don't think she's dead. I think everything is going to be okay. Let's just go for a quick walk to the pickup."

She didn't love his attempt to mollify her, but at the same time she found some relief and comfort in his words. Everything would be fine. She had to trust him.

Silently, she let him lead her toward his pickup. He opened the door and helped her inside before making his way over to the driver's side and getting in. As he did, the aroma of sweat and ash filled the small space.

He took in a long breath.

He was being so reticent in talking to her, but he'd told her everything was going to be fine. Why? "Was she inside?"

"I didn't think she was inside… I really didn't."

"Didn't?" He was speaking in past tense. Which meant only one thing…now he did believe she had been inside. "She's in there? You think she…*was*…inside?" she asked, struggling to come to terms with what she was saying.

"One of the neighbors believes she saw a teenage girl entering the house about ten minutes before the fire really took off."

"Did she see anyone leave?" April tried to remind herself to breathe. "You said you didn't think she was dead…"

"She didn't come out—at least, they didn't see her." He shook his head, concern filling his eyes. He reached over and took her hand with his. "I'm hoping that the woman was wrong. But the description she gave was consistent with that of Grace. Teenage girl. Green hair. And she believed the girl had a black eye. I think she slipped out before the fire took off. Ten minutes…that's probably how long she was in there."

Is he saying he thought Grace had set the fire?

She didn't know what to say, or how to feel. Grace wasn't likely to commit arson and she wasn't suicidal, at least not from what April knew or what she had managed to read from the girl.

"She…she has to still be alive."

He nodded, giving her a look as though he was taking it easy on her. "She is probably alive, but there's talk Grace may have started the fire." Sean squeezed her hand.

"What?" April sank deeper into her seat. "No. That doesn't fit. She wouldn't do something like that."

He studied her, like he was trying to decide if she knew something about the girl he didn't and as he did, she wished she didn't have a rising feeling that she was wrong. This girl *did* come from a family that wasn't the best, and she had been in trouble before. There was no way to really say for sure that this troubled teen wouldn't have committed arson.

Almost as though he could read the thoughts on her face, he nodded. "Just because we want to assume the best of the people we care about doesn't mean they are actually worthy

of you giving them the benefit of the doubt. Grace was...
is troubled."

"There's no doubt about that." She started tapping her
foot.

He glanced down at her nervous movement. "It's been a
long day. How about you come over to my place?"

And just like that, her nervousness amplified.

Chapter Eight

Sean added the finishing touches to his best attempt at a charcuterie board. He barely paid attention as he placed the end of the cheese back in the fridge.

All he could think about was April and how he wanted to take her into his arms and tell her everything would be okay, but nothing he could say or do would help her get through this without more pain and disappointment. He hated that he had to be the one at the epicenter of this battle she was facing, one without any clear-cut answers. In fact, the only thing he knew with any certainty was he had played more of a role in the destruction of her life than he wanted to, or could, admit.

"Look, we don't know if Grace was inside the house. Maybe it wasn't her," he said, walking out of his kitchen while carrying her a plate of salami and cheese—the only thing he'd had in his fridge on this short notice. Having a guest wasn't something he'd prepared for.

"That's what I'm hoping. I just wish we had more answers." April turned in the recliner, and he handed her the plate and the glass of wine. The wine had been the five-buck-chuck stuff from the market at the corner; he'd bought it the last time he thought he had a possibility of bringing a woman back to his place. Which, come to think about it, had been more than six months ago. He was sure this kind of wine wasn't the type that got better with age.

He had beer in the fridge, but the last time he'd bought a woman a beer at Great Northern Bar, she'd turned up her nose at him like he'd somehow committed the worst crime on the planet. He hadn't wanted to offend April.

"I have my ringer on, and as soon as Jim finds anything of use, he will let us know."

She nodded and took a long drink from the wineglass he'd bought at the secondhand store. As she drank, he noticed the chip on the edge of the glass. He wasn't sure if he should say something. Thankfully, from the way she was putting the wine down, he doubted she would really notice or, if she did, that she would say anything.

"I hope you're okay with what I've got in the kitchen. We can order something in, too. I don't have a ton of stuff on hand, sorry. About all I have food-wise is cat food."

She waved him off as she drained the glass. "You're fine. Wait… You have a cat?"

He nodded. "He's a gray American shorthair and he's pretty shy, but he is around here someplace. He doesn't usually come out unless it's really quiet."

"I like him already," she said with a smile. "I hope he's okay with me being here. And I hope you know how much I appreciate you having me over. I didn't feel like going back to my place and staring at the walls until we heard something."

"At least they have gotten the fire completely under control," he said, looking at his watch. It was nearly midnight. It had been the longest day, yet the shortest as she had been by his side. It was crazy how fast time seemed to move when they were together.

"If he calls when I'm sleeping, don't worry about waking me up. I'm a light sleeper. But he isn't going to work overnight anyway, right? He has to wait for things to cool down, first."

He nodded. "And I'm the opposite. Unless you have an alarm going off or there's smoke in the air, there isn't much of a chance of waking me up." He smiled at the thought of getting to see her when she was sleeping.

The only thing that could have made it better was if he was holding her in his arms.

She was so beautiful.

She smiled up at him. "What if I want to wake you up? If I need something?"

He wasn't sure, but he could have sworn there was a flirtatious lilt to her voice as she spoke.

"I'm at your mercy."

If only he was better at reading between the lines with women. He absolutely sucked at seeing when a woman was flirting with him. His ex used to laugh at him when they were out in public and women would talk to him. He'd think they were being nice, and she would tease him…and then be furious with him by the end of the night. Her shift from laughter to fury always made him wonder if it wasn't actually that he was being hit on or if she was just looking for reasons to fight. To this day, he wasn't sure.

He sat down on the couch next to April and turned on the television, putting on *Hot in Cleveland*. He'd not watched it, but he'd heard it was funny from Cindy.

As the show played in the background, his gaze kept slipping over toward April. Her blond hair had fallen into her face, and a piece was gently tracing the curve of her cheek—exactly where he would have given anything to trace his finger.

She laughed as she watched the show, and his heart lightened with her sound. It was a relief to hear her laugh. He couldn't recall hearing that sound from her before, and it was addictive.

She turned slightly, catching his eyes as he stared at her. "I love Betty White. She is so funny." She popped a piece of cheese into her mouth, making his gaze move to her lips. She licked them, and he tried to control his desire to feel those lips pressed against his.

He couldn't remember a time he had ever wanted a woman more. He wanted to reach across the couch and take her into his arms and make her forget about everything but him and this moment. Yet, how could he kiss her when there was such a heavy secret between them?

Maybe a kiss could be some kind of remedy. Maybe not for the secret, but at least it could take away some of the stresses they were both feeling. It wouldn't hurt their search. They were merely both volunteering. Aside from his own inadequacies and the nature of the situation that had brought them together, there was nothing standing in their way when it came to taking things a step further.

Betty White said something about breaking a hip, and April let out a long laugh. It was too much. He moved closer to her. "Do you need another glass of wine?"

She nodded, reaching over and grabbing her glass. "That would be great. It's been such a long day."

As he moved for the glass, their fingers grazed against each other, and her gaze snapped over to him. There was a soft smile on her lips, and she looked down at their touching fingers and then back up at him. Her blue eyes caught the light of the lamp on the side of the couch behind him. "I…" she said, "I think you should get a glass, too."

He nodded, but as he moved to get up, she shot to her

feet. "Do you want anything else?" she asked, her words coming fast as though she was nervous.

He wanted her, but he didn't know if he could dare to say such a thing aloud. "Wine is good." *But* you *would be better.*

She nearly sprinted into the kitchen, and he retreated to the far corner of the couch. He had screwed up. Maybe she was feeling unnerved by their being so close together and alone.

April's phone buzzed on the side table.

Though he knew he shouldn't, he was tempted to take a look at who was trying to get ahold of her.

Her phone buzzed again.

His stomach tightened as he leaned back into his seat on the couch. He didn't have any right to know who was trying to get in touch with her—that was, unless it had to do with the search.

"April," he called, getting to his feet and trying his damnedest not to peek at the screen as it buzzed again. He glanced down and spotted a man's pic looking up at him with the name "Damon." The guy looked like a jerk. He had a beard and a big, dumb smile that Sean would want to punch off the dude if he saw him in person.

He had to be the guy Summer had mentioned earlier.

He flopped back down on the couch. She should have told him that she had a boyfriend. Maybe that was why she had seemed so uncomfortable with him—she didn't want to tell him that she was taken. Or maybe she was just looking for a place to stay where she wouldn't have to be alone—maybe Damon was out of town for the night or something.

He gritted his teeth so hard that his jaw cramped.

After a few minutes, she returned from the kitchen, two beers in her hand. She handed him one. "I hope you don't mind that I made a switch. I'm not much of a wine drinker."

He smiled at her. "What's mine is yours. Plus I'm sure that wine was terrible."

She laughed as she sat down on the couch beside him. "I'm not going to say that it tasted like feet, but I'm pretty sure I got a big toe in my glass. Though…" she said, taking a drink of her beer, "it didn't really slow me down. I figure having a couple glasses must be as effective for my arm as taking a couple painkillers."

Her phone buzzed and, when she picked it up, he saw the same name as earlier. She slammed her phone down on the couch beside her and shoved it violently under her leg.

"You can answer that, if you need to." He motioned toward the phone she'd been trying to hide.

"No. I'm good," she said, not giving him any more information than he already knew.

He didn't like it. "He called when you were grabbing drinks, too."

"Oh," she said, touching the phone under her leg as it buzzed again. "Well, he doesn't need to talk to me now… or ever."

"So, that's not your boyfriend?" he asked, hope dulling some of the sharp edges of the jealousy he had been feeling.

She delicately nibbled on her lip. "We have hung out a few times, but the guy just doesn't know how to take a hint."

He wasn't sure what that was supposed to mean. "Does that mean he's still a part of your life?"

She shrugged. "I haven't been out with him for a few months, but we work together, and he thinks it's fine if he calls all the time. If I try to block him, he just changes his number. It's gotten ridiculous."

"Hold up…" He paused, putting down his beer on the table next to him. "This guy is *harassing* you?" His anger flared. "Has he *hurt* you?" The words rang funny in his ears as he heard himself speak and try to judge anyone else for doing her harm, when harm was what he had brought most of to her life.

He had to tell her the truth…*eventually*.

"The guy is pathetic. He knows I don't want to see him again, but he always manages to weasel his way back into my life. He wears me down with the constant phone calls and texts. It's easier to give one-word responses than to have him keep badgering me."

"April…" he said, surprised by her situation, "that's called stalking. Have you talked to anyone? A lawyer?"

She shook her head. "It's not that bad. He hasn't threatened me or anything. He just is *persistent*. And there are times at work when I *have* to talk to him about things."

She could call it anything she wanted, but if he met the guy, he would want to punch Damon's teeth down his throat. Damon, coworker or not, was a letch.

Her phone started buzzing again. "Do you really want him to stop calling you?" he asked.

Some of the color drained from her face. "I do. Why?"

"If you want, I will talk to him and handle this. Just hand me your phone." He extended his hand.

"I… I can handle him. It's just—"

He didn't doubt she was telling him the truth about the man, not from the look on her face whenever that phone buzzed, but he was surprised she didn't want him to help. "You can count on me to protect you. It's what I do."

"I hope you don't think that I'm some kind of damsel in distress." She chewed on her lip, harder, as she pulled her phone out and looked down at the screen.

"You've needed help this week, and there is nothing wrong with that. We all have moments in our lives when we have to count on other people to help us get through. Just think of this as me helping you out of another rockslide… just this time the rock is this piece of work."

She handed her phone over. "I don't think he's going to listen to you. He definitely hasn't been listening to me."

"What is there to lose?" He slid the green dial on the phone, answering. "Hello?" It sounded like a low, dangerous growl.

"Who is this?" the guy on the other end of the line asked. "Where's April?"

His lip quivered as he tried to control his snarl. "April is busy."

"Give her the phone. I need to talk to her about work."

"Damon, she doesn't want to talk to you…not now and not ever. In fact, if you keep harassing her, you'll have to deal with me, and you don't want that, trust me."

The guy laughed. "Boy, she has you curled around her finger…doesn't she? Listen here, she's mine and she's always going to be mine. She may play with you and tell you she loves you, but I'm the one she's always thinking about."

"She's always thinking about you because you are scaring her." He looked over at April, who had started to pace beside the couch. "Is that how you achieve power over women? By breaking them down until they feel like they have to talk? Yeah, you're a big man."

"Screw you," the guy said. "You have no idea what damage you just caused." He hung up the phone.

"Wait…" But it was too late, the phone line was dead.

As Sean put the phone down, fear filled him—not that he could admit that to April. He had promised he would help her, but now he was concerned he done exactly the opposite.

April had been right, this guy was a real piece of work.

She looked over at him with a questioning expression.

"I think you should get yourself a new cell number tomorrow." He put the phone down on the table. "In the meantime, you need to tell me more about this guy. Did he know that you were hurt on the mountain? Where was he when you were in the hospital?"

"I'm sure he heard about the accident." She took her phone and shoved it under her leg. "He's another one of the counselors at the camp."

"What? You said you worked with him, but I didn't think—" He couldn't believe that her admission hadn't sunken in until now. Of course, the guy was a counselor. "How is this guy able to work with kids?"

"Everyone has their quirks," she said, staring down at the edge of the couch like it held some kind of answers.

"Stalking and harassing a woman isn't a *quirk*, it's illegal."

"He's obnoxious and rude, but—"

"No, April. Don't minimize this. You and I both know this guy is a problem, that he shouldn't be around you or children. Have you told your bosses about him?"

She shook her head. "They have enough on their plates. It was my mistake for thinking I could date someone there."

"No, none of this is your fault."

She stared at the ground. "He hasn't done anything to harm the kids. As for me, he's harmless. He just wants my attention."

"Is he, though?"

She finally looked up and sent him a forced smile. "I can't help it if I'm so desirable that men refuse to let me slip through their fingers." She tried to laugh, but the sound was awkward and strangled. She reached over and touched the back of his hand. "Seriously, though, let's not talk about him. There're more important things we could be focusing on."

He didn't like her deflection, but he didn't want to make her any more uncomfortable than she already was. "Grace?" He moved his hand over hers.

"I know I should say yes, but until we know what happened with the fire…" She edged closer to him. "I was thinking we could relax."

He could think of any number of things he wanted to do right now, most involving kicking her ex's ass, but he tried to stuff down the feelings. Just because he wanted to protect her and keep her safe didn't mean it was what she needed.

His gaze moved to her hot pink cast. "I bet you are exhausted. You want to watch a movie or something? You need to rest so you can heal."

She nodded, and there was a tiredness in her eyes he hadn't even noticed until this moment. The kind that came more from a weary soul than the late hour. He'd seen it so many times when he'd been called to fires and he'd spoken to homeowners or survivors.

If only there was something else he could do to make her forget. Recently, he'd heard a concept about moving through pain. He couldn't remember it exactly, but from what he remembered it was basically the philosophy that everyone experienced pain—varying levels, but pain, nonetheless. What helped people keep hoping were what they called moments of "glimmer." Glimmer were small moments in time in which the heart lifted, and true happiness or relief could be found.

For him, a single glimmer in the heaviest of darkness could do more help than any words of consolation or comfort. His thoughts moved to the day he'd watched Cameron, April's former boyfriend, die on the side of the road. He had been holding his friend when Cameron had taken his last breath. It had taken Sean years to recover. In fact, there were days that the memory swept back into his life and threatened to steal his soul once again.

He'd been lost and was considering ending his life in some twisted tribute and apology; that was, until he'd found a glimmer. It had come when he'd been working as a custodian at the local high school a month after he graduated. It was the night shift, and he'd been cleaning in the shop area, thinking about Cameron and the car accident, when he'd heard a mewing come from the corner. He tracked down the sound and in an old, rusted-out engine cylinder was a tiny kitten. Its eyes weren't even open, and it had appeared to be no more than a few days old.

The thing had been tiny. He'd never seen anything so newly born and the creature had terrified him at first. He hadn't had a clue how to take care of the animal. Yet, he'd stayed near it. He'd opened the shop door slightly, waiting for the mother cat to come in and retrieve it, but she never came. After spending the night on the floor of the auto shop classroom, he'd left. It had been the weekend, but that little kitten had haunted him the second he'd gotten home.

Six hours later, with kitten formula and strict instructions on how to care for a newborn, he returned. The kitten hadn't moved, and he'd wrapped it in a towel and brought it to a vet's office, and then finally home with him. He nursed it every few hours. When the baby had perked up and started to open its eyes, he'd finally decided to name it Piston.

It was silly to admit, and he wouldn't say it aloud, but that old cat had saved his life.

Now, what April needed most was a glimmer.

Chapter Nine

April scooched closer to Sean on the couch. As sore as she was feeling, he was the one who looked to be in the most pain. She couldn't make sense of the expression on his face. At first thought, she would have assumed his discomfort was caused by the situation with Grace, but that look hadn't shown up until after Damon had called and interrupted their night.

She really did hate that guy.

Her hand moved into his and Sean smiled over at her, the pained look in his eyes finally disappearing. "Are you okay?" he asked. "Warm enough? I think I have a blanket around here somewhere if you need something."

"I know this sounds strange," she said, wishing she was better at the game she was about to try to play.

"What?" he asked, as an advertisement played on the television between scenes of *Hot in Cleveland*.

"It's been a really long day…actually, you can call it a week." She looked at his chest, yearning for his touch. "I could use a snuggle."

Though she was aware she was playing with fire in wanting to be so close and for him to touch her, she couldn't resist the desire. She needed to be held, to be touched by someone who would keep her safe—at least, in this moment.

He nodded, his smile widening. He let go of her fingers and lifted his arm, opening up his chest. "Bring it in."

She moved in close and looked up at him. "This isn't too weird?"

"I want you to be comfortable. If this is what you need tonight, you got it." He cleared his throat. "And, if this is *all* you want… I respect that. This can be a onetime, see-a-need-fill-a-need kind of thing."

She appreciated the fact that he wasn't going to pressure her for something she wasn't sure she was ready for with him. Then again, he was so hot. If she had less going on in her life, and she wasn't in a dumpster fire phase, she would have jumped on this opportunity to spend the night with him as something more than friends. Yet, as she was getting older, she was coming to realize that while sex was fun, it led to more complications than comfort.

"Thank you, Sean." She laid her head against his chest.

"For what?" he asked, his words making his chest vibrate against her face and sending gentle shivers down her spine.

"Not trying to force anything. Saving me. Being you. Take your pick." She put her hand on his chest, hoping to feel the sweet vibrato of his voice on the palm of her hand.

"If you think you need to thank me, or that I've done anything to be thankful for, you need to hang out with a higher caliber of men."

She wrapped her fingers in the cotton of his shirt as his words filled her hand like gold flecks. If only she could keep them, him, and this moment, forever.

"You've done more than you know." Her thoughts moved to the moment she'd awakened to find him beside her after her accident. From the moment that fate had brought them back together, he had been saving her.

He put his hand on hers and held it tight. "I could say the same of you."

"All I've done is bring craziness into your life," she said, with a gentle laugh.

"Didn't you know, I'm an adrenaline junkie," he said, stroking her hand with his thumb. "Really, you've brought me everything I needed."

"If you stick with me, the one and probably only thing I can promise you with any certainty is that you will never be bored."

She thought about how different her life would have been if she hadn't dated Cameron in high school and had, instead, been with Sean. At the time, they hadn't run with the same crowds. He'd been a football player and class president, while she had been hanging out outside the Grange, a small bar on the outskirts of town that was notorious for serving underage girls.

It was strange to think that as differently as they had started life, they had still been brought back together and found this moment—even if it was only temporary.

She soaked in the feeling of his skin on hers. Her plaster-casted arm started to cramp as she laid against him. She needed to move her shoulder and get the pressure off her arm, but she didn't want to give in to the pain. Shifting, she tried to take some pressure of her broken arm.

"Are you okay?" he asked, sitting back slightly as if he could tell that she was hurting.

"It's my stupid arm," she said, moving it slightly between them.

"Here," he said, moving, "sit up a little."

Moving was the last thing she wanted to do. She was finally where she wanted to be—in his arms. She shook her head. "I'll be fine, really."

He sent her a little half smile, like he could tell what she was thinking. "We can go back to cuddling, I promise."

She sighed as he let go of her hand and she sat up. He stood. "I'll be right back, wait here."

The movie played over the fireplace on the wall as she tried to patiently wait for him to come back. After a few minutes, though, when he still hadn't returned, she got up from the couch and made her way down the hallway. "Sean, is everything okay?" she called, hoping she wasn't interrupting him on the phone or something.

He didn't answer.

She wasn't sure if she should keep looking for him, or if he had forgotten about her or fallen asleep and she should just tuck back into the couch for the night. At the far end of the hall, there was a closed door. She stopped at it, giving it a gentle tap.

"Come on in," he answered.

There was a little part of her that was excited to see what he was doing, and her thoughts moved to him lying on the bed, centerfold spread, and just waiting for her to find him. If he was naked and waiting, she wouldn't be able to say no to her devilishly handsome rescuer. On the other hand, he'd promised her things wouldn't head that way…but that didn't mean a girl couldn't hope.

She pushed open the door and she caught her breath.

He was still dressed, but he was perched on his elbow and lying on his side on the bed, and he was curled around a little gray tabby cat. "Oh…" she said, smiling at the sweet picture in front of her. "Who do we have here?"

"This is Piston," he said, the cat yawning as he gently scratched behind his ears. "I rescued him when he was only a few days old."

She walked over to the bed and sat down beside the cat

and Sean. "You told me you had a cat running around. You didn't tell me he was so handsome."

He stopped petting Piston and motioned for her to take over. She was happy to oblige, and as she stroked the cat, he moved and stretched, exposing his belly for rubs.

Sean looked surprised. "You know," he said, "I've had this boy for fourteen years, and I don't think he's ever let anyone else touch him."

"I've always had a thing for cats. You're not the first person to say something like that to me." She smiled.

"You must be an animal whisperer." He patted the pillow on the other side of the bed. The television was playing, and its sound was muffled as she lay down beside Piston and Sean.

As she petted the cat, cooing softly, there was something about the moment that made her thoughts move to what it would have been like to have a family. If she had kept her baby, if Cameron had lived, if her life had been different, this could have been hers. The thought threatened to steal away the joy in the moment, but she pushed away the yearning for a life missed.

She closed her eyes as she tried to feel nothing but the happiness in her heart.

APRIL'S EYES CLOSED and soon her chest was moving with the steady breaths of sleep. Sean smiled at the serenity in her face. For the first time since he'd found her, she finally looked at peace.

There was a strand of hair caught in the corner of her mouth and he was tempted to reach over and fix it for her, but resisted the urge. She needed to rest. She needed to heal. Plus he needed to keep his hands off her. It had been so hard to resist the urge to kiss her ever since they had set foot in his house. She had been so vulnerable and stripped of all pretenses that had he been a lesser man, to take her into his arms and find respite in one another's naked body would have been easy. Yet, he had told her she didn't have to worry about an advance.

Now, he wished he hadn't given her such guarantees. He would have given his left eyetooth to simply kiss her—nothing more.

He carefully got out of bed. Piston peeled his eye open, squinting at him with an edge of annoyance, but then closed his eyes once again.

I get it, buddy, he thought. *If I was where you are, I wouldn't give up my spot, either.*

He moved to the doorway and looked back, taking in the scene on his bed for a long moment. He didn't want to be weird, but he could have watched them together all night. To see Piston so at home with this woman who meant more to him than she knew and was deeper into his heart with every passing hour, was incredible.

Going to his hall closet, he pulled out a blanket his grandmother had crocheted for him when he'd been a kid. It was blue and orange, and he'd slept with it into his teens and well past the point it was probably normal to keep childish things, but it had always been his favorite. It seemed only right that he'd use something that meant a great deal to him throughout his life to now keep April safe and warm. It was the least he could do.

He slipped back into the bedroom and gently placed the blanket over her. She rustled slightly as he stepped to leave, and she moved her hand to his. His smile returned at the honest moment. She wanted him. He could feel it in the way her skin brushed against his.

Reaching up, he moved the wayward strand of hair from

her lips. Like Piston had, she peered up at him and a sleepy smile came over her lips. "Kiss me good night."

She didn't need to ask him twice. Leaning over, he kissed the soft skin of her forehead, happy for any chance to press his lips against her. However, she lifted her chin, moving her lips to his. She reached up, placing her arm over his shoulder and pulling him closer to her and deeper into their kiss.

She tasted like beer, and he licked the tang from her lips. He could imagine that the rest of her body would likely taste just as delicious. He grew hard at the thought of taking her, all of her.

As he moved closer to her, Piston retreated from the bed, but not before throwing them a sideways glance.

He laughed at the cat before turning back to what he had been doing.

She moaned into his mouth, and he moved between her thighs. He traced the line of her jaw with his kisses and buried his face in her neck as his hunger raced through him.

"Sean." She whispered his name like it was a precious secret.

"Mmm?" He kissed the line of her collarbone.

"I want you," she said, pressing her fingers through his hair and gently tugging. "I want all of you."

He groaned as he grew impossibly harder, pressing painfully against the zipper of his jeans.

"I want you to make me forget…everything that has happened in the past."

Just like that, he was pulled out of his study of her body. He'd nearly forgotten about the hurt and pain he'd caused in her life, and now it had come slamming, fist-like into the center of his gut.

He couldn't have her…not until she knew his truth.

Chapter Ten

Sean had left the room so quickly last night that April was afraid to talk about what had happened and how she had frightened him away. In the long list of mistakes she had made in her life, his retreat from between her thighs had to be one of the worst.

Why had she opened her mouth and spoken her thoughts? If she had just shut up and let things progress, she wouldn't have woken up aching and more confused.

Instead, she'd messed everything up. If she hadn't asked him to kiss her…but she couldn't regret asking. Not that. That was the one thing she had done right last night.

As she walked out of his bedroom, Sean was up and working in the kitchen. It smelled like coffee and bacon and as she came in, he handed her a steaming mug. "Good morning," he said, sounding slightly sheepish.

He must have been feeling as awkward and confused as she was.

"Sorry I took over your bed last night," she offered, trying to dance around the real topic that was standing between them. "You know, I could have given you the bed."

"Oh, no," he said, turning away like he feared that she would read something on his face. "It was all yours. It can be as long as you want to stay here, by the way."

Even with his offer, he didn't turn to look at her. She wasn't about to grill him on the fine points, and whether or not "as long as you want" was a day or a lifetime.

She laughed at herself as she sipped on her piping-hot coffee. He even made coffee perfectly, cream and sugar included. It was a great man who met a woman with a cup upon waking. He really was a keeper.

He might have been right about her needing a higher caliber of men in her life—especially if this was the kind of treatment that was included.

"Piston stayed with me all night. I think he finally got up around five." She tried to make small talk without rubbing against the subject of his leaving.

"He must have heard me. I had to run and grab a few things at the store so I could make you breakfast." He smiled and set down a plate of eggs and bacon with toast in front of her. He grabbed a jar of grape jelly off the counter and popped open the lid.

"Thank you," she said, taking the jelly with a wide grin. "You went out of your way. I appreciate it." She didn't have the heart to tell him that she wasn't much of a breakfast eater. Besides, she wasn't going to turn down an opportunity like this.

He turned his back to her, and she watched his jeans stretch hard against his backside. She could have stared at that backside forever. He had to do at least a hundred squats a day to make it look that good.

"I wasn't sure how you took your eggs, or your coffee," he said, looking back at her over his shoulder. "Is everything to your liking?"

In all my life, I don't think I've ever had a guy make me breakfast. Or care how I like my eggs, for that matter, she thought.

She was loving the fact that she was being spoiled, but at the same time he was ruining her for all future men. If she started to get used to this level of care and consideration, she wasn't sure she would ever be able to go back to a hit-it-and-quit-it type of relationship. *Er, rather, a situationship.*

"Everything is perfect." The statement was far more inclusive than she'd intended, but she didn't care if he inferred the true meaning of her words.

He grabbed a second plate for himself and dished it up. Sitting down next to her, he took a long sip of his black coffee.

"Did you have to buy everything for this breakfast this morning, or did you have a few things on hand?"

"No…" He gave her a sheepish grin. "I had a canister of coffee."

"But you had to buy everything else?" she asked.

"It wasn't a big deal. I needed to stock up. Piston is *super needy.*" He laughed, and the sound caressed her like a hand and made goose bumps raise on her arms.

That's new. She put her hand over her arm, inadvertently attempting to cover what he could make her feel with just his voice.

He couldn't know the power he held over her. If he did, he would be able to get away with darn near anything.

Popping a piece of toast in her mouth, she chewed as he turned to look at her. "So…about last night."

If she didn't know better, she would have thought he'd picked this exact moment, that was, with her mouth full, to bring this up.

"Mmm-hmm," she mumbled, trying to chew faster.

"I hope you know how much I wanted you…and to take things further." He ran his hand over the back of his neck as if he was deeply uncomfortable.

She swallowed. "But?"

There was always a *but*.

"There's something I have to tell you…" He paused as he stared down at his plate. "I'm worried you may not take it well. But please promise to hear me out."

All of a sudden, all desire to eat left her. "Okay… What did you *do*? Did something happen to Grace? Did they find her?" Her stomach roiled.

He put his hands up. "No. No. It has nothing to do with Grace. In fact, it happened a long time ago."

She relaxed a little and reminded herself to take a breath.

"Do you remember the night that Cameron died?" he asked.

Of course she remembered that night. It had been two weeks after she'd told him about her positive pregnancy test. He'd promised her they were going to spend together forever, and he would marry her and take care of their baby. They'd had two years left in high school before they would graduate. And yet, in the blink of an eye and a single phone call later, he was gone and with him so were her dreams of a future.

"Yes," she said simply.

"I was there."

Her whole body jerked. "What do you mean *you were there*? He was the only one in the car that night." She stared at him, trying to make sense of what Sean was saying and why he would be saying it.

"No, he wasn't." The color had drained from his face and as he reached over to take her hand, she pulled it away.

She couldn't move. She couldn't speak.

"As you know, my father—God, rest his soul—was the sheriff in those years…" He paused like he was hoping she would put the pieces together for herself, but how could she? She had no idea what was coming.

He ran his finger down the cold steel of his fork. "Cameron had been the one driving. That part was true. He and I had been partying together that night."

"That's a lie," she countered, sounding breathless. "You two didn't hang out. You weren't even friends."

He looked at her, and she could have almost sworn there were tears in his eyes.

She felt no pity.

"He and I grew up together. We didn't hang out in high school. We were in different crowds, but he lived three houses down." He made a choking sound, as though his feelings were swelling in his throat.

She couldn't even begin to count the number of times she had that pressure, that pain…that tremendous grief.

"There had been that kegger—he didn't want to tell you about it. He knew you'd be upset that he was going, but he told me he wanted to have one last bender before having to really grow up and become a dad. He'd been drinking. *You know.*"

Cameron's dad had told her they had smelled alcohol in the car at the time of the accident, but no one had ever told her *he* had been drinking and driving. Many times, she had wondered, but she'd always come to the conclusion that he was smarter than that…that he'd known what was at stake. More, he'd known she was there waiting for him and needing him to step up and be the man she needed him to be in a moment when she needed someone to help her more than ever.

He'd *promised.*

She'd been so stupid. So naive.

"He was so nervous about becoming a father. It was all

he could talk about. Most of the guys actually kind of got tired of hearing about you and the baby. A few had even told him he'd lost his mind…" He paused. "I don't know why I'm telling you about that, but…"

"Just say it. Tell me everything," she said, but her voice was laced with venom, and it burned on her lips.

"He'd come by himself to the kegger. It got late. My friends wanted to stay out there and keep partying, but I'd promised my dad I would go to work the next day. He didn't know where I was…only that I was staying at my friend's house."

She got up and took her plate over to the kitchen sink and set it on the counter. She turned around, crossing her arms over her chest as she fought to control the pain in her heart. Waving, she motioned for him to continue.

"I told Cameron to let me drive. I hadn't been drinking as much as he had been. He was pretty wasted. Neither of us should have ever gotten in that car." A single tear slipped down his cheek. "He hit that tree going at least fifty. I don't remember anything about the accident except waking up and looking for him. There was a hole in the windshield. I had to cut myself out of my seat belt. I went outside. Cameron was still alive."

He looked down at his hands as though he could still see Cameron resting in them. They were as good as still covered in blood.

"I held him… I held him when he took his last breath."

Wordlessly, she walked out of the kitchen and out of Sean's life.

Chapter Eleven

He hadn't thought his revelation would go well, but it had gone a million times worse than he had anticipated. April hated him.

She had every right.

He'd wanted to tell her that he'd tried to save Cameron. That he'd done chest compressions.

More, he wanted to tell her that he'd been carrying the weight of his failures ever since that night.

So many nights, he had wished he had died, if not in place of Cameron, then right beside him. There had been no reason for him to walk away while Cameron hadn't.

Yet, April must have known he'd failed without his ever having to explicitly tell her. If he had succeeded in his life-saving measures, then she wouldn't have been standing with him. She would have had a life somewhere with Cameron and their baby, Ann, and possibly more children, in tow.

He'd cost her a future.

A renewed sense of guilt coursed through him.

He should have been the one to go that day.

He sat down on the couch in the living room and put his head in his hands. Maybe he shouldn't have told her what had happened, or what role he'd played in it. She'd still be here if he'd kept the past in the past, but no. He just had to get his trauma off his chest.

Telling her had been absolutely selfish. That night and its consequences in his life were his to bear.

He should have borne them in silence.

Then again, if she had found out any other way...

He wiped the back of his hand over his face, roughly pushing away the tears that had dampened his cheeks in yet another moment of weakness. Here he had thought he was a strong man, a man capable of saving others and making a difference when he couldn't even do those things in his own life. All he was good at was destruction and death.

Piston rubbed against his leg, pulling him from his self-loathing.

"Hey buddy," he said, reaching down and rubbing the cat's ear. "She's not coming back."

The cat sat down and looked up at him like he could understand what he was trying to tell him.

"I know you're not surprised," he said, answering the question on Piston's furry face.

The cat meowed loudly.

He perched on his elbow. "Don't yell at me. I didn't do it on purpose."

Piston meowed again and ran to the door of the kitchen and looked back at him like he wanted him to follow.

"Yeah, yeah, I'm sure you want some food," he said, getting up and walking after the cat.

It was wrong, but he was glad his furry friend was here to save him from the fiery inferno of his thoughts. Piston pranced down the hall, turning back every few feet before lurching ahead. Instead of leading him to his food bowl, he led him to the back bedroom.

"I told you, she's not coming back," he argued.

Piston meowed loudly again and rushed into the room.

Though he didn't really want to go into the room and stare at the bed, which would inevitably remind him of last night's close call, he followed.

As he walked in, Piston rubbed against the bedside table. Sitting on top was April's cell phone. In her rush to walk out, she must have forgotten it.

"Son of a…" he said, walking over and picking it up.

The screen lit up with a notification that she had missed fourteen calls.

She hadn't been gone that long—maybe thirty minutes. He wondered how many were from her stalker.

Though he wanted to open up the phone and take a look to validate his suspicions, he didn't bother. It was an invasion of her privacy, and he doubted he could have gotten past her security anyway. It was better to just give it back to her, phone undisturbed.

He put the phone in his pocket, knowing full well that she wouldn't be coming back…not even for her device. If he was in her shoes and she had dropped that kind of bomb on him, he would just get a new cell phone before ever giving in and coming back.

In order to save her the thousand bucks, the least he could do was to take her phone over to her apartment and drop it off. He didn't even have to talk to her. He could just knock and hand it off *if* she chose to answer the door.

If she wasn't there or if she refused to see him, he could leave it in her mailbox or something.

Piston rubbed against his leg, like he was looking for acknowledgment of his good deed.

"Yes, buddy, thank you." He reached down and picked up the gray beast.

Walking out, he made his way to the kitchen where he

kept everything for Piston. He pulled out a can of wet food and flopped it out into his dish. "You earned it." He let Piston down beside his bowl and he chowed down on the special treat.

Grabbing his keys, he made his way out to his pickup. As he turned toward the driver's-side door, he was surprised to find April standing there, leaning against it. She looked slightly disheveled, but it made sense. He had sprung his information almost as soon as she had gotten out of bed.

I'm such a jerk, he thought.

He didn't have a clue what to do or say to make things better between them. "Have you been here ever since you left?" He felt stupid leading with that, but he hadn't been expecting to see her.

"I started to walk toward my apartment, but I came back." She tucked her hands in tighter to her pits, hugging herself.

"Did you realize you left this behind?" he asked, pulling out her phone. "Piston found it."

She took it and clicked on the screen, giving a long sigh. "Thanks." She turned off the screen and pushed it into her pocket. "That's actually not why I came back, though. In fact, I could probably live without it for reasons that I'm sure you're aware of."

"Then why did you come back? Did you forget something else?"

"We need to find Grace."

So, she only came back because he was the only one who could help her find answers. *Got it.*

He couldn't be mad she was using him, not when they were helping someone else. Yet, he couldn't stop from coming full circle. "Why?"

She frowned like she hadn't understood his question.

"Why are you so fervent that we find Grace? Do you

know something about her disappearance that you haven't told me?"

As soon as he spoke, her calm, but guarded facade faded away and was replaced by anger. "You know, you don't always have to say and do the most wrong things."

"Gah," he said, rubbing his face angrily. "I'm sorry. You're right."

"Look, Sean, I'm going to let you just sit with what you've said and done." She sighed. "I don't need to beat you up any more than I'm sure you've already being doing for the last sixteen years."

That didn't mean that she could or would forgive him. In fact, it didn't mean anything more than she was going to let him hang himself with his guilt.

"I want you to know how sorry I am…for *everything.*" He reached for her hand, but she stepped back. Her rejection was like a slap in the face. "Please, tell me you forgive me."

"I can't forgive you for what happened." Tears filled her eyes, but she blinked them away. "What happened…it destroyed me in so many ways. It ended so many things. I'd be lying if I said I could forgive you. When it comes to that night, that accident—there isn't a single person involved who wasn't at fault—from the person who told him about the party, to the people who handed him a beer, and then later the ones who watched him get in the car to drive."

Chapter Twelve

April could tell he wanted to keep talking and begging for her forgiveness, but she wasn't ready to hear anything else he had to say. If it weren't for Grace, she wouldn't have come back, wouldn't have set foot within thirty yards of him, but there were immediate needs that were more important than what had happened.

"April, I'm sorrier than you could even know. If there was any way I could go back—"

She stopped him with the wave of her hand. "I don't want to hear any more. I can't. Let's just find our girl, and then you and I—we can go our separate ways."

"But—" He started to argue.

"There are no *buts*. There's only finding Grace. That's all." She paused, trying not to focus on the anger and pain that were moving through her. "If you can't handle it... I can work alone."

Her phone buzzed in her pocket. She didn't want to look in case it was Damon—her stalker. She didn't need to pull the pin on that grenade by answering it; there were already more emotional land mines than she could get through.

It buzzed again, and Sean looked at her expectantly. "At least look. What if it's Grace?"

She pulled her phone out and glanced at it, but was annoyed with herself for doing what she was told when all she really wanted was to tell him that he had ruined her life.

"It's not," she said, recognizing the number as one of Damon's. She shoved it back in her pocket. "Let's just go and check on the fire scene."

He walked toward the passenger's door and opened it, quietly holding it for her.

The ride to the duplex was a silent one. She had focused on her breathing and the anger that kept boiling up in her core, making her want to yell and scream and tell him about the night terrors of car accidents and lost babies that she still experienced.

What if the person I'm mad at is myself?

She pushed the thought down. She was glad she had someone else to blame for what had happened. She couldn't blame Cameron. Every time she tried to point a finger and find a reason he had died, she had always come back to herself—her pregnancy was why he had gone out that night. *She* was the one who had mistakenly gotten pregnant. If *she* hadn't, he wouldn't have gotten so drunk or at least he wouldn't have had to drive. He had been driving to get back to *her.*

Now, it really could be someone else's fault—the pain and self-flagellation, it could all be focused on *Sean. He* had been the last one to see Cam alive.

If *he* had only taken the keys and made Cam stay at that party. The anger within her rose and threatened to spill over as the new information reopened old wounds.

Sean turned left and after a few minutes, he pulled to a stop in front of the still-smoldering structure that had once been Grace's apartment. There was a van marked Fire Marshal parked outside. He turned to her and looked as though he was going to ask her a question, but he shut his mouth and turned off the engine and got out.

He walked around to her side and held out his hand to help her out of the pickup, but she carefully avoided his touch.

"April…" He said her name like it was an apology.

"Let's just worry about her being in that fire. I need to know she's still alive."

He nodded.

"Did anyone ever run a trace on her phone?" she asked.

"The police ran one on the day she went missing from the hospital, but the last time she had turned it on had been at the hospital. As far as them running another, I don't know." He pulled out his phone. "I texted the detective who was helping with Grace's disappearance."

She looked over at the duplex. Since they had left last night, the place had continued to burn. The doors and windows had been smashed in. There was a hole in the roof that was burned through and stained by smoke.

The place was a total loss.

An overweight older man walked toward them with a clipboard in his hand.

"Hey, Jim, how's it going?" Sean asked, meeting the man out on the sidewalk, which led to what had been the front door but was now a jagged, charred hole.

The older gentleman straightened the white uniform shirt he was wearing, leaving behind a black ashy handprint right at the center of his belly. She couldn't stop staring at it, even though she couldn't think why. "Hi, Sean. It's going."

"I tried to call you," Sean said. "Find anything?"

"This and that," he said, glancing over at her like he wasn't sure of what he could or couldn't say in her presence.

"She's helping us with locating Grace," Sean said, having picked up on his fellow firefighter's nonverbal question as well.

"I haven't been on scene very long. Working the perimeter before heading inside. So, no major news about the possible vic, everyone is safe and accounted for and we've been told that Grace's foster parents are out of town and unreachable for a few days, but—" He motioned for them to follow him around to the side of the building. There, where he must have been working when they'd arrived, was a black tactical bag.

As he got near his bag, he gave them a small, triumphant smile. "I believe that whoever started this fire used some sort of accelerant."

"So, you think it was an arson?" April asked.

"Absolutely." Jim nodded. "As for finding who lit the match and then proving that in court, well, that's always the highest hurdle."

"Did you find anything that could indicate who may have started it?" Sean asked.

"Nothing to do with that yet, but look." He pointed at a strange line on the ground. "See that sheen there?" he asked, motioning toward an opalescent circle on the ground near the linear burn mark. "That looks like some kind of petroleum product."

"Is it oil?" April asked. "Wouldn't it take longer to get it going than something, say, like gasoline?"

Jim smirked. "Right?" He squatted and pulled out a swab from his bag. Taking it out of its paper wrapper, he dabbed it near the linear burn mark. He wafted the smell toward himself. "*Ha!* Here, take a whiff. I think we may have our answer. *Maybe.*"

He lifted the swab for her to smell. The swab carried a strong oily smell of burned gasoline.

"They used oil and gas?" she asked, confused.

Jim glanced at Sean like he was trying to see if Sean was following his thinking or not. "Actually," Jim said, "I'm thinking that whoever did this tried to start the fire with diesel fuel first…and realized that wouldn't work well enough to get the fire really going and then decided to use regular gasoline."

"Where did they get the gas?" she asked. "Or diesel, for that matter?"

He glanced around them and toward the neighbor's house. "That's a good question. There are trucks that take diesel, but so do tractors."

No one around appeared to be driving a diesel pickup or have a tractor.

Jim took the swab and placed it in his collection kit. He took a few pics with scales and then stood up. He walked toward the back corner of the house as he continued to take more pictures of the full scene. He stopped moving and snapped another series of pictures. "Ah, hell."

She followed Sean toward him. There, near Jim's foot, was what she recognized as a yellow clip-style cap for the end of a gas can.

Jim moved toward his bag but stopped and turned toward Sean. "As much as I appreciate you guys stopping by, this is starting to look like a crime scene, so…"

"Sorry, man," Sean said, touching her arm. "We'll get out of your hair, but if there's anything you need from us—"

"Or, if you find anything out about the missing girl…" she interrupted.

"Yes, please call us," Sean said, looking at her with a small smile.

Jim nodded. "You got it. I'm hoping she isn't in there, and nothing bad has happened to her."

"We are, too," she said.

"Did you manage to get in touch with the people who were on the lease, Grace's foster parents?" Sean asked.

Jim shook his head. "I'll text you their numbers, but so far, they haven't been picking up. However, on their social media pages it looks like they have been active." He looked over at April. "And don't worry, we're going to do everything in our power to try to locate this girl—one way or another. We need to provide her family with some answers."

The way he said those words brought back thoughts of Cameron. Those were the same words she had heard when she'd gotten the news of his death. She could still hear them ringing in her ears when Cameron's father had come over and told her what had happened. *April, at least we got answers, and we know what happened.*

After Sean's revelation, and more than ever, she knew the truth about answers—they were nothing more than convenient lies.

Chapter Thirteen

It was official. April would never forgive him for what he'd done. Any hopes he'd ever had on making things right were gone—not to mention the thoughts he'd had of holding her on his chest. It was all ruined, and her hatred for him was completely justified.

The best, and only, thing he could do now was get through these days until they found Grace. *Hopefully.* He couldn't think about the possibility that they wouldn't…or that she was inside that burned-out building.

He took another look at the apartment as they pulled away from the curb. If April hadn't been with him, he was sure Jim would have had him help out on the investigation, but he wasn't about to leave her—though, it would have been easier on his head and his heart.

Plus there were other leads they needed to look into.

First things first, he needed to locate Grace's guardians. His phone pinged with a text from Jim, who'd sent him their names and numbers. He called the male and then the female, but neither picked up. He pulled up social media and went to their profiles. There, on the woman's profile, was a picture of her and her husband standing hand in hand in Playa del Carmen, thanks to her pin.

At least they didn't have to worry about them being inside their apartment at the time of the fire—or, that they'd had any obvious role in creating the fire. However, as he scrolled through the woman's page, he found picture after picture of them on vacation—all without children. "Did Grace have any siblings?" he asked. "At least, any that were staying with the same foster parents?"

"I don't think so. Why?"

He moved her phone so she could see the pictures of the vacationing couple. "From this and the time stamps, these two have been in Mexico for more than two months."

"Are you kidding me?" She grabbed the phone out of his hand and started scrolling through the pictures. "No way."

"What?" he asked, not understanding why she would be surprised or upset with the news.

"Grace has only been at Sulphur Springs for a little over six weeks." She dropped his phone on the dashboard, with a huff. "That means her foster parents had left her alone and completely unsupervised until she came and stayed with us." She ran her hands over her face.

"They can't do that, can they?" He didn't know the laws or statutes around what constituted appropriate care of a teenager in the system. From what he had heard and picked up on the job, there were some foster parents who were great and went above and beyond, while there were other guardians who were only participating in order to milk the system.

"No, they can't leave a child alone for a month and go out of the country. Are you kidding me?" she asked, looking at him like he was dumb.

"I didn't mean it like that, just that at what age—"

"Do those who monitor the foster children's welfare stop caring so much?" she said, finishing his question.

"Well…" *Yes.*

She shook her head and started tapping away on her

phone. He could see she was texting someone, but he didn't recognize the woman's name.

"Who are you talking to?" he asked.

"I'm texting my friend at child protection services. I think they should be made aware of everything that's going on— though I assume my boss has filled them in already," she said, typing even faster and grabbing screenshots of the guardians' social media posts.

For a moment, he wondered if that's where Grace had gone, but there was no way Grace would have gone to CPS to get help. He had never heard of any child, not even a teenager, who'd reached out to their caseworker. That didn't mean it wasn't possible, but very unlikely given the circumstances.

"Seriously?" April grumbled at her phone.

"Hmm?"

"Grace's caseworker hadn't been notified of anything. She hadn't even been told that Grace was in the hospital." She balled her hand into a fist. "My boss must have assumed the hospital informed them, and vice versa." She sighed. "It's just no wonder that these kids fall between the cracks. Between systematic failures, foster care neglect and the accident, well, it's no damned wonder Grace was having social problems. She's never had a chance."

He hadn't known Grace for very long, but he could say with every certainty that the world had failed her. *He* had failed her, too. He should have checked in on her at the hospital more often.

He'd become a firefighter and SAR team member to help others, and when presented with his chance, he had fallen short…again.

"What did the caseworker say?" he asked.

She shrugged. "That she was glad of the notification. She

was sorry to hear what had happened, and they would put feelers out as to Grace's whereabouts."

"But basically, they're as limited in resources as we are."

She pointed at him. "*That.* Exactly. Plus each of these caseworkers is assigned dozens of cases. They can only sacrifice so much time. And the lady made a point of Grace having a great deal of social issues. She, too, thinks Grace is nothing more than a runaway."

This poor girl was being abandoned at every turn. Except, by them.

Yet, he doubted Grace would guess they were out there searching for her.

The girl was vulnerable in many ways—unstable home, no money, she hadn't even turned to her friends. If she hadn't simply run away like everyone assumed, she would be a prime target for a predator.

Regardless of how she had gone missing, she was going to be facing a variety of possible horrors—from human trafficking to falling in with the drug culture. That was, if she was still alive after the fire.

He shook off the thought. She had to be alive. They just had to locate her.

He started to drive around the small town, slowing down as they made their way past the local movie theater, then they worked through the tiny downtown and finally drove through the residential area full of tiny houses and toward Summer's duplex.

There were resources the local law enforcement officers could tap into, but as a firefighter and even a SAR worker, some of his reach was limited. If he could have, though, he would have loved to do another ping on her cell phone.

At the thought of phones, April's buzzed on the dashboard. She reached for it and glanced at the caller's information. She tapped on the screen and answered, putting it on speaker. "Hello?"

He could hear a woman crying and then a strange muffled, shuffling sound. There was a deeper sound, like that of a man's voice, but he couldn't make out any words.

"Grace? Is that you?" April's voice was high and frantic. "Grace, are you okay? Where are you?"

The line went dead.

"Oh, my God," she said, covering her mouth with her hand as she looked over at him. "Do you think…? That couldn't have been her, right? But if it was her…she's alive."

At least, for now, he thought, not daring to speak those words aloud.

"Who was on the caller ID?" he asked.

She tapped on her phone, pulling up the information. "There wasn't a name. It was just a location. It says the number was out of Gillette, Wyoming."

He knew the town well. It was a coal mining town with a railroad that ran through its heart. Despite the rolling hills and antelope, Gillette wasn't a place he would ever have wanted to call home.

That being said, it was within the area Grace could have traveled in the time since she had been missing. Or, it could have just been a random number used by an app and it had nothing to do with the caller's actual location. "Call the number back."

It would surprise most people, but thanks to Gillette's location along the interstate and its access to a main railroad line, the town was prime country for human traffickers. From what he'd heard on the street, it was a regular thing for the Wyoming cops to bust drug runners hoping to get to Chicago and other big cities.

She called the number back, but it went straight to a generic voicemail.

"Damn it!" she yelled, slamming her hand against the dashboard.

"It's okay. Don't get too upset. Maybe it wasn't even her."

She glared at him. "It was her. I know it was Grace. You *know* it was her, too."

He had to hope it wasn't. That the crying wasn't coming from the girl they were looking for, but it was all too coincidental for it not to be. In his entire life, he couldn't think of a time when he'd gotten a random call with a woman crying on the other end of the line, and then the line going dead. The odds of it being anyone else besides Grace were astronomical.

"Sean, she's in trouble. She needs help. She needs us." She looked back down at her phone, calling the number again, but it went to voicemail. "There has to be something we can do."

He turned the truck around and hit the gas, going as fast they could safely go. He screeched to a halt in front of the sheriff's office.

She kept dialing Grace's phone, but no one answered.

The thing must have been shut off.

"Let's go," he said, turning off his truck. "These guys are our best bet if she calls back."

She nodded, but didn't look up from her phone, almost as if she thought that at any second, it would ring again, and Grace would be there.

He rushed around to her side of the truck and helped her out, but she still refused to look away from the little screen. She was typing away, sending a text to the number. From what he could see over her shoulder, it looked like she'd already sent several others.

They rushed into the main lobby of the sheriff's office, where a secretary was talking on the phone. She spotted them and motioned for them to take a seat in the hard blue plastic chairs that were in front of her desk.

Yeah, he wasn't playing that game. Instead, Sean stood at the edge of the desk. "Ma'am, I'm sorry to interrupt, but we need to talk to the officer in charge of walk-ins today."

The woman frowned at him, silently admonishing him for his rudeness, but he didn't care.

"It's important that we see him, *now.*"

She put her hand over the mouthpiece of her phone. "If it is an emergency, you need to call 911."

He wanted to take the phone she held in her hands and slam it down on the receiver, but instead he forced himself to smile. "We're here about the missing kid. We just got a phone call from her. We need to speak to someone, now… in case she calls back, we need to be prepared."

The woman's mouth moved into an O-shape. "Can you please hold?" she asked the caller. She tapped a button on her phone, and she asked for Detective Terrell.

In less than a minute, Terrell came rolling out. He met them with a smile and a friendly wave. "How's it going, Sean. I hear you've been busy this week."

Sean nodded. "My hands have been full." If he hadn't been so emotionally connected to this case and Grace, he would have joked around with Terrell. They'd known each other ever since he'd gotten started at the fire department, though they didn't often work together.

Terrell's gaze moved to April and the cast on her arm.

"This is my friend April Twofeather. She was the hiker who was hurt in the rockslide the other day. She and I are working to help find Grace Bunchen."

"Nice to meet you, April," Terrell said, with an acknowledging nod and a warm smile. "I'm glad to see you're up and running."

"Thanks," she said tersely, but her body was almost so tense that she was nearly vibrating.

"So, I hear you may have been in contact with Grace?"

April nodded.

"Why don't you guys follow me into my office and fill me in on the details." He motioned for them to follow as he used his key card to open a large steel door that led to the inner sanctum of the department.

As they walked, April talked fast about the phone call. Terrell simply nodded as they walked down the industrial-carpeted hallway and to his office, which was at the end of the corridor. There were three other officers working on computers as they walked by, which meant they were about as fully staffed as they could be at any given time during the day. Currently, there were only about ten deputies working for the vast, low-population county.

Terrell stopped and closed the door as they walked in and sat down in the proffered chairs. "So, and please bear with me here, I'm not trying to be insensitive," Terrell started, as he walked to the other side of his desk and sat down in the quiet office, "but what you're telling me is that you don't have definitive proof that this phone call was from Grace, but merely a heavy suspicion?"

When he said it like that, Sean felt foolish for bulling his way into the department and Terrell's office.

"I *know* it was her," April pressed. "I don't give my number out very often. No one else I know is currently in trouble."

"Wait…" Terrell put his hands up. "April, if I recall, you work for Sulphur Springs. Yes?"

She nodded.

"So, you're telling me that you don't get calls from other girls who need you from time to time? And again, I am really not trying to be an ass, I just want to get my bearings here. That's all."

April answered with an annoyed huff. "Look, I do *on occasion* hear from other kids who need my help, but I know with every fiber of my being that this call came from Grace."

Terrell nodded and glanced over at Sean. The detective's button-down shirt was pulled tight over his bulletproof vest as though the guy had gained some weight since he'd bought the thing.

Sean had always liked Terrell, but he could understand April's annoyance. "I heard the call as well. And, Detective Terrell, I can understand your trepidation in looking into this. But here's how I see it," he said, leaning onto the edge of the desk and tenting his fingers in the detective's direction, "if this was Grace calling, then we have a great lead. If it is some other girl who needs our help, then great...we can help her, too. Either way, we have a girl out there who needs to be rescued."

Terrell nodded and turned toward his computer. "Can you tell me the number? I'll see what we can do."

April read off the Gillette, Wyoming, number, Terrell tapping it into the computer. He moved closer to the screen and sat his chin in his hand as he scrolled through whatever results he was poring over.

"Anything?" Sean asked after a long moment.

Terrell looked back at him. "So, the number comes back to a company with an LLC registered out of Gillette. Something called Mango Tango. You guys ever heard of it?"

"No," April said as Sean shook his head.

Terrell hit a few more buttons and, as he worked, his features darkened.

"What's going on?" Sean asked.

Terrell looked over at them like he had almost forgotten they were there. He stood up. "I appreciate you guys letting me know about the call. I'll see what we can do on our end."

The detective walked around the side of his desk and motioned for them to get up and follow him out. It was awkward and forced, and it made Sean wonder what exactly he didn't want to tell them about what he was finding. Regardless, he didn't like the way Terrell was acting.

"Wait… That's it?" April asked. "You're kicking us out? You're not going to tell us what you found? Was it Grace who called?"

Terrell glanced back at his computer. "Look, I can't tell you much, but I can tell you that company is tied in with some pretty shady dealings. Lots of criminals use their tech to cover their tracks."

"So, Grace is in the hands of a criminal…" April reached over to Sean with her uninjured arm as though she needed his help to remain standing.

Sean held her hand but put his other arm around her back to help support her. "Do you need April's phone or anything—in case she calls back, or to trace the number or whatever?"

Terrell shook his head. "Just make sure that you guys let me know if you hear anything." He looked to April. "Rest assured, April, I will do my best to see if we can locate our victim."

Chapter Fourteen

April didn't care if they had to walk all the way to Wyoming to check every phone, but they would be doing something to get their hands on Grace. From the look on the detective's face, every minute that she was missing counted.

She rushed out of the sheriff's office and got into Sean's truck. He was ten steps behind, and his lack of speed irritated her. Didn't he realize what was at stake?

As she clicked her seat belt and waited, she reminded herself how invested he was in this…at least, he seemed to be. Yet, now that she knew the truth behind his motivations—that he felt guilty—she didn't feel the same as she had before.

It was crazy to think that he had played a role in Cameron's death as a kid, but as an adult, he had *saved her*. Now he was trying to save someone else. If anything, he'd saved many people.

If she accepted life for what it had wrought, and the man who'd played such a pivotal role in hers, she wasn't sure what the future would bring, and she wasn't sure she was ready to find out.

However, she would be lying to herself if she tried to refute the fact that it had been her first instinct to seek out his touch when she'd needed support in the office. Her body and her mind were at odds.

As he got into the truck, he was tapping away on his phone. She was grateful he'd gotten in and she could go back to their immediate needs instead of spiraling down the depths of her soul. Perhaps keeping things surface level with Sean was the best for everyone involved—which meant leaving the past in the past.

For now, that would be best.

"We driving to Gillette?" she asked.

"You and I both know that she could be just about anywhere. Just because a phone is registered in one state, it doesn't mean it's there."

Of course, he was right, but that didn't make her want to go there any less. "I don't care. It's our first real, verified information."

"And I'm sure Terrell will run with it. We don't have the resources he does. We have to trust that he will do his job."

Again, she couldn't argue with his logic. "Then what do you think we should do? We have to do something."

He scowled. "Terrell texted me as soon as we left."

"And?"

"He said that he thinks he has a name of a guy who is associated with the LLC. He is looking into it."

There was a slight sense of relief. The detective was working fast and had not simply been patronizing them. Finally, it felt like they were starting to get somewhere.

"What about the fire?" she asked.

"I'm hoping the phone call proves that Grace wasn't killed, but we are making some major assumptions. Again, that call could have been anyone." He started the pickup and glanced over at her like she knew something he didn't. "What are you thinking about the fire?"

"It's just weird that Grace's duplex burns down and now this…"

He tapped on his steering wheel as he backed out of the parking spot. "Just because strange things have been happening doesn't mean that everything is related. I mean… do you think someone caused the rockslide you were involved with?"

His words felt like a fist in the gut. She wasn't sure if he had meant to hurt her, but it didn't matter…here he was, once again bringing up the sore spots in her life. "No," she said, shaking her head, "I don't think anyone caused that slide…at least no one other than me."

He quirked a brow. "Why do you think you caused it?"

She paused, thinking about the moments before the slide and her begging Grace to come her way. "I shouldn't have had those kids on the mountain that day, not after all that heavy rain. I should have known the conditions were too questionable." As she spoke, her admission reminded her of his admission to her…how if only he hadn't let Cameron drive.

He looked pained, like his thoughts had gone there, too.

She wanted to address it, but instead she clamped her mouth shut.

Silence and pain filled the space between them in the truck. Until finally, she couldn't stand it anymore. "Can you please take me home?"

"If that's what you want." He nodded, but his face had turned hard. "But what about looking for Grace?"

She had no intention of stopping her search, but she couldn't stand being in this weird limbo with him any longer. She needed a reprieve and time to come to terms with everything that had happened over the course of the last few days.

"What about Wyoming?" he continued.

"Wyoming isn't the answer. We would just be chasing our tails," she said, a sickening lump in her throat. It was hard to believe how defeated she suddenly felt. "Besides, for all we know, that really wasn't her on that phone call. What if I was wrong?"

"Why are you second-guessing yourself all of a sudden, April?" He looked over at her, searching her face. "I didn't mean to make you feel bad, or to make everything that has happened somehow your fault."

"No, but you made me realize how her disappearance is all my doing. For once, Grace had been cared for and safe— while she was at Sulphur Springs. That was, until I made a stupid decision and failed her so much that it nearly cost her life." Tears threatened to creep up into her eyes.

She blinked hard, trying to keep her emotions and their tells at bay.

"I will absolutely do as you wish. I'm not going to make you stay and work with me if you're not comfortable or if I've done something to upset you, but I have to say that I think we work better as a team. You know her better than I do, but I have more resources and connections." He reached over and put his hand, palm up, on the console between them like he wanted her to touch him once again.

She wanted to. Oh, she wanted to. Yet, if she did, it would mean more than just their holding hands. It would mean that she was going to try to forgive him and the hell he'd wrought on her life. She didn't know if she was ready. Everything was happening so fast between and around them.

Her phone buzzed in her pocket, and it pulled her away from her whirlpool of thoughts, thoughts that all came back to Grace. She took out her phone and glanced at the name—Damon.

She let out a long, exasperated sigh. Of course, it would be him. He hadn't called thirty times already today; he was behind. She ignored the call.

"Is it him?"

"Damon? Yes." She nodded.

He pulled his hand back and put it on his knee. She tried not to pay attention to the little niggle of disappointment that moved up from her core.

"At least this time he is calling from his original number. He must really want me to know that *he* is still calling."

"Let's get you a new number today—"

"That's out of the question. If Grace tries to call again…" She waved him off. Putting up with being harassed by some idiot so she didn't miss a chance with Grace was worth it.

"Are you sure this guy isn't dangerous? Do you know if he owns or has access to any weapons?"

"It's Montana, everyone has access to, or owns, guns, but I don't think he wants me dead. I think he just wants me to agree to be his girlfriend. The guy is cracked, but if he wasn't, I would have to say I was almost flattered by his persistence."

Sean shook his head at her admission.

She had said too much. Of course, he wouldn't understand why she felt as she did. Logically, she was more than aware that Damon wasn't acting like a normal or rational man, but at the same time, she'd been in relationships in which the guy couldn't even find time to text her back—at a certain level, it felt good to be wanted, even if it was by the wrong person.

Maybe, the right person is the one sitting next to me. She shoved the thought away.

What would it say about her as a person if she fell for

Sean and forgave him for throwing her life off the path so dramatically?

He was the reason she'd been forced to give up her child.

But was it really fair to put the burden of that decision on him?

She groaned as the phone in her hand buzzed to life again. *Damon.*

"Do you want me to talk to him again?"

She didn't know what she wanted, or how to feel. She didn't want to be dealing with this at all, and especially not when there were greater worries in her life. So, she handed off her phone. "Knock yourself out. Maybe you can get the message to him better than I've been able to."

He pulled the truck to the side of the road and answered the phone on speaker.

"April?" Damon's voice bounced around the inside of the truck like a thrown grenade.

She opened her mouth to answer, but Sean shook his head. "This isn't April, Damon."

"Oh, so it's you again? Her little rescuer?" Damon answered with a mirth-filled laugh. "She's got you all whipped, doesn't she?"

"This is my phone now, Damon. If you keep trying to get in contact with April, I'm going to help her to file a restraining order against you."

Damon's laugh was louder this time. "Do whatever the hell you want to do. She is still going to come back to me. She may fool around with you, but I'm the man she really wants."

"No, I don't, Damon," April said. "I never wanted you." She couldn't help herself. She had to speak up.

Sean's eyes darkened and he shook his head and mouthed *no*.

Though she didn't want to, she had to say something. This was her fault and her stalker; it was her responsibility to take care of. She shouldn't have handed off her phone.

She stuck out her hand and motioned for the device, but Sean shook his head.

Damon went quiet, then, "April?"

"Yes, Damon, it's me."

Sean tilted his head back against the headrest in annoyance, but then glanced down at the phone.

"April, is he making you act this way?" Damon asked. "We both know you love me."

"No, Damon, I don't. I told you, I'm not interested." A thrill moved through her as she found pride in her resolve to say "no" to this man with Sean watching. "I don't want you, and I don't want you to contact me anymore."

"This doesn't sound like you, April."

"It is her," Sean growled. "She made her feelings clear. Now, leave her alone."

"I want to hear that from her mouth," Damon countered.

"You just did," she said, not missing a beat. "Leave me alone, Damon."

It felt so good to make a stand against him. Though she had tried before, something about this time, about the level of resolve in her voice and the stiffness in her spine…he would listen. He had to know she was serious.

The phone went dead, and Sean handed it back to her.

"I'm sorry—" she started, but the look on Sean's face made her go quiet.

"April, you have nothing to feel sorry about." He sighed. "I'm sorry I tried to silence you. I don't know why, but it feels like I'm never doing the right thing when it comes to you—no matter how hard I try."

She could understand why he felt that way. "I know how

you feel, Sean. I felt like I made a huge mistake right there, interceding when you were trying to protect me. *Again*." The word drifted in the air like a feather.

"You're welcome." He reached over and pushed a strand of hair off her face.

The soft touch of his fingers on her skin made her heart race. She loved the way he touched her, like she needed care, but also with respect.

"I just wish I knew what I could do to make him go away."

"For now, let's just go radio silence. No more contact until we can work something out with your phone." She reached up and touched the hand that was still lingering at the edge of her ear.

"I hope you know that I do appreciate your help with this," she said, clasping his fingers. She wasn't sure if she wanted to talk about the rest of her feelings having to do with Cameron, but she knew she needed to at least say something so he didn't make the wrong assumptions about how she was thinking. "As for what happened in high school…" She paused as she searched for the right words. "I need some more time to make sense of my feelings. I'm sure you can understand that there's no manual on how to feel in a situation like ours."

He cocked his head to the side slightly, his eyes catching the light, and it made the blue of them more vibrant than she would have ever thought possible. "How would you explain a situation like ours?"

She chewed at her lip. *Right man, wrong time. Wrong man, right time*, she thought. *And no matter what I think, what would Cameron say?*

"You saved my life. I'm eternally grateful—"

"But?"

She wasn't going to say *but*. In fact, she didn't really know how she was going to finish her sentence. "All I know is that I'm more attracted to you than I think I *should* be."

A smile lit up his features as he gave her hand a gentle squeeze. "It ain't much, but for now, that's enough."

Chapter Fifteen

He hated this Damon guy. He hated him with every fiber of his being. Had it not been for the situation with Grace, he would have been on the guy's porch and ready for a fight.

It took everything in his power not to tell her that how she felt about the situation was wholly and unequivocally wrong. What was happening to her wasn't her fault. Her responding like a normal, kind and polite adult wasn't why this guy had decided to be an unshakable jerk. It was just people like Damon who loved to prey on those who had good souls. He was a predator, pure and simple.

More, the guy had problems. He didn't respect boundaries, and he sure as hell didn't take sound, albeit crass, advice.

Damon would have to eventually listen, though. Sean would make sure of that, one way or another.

He pulled the pickup back onto the road. "Do you still want me to take you home? You know I will, if that is what you really want."

I'm not like Damon. He wanted to say, complete with: *You're safe with me.* But he stayed quiet. He didn't want to talk about Damon with her. In fact, for her sake, he wanted to pretend the guy didn't even exist.

"No matter what, we can't stop searching for Grace," she said, sending him a meaningful and heart-wrenching look.

In so many ways, it felt like they were beating a dead horse. The only bright spot in this was that he was pretty sure April was correct in thinking the phone call had come from Grace.

With that likely assumption, there were few remaining doubts about Grace running away or being taken. It was definitely the latter. However, they had numerous other issues to worry about, and each fear was darker than the last.

Yet, there was still hope Grace was alive.

He was glad Terrell had jumped into action.

His only surprise was that it had taken a damned mysterious phone call from the girl before the police had considered her disappearance legitimate. He could understand being woefully understaffed; it was the nature of the beast when a person worked in a county that was bigger than most states and far less populated, but it always tore at him when minutes mattered.

From the fire standpoint, ten guys ran the station, five on at all points in the day covering an enormous county. Normally, it was more than enough, until the fall fire season hit, and they were inundated with calls from those who lived in remote rural areas; then, it was nonstop calls and no sleep for anyone involved in the firefighting efforts.

"Have you talked to anyone back at the Springs?" he asked.

She shrugged. "The other counselors there haven't said anything."

"What if we run out there? Maybe we can find someone Grace had talked to before the accident."

She nodded. "It's worth a shot, but it's a drive."

He didn't care. He was with the person he wanted to be with. "I think I can suffer through," he said, sending her a playful grin. "I mean, if you can."

She returned his smile. "Being with you is not what I consider suffering…" Her smile widened. "That is, unless you listen to opera or something."

He clicked on an opera channel via Bluetooth. He had no idea what the song was about or who was singing it, but he laughed as April rolled down the window and stuck her head out.

It was so good to finally see her being comfortable with him and joking around. He wasn't sure that they would ever get to this place together again, and he wasn't going to dissect it, but he was relieved. This moment, this time and laughter, was what they both needed.

She pulled her head back in as he turned the volume down. "I take back my suffering comment…" she teased.

His heart lightened in his chest as her eyes sparkled. She really was a beautiful woman. Moving forward, if he got the chance, he would give just about anything to stare into them while he slipped inside of her.

He could almost feel it now, her warmth against him. Kissing her skin. Hell, he'd be happy just to have a chance to hold her in his arms.

"What are you thinking about?"

He jerked. "I…" He couldn't tell her the truth. Things were finally starting to go well with her, and if anything, he was a little embarrassed that he'd been fantasizing about her. "I was just thinking about how much I want to go sky-diving." He smirked.

She cuffed him on the shoulder, the action so teenage-like that it made his pulse race.

He really did have feelings for this woman. Even if she would and could never truly be his, due to the nature of their past, he was grateful for this shared moment in the midst of their continuing drama.

He turned up the radio, singing along like he knew the words. The time flew by as they made their way onto the highway and the thirty minutes out of town. Too soon, she was motioning for him to turn.

If they hadn't been on a mission, he would have kept driving and enjoying their time together.

"Turn at the main entrance," she said.

There was a large, log sign hanging over the entrance to a gravel road that led up into a timbered ravine. The sign read: Welcome to Sulphur Springs, in bold black scrolling. There were bears carved into the left and right sides around the lettering, and the effect was beautiful.

"Is this place only for at-risk youth?" he asked, realizing that for as many times as he had driven by this place on his way out of Big Sky, he'd really never paused to give it much thought.

She nodded. "And their families. We do a lot of work with foster kids."

He turned down the dirt road, driving slowly.

"Sometimes we have group therapy weekends where parents or guardians of our kids can come in and discuss the issues they're facing. Some sessions are with the kids, some without. The owners have tried to develop a location in which everyone can feel safe and secure while also promoting healing and lasting relationships."

It sounded like he needed to spend some time here as well. It had been a long time since he'd been in a lasting relationship. And, as for the healing, he had a feeling that when it came to April—that was a journey in which they could embark upon together.

A large, three-story house came into view at the end of the long, meandering driveway. To its left was a red barn, complete with many horse stalls that led out into a paddock.

The entire ranch must have been at least a hundred acres, if not more. It made him wonder who owned the facility and how it had come about.

"There is a steady flow of kids in and out. Sulphur Springs normally houses around fifteen kids, and there are two adult staff members always on duty. Sometimes we have more adults around if there are big events or if parents are here with kids."

"Is it just a camp?" he asked.

"During the school year, we host kids who need temporary housing, and we even have a couple of full-time residents—Andrew and Josie. They are great kids, but because of their ages, have had a hard time getting adopted."

"So, it's a group home?" he asked, pulling to a stop in the parking lot near the front doors.

"It is whatever the kids in this community need." She smiled proudly.

The white house had black shutters, and up close it gave off an air of a place he would have expected in the Deep South, thanks to its Grecian columns and wraparound porch. It was a beautiful, almost palatial house that put the double-wide trailer he'd grown up in to shame.

A boy came out of the front doors and waved as they stepped out of the truck.

"Andrew," April said, joy making her voice high. "How're you doing? You okay?"

The teenager nodded. "Just fine. I'm sorry about your arm," he said, motioning toward her cast. "How long do you have to wear that thing?"

"They are saying six to eight weeks. It's already feeling like forever, though," she said, stopping beside him and resting her hand on his shoulder.

"I bet. I had a cast when I broke my arm when I was

seven. I just remember how badly it itched." The teenager looked over at him. "Who're you?"

"This is Sean McCormack. He was the SAR member who found Grace and me after the slide," April said, scratching at the edge of her cast arm. "Sean saved my life."

The kid nodded appreciatively. "Well done, sir." He stuck out his hand.

"I was just doing my job," Sean said, giving his proffered hand a shake. "I heard what happened up there. If anything, Andrew, it sounds like you are the one who saved everyone. Thanks for getting the other kids to safety and making the call to 911. Without your quick thinking and action, my team wouldn't have stood a chance to reach April and Grace in time. You're the real hero."

Andrew looked at his shoes, embarrassed. "I was just doing what April told me."

She patted his shoulder. "You did a great job. Thank you for saving my life. And… I'm sorry that I put you and the rest of the group in danger."

Sean ached, as he sympathized with her and what she had to have been feeling.

"Everyone's fine." Andrew pointed toward the door. "Well…everyone but Grace. Did you guys find her yet?"

The kid's question slammed into him. "Not yet, but that's why we're here. We were hoping to take some time and talk to everyone." He walked up onto the veranda and leaned against one of the columns. "Do you mind if I ask you a few questions?"

Andrew shrugged and April's hand slipped from him. He made his way over to a porch swing and plopped down as though he was readying himself for an interrogation. "What's up?"

"Do you know if Grace was dating anyone here at the Springs?"

Andrew rubbed at the back of his neck and looked toward the front door, almost as if he was afraid someone was listening from behind it. Or maybe Sean was just connecting dots that weren't really there.

The kid shrugged as he stared at him like he had somehow just given away the fact that he was old and unhip. "I don't know if she was *dating* anyone. That wasn't really her *thing*. She liked to keep things casual. You know…without labels."

Sean nodded. "Did she and anyone here *keep things casual*…you know, hang out or whatever?" He tried to sound cool and relaxed, but he couldn't help his overwhelming feelings of lameness in the face of teenage judgment.

Andrew shrugged noncommittally, but he couldn't meet his gaze.

He really had no idea how April could handle being around these kids every day. While Andrew seemed relatively nice, he could clearly still be a handful. It had to have been hard for April when it came to dealing with the snark and emotional minefields that came with the world of teens.

April stepped closer to the kid on the swing. "Andrew," April said, "it would really be helpful if you could tell me if you know anything about Grace and her private life… We have reason to believe she is in real trouble. She needs help, and we have no idea where we can find her. I know you guys were friends."

Andrew picked at the edge of his fingernail. "We *were* friends."

"What does that mean?" Sean asked.

The kid looked at him like he was speaking out of turn

and interfering. He shut his mouth, hoping Andrew would continue to talk.

"It means that she and I had been hooking up here and there. She told me I was one of the reasons she wanted to come to the camp…you know, so we could spend more time together." He put his finger in his mouth and started to chew on his nail for a second. His gaze kept slipping to the door. "We were doing pretty good. You know, getting along. We had even started to talk about what we were gonna do when we got sprung from this place. I'm turning eighteen in like three months, ya know?" He looked at April who nodded. "But you know how things can get."

"What are you thinking about doing, Andrew?" she asked, her voice soft and caring.

"Well, I do pretty good at school, but I'm not getting any scholarships or nothing. So, I figured my best choice was to go to the marines. I've been talking to a recruiter. He's supercool and the jobs sound fun as hell. Plus I could get away from here and see the real world."

He didn't want to tell the kid that no matter where he went in the world, the problems he would face would probably stay the same and life would continue to be a struggle. The only thing that really changed was a person's location.

"You said *was* go to the marines. You still thinking about going in that direction?" April pressed.

Andrew shrugged. "The best part of joining the marines is that by the time I'd be done with school and stuff, she'd be eighteen. It's only like eighteen months away. We were talking about getting married."

"Married?" Sean choked on the word, surprised. As soon as he spoke, though, he had wished he'd stayed quiet.

"Yeah, you know…the thing where me and my guys have

a big party with strippers and all the beer and the next day the chick walks down the aisle in the big dress? That thing."

"Ah. Got it," he said, once again holding back the urge to tell him that life was about to bear down on him and show him how things really went—especially when it came to marriage, and, well, *any* romantic relationship for that matter.

"Last month, though, everything changed. I don't know what happened." He pulled out his phone and started to poke at the screen like it could help him answer the questions surrounding him.

"What changed?" April asked, glancing over at Sean as though telling him that he needed to stay quiet and not interfere.

She could run with this line of questioning all she wanted as long as they got to the bottom of everything. Besides, it was getting clearer by the second that she really was the better one when it came to relating with these kids.

"I don't know what happened. Things were good when she got to camp, but then about a week in everything went downhill," Andrew said, staring at his phone. "She was just all-in one minute and then ghosting me the next. I kept trying to talk to her and figure out what I'd done wrong, but any time I tried she would disappear."

"Did she lose interest once you guys spent more time together?" Sean asked, knowing this time that he would definitely upset the kid, but not caring. He was tired of trying to work around mercurial adolescent feelings. He just wanted answers.

"Dude," Andrew said, glaring at him.

"All Sean meant was that he wondered if you guys had a falling out…or maybe you guys weren't clicking like you'd hoped? You know?" April said, translating.

"Dude, it wasn't like we weren't together before," Andrew countered. "She and I would talk every day. When her parents were gone, I'd be at her house as much as I could."

"Nights, too?" April asked.

Andrew cringed. "You know we can't break curfew at the Springs."

"That's not what I asked." April sat down beside Andrew and leaned so she could look the kid in his downcast eyes. "I'm not upset, and I'm not going to turn you in for any breach of curfew, but I do need to know what was happening."

"What does it matter if I snuck out at night or not?" He looked away from her. "All that matters is that Grace and I were a thing and now, we aren't."

The front door to the house opened and a shorter than average, dark-haired guy came walking out. He had a sharp chin, the kind that could take a punch, and a scar across his cheek like he'd tested it. He was wearing a red Henley shirt with the arms pushed up with a towel slapped over his shoulder. Though Sean couldn't his finger on the reason why, he already hated the guy.

"Damon," April said, sounding breathless. "What are you doing here?"

"I'm working—you know, like you *should* be." He closed the door behind himself and walked toward her. He didn't even look in Sean's direction.

Andrew seemed angry as he glanced over at the guy, and it made Sean wonder who hated the guy worse—him or the kid.

Damon turned his back to him. "Things have been hard without you around. How are you feeling? Your arm okay?"

She scowled. "My arm is fine. I'm fine."

"Thanks to your little watchdog, you haven't been answering my calls, but if you had, you'd know that I was trying to check on you. It hurts me when you're hurting. I care about you, April."

April looked down at the ground.

The man's words made chills run down Sean's spine.

"Why don't you just go back inside, Damon?" Sean said, moving between him and April and obstructing Damon's view of his prey. "She doesn't want you out here."

"That's what I bet she told you. That's her little game. Did she also tell you that?" Damon countered, shifting so he could try to look over Sean's shoulder at her, but Sean moved to keep him from glowering at her in an attempt to continue to intimidate.

"Andrew," April said, sounding metered and cautious as she looked at the teenager, "why don't you head back inside. We have some more questions for you, but I'll come see you another time. Okay?"

Andrew stood up from the swing and straightened his pants, pushing his shoulders back and making himself look bigger and more muscular than the little man who'd come out from the house.

Andrew started to walk toward the front door. He glared at Damon. And just like that, Sean liked the kid a little bit more.

"Damon," Andrew said, moving closer to the man.

"Andrew, just shut up and take your ass inside if you know what is good for you. If you don't, I'm going to write you up for insubordination. If I do, you're out on your ass."

"What do I care?" Andrew spit.

"Damon, knock it off," April said, moving beside Andrew and taking him by the arm. "Just because you're having a problem with me doesn't mean you have to take it out on the kids."

It was strange, but Sean felt as though he had walked into some pseudo-world where April and Damon were the parents of the boy and the rest of the kids inside. Maybe it was the fact that they were in authority roles, or maybe it was the fact that April seemed to genuinely care about them, but something about the situation felt *off*. The air between them, April, Andrew and Damon, wasn't exactly what he had expected, and it had thrown him off balance.

What was he missing between them?

What hadn't she told him?

Though April had her hand on Andrew's shoulder, the kid stopped within a step of Damon, and he looked at the man. Before Sean had time to register what was even happening, Andrew had his fist planted square in the center of Damon's gut. Then Andrew grabbed the back of Damon's head and smashed the guy's face against his knee with a sickening crunch.

Damon dropped to the ground, blood pouring from his nose. Andrew moved to jump on top of the man, but April's scream pierced the air and seemed to pull the kid out of his blood-fueled rage.

He spewed expletives, calling Damon every name in the urban dictionary and several that he wasn't sure he himself understood.

"Andrew! Stop!" April yelled, pulling the kid off Damon.

"I'm sorry, but we both know he has this coming," Andrew said.

"Andrew, enough!" April shouted.

Sean stepped toward the kid and pushed him back. Damon might have gotten what he deserved, however, Andrew didn't need to find himself trouble—Damon was the kind of guy who would press charges. If he did, any chances Andrew had of joining the military would be gone.

Andrew's eyes widened as he looked down at the blood that was oozing out of Damon's nose His mouth opened, and he looked up at April and then at the truck in the parking lot. "I… I'm sorry if you get in trouble. I'm sorry." Andrew grabbed the railing and jumped over the top.

"Just go," April said, almost in a whisper.

He landed on the grass in front of the porch with a thump and he tore off toward Sean's truck. Sean reached down to his pocket. The truck's keys. They were still in the ignition.

Andrew didn't miss a beat as he climbed in and started the pickup. In his wake, he left them standing in a world of dust and blood.

Chapter Sixteen

April couldn't believe what had happened. Andrew was such a good kid, and he had been making the best he could of his life. She'd been proud of him for his choices, all except his last. She knew the kids at the Springs didn't like Damon, but there wasn't a long list of the adults that they did connect with—and even those people weren't unanimously liked.

She was among those who were tolerated and mostly liked, but Grace had proven that even those relationships came with some stiff rules and murky boundaries.

Damon was sitting up against the column, pressing a paper towel to his nose. He looked put out and angry, but she couldn't say that she really cared.

"Call the police," Damon growled. "I want to press charges. He needs to pay."

She shook her head. "Absolutely not. I don't know what you did to that kid, or why he was pissed off with you, but I can almost guarantee you had that coming. You are not going to get him in trouble because someone finally had the strength to stand up to you."

Sean smiled over at her. "If anyone needs to press charges against anyone, it is April against you."

"How dare you threaten me?" Damon countered, dabbing at his nose. There was a cut across the bridge, and it angled slightly to the left.

"Oh, please," April said. "Now, do you want to tell us what you did to upset him so much, or do I need to go inside and start asking the other kids what the hell has been going on?" April asked, motioning toward the house, where she could see a handful of kids pressed against the windows and watching them.

She gave them all a little wave, hoping they would know that regardless of the state of Damon, they had nothing to worry about.

The front door creaked open, and a boy started to walk out.

Sean stepped toward him, blocking him from Damon. "Why don't you go back inside, kiddo?"

The boy, Josh, looked at her questioningly, as though he wasn't sure whether or not to follow the stranger's instructions. April gave him a stiff nod. "Yes. And when you go in, would you please let everyone know that everything's okay? There's no need for concern. In fact, if everyone could please go to the living room and wait, I will come talk to you all in a second."

Sean smiled in approval.

"Are you sure, Ms. Twofeather?" Josh asked, glancing toward Damon and the blood on the ground.

"Josh, please listen. It's important," she told him. "I will be in to talk to all of you together in just a few."

Josh slipped back inside, the door shutting gently behind him.

She had no idea what she was going to tell the kids, or how she was going to spin this, but she would have to keep Andrew from getting in any further trouble. The stolen truck would be another issue, however.

They probably needed to call the detective and tell him everything that had transpired, but she was embarrassed by the thought. The last thing she wanted to do was talk about how and why she had found herself in the position she had with Damon and then the role she had played in allowing it to continue.

No matter what Sean tried to tell her about it not being her fault, and that Damon was simply a predator, she couldn't get past the fact that she had allowed him to bother her for so long. She wasn't a weak woman, but when it came to men like him, she wished she was stronger. The entire situation with him made her feel stupid.

Sean touched her arm. "Are you okay?"

She nodded, further upset by the fact that he could see her thoughts on her face so easily.

"If you want, the Springs has a car we can use until we can get your truck back." She motioned vaguely to where the van was parked behind the house. "It's not pretty, but it can get us around."

"Don't worry about the truck. I'll have Terrell start watching for it. The good news is that it was low on gas and my wallet is in my pocket. The kid will choke if he tries to gas up that beast."

She blushed.

Damon moved to get up.

"You just stay where you are." Sean pushed him back down to a seated position. "April, why don't you go inside and talk to the kids. I'll call Terrell and watch Damon until he stops bleeding."

She nodded, glad she wouldn't have to hear about her failings as a counselor and a woman while he spoke to the detective and told him about what had happened and why. If she had stopped things earlier with Damon, and spoken to her supervisor at the house, maybe none of this would have even happened—hell, maybe she wouldn't have been on the mountain with Grace. Literally, everything bad that was happening was her fault.

"Good luck," she said, turning to go inside. "Please make sure to tell him that Andrew is a really good kid. This is not his normal behavior."

"Without a doubt."

She went inside and as the door closed behind her, she leaned against it and took a long breath. She needed to stop beating herself up for what was happening. Regardless of fault, there was nothing she could do to change the events that had transpired; all she could do was keep moving forward until she was through them.

There were the sounds of kids talking from inside the sunken living room down the hall. Josh was speaking, saying something about Damon, but she could only hear bits and pieces. Collecting herself, she moved slowly down the hall, not entirely comfortable with eavesdropping on the kids' conversation, but wanting to hear what was really happening in their world while it was completely unfiltered by their needs to perform for a counselor.

It was amazing how different they were when they thought someone wasn't listening.

"Damon has been hitting on her since she got here," one of the girls said, but she wasn't quite sure who was speaking.

"She liked it," Josh argued.

In that moment, she knew they had to be talking about her and Damon.

With that, she cleared her throat and made her presence known. She couldn't handle any more lashes from the whip of public opinion. "Hey, guys," she called a little louder than the situation required.

Several of the kids who had been standing hurried to chairs and sat down.

Josh was standing in front of the flat-screen television, and his hands dropped to his sides as she strode in. "What happened? Where's Andrew?" he asked, like he was the president of the Springs kids club.

"Andrew..." She paused, having no idea what she should say as heat rose into her cheeks. "He is fine, and hopefully he won't be in any trouble."

"So, he was the one who did that to Damon?"

"Yes. But violence is never the answer even when someone is verbally provoked." She was careful in how she spoke.

"Was this because of what he did to Grace?"

The warmth she had been feeling in her cheeks drained away as the blood started to seep out of her extremities and move straight to protect her core. "What?" she said, a chill moving over her skin. "What did he do to Grace?" she asked, each syllable punctuated by her instantaneous fear-induced anger.

Josh looked at a red-haired girl, Elyse, who had run with Grace before she'd disappeared. The girl wouldn't meet her gaze.

"Elyse, tell me. It's important." April moved gently toward the girl, trying to control her rage as she silently begged for her fears not to be realized. If Damon had laid a single finger on Grace...

"He didn't do nothing." The girl stared down at her pink toenails.

There were eight kids in the room. All of them were teenagers and had been through the ringer in their personal lives, but that didn't mean she could continue to question Elyse in the midst of them.

"Elyse," she asked, touching the girl gently on the shoulder in an attempt to get her to open up and feel comfortable with her. "Why don't we go talk somewhere away from everyone."

Elyse crossed her arms over her chest and flumped deeper in the couch cushion. "I'm not telling you anything."

April looked to Josh. "Would you please help me by taking everyone and escorting them to their rooms?"

Josh looked to Elyse, as if he was torn between wanting to protect her and at the same time knowing that he needed to listen to April.

"It's okay, Josh." She smiled as she gently squeezed Elyse's shoulder. "She is fine. We are all good. I just need to get a better understanding of what we are dealing with today."

It was one thing for Damon to have harassed her, but it was another thing entirely to potentially have taken advantage of children who had been entrusted to their care.

Hopefully she was just making more of this and the potential crimes he'd committed worse than what had actually taken place. Hopefully the kids just hated Damon. Hopefully...

So far, hope hadn't been working in her favor.

But maybe this time was different.

It took a couple of minutes, but the kids filtered out of the room. One of the other girls came over and touched Elyse's other shoulder in what she could best assume was support.

There was something to be said for these kids. They had all been through hell and back, but when one of their own needed help, they were there. If for no other reason, she was glad to be a part of this world, a world where they could provide escape for the kids who had needed it the most.

Yet, if Damon had preyed on them, what good had they really been doing as a part of "the system"? What if by having these at-risk kids together in this home, they had created the perfect environment for a predator to easily find his prey?

Damon had to have just been bothering April. He couldn't have been targeting the girls here. He wasn't that bad, was he?

"Elyse." She said the girl's name like she was talking to a young child and not the surly teen who had every right to hate adults. "I need to know what you do about Damon and Grace."

Elyse turned her gaze toward the television even though it was just a black screen.

"Did Damon *touch* Grace? Ever?" The words curdled in her throat like soured milk. She hated that she had to ask such a question.

"What?" Elyse twitched. "No. No. Nothing like that," she replied, shaking her head vehemently.

Some of April's rage seeped from her. Maybe there was a ray of hope somewhere in this.

"Who were you talking about before I walked in? I think you said Damon had been hitting on *her* since she walked in. Did you mean Grace? Or did you mean *me*?" Again, the words stuck in her throat.

Elyse finally looked up at her, and she stared at her for a long moment before she started to speak. "Come on. You know how it is here. We live by prison rules."

Maybe she had been naive, but she hadn't picked up on that dynamic with most of the kids—at least their full-timers. A few of the campers would come through jaded by life and hateful, but she'd treated them with love.

"What does that mean, Elyse?" she asked.

"It means that if we can work someone to get what we want when we want it, we are going to do it."

"What did you guys have to do to Damon to get what you wanted?" Her rage started to bubble up.

"Whatever it took. It wasn't his fault that we worked him. He was just an easy target." Elyse smiled, and the action was so unsettling that April was forced to look away.

She hated that these kids had to play games and manipulated people to get what they wanted. It wasn't their fault that they had learned to live this way, and she couldn't begrudge them for the role in having to play the game of survival, but she also didn't have to like it.

There were times when she had known the kids here had been testing her to see what they could get away with and how far they could take things. But she'd always been careful and considerate to set boundaries with their behaviors and their allowances. It came naturally to her, and it made her wonder what Damon was lacking in his life that they could have used for leverage to manipulate him.

"So, you guys were flirting with him?"

Elyse giggled, the sound so abstract set against the harsh reality of what was happening. "At first he would stop us, but when you guys broke up—"

"We were never really dating," she said, correcting the girl.

"That's not what he said."

"Hold up… He talked to you about *me*?" She really did hate this man. Didn't he know how inappropriate talking about his private life with teenage girls was?

"He wanted advice on how to get you in the sack. Well, not that he said that… He just wanted to know what kind of stuff you liked…you know?"

It disturbed her that he thought asking these girls was his best way to get information.

She didn't want to know what they told him. Everything

about him made her disgusted. "So, you said *at first*, he would stop you from flirting. Does that mean that eventually he didn't? Was he flirting back with you guys?"

She shrugged. "I dunno."

"But he never touched you? Did he do anything else that you felt was inappropriate or out of line?" *Besides discussing our private life?*

She shook her head. "Not with me."

"But he did with Grace?"

"I don't know what they had going. It was weird, but I don't know if it was like dating or whatever." The girl shrugged. "When she talked about him, she said he was too old for her."

Now, Grace's actions during the rockslide and her hatred of her made more sense. Unbeknownst to April, they had been in some kind of cold war because of Damon. If Grace had just talked to her, she would have explained what an immoral piece of human garbage he was.

She had never believed in vigilante justice more than she did in this moment.

Whether or not he had physically harmed these girls, he'd wreaked havoc in their lives.

In allowing that, she and the system had failed.

"If you want to know who Grace really had a problem with," Elyse said. "Her foster parents."

April knew she was about to get a very necessary earful.

Chapter Seventeen

An hour later, Andrew still hadn't been found and they had been forced to call Terrell. Sean was standing with him outside, staring down the driveway in hopes the kid would return. Damon had gone back inside after Terrell had finished questioning him about the events earlier in the day. Of course, Damon denied knowing anything about Grace or why Andrew was upset, and he'd come out looking like a hapless victim.

The entire situation made Sean want to rage and fight, anything in his power to make things right. Yet, it kept feeling like they were coming up against roadblocks.

"I'm sorry," Detective Terrell said, leaning against the back of his black SUV. "From what you are telling me, Damon is a piece of work, and he shouldn't be working around kids, but he hasn't done anything I can arrest him for—April could hit him for harassment, but that would be about it." He dug the toe of his black boot into the gravel driveway. "Unfortunately, Andrew on the other hand… If either you or Damon wished to press charges…"

"Absolutely not," Sean said. He had a strong feeling, based on what he'd learned from April, that Damon wouldn't risk what the kids might reveal about him.

April came walking out of the front door of the house,

a red-haired girl by her side. She gave them a slight wave, as she made her way out to them. "This is Elyse, she's a really good friend of Grace's." She looked to the detective. "Elyse, do you wanna tell the detective what you told me about Grace's foster parents?"

Elyse looked over at April as if the last thing she wanted to do was talk to law enforcement. "I don't want things to get out of control. I mean, she didn't really even tell me much. Hell, I don't even know if what she told me was true. You know how Grace could be. For all I know she was just being dramatic."

Sean could understand all of the reasons the girl would want to minimize and downplay any information she had that pertained to the case. From what April had told him, the children who passed through the doors of this house were kids who typically had a great deal of experience with law enforcement and not always in the most positive ways.

This young lady probably had more insight into Grace's mindset than anyone else. Thankfully, though she appeared to be reticent, she seemed to be more helpful than Grace's other friends. Yet only time would tell.

"Elyse," Terrell said, "first of all just know that no matter what you say to me, neither you nor Grace will be in trouble. All we are concerned with is getting Grace back and making sure that she is safe and unharmed."

Elyse glanced over at April. "You guys think Grace was kidnapped or something?"

Terrell nodded. "Do you know of anyone else who would have wanted to take her, or harm her in any way?"

She shook her head. "The only people who Grace truly had a problem with were her foster parents." She paused. "She even told me that they had put a calendar up in their house marking down the days until they got the last check from the state for her care. They'd get really drunk some-times, once even when I was there, and tell her all about how much they wanted her to just die."

Terrell frowned.

"Hold on a minute," Sean said. "If they were so wrapped up in getting money for taking care of her, then why would they want her to die?"

April made a slight choking sound, and he wanted to tell her it would be okay, but now wasn't the time or the place to indicate that they had anything more than a friendship type of relationship. The waters around them were murky enough without him allowing their own personal trauma to seep in.

Instead, he looked to April, and he gave her a slight nod, hoping she would see it as reassurance and could understand why he was holding back from further action.

"You know exactly why they treated her like they did," the girl said. "They're just like all the other foster parents out there. At least, all the foster parents I've ever come across. These people really don't care about us. All they care about is getting their monthly checks."

"Do you know when Grace's foster parents left the States?" Terrell asked.

The girl shrugged. "They were gone all the time. They left like two weeks before she went to camp, this round, but I honestly don't think they were around more than a week a month or so."

Terrell glanced over at him with a look of concern upon his face. He turned to April. "Did you know that these folks were not providing an adequate level of care?"

April shook her head. "I'm learning that I didn't know nearly as much as I thought I did."

Her statement made Sean's chest ache. "I think that's going around." He pursed his lips, as he hoped she would take some level of comfort in the fact that everyone was coming out of this situation humbled. The only hope that still resided was that Grace would make it through this situation alive.

If things continued the way they were, however, even that hope was minimal.

"Do you know where Andrew may have gone?" Terrell asked Elyse.

The question caught Sean off guard. He wasn't sure how Andrew's possible location was related to Grace's caregivers.

The girl wouldn't look at Terrell, but she shook her head. "I know he's upset with Grace. He thinks that she was egging Damon on with her flirtation, and he's not wrong. But I think he knows that Grace still loved him. She was just playing a dangerous game."

Terrell stuffed his thumbs in the edges of his vest near his armpits and sat quietly in thought for a moment. "Do you think Andrew still loves Grace?"

The girl pointed at the house, where Damon was sitting inside. "If he didn't, I don't think he would have done that to that guy's face. Andrew isn't one who is quick to get pissed off."

"Do you think that Andrew went to look for Grace?" Terrell asked directly.

"I'd put money on it." The girl glanced back at April. "Can I go back inside? I'm hungry."

April nodded. "Go for it."

"Elyse, I may need to ask you some more questions, please don't go too far," Terrell called after her.

She sent him a backward wave in acknowledgment.

The three adults watched as the kid retreated back into the house. Sean tried to tell himself that she was safe inside there, but his attempt to lie to himself was met with a mixture of feelings. Safety for any of these kids was tenuous at best… Hell, it was tenuous for everyone. Safety was never more than a hair's breadth away from becoming danger.

"What are we going to do?" April asked, crossing her arms over her chest. "We aren't any closer to finding Grace."

Terrell sighed. "No, but I've put out a MEPA, or a Missing and Endangered Person's Advisory, for her and I'll send one out for Andrew as well. You know, the kind of alert that you see on the television and social media sometimes."

"Don't those only last for twenty-four hours?" April asked.

"So, you do know a little bit about them?" Terrell asked.

"A little. We had a runaway a few years ago, but they ended up coming back after a day."

"Well, if Grace isn't found or doesn't come back, we can extend the advisory as long as we need. As you know, we use them in cases like this or where there have been parental custodial disputes that resulted in one parent absconding with a kid."

Though Sean had heard about custody battles, in his line of work, he wasn't privy to the ins and outs of the legal system.

Sean's phone rang. He pulled the device out of his pocket and stepped away from April and Terrell for a moment. Jim was calling. "Hello? What's up, man?"

On the other end, Jim cleared his throat. "How's it going? I hear you are light a truck."

Word traveled fast in a small town, a whole heck of a lot faster than he would have liked.

"Yeah, working on getting it back now." He tried to sound like he wasn't worried, but he was sure his friend had a pretty good idea of the emotional turmoil he was feeling without Sean having to tell him. "What's happening at the station? Everything good?" He glanced down at his watch. He wasn't supposed to be working until tomorrow at this time.

"Actually, I'm calling because I managed to pull a little bit more information from the fire scene. Do you have time to talk about it? It's nothing major, but I thought you'd like to know."

He looked over at Terrell, who was getting into his squad car and doing something on his computer. "Sure, what's up?"

"So, some of the lab work came back. I was right about it being diesel fuel. Which sent me down a rabbit hole today. So, I had them try to pull prints off the gas cap I showed you in the yard. I got a match."

"And?"

"This is where things get weird. The fingerprints came back as a match to your friend, April Twofeather. I think she may have started the fire."

Chapter Eighteen

April unlocked and opened the door to the Sulphur Springs' main office and slipped inside. The place was dark and though she had been granted access, it still felt as though she was somewhere she shouldn't have been. When she was working, she rarely had a need to come in here unless it was to talk with Brenda Dex, the director of the Springs.

She sat down at the desk that was pressed against the wall in the small office and picked up the phone to call Brenda, who was on vacation for a few days. Her phone went straight to voicemail. Carefully selecting her words, she let Brenda know about the situation with Andrew and what had happened with Damon—leaving out no details about his alleged flirting with campers and his using them to continue to harass her.

As she hung up, there was a chalkiness in her mouth. She wished she had the authority to fire Damon right now. He had no business continuing to be here and around the kids.

She was almost glad that Brenda hadn't picked up and she could just relay the details as they happened unencumbered by questions. She wasn't sure she was ready to talk about all the things Damon would have continued doing and the problems he would have created had things not been brought to a head.

Turning to go, she eyed the filing cabinet in a corner of the room. Inside was all the campers' and residents' personal information for the last few years. Opening the drawer, she pulled out the yellow file marked with Grace's name.

She scanned through the paperwork. From everything she had managed to pull up on Grace and her history, it appeared as though the girl had been in the system since she was put up for adoption when she was less than a year old. There wasn't an age that she was given up, or a date, but the documents noted that the parents were young and unable to provide care. Nothing more.

The words "young parents" jumped out at her as if in bold type. It was strange how a mind had a way of picking out the things that could hurt the most.

What if her daughter was out there somewhere fighting against the world like Grace was?

Her knees grew weak, and she was forced to sit down. Grace wasn't her daughter. Ann was. Ann had gone to a good home with a stable set of parents, probably in some tropical state where she was living her best life and growing up with stability, reliability and resources that, even now, April wasn't sure she could have provided.

These pervasive thoughts, the ones of guilt and the overwhelming sense of failure, had been a constant in her life, but she had been good at talking herself down from the ledge and keeping them at bay. Yet now, her normal composure and ability to compartmentalize were completely lost. Her emotions were out of control.

She needed to stay in check. If she didn't, she couldn't do her best for Grace. Every minute counted when it came to finding her. And, as they ticked by, feelings of desperation and failure were starting to seep in. Those cracks were just letting in every other feeling as well. She had to stay strong.

She had to focus on the now and on doing everything in her power to get potentially helpful information.

Dipping her toes in the past wasn't helping.

She flipped to the next page in Grace's file. She'd been functioning at school, but according to her teachers was not performing to the best of her abilities. Which made sense, given that it appeared as though she was, for all intents and purposes, living on her own. Which meant the girl must have been working, but she didn't find any mention of Grace having a job or any form of steady income.

Perhaps that was why Grace hadn't tried to be emancipated from her current guardians. To do so, she would have to prove she had a good paying job and a stable place to live. Not to mention the fact that the girl likely didn't have the resources to seek legal counsel in helping her to remove herself from her situation.

If only Grace had spoken up and asked for help, April would have done everything in her power to extricate the girl from a bad situation.

She scanned through more of the background information the Springs had on Grace. Most of it was old medical records, nothing that seemed to have any bearing on her disappearance.

The next pages, however, were interesting. According to the paperwork the family had filed with the state, they had been fostering another girl as well—Summer Averian. The same Summer who she had last seen sitting out on the porch and refusing to answer their questions.

Why hadn't Summer told them that she was more than just a friend of Grace's? More, that they had shared foster parents?

Summer had to have known that eventually the police

looking into Grace's disappearance would find out and start to ask questions.

Then again, Summer had no reason to tell April and Sean the truth. They weren't the police, and they hadn't known what to ask. However, something about Summer not telling them the truth and speaking up when she had the chance felt strange. If nothing else, April would have to tell Terrell what she had found.

It was possible, and even probable, that he already knew. He had access to databases that had all of a person's information, including siblings, parents, known addresses and everything all the way down to every car they had ever owned.

Maybe she didn't need to tell him after all.

She closed the file, slipping it back into the cabinet. Stepping out of the office, she locked the door behind her.

The next shift of two counselors had shown up to take over for Damon, who'd been alone after the other counselor had called in sick. She could hear them talking in the kitchen when she walked by, but she didn't have any desire to take part in getting them up to speed. Regardless of how Damon wanted to spin this, the truth about him was going to come out—she'd make sure of it.

Hopefully Brenda would get the message before too long and Damon would never be allowed to set foot back on the grounds. Until then, she was going to steer clear of him— she didn't need him harassing her any more than he already had been since they'd met. He wasn't to be trusted.

The sun was bright as she walked outside, and it sat falsely against the darkness that was filling her soul. Sean was standing beside Terrell's vehicle, talking on his phone. He looked serious, and as he spoke she couldn't quite make out his words, but from the baritone of his voice she could tell he was angry.

She could only imagine what was happening now.

Sean looked up and he scowled as he looked at her. He quickly turned away.

Though she was sure it wasn't intended as a snub, his cold shoulder cut.

Terrell was in his car, typing on his computer.

She pulled out her phone, praying she would receive more information about Grace, but there were no new messages.

Walking over to Terrell, she gently tapped on his window to draw his attention. He looked away from his screen, closing it slightly, and he rolled his window down. "What's up?"

"I called the director and let her know what has happened." She paused. "I've been thinking—I want to file a report against Damon for harassment. Let's get the ball rolling for a restraining order. At the very least it will keep him away from here until Brenda can do a full internal investigation."

Terrell smiled. "You don't know how glad I am to hear you say that. Why don't you come on into the car, and I'll take your statement and write it up. From there, you'll need to talk to a Crime Victims Advocate who can help you get a temporary order of protection until you guys can get in front of a judge and make it more permanent, if necessary."

She nodded, but there was a sickening feeling in her stomach. She hadn't wanted to do this, but now it wasn't just her welfare at stake.

TWO HOURS LATER, after Terrell had dropped her off at the CVAs offices and she had filed her thirty-day temporary order of protection against Damon, she was relieved to finally be out in the fresh air again. It had been draining to go over everything that had happened between her and Damon, and then show proof of all the text messages and attempts he had made to contact her after she had written him off.

It wasn't going to be pretty when they went to court, but at least she had legal recourse if Damon attempted to contact her or try to get close to her. The only thing she feared now was the reality that often occurred when someone was slapped with a TOP—the violence and stalking behaviors escalated.

With any luck, Damon wouldn't go off the rails and he would see this as what it was—an attempt to make him realize his actions were out of line and that using children to get to her was absolutely despicable and couldn't continue.

As she walked outside, Terrell and Sean were sitting in Terrell's squad car, talking.

Sean had been *off* since everything had happened with Andrew, but they'd been so busy that they had barely had time to talk openly about what had gone on. Terrell gave her a tilt of the head and a smile, but Sean couldn't seem to meet her gaze.

"How'd it go?" Terrell asked, motioning her toward his window.

She lifted the copy of the papers the CVA had given her. "It's done. I have a hearing in thirty days. Until then he can't contact me or be within a thousand yards of me in any way." A sense of relief filled her, and a smile fluttered across her lips.

"That's great," Sean said, finally looking at her and smiling.

She hadn't realized how much she had needed his support. "Thank you, Sean. I'm glad you were here. I appreciate it."

He gave an acknowledging nod. "I'm glad you got it taken care of."

Yes, something with him was off. Everything he did and said just felt so *stilted*.

Was this because he had finally met Damon? He seemed in support of her taking the steps that she had to protect herself, but was he also judging her for allowing herself to get into such a predicament?

He didn't seem like the type to blame the victim, but maybe she was wrong in making that assumption.

Gah.

"Detective," she said to Terrell, "I know you're not a taxi, but I was hoping that maybe you could give us a ride back to my place. I'm *exhausted*."

Terrell sent a questioning glance to Sean that made her wonder what they had been talking about for the hour or so she had been inside the CVAs office.

"Sean?" he asked.

"Terrell and I were talking…" Sean started, but he seemed deeply uncomfortable as he shifted his weight and was entirely too preoccupied with a loose thread on the cuff of his shirt. "We both agree that it's probably not best if you go home. Damon is going to be served with the TOP sometime in the next day, and he may well come looking for you."

"I was thinking about that, too," she said, realizing that she hadn't really thought about Damon showing up at her door nearly as much as they had. "I guess I can get a hotel room."

Sean twitched and Terrell shook his head like they were having a completely wordless conversation. She hated feeling like she was being left out from whatever was happening, but at the same time maybe she was glad she didn't know what was going on. She already had enough to handle.

"How about you stay at my place?" Sean asked, but there was hesitancy.

"Sure." She tried not to notice it as all she really wanted was a safe place where she could get some rest. "But what about Grace?"

Terrell shook his head. "You guys don't need to worry about her tonight. I've got my people working around the clock, and we're going to look into a couple of leads we heard about today."

"What kind of leads?" she asked, a new sense of excitement filling her.

"Get in," Terrell said, clicking his computer shut and getting out of the car. He opened the back door for her. "I know it's not great to be seen riding around in the back of my car, but Sean's place isn't far. I'm sure no one will notice."

She was nearly certain someone would see, but she didn't care. Let the gossip mill run. It wasn't the first time she'd been the target of small-town chatter. As she got into the hard plastic, bucket-style seat, she clicked her seat belt into place. She tried not to think about all the people who had been cuffed, stuffed and escorted to jail in this seat.

The hard black seat bit into the back of her thighs as Terrell pulled out of the parking lot and onto the main road. The seat reminded her of sitting on a public bus, and it smelled about the same thanks to the scents of sweat, fear and bodies.

"So," she said, shifting her weight as she tried to get a better view of Sean and Terrell in the front seats through the hard Plexiglas window between them, "what new leads did you get?"

Terrell gave a quick glance back over his shoulder at her. "We've received two calls from our tip line. Like I said, I still need to follow up on them, but right now it sounds possible that Grace was spotted at a gas station in Bozeman."

"Who saw her?" she asked, wiggling with excitement.

"A gas attendant thinks he spotted her last night."

"Was she alone?" she pressed.

Terrell shrugged.

"What about the other call?" she asked.

It was quiet for a long moment, and the air conditioner fan and the road noise were the only sounds in the tight space.

"That one is a little more concerning. According to the caller, Grace was being trafficked to Chile to work as a housekeeper."

A housekeeper? She hoped that wasn't slang for something else, but the ache in her gut held her back from asking.

"Do you know who made the call?"

Terrell shook his head. "We didn't get a name, but we have the caller's phone information and last known location. I have a deputy out of Gallatin County working on that call as we speak." He pulled to a stop in front of Sean's house. "I'm going to run to Bozeman right now and link up with the other department. We'll go through their findings. If I get my hands on Grace or Andrew, I'll let you know. In the meantime…" He paused. "Please…stay safe."

Chapter Nineteen

Sean didn't want to leave April alone, but he also wasn't sure how he wanted to handle the situation with the gas cap. He hadn't told Terrell about the fire marshal's findings, and he wasn't entirely sure why. Perhaps it was the fact that he didn't want her to have played any kind of role in the fire.

No matter how many scenarios he went through in his mind, he couldn't make sense of how her fingerprints would have been on that cap. She had to have been the person who'd touched the plastic last, but there was no motivation for her to have torched Grace's foster parents' apartment. Well…except…maybe…if she had decided she hated Grace's foster parents for their having left her, but even that wasn't a good enough reason for her to burn down the one place Grace called home.

It just didn't make sense.

There had to be some reasonable explanation. She hadn't given him a reason not to trust her, in fact, quite the opposite.

The house was quiet when they walked in, and though he could understand why, he was a ball of nerves. It wasn't like they hadn't been alone before, and it wasn't like either of them were wishing to take things between them to another level.

"If you'd like, there's the guest bedroom. Or, you can have the couch," he said, motioning toward the place where he'd held her in his arms.

Things had gone haywire since he'd told her his truth, but he wished they could try again. She was everything he wanted in a life partner, but he couldn't help but wonder if they had gone through too much to come back from.

"What are we going to do without your truck?" she asked.

"I have an old Mustang in the garage. I haven't driven her in a month or so, but I know she has gas."

"She?"

He sent her a guilty grin. "She's fast, beautiful and a little temperamental."

"Should I be offended?" she teased with a gentle giggle.

"Not even a little, I was totally kidding. I really have no idea why I call it 'she.' It's just a habit I got from my dad."

Some of his nerves slipped away. She wasn't a criminal, and there was no way she could or would have done anything to hurt Grace.

Her smile faded, and he could tell she was thinking. After a moment, she turned to him. "Do you think we are going to get Grace back?"

"I want to think we will." He sighed, tired. "Do you want a drink or anything?"

"Sure," she said, but her smile didn't reappear. "Do you think the calls to the tip line were legitimate?"

He didn't want to tell her that she was probably right in being concerned on both fronts. She knew as well as he did that many of the calls that a tip line received were nothing more than prank calls, people with mental health issues or well-meaning folks who got it wrong.

He knew that in the case of Jim and his investigations, he often got dozens of calls and more often than not, they led to nothing. The only good news was that they only needed one real lead and they stood a chance.

"Terrell will get something from this. We just have to have faith in him." He grabbed two beers out of the fridge and smiled as he glanced over at the open bottle of wine from the other night.

It was strange how much things could change and evolve in just a matter of hours, and even minutes. Last week, he hadn't even considered having a woman in his life, and now he found himself silently begging that the red flags he saw in her were nothing more than decorations that might have matched his own.

He carried the beers out and handed one to her on the couch. She took a dainty sip and started to pick at the label. He felt the same need to keep his hands busy and as he sat down beside her he pulled at the silver corners of the label as well.

He glanced at her and caught her looking at him from under her eyelashes. Maybe history really did repeat itself.

He smiled at the thought.

"How's your arm feeling?" he asked.

She looked down at it like she had nearly forgotten about it. "It's a little achy, but fine. You know, I've never broken anything before."

His thoughts instantly shot back to the night Cameron had been killed. Sean had fared well, but he'd broken two ribs and sometimes when he worked out hard, they still ached. That had been the only time he'd broken bones, but he feared bringing it up. They had finally seemed to put the memory and pain of Cameron's loss behind them.

Then again, there was only sweeping it under the rug for moments, not forever.

"It wasn't your fault," she said, almost as though she could read his thoughts like they were headlines upon his face.

"Huh?" he asked, hoping he was wrong, and she was talking about something other than Cameron.

"His death." She sighed like she was resigned to the fact that they needed to talk about all the emotional pitfalls in the way of their being closer.

He grunted, noncommittal.

"If I've learned anything this week, it is that bad things happen to good people…especially to the kids and young people who have done nothing to deserve the hardships and losses they've been forced to endure."

"I deserve whatever happens to me. You can say it wasn't my fault, but—"

"You were a kid," she interrupted. "If your father hadn't shielded you, you would have been put through the wringer, too."

He looked at the silver label on the bottle. He still hadn't taken a drink. "Maybe you wouldn't have had to have gone through it alone if I had been made to pay for my role in his death."

"What role? You were just in the car. You were just a passenger. It was lucky he didn't kill you, too."

"That isn't entirely true. A deer jumped out. I yelled at Cameron to jerk the wheel. When he did, he was going too fast. We spun out and Cameron had overcorrected. It was my fault, April."

"You were doing what anyone would have done in that situation. Cameron was an inexperienced driver in the wrong place at the wrong time—and intoxicated. So were you." She ran her hand over her hair, soothing herself. "There's no going back. There's no making different choices. I can't bring him back and neither can you."

He took a deep breath to control his guilt and pain. He had to be strong.

PISTON'S FOOTFALLS PADDED down the hall, breaking the silence as he thought about what April was saying. The cat rubbed against his legs, and he gave him a scratch before Piston did the same to April.

Piston purred as she touched him. He could understand the cat's reaction. Getting enough love, the cat disappeared behind the couch.

"So, I've been thinking..." she said, moving closer to Sean.

Her nearness made him inexplicably nervous. *What is she doing?*

She put her hand on his and looked up into his eyes. She was so incredibly beautiful. "You touched on it, but we can grow from these horrible things that have happened to us, together. We can find strength from one another on the days when we need it."

"We?" he asked, a smile trembling on his lips. He couldn't believe what he was hearing. She couldn't possibly be forgiving him—not after all the ways he had screwed up her life and caused her pain.

"Yes, we," she said, putting her hands on his face and looking him squarely in the eyes. "*We* can be together tonight. If you want?"

He took hold of her hands on his face and pulled one back, kissing her palm as he closed his eyes. There was nothing that felt quite like this, her skin on his. The scent of her hand, lavender soap with a faint hint of her perfume still on her wrist from this morning. He loved her smell. And he loved the way she made him feel.

"I want everything. I need *everything*," he whispered into the cup of her hand as he looked at her beautiful face. Her blond hair was caressing her cheek, and he took a strand of it between his fingers. It was nearly as soft as her skin. "Do you know how beautiful you are?"

She smiled. "I already said we could be together. You don't have to butter me up now."

He wanted to ask her what being together meant—she had first said for only tonight, but then just generally together. From the way she spoke about the future, it sounded as if she wanted a relationship. Maybe she was just as torn about them being together as he was. There were more reasons for them not to be an item than there were for them to try to make a relationship work, but at the core of his desire was his attraction for her.

He leaned in, moving his hands down her as he took her lips with his. Even her kiss was perfect. Her mouth yielded to his, but she was strong and passionate. Her tongue flicked against his, massaging him and teasing him.

His hand cupped her breast. Her bra was thin, and he could feel her nipple grow hard under his thumb. He wanted to take her nipple into his mouth and gently nibble as she moved to climax, but he wasn't about to rush the moment. Now, he wanted to make her moan his name—extra points if she breathed it into his mouth as his fingers explored the warmth between her thighs.

She reached down to pull her shirt over her head, but he stopped her with the touch of his hand. "I like to unwrap my own presents." He sent her a sultry smile. "Stand up."

She moved to her feet, but her movements were unsteady.

He took hold of the edge of her pants and pulled her closer to him so he could touch her soft belly with his lips. He loved her body. The way her curves pressed against the coarse fabric of her jeans. He pulled open the button of her pants, kissing the little red mark left behind by the confining button.

He took hold of her hips and pressed his face into her, kissing her hard as he took the zipper in his mouth and pulled it down. She giggled and it made him grin. He pulled her jeans down to her thighs. They held there, and he took his opportunity to sit back and stare at her white cotton panties.

"I should have changed," she said, pushing at her panties like she was embarrassed.

"I think they are perfect." He loved the feel of them on his mouth as he moved lower, pushing her jeans down and taking her into his mouth through her panties and sucking on the hard little spot he knew would drive her to ecstasy.

She threw her head back and grabbed his hair, pushing him harder against her. He hummed, tapping his tongue on her with his every break for breath. She tasted so good, like a mixture of pennies and sugar.

He pulled down her panties and licked her harder. Her legs started to shake as he pressed his mouth against her, using his chin to hit the other sensitive spots. He swirled his tongue, working figure eights of pleasure until her breaths quickened.

"I want to feel you inside me," she said, moaning.

"Am I doing something wrong?" he asked, pulling back from her.

"No." She shook her head. Her pupils were dilated and her eyes opened wide, and she pressed his head back down between her legs. "I… I'm close. If you keep going…"

Oh, hell yes…

He buried his face, letting her juices run down his chin as he moved with her body. He ran his fingers above her hard little spot, rubbing gently and flicking his tongue. She quaked, and he wrapped her in his arms as she released.

She called out, the sound echoing of the walls and settling deep in his heart. "Sean…"

Chapter Twenty

April woke up before him, and she rushed to the bathroom. Piston mewed lightly and, giving his head a good scratch. She cleaned herself up, then snuck back into Sean's bed, where they had finally come to rest after a night of love-making. He looked peaceful in his slumber, but she wasn't done. She would never get enough of him.

She slipped down under the sheets, taking him into her mouth.

"Mmm… Yes." He sucked in a long breath, gently waking as she moved up and down on him.

"April…" He said her name like it was a taffy, stretching and sweet on his tongue.

She moaned on him as she worked his hard, enormous length.

Everything about this man's body was perfect.

And don't get her started on all the things he could make her body do. He knew his way around a woman.

He lifted the sheets and smiled down on her, groggy. "Should I call you breakfast?"

She paused, taking him in her hand and stroking as she looked up at him. "What?"

"Well, you are going to be the first thing I eat this morning," he said, sending her a devilish grin.

She giggled, hard.

Taking it as a sweet weakness, he lifted her up to him and kissed her lips. "I hope you are ready for more," he said. "Get on your knees."

She followed his direction, her body ready for anything he wanted to do to her. He was a demigod in bed—complete with pecs that made her want to take a bite, and his abs were nearly washboard. Any more chiseled and she would have sworn he was made of stone and not right for a mere mortal like her.

He moved behind her and ran his fingers down her body, getting her used to his presence. Then she felt his tongue dip into her. She nearly lost control of her arms and she lowered her face onto the pillow, moaning as he kissed her gently on all the places he had played with last night.

His tongue flicked on her again, and as he played, she felt herself nearing closer and closer to the edge. When he ran his tongue over her and pressed it inside of her, the sensation was too much. She'd never experienced anything like it, and as he took hold of her hips and circled back to her mound with his tongue, she couldn't hold back.

He licked every drip from her as she quaked for him.

"That's my beautiful queen," he said, helping her move from her knees and laying her down. "Now, I'll make you your breakfast, my beautiful queen. You just stay here and rest. If things go our way, you are going to need your strength for more of this again tonight." He pushed her hair behind her ear and wrapped her in the sheet and light blanket. He started to get up, but turned back and gave her a playful smack to her butt, making her giggle.

"If you're lucky," she teased.

"I have a feeling that things are going to go my way." He popped up from the bed like her body had been some kind of energy drink. She could hear him humming a song as he made his way down the hall and toward the kitchen.

He really was incredible.

She didn't know how she had gotten so lucky—not only had she found a man who was smart, kind, courageous and charming, but he was also her perfect match in bed. She'd heard about the unicorns out there who could make a woman howl and forget their names. Before last night, she wouldn't have believed it. Finishing had never come easily, until he had his way with her.

He had awakened parts of her that she thought were nothing more than urban myths.

She couldn't be more grateful, but hopefully she had pleased him in the same ways.

Her phone buzzed on the bedside table. *Ugh.*

It was fine. She could ignore it; it was still early.

It buzzed again, making her think about the Springs, Damon and Grace. There were too many things to worry about for her to bask in the glow of what she had just experienced and forget about the world—no matter how badly she wanted to.

It was an unknown number. Damon had been using unknown numbers, so she was fearful to answer, but if it was Grace then she would hate herself if she didn't pick up.

No matter what, Damon couldn't hurt her through a phone.

"Hello?" she asked, her voice rough.

"How could you?" Damon growled through the phone.

"Damon, I'm hanging up and I'm calling the police. You know you can't call me."

"Shut up. *You* know you don't feel like this. I know *he* made you do this. You are mine. You've just been too…too *shy* to give yourself to me. And yet…you'll give yourself to him." He sounded hurt and furious.

She wouldn't have cared except for the fact that his knowing what had happened between her and Sean last night meant that he had been watching. The realization made goose bumps rise over her entire body.

"You…you have no right."

"You are the one who has no right. You are mine. You were mine before you were his, you are cheating—"

"I'm not cheating, Damon. I'm not yours. I've never been *yours*. I wouldn't be yours if you were the last man on earth. Why can't you understand?" Her words nearly choked her.

He laughed, the sound maniacal and high on the other end of the line. "That's fine… Just fine."

His laughter was terrifying.

"I'm going to hurt you, just as much as you've hurt me."

The line went dead.

She sat on the edge of the bed, staring at the phone in her hand. That couldn't have just happened, but it did. She should have known he'd break the order of protection and threaten her. Though she didn't want to, she would have to tell Sean and call the police and report what had just happened.

She had known that the threat of violence would escalate. Damon had never been well-adjusted, and her actions had definitely thrown him over the edge. She could only guess what he was going to do now. She wasn't safe anywhere she went.

If only she had trusted her gut when she'd first met this guy and not wanted to see the best in him. She felt so stupid and utterly terrified.

If she'd just kept him at arm's length, she wouldn't have had to file the restraining order or worry for her safety.

She captured a screen grab of the phone number and time of the call. It wasn't his number, or associated with his name, but her word would have to be enough. If something like this happened again, she would have to do things differently and record the call or something. She'd been in enough courtrooms to know that she'd need proof of his call and threat for the violation of the TOP to stand up in front of a judge. It would be her word against his in thirty days. He could easily deny that he'd called and threatened her.

She looked at the window. What if he was just outside and waiting for her to stand up so he could shoot her through the glass? At least there wasn't a car parked outside for him to booby trap. That was one less worry.

There were the sounds of Sean cooking coming from down the hall. He was still humming. Just like that, she was going to ruin his day and crush his feeling that things were going to go his way. By now, they should have both known better than to call up the fates by speaking hopes aloud.

She quickly got dressed and slipped to the window, staying behind cover as she carefully looked outside. From where she stood, she didn't see Damon or his car, but it didn't bring her much comfort. He wouldn't have been so stupid to be out in the open if he was going to try to kill her.

Then again, he wasn't smart enough to take a hint or follow police orders.

She pushed the curtains closed, careful to avoid putting her arm out in the open.

It struck her that this was how things were going to be. She would always be afraid and waiting for the bullet to strike.

What kind of life would this be if she was living in constant fear?

She checked herself. For now, it was *her* life. She was going to have to fight to keep it.

Sean smiled widely at her as she made her way out into the kitchen. "Hey, babe," he said, leaning over to her and giving her a kiss on the cheek. "Breakfast is about ready." He motioned toward the scrambled eggs with the spatula in his hand.

"Did you just hear me in there?" she asked, motioning toward the bedroom.

His smile grew impossibly wider. "Oh, I heard you all right." He laughed, but as he looked at her face he abruptly stopped.

"No." She shook her head and lifted her phone slightly so he could see what she meant. "Damon just called."

He stopped moving. After a long moment of silence, he turned away from her and carefully put the spatula down and turned off the stove. "Let's go."

She wasn't quite sure what he meant. "Where?"

"Let's run to the police station. We will file a report and have his ass brought in for violating his TOP."

He hadn't even asked what Damon had said; it was like he already knew. She appreciated not having to explain it to him. He probably knew that whatever Damon had said wasn't something he wanted to hear or give attention to.

Grabbing the keys that were hanging on the wall by the door leading to his garage, he motioned for her to follow him. She wasn't sure what she feared more, Damon or Sean's eerie silence.

The mustang was a pearly opalescent white and it sparkled in the sun as he opened the garage door. He moved to the passenger side and opened her door. She climbed in, almost afraid to speak.

It wasn't until they were approaching the police department that Sean finally made a sound. "I've been meaning to ask… Jim brought something up to me…"

"The fire marshal?" she asked.

He gave a stiff nod. "He located fingerprints on the gas cap we found at Grace's apartment." He slowed to a stop at the light. No other cars were around, and he turned to face her. His eyes searched her face in a way that made her deeply uncomfortable. "Was there anything about the fire at Grace's that you haven't told me?"

"No." Her stomach ached. "Why?"

"It was *your* fingerprints."

She stared at him, trying to make sense of what he was saying to her and all that it implied. "You don't think I *actually* had anything to do with the fire at Grace's, do you?"

He ran his hand over his face like he was trying to wipe away wayward thoughts. "No. I have been going over it and over it since he brought it to my attention. I just want to make sure that I'm right."

"The last thing I want to do is cause Grace more heartache," she choked out. "Hell, all I've wanted to do is help her—since the moment she and I met." Her anger roiled within her, making heat rise up from her core. The mere thought that someone could think she'd intentionally hurt a kid made her want to scream.

"If I thought you had anything to do with the fire, or if you were the kind of person I had to worry about, last night wouldn't have happened. I'd like to think I have a pretty good idea of the incredible woman you are, but I had to tell you about the fingerprints." He extended his hand, and she slowly put hers in his.

She wasn't sure how she felt; there were so many things going through her mind right now…but at the center of it all, she held no doubts that Sean was there for her. He was the one person in her life who was safe.

"Do you have any clue how your fingerprints would have been there? Did you fill a gas can anytime recently?" He squeezed her hand as though he was trying to reassure her.

She thought back to the last time she'd even held a gas can. "I bought some diesel for the camp's lawn tractor a week ago. I normally don't mow, but they gave me a bonus if I did it, so…"

"There we go. Grace probably stole the can from the group home," he said. He pulled to the right, instead of continuing to go toward the station. "Let's swing by your apartment." He motioned to her phone. "Why don't you go ahead and text Terrell and let him know about the thing with Damon and that we will be dropping by to file a report."

She sent a text off to the detective, careful to include the picture she'd taken of the phone number and carefully quoting what Damon had said. As she typed, bile rose in her throat.

What if Damon was following them? He had made it clear he'd been watching her. She glanced up from her phone, but she didn't see anyone but a lady out watering her flowers.

"Sean," she said, trying to quell the fear she was feeling and not let it leak into her voice, "Damon said he was going to hurt me. If he's following us…" She motioned her chin in the direction of her apartment, just minutes away.

"If he's there, then he will have to deal with me."

She wanted to point out that Sean didn't have a gun. What was he going to do if Damon came at them with a weapon? She wanted to feel completely protected with Sean by her side, but her anxiety was weighing on her. There were too many variables—and the one common denominator was unpredictability.

Chapter Twenty-One

As he turned the corner and April's apartment building came into view, the first thing he spotted was his pickup truck.

"What in the hell?" he said, pointing toward his truck.

She looked up from her phone. "Oh…"

He pulled to a stop beside it, hoping that Andrew would be inside. He was nowhere to be seen outside the building.

"Why do you think he came here?"

Sean shrugged. "I'm hoping that he knew we'd find the truck if he dumped it here."

April nodded. "I told you. Andrew is a good kid. He just needed a way to escape."

It would have been nicer if the kid had dropped it off at his place, but he doubted that Andrew would have known how to find him, or his address. Which made him think. "How did he know where you lived?"

April shrugged. "I have no idea."

He knew she thought of Andrew as a good kid, but the teenager had kicked the living snot out of Damon. Which meant he was capable of violence.

"Let's go inside and check on things," he said, turning off the car and getting out.

She motioned to her apartment door, which was slightly ajar. "I know I locked it when I left the other day."

They walked toward it, but before he had even gotten close, he could see that dead bolt had been broken and the inside of the door frame was dangling loosely just inside the door, which was keeping it from closing.

He didn't dare to touch it. "I think we need to get Terrell over here."

She was already tapping away on her phone. In a few moments, she said, "He'll be here in ten." She snapped a picture of the lock and the door and sent it off to the detective. "There."

"Let's take a look inside your apartment and see if Andrew's behind this." *Or if Damon or someone else had broken in.*

Her face blanched slightly. "Don't you think we should wait for Terrell or a deputy? Damon…"

"Probably didn't do this," he said, motioning toward his deserted truck. He touched her arm. "You're fine. Everything's fine." Even as he spoke, he wasn't quite sure that he believed himself. "Let's just go take a quick look."

He pushed open her door. There, stuck inside the wall by the light switch, was a note. It simply read: "I'm sorry. I have to find Grace. —A"

The poor kid. He felt for Andrew, he really did. If he had a chance, he would have assured him that he and April would stand by him if he was worried about getting in trouble for fighting and running away, and that they *all* wanted to find Grace, in every sense of the word. Everything Andrew had done was understandable, especially given his age.

"Well, I think he's proven that he's not the kind of kid without a conscience," he said, pulling the note off the door and handing it to April.

"I tried to tell you that before."

They went inside. Even though the door had been slightly ajar, the place held the stale smelling air that came with enclosed spaces and summer heat. Masking it, though, was the sweet scent of her perfume.

Her apartment was clean and meticulously organized, even the mail on the counter was sorted by size, largest to smallest. "I'm guessing everything is undisturbed?" he asked.

She walked over to the kitchen island where the pile of mail sat waiting for her. She picked up the envelope on top and flipped it over, reading the back. "So far, except the door, we are good."

They walked back toward her bedroom. As he followed her there was the sound of breaking glass behind them in the living room, and then a distinctive *whoomph*.

He instantly knew that noise.

Fire.

His realization was met with the faint aroma of gas.

There was an explosion, and as he turned, the heat of the gas-fueled flames blasted against his face. His eyelashes curled from the heat. As if time had slowed, he turned back to April and threw himself on top of her as the fire rushed overhead at them. It was only a millisecond, but it could have been a minute as he watched her fall to the floor under his body. He pressed her down as the fireball ballooned over them.

"Are you okay?" he called to her.

She nodded, but her eyes were wide with terror.

"Stay low," he ordered. "Move toward your room as fast as you can. I'm right behind you."

She nodded, army-crawling the distance to her room, using her pink cast as well as she could. The air was thick with smoke, and he could detect the faint smell of burned hair…likely his own.

They didn't have long before the smoke would overtake them. It was a matter of minutes. In events like these, time worked in mysterious ways. There were instances when he'd been donned up, masked and working that it had felt like he'd been in a building just a matter of seconds when in fact he'd nearly run out of air in his tank. And then, there were times like these when seconds felt like forever.

Though he knew she was moving as fast as she could, he needed her to go faster. As he moved to speak, there was a strangled cry from her second bedroom.

"April?"

She looked back at him.

"Was that you?"

She shook her head.

There was someone else in this apartment.

"Call out if you need help!" he yelled.

The fire roared around them, but he heard a man's voice. He was calling for help, but his words were muffled by the closed door and the sounds of the fire.

"Is there a window in your back bedroom?" he asked April, motioning toward the room.

She shook her head and stopped moving to talk to him.

"No! Keep moving. Don't stop. I want you to get to your bedroom and get out that window as fast as you can."

She wanted to say something, to argue, but he shut her down. "Move. Now. Go!"

She hustled forward turning the corner into her bedroom. He moved behind her, closing the door to her room in an attempt to stop the smoke from getting any heavier in there, but in doing so it immediately made the smoke downdraft toward him, filling his lungs.

He coughed, fighting the terror that rippled through him. That had been a mistake, but he didn't care as long as she got out. She came first. Not him. He'd promised to protect and keep her safe. He was going to stand by his word, no matter the cost.

The smoke thickened around him, and he tried not to breathe, but his coughing fit had cost him, and he could feel the smoke burn at the insides of his lungs.

He forced himself to get lower, his face almost on the carpet as he moved toward the second bedroom. The door was closed, and he reached up, grasping blindly until he found the handle. Twisting it, he pushed it open. The smoke from the hall cascaded like billowing water into the room.

There was another *whoomph* sound as the oxygen from the room met the flames, feeding them. He rushed into it the bedroom, closing the door behind himself hoping that it would stop the fire and smoke from its rapid advance.

"Hello?" he called, using his sacred breath to help this unknown man.

"Help!"

He followed the man's call and found him huddled in the corner of the room, against the back wall and across from the bed. As he drew close, he recognized Andrew's face immediately.

What was he doing in here? Why was he hiding? His note said he was out looking for Grace, but he must have surprised him when he'd been leaving the note. Maybe the kid had been trying to hide.

Sean was mixed with a sense of relief and terror for the boy who sounded all too much like a full-grown man.

Andrew was breathing hard, pulling way too much smoke into his lungs. A tear was running down his cheek.

"Are you okay?" Sean asked.

The kid nodded, but he could tell something was wrong. As he opened his mouth to speak, Andrew started coughing.

Sean glanced around the smoke-filled room. Through the haze, he spotted a bottle of water on the table near the bed. He rushed to grab it. He pulled his shirt over his head and doused it with the water. He threw the empty bottle on the floor.

"Andrew, take this shirt and loosely put it over your head and around your mouth and nose." He handed the kid his shirt.

He wrapped it around his head as Sean had instructed. "Okay, we are going to move to the other bedroom. There's a window there, we can crawl out. Okay?"

Andrew nodded.

"I want you to stay close to the floor, as close as you can get while moving as fast as you can. Okay?"

Andrew nodded again.

"All right, kiddo, let's go." He moved toward the door. The smoke in the room was stinging his hurting lungs, and he tried to control his breathing.

He would be okay. They'd all make it out of this fire alive. This was his job.

He kept checking over his shoulder to make sure that Andrew was following him through the smoke. There was a cord on the floor, and he yanked at it, pulling it from the wall. The small lamp it was attached to crashed to the ground. He took hold of the lamp and handed the end of the cord to Andrew.

"Out there," he said, motioning toward the hall, "it's going to be impossible to see. You need to keep hold of this. I'll lead us out. Got it?"

Andrew nodded as he looped the cord around his wrist. *Everything is going to be okay*, he told himself. As he did, he was reminded of his telling April that exact same thing not all that long ago. Even then, he hadn't been sure everything would be okay, and he was even less sure now, but he had to calm himself.

He had enough experience. He'd been through hundreds of fires and training environments. None were exactly like this, but they were close. He just needed to keep his emotions in check and allow his muscle memory and training to take over.

Tapping the door handle to make sure it wasn't too hot, he then turned the knob. His body was instantly flooded with heat and the stinking, acrid smoke of the house fire. In the few moments he'd been in this room with Andrew, the fire had taken over. Though he couldn't see the flames because of the black, tarry smoke, he could feel the heat of the active flames overhead.

Though he knew April's bedroom door was close, his heart thundered in his chest as he blindly swept his hands on the floor, trying to find where it met the carpet. He edged forward, finding the wall and moving down it. The wall was warm and gritty from smoke and ash.

He tried to keep his breathing as slow and metered as he could, but his heart was racing, and he found himself struggling to win the battle against nature.

He reached up and tapped the doorknob. It was hot and stinging, but he didn't have a choice. He moved fast, twisting the knob as it burned his fingers, and he forced the door open and tugged on the cord. Andrew moved closer, and he brushed against his foot as he rushed into the room.

Glancing around the room, he was semiblinded by the smoke, but he didn't see April. Her bed sat at the far side of the room and her closet was open. Everything seemed in place. He looked up and watched the smoke pour out of the bedroom window. Helping Andrew over the edge, he lifted him outside and into the fresh air. He followed, slipping over the windowsill, and scraping down the siding of the building until he hit the sidewalk.

Getting his feet on solid ground outside of a fire had never felt better. He took a deep gulp of air and tried to blink away the stinging in his eyes. His lungs felt like he'd smoked three packs of his grandmother's cigarettes. He hacked, trying to take a breath that didn't ache.

Andrew walked into the parking lot, pulling the shirt from his face. The areas of his head that hadn't been covered by the wet cloth were covered with dark soot, and his eyelashes were caked with ash.

Sean could guess how he looked after crawling all over the floor. His chest was sweaty, and he touched his skin. It felt gritty with dirt and ash. His fingers ached with burns, but all in all he was going to be okay.

"April?" he called, looking around the parking lot.

There was no answer.

She had to be outside. She had to have gotten out. The window was open. There was no one else in the bedroom.

He panicked.

Was she still in there? Had she gone back in?

"April!" he yelled, hoping she simply hadn't heard him.

He started back toward the window. On the siding near the bottom of the window was a small, bloody handprint. One too small to be a man's. It had to have been April's.

He called her name again; he sounded frantic.

There was still no answer.

April was gone.

Chapter Twenty-Two

What in the hell?

April had no idea where she was or what had happened. She remembered she had been coming out of her bedroom through the window. Something hit her. It hit her hard in the head. There was pain. So much pain. And blood. She remembered the blood.

A blindfold covered her eyes, but she guessed she was in the trunk of a car as she heard the muffled sounds of a radio and road noise beneath her. They hit a bump, and it threw her up in the air a couple of inches before she came down hard on what must have been the scratchy industrial carpet lining the area.

Her hands were tied together in front of her. Reaching up, she touched the tender spot on the back of her head where there was an open cut.

There was a pounding in her head.

Using her bound hands, she rubbed at the blindfold on her eyes, slipping it up on her forehead. It was pitch-black around her, but she was less afraid than she had been when she'd been blindfolded.

She listened hard to try to make out the sounds of anyone talking, hoping to identify who had taken her. Instead, the stifling hot air of the trunk seemed to grow impossibly hotter, and it amplified the sickening scent of smoke that had been on her skin.

It had to have been Damon who had taken her. There was no question in her mind, even though she hadn't heard anything to confirm. He drove a late-model Toyota Corolla. It had a small trunk, and as she stuck out her legs, they jammed into the sidewall of the trunk before she could even extend them.

Yes, it had to be Damon's car.

The police must be looking for him. They had to know he started the fire. At least, as long as Sean had gotten out of the apartment. He had been right behind her.

Did he know she was gone?

That she had been kidnapped?

If he did notice, how long had it taken before he'd realized?

She was flooded with questions as she tried to make sense of the situation in which she found herself.

Yet, she couldn't worry about that. She needed to come up with a plan to get out of this trunk. Or, what to do when Damon would finally stop to let her out.

He had to be taking her somewhere to kill her.

The only luck she'd had in this was the fact that he hadn't pulled the trigger when she was coming out the window. If he'd wanted to, that would have been the perfect opportunity. She'd had her back turned. She was focused on just getting out of the fire alive.

He had set the whole damn thing up.

The worst part was that she had known he had been gunning for her, and yet he had still gotten the drop on her.

She'd never thought he would actually do something like this. He hadn't been homicidal. Pathetic, yes. Needy, yes.

Manipulative, yes. But why, if he professed to love her so much, would he have wanted her dead?

Maybe he didn't intend on killing her. Maybe he just wanted to kidnap her for his own use.

She wasn't sure which would be worse.

No matter what his plans were, she was going to fight like hell.

EVERY FEAR HE'D ever held was being realized in a single second.

Sean sat on the edge of the sidewalk watching his team as they battled the blaze at April's apartment complex.

The black smoke curled up into the sky, filling what would have been a beautiful blue-sky day with dark clouds.

He sniffed at the air but couldn't smell anything but the smoke that had penetrated his lungs. The EMS worker was standing over him, making sure he kept on his oxygen mask as he tried to control his emotions. The woman looked down. "How are you feeling?"

He couldn't tell her that he was scared out of his mind. That he felt like a failure. That he'd never forgive himself if April had somehow gone back into the building and he'd missed it.

"I'm going to be fine." He motioned to the kid who was lying on the gurney inside the ambulance with his eyes closed. He looked almost asleep. "How's Andrew doing? Did everyone make it out okay?"

"Everyone made it out and is going to be fine. We are going to run Andrew to Bozeman to receive care." She reached into her pocket. "He asked me to give you these." She handed him his truck keys. "And to tell you he was sorry." She made her statement sound like a question, but he didn't want to go into the details with her as he took the keys.

"Was anyone else outside when my crew got here, do you know?" he asked, his voice was raspy, and he had to suppress a cough.

She shook her head. "I have no idea. Why?"

Someone had tried to kill them *that* was why. "Did anyone see a vehicle leaving the scene around the time the fire started?"

The EMS worker shrugged. "You'd have to ask the police officers." She motioned down the road.

In the distance, he spotted Detective Terrell. The guy looked deadly calm, which only meant one thing in their first-responder world—it was go time. Things were getting real. Now, he was truly terrified.

"If I promise to keep on my mask, can I walk over there?" he asked, motioning toward Terrell.

She nodded and handed him the green oxygen tank.

He walked over to Terrell and the detective gave him a deep tip of the chin in acknowledgment. He put his fingers up, motioning for the officer he was talking with to be quiet.

"Did anyone see anything suspicious at the scene?"

Terrell turned toward him. "We have a car matching the description of Damon's leaving the area. They couldn't see who was driving, but I think it's safe to say it was likely Damon. I've put out a BOLO for him. Highway patrol will be on the lookout for him if he tries to leave the area, but he may have gotten past them already."

He nodded. As much as he wanted to tell them to shoot to kill if they saw the bastard, he stayed quiet. "Besides, Damon had April. They'd all have to be careful."

"Andrew looks a little worse for the wear." Terrell motioned toward the ambulance. "I'm going to try to talk to him as soon as Brenda gets here from the airport—she came home early from vacation when she heard what happened. She said she'd meet us at the hospital. Did Andrew say anything to you?"

Sean shook his head. "Just that he was sorry."

Terrell's features darkened. "I'm sure he is. Anything else? Anything as to why he was in the apartment at the time the fire started?"

He hadn't realized until right now that from the detective's perspective, it made sense to think that Andrew was likely the one who had set the place ablaze. Sean clearly hadn't explained the situation well enough. "He was hiding in the back bedroom when I was trying to get April out."

"And she came out of the window before either of you?" he asked, even though he'd already given the guy a brief about what had happened when the EMS workers had started treating him.

"I thought she did, yes."

"So, you know for a fact that she didn't go back into the apartment?"

He popped his neck, purely out of stress. "I don't think she went back inside. I think Damon took her. He threw the bomb into the house. Hell, he probably started the fire at Grace's, too. He seems to have a thing for fire."

Terrell's features went impossibly darker. "I hear what you are saying, Sean. The thing is, Damon had an alibi for the time that the fire was started at Grace's apartment—he was working at the Springs. The kids reported seeing him. He couldn't have been the one to set it."

"Okay…" He felt the wind leave his sails. "That doesn't mean he didn't have something to do with these fires…and April's going missing."

Terrell nodded, but the action was placating. "Jim told me that the prints he found at Grace's fire came back as April's."

"Yes, she had filled up a gas can the week before. She had mowed the lawn at the group home."

"I got the video records for the gas station nearest the Springs, and I did manage to find her filling it up as she said."

"I'm not surprised," Sean said. "She has no reason not to tell you the truth."

"Yes and no, Sean." Terrell shifted his weight like he was about to throw a bomb. "According to some of the folks where she worked, she and Grace did not get along. They had a very antagonistic relationship."

"I would venture to guess that most of the kids didn't get along with authority figures there. Did you talk to Andrew? Andrew loves April, and he knows just as much as I do that she wouldn't have done anything to hurt anyone in her care."

"Did she tell you that Grace is her biological daughter?"
What in the actual hell?

"No. Grace isn't her daughter. There's no way."

Terrell arched his brow. "I spoke to Damon after you left the house last night. He was the one who told me. He had the adoption paperwork from both sides on his phone. He made it sound like April knew all about Grace. Are you saying she didn't tell you or you think she didn't know?"

"I swear, I don't think April knows." How did *Damon* know?

"Really?" Terrell looked surprised. "You think she wouldn't have had access to the same files as Damon? That she wouldn't have put it together?"

"How did Damon get the files?"

Terrell shrugged. "He didn't say, but the paperwork was notarized."

He thought about the strange situation between her and

Damon. Was this what he was holding over her head and why she hadn't wanted to move against him and get the TOP until he'd forced the issue? Was it possible that she was afraid that Damon would tell Grace that she was her birth mother or vice versa?

If Grace had known the truth, perhaps that was part of the reason she had disappeared. But that didn't help Sean make sense of the strange, garbled phone call they had gotten from Grace.

"Did you actually look into Damon's documents? Wouldn't that be something you would have access to through your database, NCIC?"

"Adoption records?" Terrell shook his head. "Absolutely not. Those are sealed by the courts in most cases."

Then how did Damon get his hands on them? "Can you get the documents?"

Terrell sighed. "Maybe, but in this case, I think we need to focus on finding Grace and April."

"Are you going to arrest April?" he asked.

He wasn't sure if working with Terrell would be in his best interest if the man was going to arrest her for a role he knew with almost complete certainty she didn't have in the fire. However, Sean had questions and there was a tiny bit of doubt within him because he didn't know what was going on with April. What she knew or didn't know. Yet, even at the thought of the possibility that April had started the fire at Grace's, he found that he was shaking his head. There could be some kind of motive there, but this was a case of Damon trying to clear his name and create a shadow of doubt to avoid trouble.

Terrell was watching him. "I just need to talk to her and see what she has to say about her fingerprints being at the scene of the arson. I also need to see if she had any desire to harm Grace."

He opened his mouth to argue that April had been in the hospital when Grace had initially gone missing. There was no way she could have kidnapped the girl.

"Before you say a word, think about it…" Terrell put up his hand. "We all know not to go up on that mountain in those kinds of conditions. I'm not saying April set up the slide, but she was an avid hiker—I'm sure you can see why I'm concerned. And while she may not have kidnapped Grace initially, I believe she may have known Grace had returned to her apartment—there, the girl was a captive target."

"April was with me the whole time."

"When I questioned Damon yesterday, he told me you'd say that. He also said she wasn't above getting someone to do her dirty work."

"Damon is the one who you should be digging into, not April. She has an alibi. April wouldn't hurt anyone."

"Just like you wouldn't?" Terrell countered.

His sharp words stabbed deep. "What do you mean?"

"Damon told me about you and your role in your high school friend's death."

"I didn't kill him. I didn't hurt him. I was just in the car."

"That's not what Damon said."

"That case was closed. I was cleared."

Terrell nodded, but he studied him. "And your father was who he was—you and I both know your dad pulled strings. I know how these things work. Your father didn't want you to ruin your life. One kid was dead, another one was looking at a possible court battle. He did what he needed to do."

"Screw you, Terrell," he said through gritted teeth. "You know I was just a kid in the wrong place at the wrong time.

My father was a good man. Don't discredit his memory or me based on some stalking jerk's word. Damon's the one who you need to dig into—not some stupid conspiracy theory he tried to get you hooked up on. You know how these games are played…he's a con man."

Chapter Twenty-Three

April waited until the car came to a stop and the engine turned off. From the earlier sounds of the tires and the number of ruts, they had to have been somewhere on a gravel road. Her heartbeat was thrashing in her ears, muffling the car door as it slammed shut. The car bounced and a second door slammed shut.

There were two. Two people who wanted her dead.

They were going to kill her.

They were going to get rid of her body deep in the woods where only the bears and vultures would find her.

Her emotions welled in her throat, and she tried to swallow them back. She was going to have to fight. She pulled at the paracord that was tied tight around her wrists with her teeth, frantically trying to get free. All her pulling did was yank the cord tighter and make her hands tingle from a lack of blood flow.

She twisted her hands, trying to loosen them. But her captors had tied the knot through the thumbhole in her cast. As she pulled, the hard cast rubbed her skin raw.

Thankfully her feet hadn't been tied. She could kick.

Or, what if she played dead?

What if they opened up the trunk and had a gun in their hands? One pull of the trigger and she'd be gone.

There was the jingle of keys and footsteps approaching the trunk. A key slid in the lock and ground as the teeth clicked into place. The trunk popped open. The slit of light blinded her and burned her eyes, and she was forced to close them for a moment.

Silhouetted by the sun was a dark shadow of a person. From the round shape of the body, it was a woman. A thin breeze kicked up, filling the stagnant air of the trunk with fresh air. As the wind blew, the woman's green hair lifted and shone in the light, giving her a strange swamp-colored aura.

Grace.

The fight left her body. What was Grace doing here?

"What… Grace? Why?" she stammered.

The girl grabbed her ankles and swiveled her legs out of the trunk. "Just be quiet."

There was another set of footfalls as someone walked around from the driver's side.

"Stand up," Grace ordered.

April wiggled forward, struggling to sit up with her legs arched over the metal edge of the trunk. Grace grabbed her arms and pulled her up, her thighs scraping on the plastic weather stripping and scratchy industrial carpet. Grace's fingers dug into her flesh as she tried to right herself and find her balance.

Damon stepped around the back of the car. "How was your ride?"

She couldn't stand looking at Damon's weasel face, with his long, crooked nose and beady little dark eyes. She hated him with every cell in her body.

"Grace? What are you doing with him?" Her words came out as whispers. She couldn't believe it.

Didn't Grace know what kind of man she had found herself with?

She glanced down at her bound hands.

Grace had to have known. She was complicit. She had kidnapped her. *They* were going to kill her.

"Why?" April asked, trying to sound stronger and more dangerous than she felt. "What do you want from me?"

Damon smiled, and tendrils of saliva stuck to his bottom lip from his canine teeth, reminding her of the predator he was. "I want everything from you. Do you know how much you've hurt me? What you've done? You've ruined my life."

She looked to Grace, who was looking adoringly at her mentor.

"I... I'm sorry, Damon," April said, playing along in an attempt to mollify the crazed man. "I didn't mean to hurt you. You were just...*scaring* me." She tried to look coquettish and supplicating.

His spine softened and he licked the saliva from his lip. "I didn't mean to scare you. All I ever wanted was for you to know how much I cared about you. How much *I love you*."

Her thoughts instantly moved to Sean. He was the man she wanted to love her. He had to be searching for her. She silently called to him, hoping he would feel her soul reaching out.

She glanced around, trying to figure out where in the world they had taken her.

"Do you love me, too?" Damon pressed. He reached forward and took her hand, lifting her bound fingers.

She nodded, afraid that if she tried to speak those words aloud to him that she'd retch.

"I knew that Sean had made you act the way you did." He picked at the rope on her wrists. "If I untie you, will you behave?"

She nodded, clamping her lips shut.

Hate filled her, taking the place of the fear she had been harboring. This man was nothing to fear. He was no longer human; he was nothing more than the embodiment of all the judgments, opinions, dismissals, pettiness, overt hatred and lies everyone in her life had ever placed upon her. He was just something she had to conquer. She would.

He took a knife out of his front pocket and gingerly placed the tip under the rope and started to saw next to the knot. The knife was dull, and it struck her how ill-prepared the man was if he was going to hurt her.

It made her wonder if he'd not planned her kidnapping or if it had been more of a desperate act by a desperate man.

Or, maybe, Grace had been the brains behind this.

She looked over at the girl. There was something familiar in her eyes—if she had to guess what it was, it was resolve. This girl was determined to do something, but she wasn't quite sure what. All April could hope was that it wasn't to murder her. Because she wasn't already dead, she had to guess the odds were in her favor.

As he cut her loose, the rope fell from her wrists. She turned slightly and there, lodged in the corner of the dark trunk, was her phone. It must have fallen from her pocket when they'd put her in the trunk. She looked away as quickly as she could so as not to draw their attention to the device.

"I have to use the restroom," she said, saying the first thing that she could think of in order to get a moment alone.

"She's fine," Grace argued.

Finally, the girl had found her voice. Unfortunately, it didn't seem as though she would be finding an ally with her.

"It will only take me a second. I can pee right here." She motioned toward the front of the car. "If you guys just step up there. I'll be two seconds."

Grace frowned.

"Okay," Damon said. "Be quick. I want to get to the hunting shack before it gets dark. I don't want to have to worry about bears."

Yes, the last thing she needed to worry about was another thing that wanted to kill her.

Damon motioned for Grace to move. "Let's give her a second."

"I don't trust her," Grace said, glancing around her and then into the trunk.

Her heart raced with fear that the girl would see her phone and know what she was thinking.

"Come on," Damon said. "And you, April, be my good little girl."

Oh, she was *so* going to make him pay for saying that to her.

As they stepped toward the front of the car, she reached into the trunk and grabbed her phone. She went through the motions of using the restroom. As she squatted, she texted 911.

For the first time since awakening the trunk, she felt hope that she could possibly make it out of this alive.

Chapter Twenty-Four

Sean's foot tapped on the floor of the car as Terrell drove toward the sheriff's department to take his official statement. He didn't want to be here. He didn't want to be playing this game. Yet, he knew Terrell had to check everything off his list.

"Look," Sean said, "all I'm saying is that we run a trace on Damon's phone."

"It's not that simple. The man has burner phones."

He knew it wasn't that simple, but logic wasn't in control. He needed to find April. He had to get her back.

"I know he has her." Sean's foot tapped faster.

"First, there's no proof."

"You know he's been stalking her. She disappeared after a suspicious fire. He was seen leaving the scene of the crime at April's apartment. What other proof do you need?" Sean tried to control his fear-based rage. "You can't possibly think that she started this fire and that she ran away. I thought we've been through that. She is not the one at fault."

Terrell sighed. "I know you are close to her. I know you guys have some kind of relationship happening, but you need to look at this situation from my perspective. I have a job to do, and sometimes that means looking at the story from a variety of perspectives."

"So, you think that Damon was telling you the truth? That he wasn't stalking her? You know he was. You saw the way he looked at her at the Springs. He is a piece of human garbage."

Terrell halted at the stoplight and looked over at him. "I know Damon isn't innocent. I know he was stalking her, but without some kind of witness statement that blatantly states they saw him throwing the Molotov cocktail, I can't get a judge to sign off on a warrant that allows me to go down those rabbit holes. You know this, Sean."

He did. He knew how the justice system worked. But he didn't have to like it.

Terrell's cell phone rang, pulling his attention away from his passenger.

Sean glanced out the window and watched as a mom and daughter walked hand in hand on the sidewalk in front of the small shops that lined the historical downtown.

That could have been April and Grace in another life.

He tried to stop the wave of emotions and thoughts from crashing on him by taking a deep, calming breath.

April couldn't have known that Grace was her daughter. If she had, she would have told him. They'd had so many honest, candid conversations about the past. She'd not hid anything from him that would make him think she'd known that Grace was her daughter. *If* she was her daughter.

Terrell picked up the call. "Hello?"

There was a woman's voice on the other end of the line, and he could tell it was dispatch from the cadence of the words. He tried to listen, but he could only pick up a word here and there.

"Got it. Thanks for the update," Terrell said before hanging up. "Did you hear that?" he asked, turning to face him.

"What's going on?" Sean asked, his core clenching with

nerves. Something was wrong. "Is April okay? Did they find her body?"

Terrell shook his head. "Thankfully, no. That's not it at all. Actually, we got a ping from her cell phone. She texted 911."

"What did she say? Is she okay? What happened? Where is she? Damon took her, right?" All of his questions spilled out at once.

"Hold on. All they got was that she needed help." He spoke slowly and carefully, trying to speak in a metered way that Sean knew was to keep him from blowing his top.

"What kind of help? Medical?" he asked, trying to mirror Terrell's tempo to prove that he would be okay, even if everything about the way he was feeling told him otherwise.

"She didn't tell dispatch, just the text and then radio silence. They, however, did manage to pull a location on the device." He flicked on the lights. "We're going to find her."

GRACE WAS STANDING on the side of the trail, looking down at her as she tried to slowly pick her way through the rocks and debris that littered the trail. "You and I both know that you can hike faster than that. I've seen you in action," Grace growled.

Damon put his hand on April's lower back as she stepped beside her. "How's your arm feeling? Are you doing okay?" he asked, sounding like an overly concerned boyfriend and not the man who could just as easily kill her as kiss her.

"I'm okay, just hurting," she said, trying to sound weaker and frailer than she was actually feeling. She ran her arm over her breast, feeling for the phone she'd stuffed in her bra when they hadn't been looking.

"We aren't in a rush, just take your time," he cooed.

Grace rolled her eyes. "She's playing you. She's just fine."

April batted her eyelashes at Damon. "I'll be fine, she's right," she said, stumbling gently and allowing him to help her.

As much as she hated acting like this, especially since she'd been so hell-bent on fighting, she felt as though she was doing the right thing...the thing that this situation required.

"Grace, knock it off," he countered. "She is hurt because of you and your attitude."

Grace's lip curled as she looked down at Damon. "Look, as much as you want to play house, you're not my dad."

April was relieved to see that there was a rift in their alliance. "Wait, playing house?" she asked, her voice soft. "Are you guys—"

"No." Damon shook his head, like any sort of questions about their relationship was out of line and out of the question.

"Why...why all this?" She really didn't understand how the two of them had aligned against her and how she had found herself here if they weren't together in some way.

"Damon, you didn't tell her?" Grace looked at her and smirked, the evil look in her eyes returning. "April, you're my biological mother."

Once again with this girl, it felt as though the ground was giving way under her feet.

Grace couldn't be her daughter. Ann had found a good home, with good parents, people who were going to take care of her and do better than April could have. The adoption agency had told her she was making the right decision, that her daughter would be in good hands.

"What?" April asked, the sound choked and high. "No. My daughter was named Ann. She was adopted by someone out of state. She went to good parents. They promised me..."

"Well," Grace spat, "they lied."

She stared at the girl, trying to find bits of herself or Cameron in her face, but all she could see was a hateful teenager. Maybe, in that, lay the proof that she truly was her child. The only difference was that, at Grace's age, April was pregnant and hoping for a future that had never played out.

"Grace…" She whispered the girl's name like she was speaking it for the first time. "I'm so sorry this happened to you…that I put you in harm's way when I thought I was doing what was best."

Grace waved her off. "You can apologize all you want. It doesn't change a thing." She turned her back on April and started hiking up the hill. "You abandoned me."

This time April didn't hesitate or try to slow their assent. With each step, she moved closer to the girl who claimed to be her daughter.

Damon touched her arm and handed her a tissue. Until now she didn't realize that tears were streaming down her cheeks. "I'm sorry, April. I wanted to tell you before. I thought maybe you knew, but when it was clear you didn't, I knew I had to get you alone with her. I knew we all needed a chance to be a family."

And just like that, regardless of the status of Grace's lineage, she was pulled back to the reality that she and the girl were at the mercy of a man who wasn't in his right mind.

"How did you find out, Damon?" April asked.

"It took some digging after you told me you had given up a child for adoption. It took a lot of cyber-sleuthing, but I managed to figure out that Grace had been adopted by a family in Cody, Wyoming, a few days after you put up your Ann. A few years later, they moved to Montana for work and when Grace was five, her adoptive parents were killed in a car accident on I-90 and she became a ward of the state of

Montana. It was all tough for her after that point. She was moved from home to home."

She made a strangled sound as though his words were a punch straight to her gut. This wasn't what she had wanted for her daughter. And whether or not Grace was Ann, she hated that this had been the girl's past. No child should be treated like chattel and passed around.

"I know that you don't believe me," he continued. "But I ended up running a DNA test on her."

"And me?" she asked, feeling violated as she guessed what he was about to say.

He nodded. "I managed to get a couple hairs of yours. I'm sorry for invading your privacy, but I had to be sure. The results didn't take long, and they were conclusive." He motioned up the hill. "I have all the paperwork in our cabin... even from the state. I'll be happy to show you."

She stared after Grace, watching her move up the hill like she had made this hike many times before. The girl was beautiful, and for the first time she wondered what the girl's natural hair color was—whether it was that of Cameron's or something closer to hers. Her heart ached as she looked at the living reminder of a past she thought was gone forever.

"After I was sure," he continued, seemingly oblivious to the effects his words were having on her heart, "I talked to her foster parents and I made sure that Grace was enrolled at the Springs. I wanted to see you two together. After that, there was no doubt. And I knew what I had to do."

"Damon," she said, knowing she had to be careful in how she approached what she was about to say, "thank you for all of your hard work. You don't know how much I appreciate having the chance to get to know my daughter."

He smiled, his teeth shining brightly in the sun. "I knew you'd appreciate it...that you'd love me for what I'd done."

Love was the wrong word, but she wasn't about to correct him and tell him that what he'd done *terrified* her. Not only was it a complete invasion of both her and Grace's privacy, but he'd upturned two worlds in his unilateral decision to expose the truth. She was truly grateful to finally be reunited with her child, but she hadn't been ready. In finding out this bombshell, it made her feel things that she hadn't been prepared for.

Then again, none of this was really about her.

This was all a game devised by Damon to win her favor.

"How did Grace take the news?" she asked, watching her daughter move behind a ponderosa and disappear into the woods.

"She was upset at first. You know how teenagers can be. She's gone through a lot." He smiled with a weird look of pride—almost like that of a parent. "We spent a lot of time talking about her feelings and what all of this meant to her. She was the one who didn't want to tell you at first. I agreed to give you both time."

"Did she know that you wanted this?" she asked, motioning vaguely at the cabin in the woods.

His features darkened. "Not right away. I had to do a bit of convincing to get her to go along with my idea."

Convincing? Or do you mean grooming? She wanted to challenge him, but she bit her tongue. She already knew that he'd manipulated the girl and made her an accomplice in his screwed-up game.

"So, she was on board with us being a family?" she asked, playing along.

His smile widened. "She did. This house was her idea. She thought we could use the privacy and get used to being a family. In truth, I think she was really looking forward to it—you know, she'd finally have a bit of stability in her life." He paused, looking up like he was trying to see if she was close and listening. "She was really having a hard time with her foster parents. They were just using her and other kids for a paycheck. They regularly left her, and the other kids who had been in their care, alone."

"Is that why she burned their place down—she was angry?" she asked, though she felt as though she already knew the answer.

"I didn't like the idea, but she was hell-bent." He made a *tsk* sound. "We are going to have to watch her around fire. I think she likes it just a *little bit* too much."

When and if she got them away from Damon, she would make sure Grace got everything she needed—including every therapist and counselor. She thought about several whom she had worked with at the Springs over the years. That was, if Grace safely made it through juvenile court and didn't face charges.

Moving up the mountain, her thoughts were a flurry of what-ifs and hows. She had so many questions, but as her breathing grew labored from the hike, she savored the physical pain as it brought a reprieve from the pain in her soul.

Her well-intentioned past had led to this agonizing present and a potentially even more painful future if Grace hated her or ended up in jail for arson; and her only hope lay in a civil system that had let her down.

Chapter Twenty-Five

Sean had grabbed his pickup and followed behind Terrell up the mountain. It hadn't been hard to find the Toyota Corolla at the bottom of the mountain; it was exactly where 911 had told them it would be after April's text. Unfortunately, as Sean and Terrell walked around the car, it appeared to have been abandoned. There was nothing inside from the visual scan that could give away where Damon had taken her. However, thanks to 911's tracking software, they knew that April's phone was continuing to send a signal, and it appeared as though she was moving up the mountainside.

Their last pin on her phone was about a mile from where he stood and, though he knew they had to be careful in how they approached, Sean wanted to run to her.

When he found her, he wanted to pull her into his arms and beg for her forgiveness. He'd promised he would protect her and keep her from any kind of harm. Instead, he found himself standing beside the car a madman had used to abduct her.

He didn't know what Damon planned to do with her, but if he hurt a single hair on April's head… Damon would pay for what he had done.

Deputy Collins, who had been first on scene, stepped out of his unit. "What are you guys thinking?"

"I think we are going to be in for a hike." Terrell sighed. "It's starting to feel like I'm on patrol again," he added.

Collins gave a dry chuckle. "Don't you miss it? You know, you're always welcome to come back and work the beat with us."

The good-natured ribbing was somewhat of a relief for the tension between the men, but it didn't help when it came to Sean's anxiety. They needed to move. They needed to get to April.

Collins walked up to the trunk of the abandoned blue Corolla and stopped. "Did you see this, Terrell?"

They stepped around, stopping beside Collins. There, barely sticking out of the edge of the closed trunk was the edge of what looked like orange paracord. The end of the cord was frayed and jagged like it had been sawed through. His heart launched into his throat.

"Do you think…" Sean started, trying to control his fear and anger and stop it from smattering his voice. "Do you think Damon had her tied up in the trunk?"

"Let's not jump to any conclusions here." Terrell squatted and stared at the cord for a long moment. "I'm not saying you're not correct in your assumptions, but for now we just need to collect information and get to April."

More than ever before, he feared for April's life. Damon was unstable, and he was capable of just about anything.

Collins took his phone out of his pocket and started taking pictures of the car.

"Are there any other deputies headed this way?" Sean asked.

Terrell nodded. "They are on their way, but as you know it's a bit of a drive."

"Please tell me that we aren't going to wait to go up after April." He could hear the panic in his tone. "You both have to know that every minute we leave her alone with Damon is a minute closer to her being killed. We have to help her."

That is, if he hadn't killed her already.

She was alive. She had to be alive. As strange as it sounded, he could feel her.

He grabbed his search and rescue pack out of the back seat of his pickup. Say what they will, Andrew hadn't stolen or messed up anything in his rig. The kid would be all right.

From inside his bag, Sean grabbed his holstered Glock 19 and placed it on his belt. He pulled his shirt over to conceal it as much as possible. Closing his pack, he put it on and met up with Terrell and Collins, who were waiting at the start on a barely visible trail.

Terrell was staring at his phone. "It looks like they are moving pretty slow. We should be able to catch up with them in about twenty minutes if we move fast."

"Let's make it fifteen," Sean said, charging up the hill.

The ascent was steep, and the path was nothing more than a game trail. Roots stuck up like grasping hands, threatening to pull him down.

He was breathing hard, and his legs were burning after the first half mile thanks to the pace. He hiked quite a bit with Big Sky Search and Rescue, but short of running he didn't think he could hike any faster. The pain felt good, like it was payment to the Fates to keep the woman in his heart safe until he could reach her.

That was, if her phone was still in her possession.

It was. She was smart.

It struck him, as he led the charge, how this wasn't the first time he had raced up a mountain to get to this woman. He would do this for her for the rest of his life if it meant she would come home safe—and to him.

She had been through so much. If given a chance, he

wanted to be her safe place and the man she could rely on to stand by her side and help her through whatever life threw at them. After their time together, he had to think that she wanted the same.

"Hey, speed goat," Terrell called from behind him, sounding winded, "I know you can run up this hill, but you need to let us be in front in case something happens."

He stopped, waiting for them to catch up. Collins was sweating and laboring for breaths, but he wasn't as bad off as the cherry-faced detective.

Terrell looked at him. "I know you're probably still upset with me, but you don't need to give me a heart attack on this hillside. Damn, man," he said, chuckling.

Sean slapped him on the shoulder. "You know, strangely enough, I am almost enjoying kicking your butt up this hill. Let's call what happened earlier water under the bridge. I know you were just doing your job. I don't have to like it."

"Fair." Terrell gave him an appreciative nod. "You're all right."

"Now, hurry up," he said with a slight grin as he motioned for Terrell and Collins to take the lead. "How far are we out?"

"They haven't moved in a few minutes. I'm thinking they made it to their desired location, or they are taking a break. Either way, we are only about a quarter of a mile to where the phone signal was last picked up." Terrell, in point position, moved up the hill.

Sean's nerves crept up. They were so close.

The men grew silent. The only sounds were of their feet on the gravel and the rub of their backpacks as they pressed on.

Terrell stopped ahead as they neared the top of the hillside, putting his fist up in the air. He dropped down to his knee and Collins moved into position by his shoulder. Not entirely sure what to do, Sean dropped down to his knee behind the two officers.

As much as he loved to have a little good-natured ribbing with his friends on the police force as to who did the real work, they knew what they were doing—not that he would ever admit that to them.

Terrell whispered something to Collins. They unholstered their weapons, getting into a low-ready position. He looked over his shoulder to him. "You wait here, let us clear the area."

Sean nodded, but he hated that he couldn't be rushing in on the scene with them.

The officers moved to their feet, roll stepping quietly up the trail and moving to the top of the ridge where the mountain saddled out.

"Get down on the ground! Police!" Terrell ordered, using a voice Sean had never heard come out of the cop before.

He moved slowly behind them, staying out of sight, but unholstering his gun in preparation.

Terrell and Collins were pointing their weapons at someone he couldn't see from his position.

"Drop your gun!" Terrell yelled. "If you don't lower your weapon, we will shoot!"

A man released a string of expletives, telling Terrell exactly where he thought they should put their orders and their guns. He recognized the voice as Damon's. "Is Sean with you?" Damon yelled. "If he's with you, I'll trade him for Grace. Then you have to leave."

Grace was with them?

Sean edged upward, unable to control his curiosity but still trying to stay out of the officers' way in case things went sideways. As he moved upward, Damon came into view. He looked crazed, his eyes wide with fear as he stared down the two officers. He had his gun drawn, but it was low by his side.

Grace was standing behind him. Her face was pinched, and there was a smudge of dirt on her cheek. She looked much better than the last time he had seen her, but this time she looked…well, *angry*.

Where's April?

He panicked as he scanned the area. He was tucked behind a small huckleberry bush and some thick bladed grass that obstructed his view. Moving, but careful to stay behind the concealment, he tried to find her.

Where was she? She had to be here. She had to be with Damon.

What if he had killed her and taken her phone?

What in the hell had happened?

His hands started to shake. All he had to do was point and shoot. Damon would be dead.

First, he had to find April. He had to know she was okay. He *had* to.

"Damon, if I come out and trade for Grace, you have to let April go, too!" he said, breaking his concealment.

"Sean?" Damon asked, a dark smile taking over his face.

Damon was going to try to kill him the second he stepped out—that wouldn't help April. He had to be careful.

Collins moved toward him, sticking out his hand like telling him to shut up. Yet, he didn't look away from Damon.

"Is April alive?" Sean asked.

There was a thin line between not putting his brothers in blue in further danger while also making sure that he saved April. As for his life, he would happily exchange his for hers. And he damned well knew that Damon would take the deal, too, as the only thing they had in common was their abnormal love for the same woman.

"If your buddies put their guns down and you show your face, I will let you all see her." Damon put his hand up, almost as though he was telling her to stay put.

"Sean!" April yelled.

She's alive.

He let out a long exhale. That's all he needed to know. Everything else was just details—including Damon's life.

"April, you know better!" Damon countered, looking in the direction she'd called from.

Terrell took that as his moment, and he and Collins charged toward Damon. Sean stood up, weapon ready. As they moved, Grace stepped forward and grabbed at the gun in Damon's hand. He turned to the teenager, a look of surprise on his face. She tried to twist the pistol out of his hand, but he lifted the barrel and pointed it right at the girl's center mass.

"What are you doing?" he stammered, shocked at the girl's sudden change of heart.

"I'm doing what I should have done all along, I'm stopping you. I can't let you destroy anyone else's life." Grace moved closer to the gun.

His finger moved on the trigger.

April came running out and hit Damon square in the back. He made a strangled sound as he lurched forward. Grace grabbed at the gun as he lost his balance, trying to wrestle it out of his hand. As she did, the gun skittered out of Damon's grip and fell to the ground.

Grace lurched for the gun and picked it up. As she moved, the two officers rushed the scene.

They weren't fast enough.

Damon lunged for Grace, murder in his eyes. The girl pointed the gun at him and pulled the trigger.

The sound of the gunfire echoed off the mountain. April looked over at him, fear in her eyes.

Grace stood, motionless. She stared at the man at her feet. "You were never worthy of being a father."

She moved to turn the gun on herself, but Terrell threw his body against hers, throwing her to the ground. Hard.

He pulled the gun out of her hand and threw it to the side and pulled a set of cuffs from his belt. He snapped them on the girl's wrists.

Sean ran to April and pulled her into his arms. She smelled of sweat and fear. He couldn't hold her tightly enough. "You're okay, honey. I've got you. You're safe."

Chapter Twenty-Six

One year later...

The county attorney had decided not to press charges against Grace, calling her actions on the hillside self-defense. In the attorney's statement, they had deemed her roles in the crimes committed by Damon as a product of grooming and manipulation by a man who clearly had mental health problems. As a result for her role in the crimes, they required she seek counseling until she turned eighteen, and moving forward.

Her foster parents, clearly having heard about the fire and Damon's death, hadn't come back. There had been talk that they had cashed out everything they had and fled to Brazil. If they ever returned to the States, or if they were found, charges of negligence and child endangerment awaited them.

Since then, April had been working diligently with members of the state Department of Health and Human Services to create a stronger background check for parents who wished to be licensed foster care providers as well as to help conduct spontaneous inspections for those three thousand kids who were currently in the system in just Montana. It was her goal to make a difference on a national scale in hopes that no child would ever fall through the cracks.

It was her biggest mountain to climb, and she wasn't sure she would ever reach the top or make the kind of difference she wanted, but she wouldn't stop fighting for the kids who felt as though they stood alone. She would forever be their advocate. No kid was perfect, but they all deserved to be treated with decency and given a chance.

For the last year, Cameron's family had refused to have a relationship with Grace and she had been staying with April some nights in her new house and many at the Springs, where she had been working to finish high school. Things between mother and daughter were slowly progressing, but April held out hope that their relationship would keep getting better. No matter what happened legally with her case to adopt Grace, she would be whatever Grace needed her to be—a mom, a friend, a confidant or just a safe place.

Thanks to therapy and time, Grace had granted her forgiveness for the choice she'd made when she was a child—and even younger than Grace was now. April would be forever grateful, and aware that there would still be hard days ahead.

She loved her child just as much as the day she had been placed in her arms.

Today, Grace was staying at her house and lately, things had been going pretty well. Grace was starting to come out of her shell a little more, and today she had even cleaned the kitchen without asking—a major win for any parent, as far as April had been told.

Her house was small, just two bedrooms, but she'd finally managed to get a good deal on her own home and a down payment put together thanks to her renter's insurance payout and savings.

"Grace?" she called.

The girl walked out from the bathroom, drying her naturally blond hair with a towel. "What's up?"

Her daughter had really grown into herself, and she looked more and more like Cameron with each passing day. "Sean and I are going for a hike. He's about to pick me up. Do you need anything while we're out?"

"Give me a second, I'll come with you." Grace moved toward her bedroom. "That okay?" she asked, but not really waiting for an answer.

She loved that her daughter wanted to be a part of her life. It felt like they were becoming a family unit more and more by the day.

"I'll be outside when you're ready," April said, thinking about how lucky she was and how great her life was turning out to be.

Walking outside, she was met with a surprise. Andrew was standing with Sean. They were each holding a hiking pack.

Sean waved at her. "You ready?"

She smiled as she took in his handsome face. "So, Grace told you she wanted to go with us?" She motioned toward Andrew.

Sean's smile widened. "I'm glad she decided to face her fears." He motioned toward the mountain in the distance. "Andrew even picked up everything for a picnic."

The young man lifted the hiking pack in his hand, slightly like it was proof of his kindness.

"Hey, kiddo," she said.

"Hello, Ms. April," he said, lifting the bag and putting it into the bed of Sean's truck.

Sean walked toward her, meeting her halfway from the front door of her little house, which was starting to become a home. He took her hand and she stepped beside him, expecting him to walk her to his truck. He slipped his hand into hers as she stared up at Lone Mountain, where she had first saved her daughter, and then her daughter had saved her. Those mountains were her home.

"April." He said her name like it was full of unspoken promises.

She could listen to him say her name like that forever.

"Can you believe it was a year ago today?" he asked.

Before she could answer, the door to the house opened and Grace came jogging out. She was pulling her hair behind her head and putting it up with a hair tie. "You didn't do anything without me, did you?"

Andrew groaned. "Seriously? Babe, you're gonna ruin it."

"Not at all," Grace said, laughing as she rushed into the yard. She touched her arm. "Mom, don't listen to him. I'm not going to ruin anything."

April smiled widely, her heart light as Grace called her "Mom." It sounded so beautiful.

Everything about their lives now was a flurry of motion and *life*. It was an ethereal feeling to be in this whirl of activity and love. They were building, all together.

"It's just a hike, guys," April said. "No one's going to ruin it. We're not in a rush." Her thoughts moved to the fateful day on the mountain in the distance that had forever changed all of their lives—in most ways, for the better.

Grace sent her a bright, excited smile and then looked to Sean. "Yeah, just a hike." She giggled.

"What's that supposed to mean?" April asked, looking to Sean.

He had a guilty, excited look on his face.

Andrew jogged over and took hold of Grace's hand. "Babe…"

"Just do it already," Grace urged, looking at Sean.

Sean laughed. "Do you know that your daughter is just a little bit bossy?" he teased, winking playfully at the girl.

Grace stuck out her tongue.

Sean dropped to his knee. "I was going to wait until we were at the top of the mountain, but Grace is right—I can't wait another second."

Her heart thrashed in her chest as she stared down at the most handsome man she had ever laid eyes on. There would only ever be one man who she would see or want.

"April Twofeather," Sean said, "I love you in ways I never knew possible." He pulled a black velvet box out of his pocket. He opened it. Inside was a beautiful channel band fitted with a line of diamonds. It was dazzling, just like him. "You and I have been through hardships in life that most people could never imagine, and yet we have come through it stronger and more in love than any other couple I've ever met. I never want to spend another day without knowing for sure that we will be together forever. Would you marry me? Let's become a family."

She hopped from one foot to the other with pure joy. "Yes, Sean." She looked to Grace and Andrew. "Wait, Grace…"

The teen rolled her eyes. "Come on, Mom, don't you think he already asked me? Of course I told him to do this. I want the best for you. Sean is definitely the best for you. You guys are freaking perfect."

She didn't know if she agreed with the perfect part, but she held no doubts that this moment and this family they had built through hardships and tribulations would be one that stood the test of time.

They were each other's forever.

* * * * *

A COLTON KIDNAPPING

JUSTINE DAVIS

Chapter One

Greg Colton was sound asleep when he heard the pounding on his door.

It wasn't the mare's fault. The sorrel with the flaxen mane and tail was one of the sweetest horses on the ranch, and the fact that she was Dad's favorite meant if she needed help, they'd be all hands on deck. Even on a Friday night.

The ranch foreman had sent his nephew Mitch to get Greg when, on a routine check of the pregnant animal, he'd found her down in the stall, apparently in labor but with no sign her water had broken. Greg scrambled up, pulled on his jeans and told the kid to go get his dad at the big house.

"Mr. Buck?" Mitch looked almost scared.

"He won't bite," he assured Mitch. "And he'll want to be there. Lily is his girl."

Mitch nodded and left. Greg pulled on his boots, grabbed a shirt and ran, pulling the long-sleeved thermal on as he went. He snagged a jacket from the rack beside the door without breaking stride and headed for the barn. From here he could see the light on in the bigger foaling stall.

When he got there, Mitch's uncle, Marty Gibson, was outside the door with the case of medical and veterinary basics. Lily was down, her breathing elevated. Horses had such a wide range of what was their "normal" gestation that this was early but not unheard of. And it was her first pregnancy, so entirely unpredictable.

"You had to make it complicated, didn't you?" he crooned to the horse as he knelt in the straw beside her. She snorted inelegantly. He laughed back reassuringly.

But he knew forty minutes of stage two labor was the magic number, that after that the chances of foal mortality went through the roof. Since they didn't know how long ago this had started, he had no idea when to start worrying.

Save time, start now.

His brother Malcolm's joking suggestion, usually referring to his search-and-rescue assignments, went through his head and made him smile inwardly.

"Boss? It's starting, but this looks weird."

He moved to where Marty was watching for the emergence of the foal, which had begun. But he saw not the expected amniotic sac but what looked like a bumpy red mass. He swore under his breath and his instincts instantly went into overdrive.

"Hand me that," he snapped, gesturing toward the case of medical gear they kept on hand. He was no veterinarian like his cousin Ruby, but he knew what he was dealing with. A red bag delivery. The placenta had separated prematurely, and the foal was essentially being born inside it. Which explained why her water hadn't broken. And unlike the normal sac, the foal couldn't break through the much stronger placenta.

Which would mean the baby wouldn't be able to breathe.

He heard a sound behind him but was utterly focused on what was happening in front of him. He'd never dealt with one of these firsthand but he'd seen one once, and knew every second was critical. He hastily gloved up and grabbed at the first tool at hand that could do the job, the utility knife he always had in a sheath on his belt. He swiped the blade quickly with sterilizer, then cut through the placenta, ignoring the flood of fluid to examine the foal. Saw head and both front feet first, normal delivery position. He gently made sure everything was aligned properly, then reached out to press on Lily's belly, urging her to go to work. The mare seemed as eager as he was to have it over, and soon the foal was sliding the rest of the way out.

Greg immediately cleared the baby's nostrils, and he—it was a colt, Greg noticed—was quickly breathing on his own. Greg grabbed the battered stethoscope from the case, but realized he didn't have his watch on to time the pulse.

Then someone was crouching beside him. Dad. "Go," was all he said, holding out his own left wrist, which did bear a watch. Greg applied the stethoscope, and once he had the heartbeat steady in his ears, he began the count.

"Hundred and ten," he finally announced.

"A little high, but not abnormal," Dad said. "We'll have to monitor him for a while. And maybe have Ruby come out and verify everything's all right."

"Good idea," Greg said. "Although he looks fine."

The colt was wiggling now, trying to get free of encumbrances both biological and human. Greg went about the last details of cleanup, clamping and cutting the umbilical cord and sterilizing the cut. When he was done, he sat back on his heels, watching. He was certain now the little one was going to be okay. The foal's head was up and he was looking around curiously at this strange new place he'd been deposited.

Greg knew he probably looked like he'd survived some kind of bloodbath, from knees to chest. The arrival of new life was wondrous, but nobody ever said it was tidy. He remembered his best friend, Rick Kraft, talking about when his son, Justin, had been born.

"You know intellectually it's messy, but until you see it live and in person…"

He'd ended with a bit of a shudder, and Greg had laughed and gotten him another beer. By the time little Jane had come along, Rick was a pro with the dad stuff and barely blinked.

Greg felt a steady hand gripping his shoulder, taking him out of the memory, and for the first time he actually looked at his father. Who was smiling, widely.

"Proud of you, son. You did what had to be done and saved this little guy. You're a true horseman."

Greg felt a sudden tightness in his chest. Funny, his father was never stingy with praise, yet every time he earned some it still made him feel this way, even at thirty-seven. A measure of the man his father was. The man he admired beyond all others, for the way he loved his family more than himself, the way he never dwelled on the dark times Greg knew he'd seen in the service, the way he was ever and always fair, and even for the silly jokes he told that made them all groan. Steady, solid and stalwart, the man would die for any one of his children and they all knew it.

Unlike their mother, who had walked away from them when Greg was ten years old, betrayed them all completely, gone off to have an affair and two other children—that she'd stayed around to raise—and never looked back.

That the affair was with Dad's brother Robert was the bitter icing on a very sour cake.

But Dad had stepped up for his children, and Greg had decided long ago they were better off without her. With a father like this, they didn't need her.

"Thanks for trusting me to do it," he said, his voice tight.

Buck Colton met his gaze steadily and gave him another squeeze of his shoulder. "I trust you with a lot more than this."

Greg had to wait a moment before he could speak again. "She's your special girl, and I know you've been eager to see what she and that fancy stud produce."

"That spendy stud, you mean?" his father said with a wry grimace.

He grinned then. "Yeah, that one."

He got that smile again. "Thanks to you, I'll find out." He looked Greg up and down. "And now you'd better go clean up. Go back to bed, I'll take it from here."

"Thanks, Dad," he said, rising to his feet. He started to head for the door to the stall, then looked back. "For everything," he added, meaning it completely.

"Get on with you," his father said, but Greg saw in his expression that he was pleased with the emphasis and the emotion behind the words.

Greg headed back to his place, which was the guest house on the ranch, not too far from the main house. It was small, but enough for him. And since it seemed likely that it would always just be him alone, he didn't think about it much anymore. He'd been close to marriage once, but it turned out ranch life wasn't for her, and he couldn't leave. Or, according to Jill, wouldn't. The commitment to his family and this land was something the city-raised woman just didn't get.

Just as well. He had work he loved, a big family—complicated and recently even bigger not only with cousins and a brother finding their life partners, but with the revelation he had two half siblings they'd never known about—good friends, and he got to play uncle to Rick and Wendy's little ones. It was enough.

It had to be enough.

He hit the shower smiling, remembering the moment when the colt's head had come up and he started inspecting his new surroundings with wide eyes and swiveling ears. There was definitely something about helping a new life into the world that felt good. Really good.

The shower felt good, too, and he lingered longer than he'd planned. He finally got out, dried off, then ran a towel over hair that had gotten long enough to tickle the back of his neck. He went back into the bedroom, wondering how much sleep he could get before he had to roll out again. It had been nearly midnight when he'd headed for the barn, and he was guessing it was now after two. He could get maybe four hours before his regular workday had to begin. It would still be fairly dark out at six, but sunrise was late this time of year in Idaho, not until nearly eight, so the first couple of hours of work were usually done in the dark anyway.

He yawned, stretched and slid back into bed. And was sound asleep when the second interruption of the night came. The annoyingly loud ringtone of a phone call, which he'd often been tempted to change but never had, afraid he'd sleep right through anything gentler. Because he had, which was why Marty had sent his nephew in person.

Groggily, he reached out for the phone, knocking the earbud he always used to avoid that ringtone, spooking a critter off the nightstand in the process. He opened one eye enough to swipe the screen to answer.

"'Lo?" It was all he could manage.

"Greg, it's Chase."

He rubbed at his eyes, wondering what on earth his cousin was calling about at this hour. "You okay?"

"I am."

Even as half-asleep as he was, he couldn't miss the implication that someone else wasn't. He wasn't sure he could handle another emergency. "What is it?"

"Rick and Wendy Kraft."

That sent a jolt through him. He was instantly wide-awake. He sat up, half-afraid to ask for fear of what would come next. For fear of why his cousin who barely knew them would be calling him about Rick and Wendy.

"What? Are they all right?"

And then Chase said the words that would change his life forever.

"I'm afraid not. I'm sorry, Greg…"

Chapter Two

Briony Adams was a little amazed she'd gotten here without crashing.

Even as she had the thought, she recoiled from it. How could she, even jokingly, be thinking about crashing?

She wanted to see them. Had to see them. How else could she believe the impossible? Wendy and Rick, dead?

No, it couldn't be. It just couldn't.

She tried taking some deep breaths but couldn't manage it yet. She'd been beyond revved up since the call had come, and the drive to the hospital in Conners had seemed to take forever. She'd had to work her way through three staff people, insisting vehemently she was Wendy's emergency contact, before she got to the ER doctor who had finally, gently, even though she was obviously harried, broken the news to her.

"You're related?" she had asked.

"No. B-best friends." She could barely get the words out.

"Someone will be out to talk to you soon," the doctor promised. "We'll need some more information."

And so she was left standing here, feeling more at sea than she ever had in her life. Which was saying something, given her painfully shy nature that made her uncomfortable in any gathering of more than a half dozen people. The last time she'd tried going to a big party, a few months ago, she'd been exhausted and practically nonfunctional the entire day after. Her business had suffered, since being an accountant and being exhausted did not mix well.

That party had been Wendy's birthday.

Today—or rather yesterday, since it was now 4:00 a.m.— had been Rick and Wendy's wedding anniversary. So it couldn't really be true, could it? The universe couldn't really be that cruel.

Of course it can. Hasn't life proven that to you from the day you were born?

"Briony!"

She spun around at the sound of her name. She knew who it had to be. Wendy had listed her as her first emergency contact, with Rick's best friend, Greg, next, and Rick had done it in reverse order.

She saw him striding across the waiting room—which in her opinion would be better named the torture room, or simply hell—toward her. He moved like the strong, powerful man he was. Someone who could wrestle a cow or a horse and anything else that needed wrestling on a ranch. She hadn't seen him since that party, and he looked as if he hadn't had a haircut since. She liked the slightly shaggy look. But then, she liked most things about Greg Colton.

Memories suddenly flooded her, of all the times Rick and Wendy had tried to set them up. She and Greg had both laughed it off, saying they were only doing that because they were the only single people the couple knew. She knew Greg thought her work boring and probably her as well, while she had no idea how to even talk to the sometimes-gruff cowboy. She couldn't read him at all, and she imagined he liked it that way. After all, why would he, or any strong, competent man like him, want anything to do with her?

But that hadn't stopped her from developing a little crush on the guy. What woman could look at the rugged rancher, with that strong jaw, warm dark brown eyes, that pure, solid man, and not feel her pulse kick up a bit? That he was kind, funny and a loyal friend only made him more attractive. But they had nothing in common, on any front. He had a big family he was close to and loved the challenge of managing the family ranch, working with unpredictable animals she knew nothing about and was wary of. She had no family, at least that she knew of, preferred numbers because they were consistent and knowable, and quiet nights alone to read were her favorite times. It would never have worked, even if she'd had the nerve. Or if Greg had shown the slightest bit of interest.

And then he was barely three steps away. He stopped abruptly, staring at her. She looked up at him, his face a little blurry now as tears welled up again.

"You know?" She could barely get it out.

"Yes. My cousin…he was there. At the scene." His voice sounded beyond gruff, almost hoarse. As if his throat was as tight as hers.

Greg crossed the distance between them in one long-legged stride. His hands came up and gripped her shoulders, gently but firmly. As if he wanted to steady her, which, surprisingly, worked.

"You haven't seen them?"

She shook head. "Not yet. They won't let me yet."

She saw his eyes narrow, saw the very slight wince, and knew he'd reached the same conclusion she had about the probable state of…the bodies.

"The kids," he began. His voice audibly broke this time.

"Mrs. Matson is staying with them for the night," she said quickly, guessing he was fearing they'd also been in the car.

But Wendy had told her about the kids' reliable babysitter staying with them overnight right before she and Rick had left for their night on the town here in Conners.

Their fifth anniversary celebration.

And now they'd never see their sixth.

The reality of this, standing here in a hospital, with Rick and Wendy's other best friend, staring at each other, suddenly overwhelmed her.

It was true. Dear God, it was true.

They're dead.

Something must have shown in her face, some flash of agony, because Greg moved suddenly, wrapping his arms around her, holding her in a fierce, tight hug. He was so strong, so warm, she actually took some comfort from the embrace. He was feeling this, too, she reminded herself, or some version of it. He and Rick had been friends since early grade school, after all. Not quite as long as she and Wendy, but that was because they'd both ended up in the foster system together and had first met as wary, untrusting eight-year-olds.

"Ms. Adams?"

The quiet voice came from close behind her, and if she'd had the energy she might have jumped. But it had all drained away, and with Greg's arms around her she didn't even need strength enough to stand up. She only turned her head to see a small dark-haired woman in business clothes and a hospital name tag, carrying a tablet and smiling at her gently.

"I…yes," she finally got out.

"I'm Barbara Crane." She glanced at Greg, then looked back at Briony. "Would you come with me so we can speak privately?"

"Greg has to come, too," she said quickly when she felt Greg tense.

The woman's expression changed. She glanced down at the tablet she held, then looked up at Greg. "Greg... Colton?"

"Yes," he said, his voice still rough, but with a note of challenge in it now. Whatever this was, he wasn't about to be shut out of it if it involved Rick. And if his last name and the standing of the Colton family in Owl Creek eased his way, so be it.

"All right, you're the other person on the list, so you should come, too."

Moments later they were in a small room with a table and several chairs, one chair on one side, the rest on the other. Clearly the hospital worker was meant to take the single chair, and did. Greg politely ushered Briony to one of the chairs on the other side of the table, then he pulled a second one up close to hers and took a seat. In her dazed state, all she could think was that that was typical Greg—polite, thoughtful and handling it.

When Mrs. Crane spoke, her voice was still quietly gentle. Briony wondered if this was her job, dealing with people in horrible shock, and if so, wondered how she did it.

"First, I have to confirm, neither of you is a blood relative of Rick or Wendy Kraft?"

Briony only realized she was clenching her fist when her nails dug into her palm. "As good as," she said.

The woman looked thoughtful, but before she could speak Greg did. "Rick only has his father, and he's had no contact with him for more than ten years. The man's a..." He ended with a grimace and a shake of his head that managed to express his opinion of Rick's father perfectly.

While Mrs. Crane made a note, Briony added, "And Wendy has no family. She was orphaned at a young age."

The same age I was when my so-called parents aban-doned me.

"I see." She studied whatever form she was filling out. Then she looked up at them both. "So there's no other blood family for either of them?"

"No," Rick said flatly. "*We're* their family."

Briony felt a sudden tightness in her chest as he put into blunt, firm words exactly what she was feeling. Wendy had been her sister-by-choice most of her life and when they'd married, Rick, bless him, had embraced her as if the relationship truly was one of blood and DNA.

"Can we…see them?" Briony asked, bolstered by Greg's strength.

"I'll look into that," the woman said, and it came so quickly she knew it had to be a practiced answer to a frequent question.

"Do that," Greg snapped. Then, as Mrs. Crane gave him a rather startled look, he drew in a breath and said, "Sorry. I just can't wrap my mind around this. Since the kids came Rick was such a careful driver. He was a pain in the ass sometimes, even, so I can't see how this could happen."

"Me, either," Briony said quietly. "I don't think we'll believe it until we see them."

"I understand," Mrs. Crane said kindly. "If you'll wait just a moment?"

Alone in the little room now, Briony consciously tried to slow her breathing, hoping that would ease the hammering of her heart. Her well-trained logical brain tried to tell her it was all true, that they wouldn't make a mistake like this, but her silly heart couldn't help but hope. The conflict made her more than a little shaky.

Then, to her surprise, Greg reached out and took her hand. The warmth, the gentle but firm grip, steadied her once again. And her mind darted for refuge in the oft-wondered thought—what would have happened if she'd had the nerve to tell him they should give in to the Krafts' matchmaking efforts? She'd even worked out how to do it with the least embarrassment to them both, by telling him that then they could tell their friends they'd tried, so maybe they'd then back off. Behind all that Briony harbored the harebrained hope that something else might happen instead, that they might find that Rick and Wendy had been right about them being good together.

Rick and Wendy. Who were right now lying lifeless somewhere in this building.

A light tap came on the door in the moment before it swung open. Briony looked up, expecting Mrs. Crane. Instead, she saw a man she would have recognized even without the uniform. Police Chief Kevin Stanton had been all over the news when that story of the serial killer had broken. She'd paid more attention than she usually did to such horrific things, in part because Greg's FBI agent brother, Max, had been involved.

Greg stood up as the man stepped into the room. Briony didn't think she could; she was too wobbly.

"Chief Stanton," Greg said, rather neutrally.

The man's brow furrowed, then cleared. "You're one of the Coltons, right? One of Buck's boys?"

"Yes." She didn't think she was wrong about the edge that came into Greg's voice when he added, "I'm Max's brother."

The chief looked at him appraisingly. "You as stubborn as he is?"

Greg never flinched. "When necessary."

And Briony suddenly realized that, along with everything else he was, Greg Colton was a man she would not want to cross.

But he was exactly the man she would want to have on her side.

Chapter Three

His brain was acting like a skittish calf at branding time. Darting this way and that, spinning and running back the way it had come, all trying to avoid that smoking black hole in the middle.

Rick was dead.

Rick. The guy who had been at his side ever since they'd joined forces to stop those two jerks who'd been tormenting a puppy back in elementary school. The two had been older and correspondingly bigger, but the whimpers of the puppy had galvanized Greg and Rick into action and made them pretty much unstoppable. It had been the beginning of a friendship that had been solid for over twenty-five years.

Until now.

Desperate to do something, anything, he zeroed in on the chief. He already knew the basics from Chase, but he wanted the official version. "What happened?"

Stanton hesitated, glancing at Briony. Greg glanced her way, too. He saw her almost visibly pull herself together as she got to her feet.

"Don't sugarcoat it on my account," she said, her voice remarkably steady. It would seem there was more spine to Briony Adams than he would have thought. He'd known she was a good friend to Wendy, and that they'd been friends for even longer than he and Rick, and thanks to that connection he'd been around her a bit, but he'd never seen her under stress like this.

Stanton nodded. "They went off the road and wrapped around a tree." He hesitated, then added rather quietly, "They never had a chance. Their car was bent almost double."

Briony let out a tiny sound but stayed upright.

"There'll be photos in the news," Stanton said, as if in warning. "Just be prepared, it's not pretty." He eyed Greg a little warily before saying, "We're waiting on the blood alcohol results on Mr. Kraft."

Anger started to spike in Greg, but he held it down. *It's routine. You know they have to.* "He won't be over the limit. He never drinks much." *Drank much. Past tense.*

"I'm not expecting he will be," Stanton said. "From what I saw at the scene, Mr. Kraft's driving was not a factor."

Greg went very still. He sensed rather than saw Briony look at him, but he kept his gaze on the man in uniform as he asked, as calmly as he could, "What was?"

"They were sideswiped and pushed off the road. As far as we can tell—so far anyway—it was a hit-and-run."

Greg stared at Stanton. "And the other car?"

"A black something. Big, judging by the height of the paint transfer. We'll be sending that to the lab, see if we can pin down a make and model."

"Did anybody see it happen?"

Stanton shook his head. "We don't even know exactly when it happened yet. It was called in by a passerby just after 2:00 a.m."

"Were they…?" Briony began, but her voice faded away.

"They were already gone, Ms. Adams. I'm no doctor, but I'd say on impact. I'm sorry."

It registered with Greg that the man was being pretty kind. He hoped it wasn't from lots of practice. He wouldn't have thought the chief of police would be involved in something like a traffic accident, but Owl Creek was, at its heart, a small town. Quiet, for the most part, especially if you took the tourists out of the equation and stuck with the locals.

Things like this didn't happen often. Thankfully.

"Now, excuse me. I'll go let them know you can make the positive IDs."

He left the room quietly. Silence spun out for a while, until Greg, taking a deep breath, turned to Briony. "Are you sure you want to do this? I can…verify for us both."

Her head came up sharply. "Of course I do."

"I just thought…maybe you wouldn't want to carry that image around in your head forever. Maybe you'd like to remember them…the way they were."

She just looked at him for a long moment before she said, softly, "Wouldn't you?"

He laughed, and it came out the harsh and bitter sound that matched what he was feeling. "Of course I would. But it's not an option. Besides," he added, his voice more under control now, "you were right before. I don't think I'll truly believe it until…"

She continued to look at him, as if studying him. "Thank you," she finally said, her voice soft, and with an undertone of…something. But he wasn't sure what she was thanking him for.

"For what?"

"Being willing to carry that image alone, for my sake."

He had no idea what to say to that, so he only shrugged. Which for some reason made her almost smile. As much as either of them could, he supposed, under the circumstances.

Ten minutes later they were standing outside the hospital

morgue, both of them shaking. Greg knew he'd been right. Those were images he would carry forever. Briony reached for him, and once more he hugged her, but this time it was to share the blow, because he felt as rattled, as devastated, as she looked. They'd both lost their best friends, friends of decades, and if she felt anything like he did the fact that she was still standing was amazing. The only reason he was still on his feet was because he couldn't bear to collapse on the floor and cry in front of everyone.

Another person in hospital attire, a man this time, approached them, accompanied by the chief again.

"The kids… They have two children," Briony said, sounding a bit numb now.

"We're aware," Stanton said. He looked at Briony. "You provided that contact information? For a—" he glanced down at a notebook, apparently still going old-school "—Lucy Madison?"

"Matson," Greg said as Briony nodded.

"Ah, yes. She's been advised of the situation but hasn't told the children yet."

He cringed inwardly. Clenched his jaw against the reaction. Then said what he had to say. "We should do it."

"Of course. We're their godparents," Briony said at the two men's looks.

Stanton seemed to relax a little. "I see."

Greg only nodded. It was all he could manage. Somehow Briony's instant agreement that they should be the ones to deliver this devastating news, together, helped him get past the realization that he didn't think he could have done it alone anyway.

And that he was glad she'd been there with him when they'd had to identify the bodies of their friends. He'd made the offer to do it alone genuinely, but now that he had that image in his head, he was truly glad he wasn't the only one who would be lugging that memory around. Shared misery, maybe.

They walked down the hallway that seemed chillier than it had been.

"What do we do now?" She sounded so forlorn he wanted to hug her again. Maybe misery really was lessened by sharing.

He glanced at the watch he'd remembered to grab this time. "I need some caffeine before I start trying to figure that out," he said. "This place must have a coffee shop or something. Someplace where we can...think."

They found the listing on a board near the elevators and made the trip and the walk down another hallway in silence. It wasn't just the hallway that felt colder. The whole place did. Which told him it wasn't the surroundings, it was him.

After Briony had ordered some fairly complicated-sounding coffee drink, he asked the young woman behind the counter, "What's the most opposite of decaf?"

The barista smiled at him. "We have an espresso machine, if you'd like that."

"Doubled," he said. "Straight."

He sensed rather than saw Briony cringe slightly and gave her a rueful grimace. "For the hit, not the taste. I'm going to need it. It was already a long night, and now..."

Now that night was going to last forever.

"What happened...before this?" she asked as they found a small table and sat for a moment.

The first part of his night seemed eons ago. "Nothing that matters now." *At least it had a happy ending.*

"I just need to think about something else for a few minutes." She said it as if he'd accused her of something. As if she felt guilty for wanting to escape the horror, even if only for those few minutes.

And so he told her about Lily and her foal, focusing less on the complications of the birth and more on the fact that the baby would be all right. He saw the faintest of smiles curve her mouth, as if it were all she could manage. But at least it was there, so he counted the diversion worth it.

"It must be so different, living on a ranch," she said.

"It is. That's why I love it. Plus, it's my family."

He thought he heard the faintest of sighs. He wished he hadn't added that, wasn't sure why he had, except that it was true. But he knew Briony had no family, had grown up in the system, because Wendy had told him that's where they'd met and bonded as children even younger than he and Rick had been when they'd connected.

She was staring down at the table as if it held some fascinating design and was more than a chunk of ordinary laminate surface.

"When they got married," she said, so softly he had to focus to hear it, "I was afraid I'd lose Wendy."

"She'd never let that happen," Greg protested.

"I know. I should have known then. And now…now…"

And there they were, back in the morass of reality, sitting in a damned coffee shop while their friends lay dead in the hospital basement. Greg's gut knotted fiercely, and for a moment he thought he was going to lose what coffee he'd drunk.

"They looked…so peaceful," she whispered.

Greg guessed the hospital staff had made an effort to see to that, because from Stanton's description of the accident it was likely they were a mess when they'd arrived. He'd witnessed a much less serious accident once, and it had been bloody enough. He didn't want to think about what this one must have looked like.

"Their worries are over," he said, a bit more harshly than he'd intended, because it hurt so damned much.

Briony looked up at him at last, and he saw the sheen of tears in her eyes, a sheen that made them seem even more green than usual. She drew in a long, deep breath before she spoke.

"But ours are just beginning."

Chapter Four

Briony watched Greg toy with the keys on his key ring. She knew when he'd found the right one, because he clamped his fingers around it as if it were trying to escape. Or maybe he just needed the pain of the metal digging in to distract him. She could understand that.

They'd left the hospital together in his truck. She wasn't even sure why, since now her car was stuck back there. But he'd suggested it, and somehow the idea of staying together for this heinous task seemed much more preferable than driving to Wendy and Rick's house alone with her thoughts. At least with Greg there, she'd feel compelled to hold herself together. Without him, she was afraid she'd fly apart into a million pieces. So here she was in his truck, trying not to stare at the rifle in a rack above their heads.

For the first time she let what had been brewing under the surface since they'd learned it was really true bubble up to the surface. Justin and Jane. They were going to have to try and explain to a four-year-old and a fourteen-month-old that their parents weren't coming home.

Ever.

And what would happen to the kids now?

One thing at a time.

Owl Creek was quiet this time of the morning anyway,

but this time of year especially so. It was still dark, the first hint of light not arriving until after 6:00 a.m., and full sunrise not until nearly eight. Snow season and hence ski season would not really arrive until next month, when they went from maybe an inch or two to a foot or two of accumulation.

Briony had called Mrs. Matson when they were on their way. The woman told them she could stay until noon, if necessary, before she had to leave to see to her own family. She knew them both, at least, and knew they were the kids' godparents, so had no problem about them coming for Justin and Jane.

Briony remembered with a jab of agony the day Wendy had asked her to take on that title.

"First thing, we are *not* trying to force you and Greg together again," she'd begun.

"I'm glad. I'm not his type, and vice versa." She'd managed to say it evenly, and—she hoped—to hide any trace of the lie that was on her part. Because she'd always thought Greg Colton one of the most attractive men she'd ever met. But clearly the feeling wasn't mutual, and she wasn't about to set herself up for that kind of humiliation. Again.

But that didn't stop her from being delighted Wendy had found such joy in her life. Even if it wasn't in the cards for her, her kind, wonderful sister-by-choice deserved it.

"That said," Wendy had gone on, "we want you two to be the kids' godparents."

She'd been pleased. Flattered. And thrilled to have a special part in her best friend's children's lives, even if it was mostly ceremonial.

Or was supposed to have been.

"Damn." Greg said it softly, more in the tone of somebody who'd just thought of something than anger.

"What?" she asked.

"I just remembered something. Rick gave me an envelope to keep, back after Justin was born. Then after Jane came along, he asked for it back and gave me a new one."

She tilted her head slightly. "What was in it?"

"I don't know. He just asked me to keep it locked away, and...only open it if something happened to him." He sucked in a long breath before adding, so bluntly it startled her, "If he died."

Briony's breath caught. "You don't think he expected something to happen, do you?"

"He was a little...odd about it," Greg admitted, "but I think it was a just-in-case kind of thing." He frowned slightly. "But it was also something he didn't want only in digital form."

"Could be a few reasons for that," she said, but it still made her edgy.

She studied him for a moment, in the faint light inside his truck. In profile he was just as handsome, jaw strong and masculine, his nose straight and perfectly shaped. And as they stopped for one of the few traffic lights in town, she saw him close his eyes. It was for barely more than one second, but it was enough to draw her gaze to the thick, dark brown sweeps of his eyelashes, something she'd always thought unfair when she required mascara to get even close to that. But right now, all she could think was that he was hurting just as much as she was, and that his blunt statement about Rick dying was probably just him saying it out loud, trying to get his mind to accept it. She'd done that herself, after all.

"Do you think you should look at it now, before we go to the children?"

He glanced at her, an almost startled look. "I was...kind

of thinking that, yeah. Not sure why." He grimaced. "Maybe I'm just stalling."

She was a little surprised he'd admit that, but then realized she shouldn't be, because on top of everything else, he'd always been one of the most honest people she knew.

"I think it's a legitimate concern," she said. "Maybe there's something in there about the kids you should know first."

The light changed, but in the moment before he looked away and hit the gas, he gave her a smile that was both sad and grateful at the same time.

"Yeah," he said as they rolled through the intersection. "Maybe. So you don't mind if we stop at the ranch first?"

"As long as they don't mind how early it is."

To her surprise he let out a short laugh. "It's after six now. Dad's likely been up and at it for an hour already, and most of the hands almost that long."

"Does he know where you went?"

He went silent, then nodded. "I left him a note. He'll cover what I'm supposed to be doing."

"With time out for cooing over the new baby horse?"

This time the glance and smile he gave her were better, more solid. "Yes. Lily is really his girl, and he's been looking forward to this foal a lot."

"Good thing you were there to help, then."

"I'm just glad I realized what was happening in time."

"Do they do cesareans on horses?"

"They do, yeah, but since the birth had already started, the foal would have been dead by the time we got a vet out. But he—"

He broke off suddenly. She saw his jaw tighten, the muscles there jump a little. As if he were biting back fiercely whatever he'd been about to say. She started to speak, then hesitated. What did she know? Either about what he'd been through last night, before the news came about Rick and Wendy, or how he was feeling now?

He and Rick had had that kind of guy relationship she'd sometimes admired. Even if they hadn't spoken in a month, the other would be there at the drop of a hat if needed. She always felt as if she had to stay in touch constantly or be forgotten. Or maybe be reminded no one much cared if she was around or not.

Except Wendy. Wendy had always cared.

Memories flooded her, and somehow converted to a literal flood from her eyes as the tears won out again. She quickly swiped at her eyes, hoping he hadn't seen her about to turn on the waterworks again. She swallowed, steadied herself, and when she thought she could get the words out, spoke quietly.

"There's nothing wrong with welcoming a new life, even as you have to say goodbye to others."

His head snapped around sharply. "How did you…?"

So she'd been right. She'd taken the chance, and she'd been right. It was a nice feeling, amid all the pain. "You just looked as if you were feeling bad that the baby horse you saved made it, when Rick and Wendy didn't."

He looked back at the road ahead. They were out of town now, in the countryside and headed north. Then, in an almost wry tone, he said, "For a quiet little thing, you're pretty observant."

"Maybe I'm observant because I'm quiet."

This time when he gave her another look, it was a kind one. "Point taken."

She realized with a little jolt that this was likely the most time she'd ever spent alone with him. She'd always thought of him as gruff and hard to read, but that was with the knowledge that she sucked at reading, understanding or having any kind of close relationship with anyone. Wendy was her sole true friend, and Rick had accepted her as that and always been incredibly kind and welcoming, but Briony knew that was because of Wendy.

She'd known the two had found such comfort in each other, Wendy who'd been orphaned even longer than Briony, and Rick, whose father was the worst kind of grifter, tied to that awful cult thinly disguised as the Ever After Church. Rick had cut off all contact with his father a decade ago, and she could only imagine the kind of inner strength that had taken. But he had especially not wanted the man anywhere near his children and had made sure it never happened.

Maybe that's what whatever was in that envelope was about. Making sure it stayed that way, even if—

She cut off her own thoughts sharply. It wasn't an "if" anymore. It had happened. The impossible, the unbelievable, the horrible had happened. Wendy was dead. Dead.

She wondered if she repeated it in her mind enough, her mind would wrap around it, process it, accept it. Ever.

"Briony?"

She gave a little start. "What?"

"Are you okay?" He seemed to instantly realize how that sounded under the circumstances and added, "Aside from the obvious, I mean?"

It was a question she would normally answer with a short, "I'm fine." Because she knew people who asked that generally didn't really want to know. At least, not about her. But Greg was in the very same boat she was, so maybe he really was interested.

"I'm just trying to batter my brain into accepting the reality. That she's gone. They're both gone. Really, permanently gone."

"Hope you're having more luck than I am," Greg said, sounding exhausted. "At this rate it'll be summertime before I get used to using the damned past tense."

"Yes," she said, fervently. "Exactly."

A strange sort of warmth blossomed in her, at a time she would have least expected it. The warmth of knowing it was true, that he was in the very same boat, and so was interested in how she felt. More interested than he ever would have been before, anyway. Odd how knowing he was having trouble with this, too, knowing this wasn't her pain alone, made it...not easier, but a tiny bit less overwhelming.

Briony had only been to the Colton Ranch once, for a surprise birthday party Greg and Wendy had conspired to throw for Rick. She'd helped a little, although not much since it had been tax season and she'd been buried, but she hadn't actually set foot on the ranch until that day.

And she'd been overwhelmed.

She was used to open spaces—this was Idaho, after all. And she loved it, loved the quiet, the expanse of trees and rolling hills up to mountains, and always had. But there was something different about this big, sprawling ranch. Maybe it was the difference between it being a grand vista you enjoyed and a vast expanse you were responsible for. The very idea of being responsible for so much land, let alone the animals that grazed upon it, was nearly overwhelming. There was a reason she'd bought her compact, tidy condo in town. Eight hundred square feet was a lot easier to handle than eight hundred acres, which is what Greg had said the ranch was.

But when he'd followed that up with "So, not that big," she'd choked on her lemonade.

He'd laughed. "Hey, big is twice that. Texas-big would be four times as much acreage."

He was grinning at her, all his usual gruffness vanished on this day of celebration for his best friend. And of all the times in her life when she'd been laughed at, this time she was certain it wasn't really aimed at her. And looking at his smile, and the way that trace of a dimple appeared, then vanished, she felt a rush of all those feelings she thought she had successfully quashed. All those feelings that had had her fantasizing about working up the nerve to suggest they get a cup of coffee or something sometime.

Then you'd find out what it's really like to have him laughing at you.

No, she'd run from that idea, determined not only that she would never make that move, but that she'd never even think about such folly again.

So she'd just listened to him explain they were more of a custom provider, of beef and produce. His dad, he'd said, had the green thumb to end all green thumbs, and loved tinkering around with all kinds of plants to get the best possible yield, in both quantity and quality.

"We don't have the longest growing season, so what he's done is amazing," Greg had said, and there was no way to miss the love and pride in his voice. What it must be like, to have a father you loved so much…

It was a longer drive than she remembered from the gate to the house. But the building looked the same, a three-story block painted barn red, with a deck built out over the patio on the bottom level. And off to one side, some yards away, was a smaller building painted in the same color, which Greg had mentioned that day was the guest house where he lived.

"You want to come in?" he asked. "It'll only be a minute."

She hesitated, then said, "Yes, please." She did want to and was honest enough to admit it wasn't just that she didn't want to be alone just now, but also curiosity about where he lived.

"You're still in the guest house?" she asked, nodding toward the secondary structure as they slowed.

"Yeah." He gave her a sideways look. "I love my brothers, but all of us under one roof...not so much." Then he let out a compressed breath. "Although Max isn't around much anymore. He's usually with Della."

"Wendy mentioned recently...he really quit the FBI?"

He nodded as he pulled up to the shed that she guessed served as a garage. He didn't pull into it, probably because they'd be leaving again soon. "Says it ain't what it used to be, and the bureaucracy running it was wearing him down."

"I can imagine. Every year the IRS about kills me off—"

Her breath caught, audibly. Her eyes stung, and she couldn't even swallow past the sudden lump in her throat.

Greg turned off the engine and twisted in the driver's seat to look at her. "Funny, isn't it, how many of our common sayings are linked to death," he said in a steady tone that helped her steady herself.

"Too many," she managed to get out.

"Because it's the shadow that hangs over us all."

And that was an almost poetic philosophical observation that she never would have expected from the gruff, sometimes laconic cowboy.

Chapter Five

Dad came out of the barn before they were even out of the truck and headed toward them. Greg suspected he'd been listening for them.

"Is that your dad?"

He'd forgotten Briony had never met him. "Yes. I'll make it quick," he added as he walked that way, as if he sensed her nervousness.

"I'm fine," she said, and he wondered it was a real "fine" or one of those ones that meant the exact opposite. But then Dad was there, his gaze skipping from him to Briony and then back again.

"It's true?" he asked, his voice a little rough.

Greg nodded. His father swore. Then, in a very Buck-like move, he pulled them both into a powerful hug.

"I'm so sorry, both of you. I know how important they are to you."

For a moment Greg closed his eyes, taking in the comfort this man had always been there to offer. He sensed Briony's stiffness, and felt a pang that, like Wendy, she had grown up without this heartfelt kind of support he couldn't imagine living without.

When Buck let go, he looked at them both in turn again.

"If there's anything you need, anything I or anybody on the ranch can do…"

"I know, Dad," Greg said.

"I'll see to your chores as long as necessary, so don't even think about it. And when you're ready, I'll make any calls that need making, if you want."

Greg heard Briony make a tiny sound, and guessed she hadn't even thought about that yet, that there were other people that were going to need to be notified.

"Thanks, Dad."

"You're heading for the kids?"

He nodded. "I just needed to pick something up first."

"All right. Bring them back here, if that seems best. We can keep them entertained until things settle."

Greg only nodded. He didn't think he could say another word about it. So instead, he shifted gears. "How's the foal?"

Buck smiled then. "Oh, he's gonna be a terror."

"Up on his feet?"

"Yep. Within an hour after, and he's already nursing like a champ. And curious. Very curious."

"Good. I'm glad."

"It's all thanks to you, son. Now, get what you need to do done. I'll keep the phone handy in case you need some help. Don't hesitate."

They were almost back to his place before, very quietly, Briony spoke.

"I get it now."

"Get what?"

"Why you're…you."

He turned his head to look at her. Who else would he be? He must have looked puzzled, because she spoke again, just as quietly. "I mean why you're so nice, so kind, and do things for people, even though you refuse to take any credit for it."

He blinked. That was a heck of a compliment. From someone who was usually so restrained she almost seemed frightened sometimes. Wendy said she was just shy, but he hadn't had much experience with that.

Then she glanced back toward the big barn, where his father was just going back inside. And he understood. No one raised by Buck Colton would be shy and uncertain. They'd know their value, their worth, from childhood. And he felt a sudden need to give his dad his due.

"He's the only reason any of us made it to adulthood relatively sane. Our worthless mother bailed on us when I was ten. My sister, Lizzy, was only three. But Dad stepped up. He made it clear from the day he told us she was gone that he was here for us, that he loved us, that he'd…die for us. And we all knew he meant it. I think even Lizzy knew it. Or she did by the time she was five and Dad took a rattlesnake bite for her."

Briony gasped, her green eyes widening. As if the very idea astounded her. And not for the first time Greg said a silent thanks that it had been that worthless woman who'd abandoned them, that she hadn't managed to drive Dad away with her faithless betrayal of vows she'd apparently never meant. Buck was their rock, and Greg couldn't—didn't want to—imagine their life without him.

"Your mother," she began.

"No," he said bluntly, taking the two steps to the porch in one stride. "I don't talk about her. She's cold, totally self-centered and not worth the effort."

He yanked the door open and held it for her. For a moment she didn't move, then she stepped inside. He followed, then went past her.

"I was just going to say that maybe her leaving was…the best thing that could have happened," Briony said.

He'd been headed for the desk that served as his office space but stopped now and turned around. That surprised him, coming from a woman who'd never known her mother at all. He would have thought she'd consider any mother better than none.

"I think it was," he said honestly.

It hit him then, somewhat belatedly, that she had lived the life Justin and Jane were facing now. A life without parents. They were so young—would they even have any memories of them? Justin, maybe, but Jane? He didn't know enough about kids' development to even guess.

"We've got to make sure they know." He said it under his breath, but Briony heard him.

"Know what?"

"Know Rick and Wendy. How much they love them. Loved them," he corrected to past tense, hating that one single letter could change their world.

"Yes. Above all, they need to know."

He gave a short nod, then turned and walked to his desk. He'd purposely put the thing in the small, fireproof box in the back of a bottom drawer, the box that held his own important documents, a picture of his mother from back when he'd thought she loved them, and a couple of other mementos—including a locket he'd bought for Jill when he'd thought they'd eventually be getting married. Before she'd told him life on a ranch was not for her, but if he'd move to the city with her, she'd think about it. He'd been, or had convinced himself he was, so in love with her that he'd actually considered it. Until he found out the city she meant was Los Angeles, and she had Hollywood dreams.

He'd kept the locket as a reminder. Some people just

weren't cut out for ranch life, and it was foolish to think they might change.

Why he kept the picture, he wasn't quite sure.

He bent and yanked the drawer open. The heavy metal box slid forward, and he was able to just pick it up.

He pressed his left thumb—his right one didn't work because of the scar that slashed diagonally across it from that day as a kid when he'd gone to help his dad free a calf who'd gotten tangled in a thorny hawthorn bush—on the fingerprint reader, and the box latch released. He reached in and lifted everything on top, until he could grab the envelope on the very bottom. He hesitated, not wanting to do it, wanting to do anything else, to deny it was necessary, to relegate all of this to the realm of nightmare.

If wishes were horses…

He yanked it out, slapped the lid of the box shut and locked it, then slammed the drawer shut. He straightened up, staring at the envelope as if it held something horrific. He could feel it held something heavier than paper, and remembered thinking it must be a key or something when he'd first shoved it in here, over a year ago. After Jane had been born.

"The thing you never wanted to open," Briony said. He looked up to see her staring at it much as he was.

"My dad wrote a couple of these," he said.

Briony drew back slightly. "He did?"

He nodded. "To his family. When he was in the army. They recommended it whenever troops were headed into a combat zone. The army kept it, to be added to their effects if…it happened."

She was still staring at the envelope. "I suppose when you have kids, you have to think about things like that, even if you're not military or law enforcement."

"Yeah."

Silence spun out for a long moment. Finally, very gently, Briony asked, "Do you want me to open it?"

He looked up at her then, and their gazes locked. Pain spoke to pain, and it was as if a conduit had opened between them. He could feel her pain, and he saw in her green eyes, shiny with tears, that she felt his.

"Yes," he said roughly, "I do want you to open it. But… no."

It made no sense to him even as he said it, but Briony looked at him as if she understood completely.

With one of the greatest efforts of his life, he slid a finger under the envelope flap and peeled it open.

A key fell out. No identifying information, no tag, just a number stamped on what looked like brass. He assumed the explanation was on the single sheet of paper. The one he dreaded looking at.

Now's not the time to become a coward, Colton.

He looked down at the front of the envelope. Saw the familiar scrawl, his name on the front. Had a sudden flash of memory, of a night long ago spent here at the ranch house, him and Rick wrestling with a tough homework assignment. Well, tough for ten-year-olds, anyway. They were supposed to write a story. About anything they wanted, but it had to have a beginning, a middle and an end, and be at least three full handwritten—computers hadn't yet invaded elementary schools—pages. They'd wasted at least half an hour complaining about the assignment. It was stupid! Write about what? How were they supposed to just make it up? Three whole pages?

It was Dad who'd gotten them started. He'd listened to their complaints, then made a suggestion.

"Why don't you pick something you'd like to do, and

write about what you think would happen to someone who did it?"

That had gotten them started. Greg vaguely remembered his own story about a guy becoming a Major League Baseball player and how he'd hit the home run that won the World Series. But he remembered very clearly Rick's story. It had been much less grandiose, consisting mainly of one thing.

He ran away from home and went to live with his best friend's family.

He remembered seeing his father's face when he'd told him about Rick's short story. He'd looked incredibly sad.

"Next time you and your mother get into it," he'd said, "think of this. To some kids, this is paradise."

He'd tried. He really had. But his mom was so...flaky sometimes. No matter what they did, no matter what she had, it was never right or enough. Secretly, and a little guiltily, he'd admitted he much preferred his aunt Jenny, whom they all called Mama Jen. How twin sisters had turned out so differently he didn't know. He only knew Jen was warm, kind, generous and loving, and his mother was...that flake.

And about a month after they'd done that assignment, she was gone anyway. Out of their lives for good and with barely a word, even to Dad. Dad, who had kept them together, from him down to three-year-old Lizzy, who'd been so bewildered by the change it had taken Dad, him, Malcolm and Max to keep her anywhere near calm.

Little Justin and Jane had had a different start, with two loving parents who'd adored them both. But now both those parents were gone. Forever. And he'd lost his best friend.

He hadn't even realized how rapidly he was blinking, how close he was to breaking down like a blubbering fool, until Briony was there, putting a hand on his arm and squeezing gently. She knew this pain. She'd been as close to Wendy

as he'd been to Rick, if not closer. He remembered thinking once how amazing it was that either of the two women
were functional, given they'd grown up in much worse circumstances than either him or Rick.

They might never have gone along with Rick and Wendy's efforts to match them up, but right now they were sharing this great, ripping pain, and that made him grateful for
the support.

And at last he did it, slid the single page out of the envelope. A page covered with that familiar scrawl.

Dear Greg,
Well, hell. You weren't supposed to be reading this,
unless maybe before my funeral years from now. But
here you are, so I gotta think the worst has happened.
I'm doing this by hand so there's no question about
who wrote it. There's a list of stuff on the back of this,
details and such. But now…

First things first: Thanks for being my friend. You
know my life was a little wild growing up, and with
your mother you can relate. But you were always there
for me, and I hope I was for you. I need you to thank
your dad for me as well. He was as close to a real father as I ever got, and compared to mine he's a saint.
But you know that. Hanging out with you, at school,
at the ranch, wherever, was the only taste I ever had
of normal. And that was thanks to you and your dad.
If I've been the slightest bit of a good dad to my kids,
it's because of you.

I know I don't have to ask, but if you're reading this
and I'm gone, look out for Wendy. She'll be devastated,
and this is the last thing she deserves after her rotten
life. (Quite a little nest of the wounded we've devel-

oped, isn't it?) When the time seems right, tell her I tried so hard to make sure nothing like this ever happened to her. Guess I didn't try hard enough, because here you are. But you of all people know how careful I was, because I knew I had to stay alive and healthy for my family.

My family. Yeah, there's the big one. The biggest ask. See to them, will you, Greg? I know it's a hell of a burden to dump on you, but you're the only one I know who's both strong enough and generous enough to do it. And I know you will, but that doesn't mean I'm not sorry about it. But you know the bottom line:

No Way In Absolute Hell is my father to get anywhere near my kids. Period.

I don't think I can say any more without getting ridiculously schmaltzy, so I won't. Just know I never had a brother except you, and I used to wish endlessly it was by blood.

I loved you, bro.

Rick

Greg knew he was swaying on his feet but couldn't seem to help it. He could barely breathe, nor swallow past the huge lump in his throat. He felt the trickle down his cheek and couldn't even muster the energy to swipe at his eyes. He was going to stand here wobbling and crying, and he couldn't do a damned thing about it.

And then Briony grabbed him, hugged him fiercely. She didn't say anything, just held on, so tightly he doubted he could have broken free.

He didn't even try.

Chapter Six

Briony knew one thing Greg didn't about the letter he held. It had been Wendy who'd told Rick to write it. Just in case.

"You and I, we talk so much you already know everything," she'd said when she'd told her about it. "But guys... they're different."

"That they are," Briony had agreed, rather wryly.

"Next to Rick, Greg's the best man I've ever known. I wish you two would—"

She'd cut her friend off there, not wanting to get on that merry-go-round again. Greg wasn't interested in her, and she understood why. He was so gruff and she so shy, they could probably spend an entire evening together without saying a word. But then, most of her evenings were spent in silence, as she was engrossed in her main passion, reading. It had been an escape for her when she'd so badly needed one as a child, and the kindest adult she'd known while in foster care had been the librarian down the block.

But that didn't matter now. Nothing mattered except that the letter he'd just read had nearly put this strong, steady man on his knees. She could only guess at what he must be feeling inside to let so much show on the outside. And for him to let her hold him like this, even hug her back, as if he was grateful for the human touch. Maybe he was. It probably wouldn't matter who it was; right now he just needed some human contact. For that matter, so did she. As far as pain and grief went, they were in this together.

She didn't know how long they'd been standing there when Greg finally moved again. Let go of her and turned the page over to look at the list Rick had mentioned. Briony read it with him.

1. The key's to our safe deposit box. Our will is there, along with the kids' birth records and our own documents. You're on the access list. The name of our attorney who drew up the will is there, too. She's good, and smart, if there are any questions.
2. The insurance policy is in the deposit box, too. It's pretty big, and should cover anything the kids need, up to and including college if they want to go.
3. Bank account info is on either of our laptops, in a password protected file labeled "Trust No One." The password is the last name of your and my favorite teacher mixed with the name of your dog at the same time, the cattle dog, alternating letters, and bracketed with the year we graduated high school split into two parts.
4. I know I said it in the letter, but I'll repeat it here. Do whatever you have to but keep my father away from the kids.

"His father's really that bad?" she asked. Wendy had told her Rick had no contact with him at all, but said even she didn't know all the details, only that he hated the man and was better off without him in his life. It was peculiar to her, to think that someone might actually be better off without a parent, and now she'd thought it twice. She'd spent so many years thinking her life would have been so different if either of hers had wanted her.

"Rick always said he was a grifter, as crooked as the Kickapoo River."

She blinked. "The what?"

He looked away from the paper for the first time. "It's a river in Wisconsin."

"A crooked one?"

"Very. And Rick just liked the name."

She smiled, although her eyes were stinging again. "That sounds like him. Did you know he was the one who wanted both the kids' names to start with the same letter?"

He drew back slightly, giving her a quizzical look. "No. Why?"

"He thought it would help remind them they were connected, and to always be there for each other."

Slowly, he nodded. And repeated her words. "That sounds like him."

A shout from outside, someone yelling to someone about an open gate, snapped her out of the sweet but painful thoughts. She glanced at the clock that sat on his desk, an old-fashioned analog version. It fit the eclectic furnishings that looked as if they'd been chosen for function over form, with no real concern about matching pieces or style. It suited him, she'd thought when they'd first come in. Of course Greg would care more about how well something served its purpose than what it looked like while doing it.

It was nearly 7:00 a.m.

"We should go to them," she said. "Be there when they wake up."

"If they aren't by now, with all the fuss and phone calls," he said, but he was already moving.

She followed him back through the living area of the house. Noticed what she'd missed in the rush on the way in, a bookshelf on the far wall that was crammed full, including some books lying sideways atop the rows on the shelves. Rick had once teased Greg about reading but she'd thought it was a joke, meaning he didn't. Obviously it was not.

It was silly, and she knew even as it happened that it was probably an escape mechanism her mind was using to avoid thinking about the reality to come, but an image formed that was so vivid it took her breath away for an entirely different reason. It was a revised version of the thought she'd had earlier, of indulging her passion for the written word. This time, an image of her in her favorite reading chair, and in the chair opposite... Greg, as deep into a book as she was.

She shook it off and picked up her pace. He was already at the door.

Back in his truck, they were out to the state route before she broached the subject that was now beating at her.

"How on earth do you explain this to kids so young?"

"I don't know. I'd say we should talk to somebody and find out, but that would really be stalling."

She thought for a moment. Then said, "Maybe we shouldn't immediately tell them. I mean, they're used to us being around, maybe we can just be there, take care of them like it's nothing unusual, then during that time maybe research or talk to someone about how to go about it."

There was silence as a big rig passed them going the other way, the headlights lighting up the cab of the truck. Lighting up Greg, showing her once more just how good-looking he was. As if she'd ever forgotten. She also saw that his right hand was resting on his leg, curled into a tight fist.

A white-knuckled fist.

After the cargo truck had safely passed them, he looked at her. "That's a good idea."

She felt pleased all out of proportion to the words. Because they came from him.

Danger zone!

She'd once sworn to herself she wouldn't be caught alone with him, because she needed the buffer of Rick and Wendy, or at least one of them, so she wouldn't do or say anything stupid.

One more thing lost in the tragedy of tonight. A small, minor thing compared to the rest, but still, another weight. For her, anyway.

I loved you, bro.

The last line of Rick's letter rang in her head. The past tense sliced at her painfully.

She and Wendy had said it often, almost every time they parted. *Love you, girl.* With a hug. And sometimes they'd done as Rick had done, calling each other sister because that's how it felt.

From what little she knew about guys, that's not something they said to each other, except under extreme duress. Like now. She could only imagine how it must feel to him to see it in writing, when it could well be the first time it had ever been said.

They lapsed back into silence. Briony noticed his still-clenched fist, now bouncing on his leg, as if he were trying to punch himself. It hurt just to look at. And before she thought, before she could talk herself out of it, she reached out and wrapped her fingers around that fist.

He froze. His fingers were still curled tight against his palm, but the hitting himself stopped. He didn't pull his hand free. He didn't look at her. In fact, she had the strangest feeling he was purposely not looking at her. Her innate uncertainty rose in her, and she wondered if he was imagining someone else holding his hand. She knew he'd gone out with the owner of a coffee shop in town couple of times a while back. And Wendy had told her of some years-ago love where they'd come close to making it permanent, but it hadn't worked out.

"Rick says she expected him to leave the ranch and go with her to some big city," Wendy had said.

Briony remembered laughing out loud at that, at the idea of Greg ever leaving the Colton Ranch. Even she knew better than that. And the idea of Greg Colton trapped in a world of concrete, asphalt and high-rises was almost laughable. No, he was a man of the outdoors and open spaces and always would be.

She thought of the story he'd told her about last night, and the abnormal delivery of the foal. No city boy would have been able to deal with that. And the fact that it was him they'd run to when it happened spoke volumes about his standing at the ranch.

"Sometime soon you should take the kids to the ranch like your father said. Show them the new baby. I bet they'd like that. Especially Justin—he's so aware of animals now, and he's fascinated by them."

It was a moment before he answered, and she wondered what he was thinking. As usual. The only thing she was sure of was that he hadn't yet pulled his hand free of hers.

"Including spiders?" Greg said, his tone a little too neutral. "Like you, that day at the lake?"

She gaped at him. "I can't believe you remember that!"

She saw his mouth quirk at one corner. "It was…unforgettable."

It certainly was for her. She knew she would never forget the time when, on a picnic with Rick and Wendy and at the time baby Justin, Greg had reached out to touch her hair. Her heart had leaped; he'd never made a gesture like that before, as if he…cared. She'd held her breath, trying frantically to decide what to do.

But a moment later, dangling from a silken thread in front of her eyes, was that spider. That he'd clearly just plucked from her hair.

"And humiliating. I shrieked like a banshee."

"You did. And it was just a garden spider. They're actually kind of pretty, with the stripes."

"Did you actually use *pretty* and *spider* in the same sentence?"

"I've become a lot more tolerant of them lately. Had an ant invasion a year or so ago. Real tiny ones. I got tired of having to clean them out two or three times a day. Didn't want to use poison, because Pacer—my brother Malcolm's dog—likes to come in and inspect every corner. Then a spider showed up, and I decided to give him a shot. Two weeks later, pfft. No more ants."

Funnily, what struck her most was his concern about his brother's dog. Not that it surprised her; she knew he was that way about all animals. Apparently even spiders.

"Is that his search-and-rescue dog?" she asked.

He nodded. "And he's the perfect combination. He's got the tenacity and the protectiveness of a German shepherd, and the nose of the hound that's his other half."

She hesitated a moment before asking, not wanting to bring the subject of death front and center again. But then she realized it still was right there, even if they weren't talking about it. In fact, she was fairly certain all this normal-sounding chatter was in fact trying to put a buffer of sorts between them and the reality they hadn't processed yet. So she went ahead.

"How is he doing, after…his fiancée died?"

Greg's jaw tensed slightly. "About how you'd expect. And being Malcolm, he blames himself."

"But…he went into the lake after her, didn't he?"

"Not fast enough, according to him."

She sighed. These Colton men certainly carried heavy loads and added to those burdens by taking on responsibilities that weren't really necessary or theirs.

She managed not to look back over her shoulder at that lake. And lapsed into silence, sorry now she'd asked. Especially since he'd pulled his hand free of hers and put it back on the wheel.

Greg drove on, steadily, smoothly. Interestingly, she often got a bit carsick when she wasn't the driver, but not with him. He was that smooth. When he started tapping his finger on the steering wheel she wondered if he was still thinking about his brother, or if he was back to their chaos. Then he startled her.

"I bet Justin would like fishing spiders."

She blinked. "He would?"

"Sure he would. How could a kid possibly not like a spider that can walk on water?"

She stared at him, certain he must be joking. "Walk on water?"

"And dive under the water, too. I read all about them after I saw my first one as a kid, at a pond on the ranch. They've got hairs on their legs that don't get wet, so when they—"

He broke off suddenly. She saw his hands had tightened on the steering wheel as he stared out the windshield. She looked the same direction, away from him, only then realizing how intently she'd been watching him.

Then she saw where they were. Approaching the turn to the street Rick and Wendy lived on.

And they couldn't put this off any longer.

Chapter Seven

"Unca Greg! Aunt Briny!"

Somehow the pronunciation that had always made him smile—Justin had always dropped the *L*, and found the *I* and *O* combination hard to pronounce—made his eyes sting yet again. The first time it had happened Briony had laughingly told them all she didn't mind sounding like a salty old sailor. Greg remembered the day she'd said it, and how they'd all laughed. He'd wondered then about how she was so at ease with them and yet so quiet and shy around anybody else.

And now the whole world was different.

Justin's face lit up and he scrambled down from his chair—the higher one with the ladder side he and Rick had built for the boy so he could sit at the big table after he'd graduated from the high chair his little sister was now sitting in—and ran toward them. Greg tried his best for a smile as he bent down to the boy, who threw his arms around his knees. He picked him up and hugged Justin back, his throat once more so tight he could barely breathe.

He was aware of Mrs. Matson, the older woman who lived two houses down, watching them all, and could see the sheen of tears in her warm brown eyes. Her own kids were teenagers now, and she'd insisted she was glad to help

Rick and Wendy out with the little ones, since she so missed that stage.

Justin leaned out from where Greg held him against his side, reaching with one little hand toward Briony's face. She took the proffered hand and kissed it with a loud smacking sound that made Justin giggle and Greg smile even through the pain.

A sudden burst of noise came from the table, a babble of sounds and coos and a couple of almost intelligible syllables, punctuated by a couple of solid blows to the tray of the high chair. A glance told him Jane had already wearied of being ignored by the new arrivals.

"I'll get her," Briony said, and went to lift the tiny girl into her arms before the recently introduced sippy cup went flying. They'd deduced she was By-By and he was Geg, also a fairly recent development.

First people she's "named" after Wendy and me. You should feel honored.

He'd laughed when Rick said it, at Jane's one-year birthday party a couple of months ago, and he had bowed to the baby in his friend's arms with an elaborate flourish. Jane had giggled delightedly at him, and he'd felt an unexpected sense of…well, honor.

And now, here they were, and… Rick and Wendy weren't.

It seemed both more impossible and more real at the same time, here now with the kids in their arms. It wasn't that this was unusual; he'd often ended up playing with Justin, easier for him than entertaining Jane, which Briony appeared to have a knack for, probably because she had no problem getting silly with the baby talk. Not that she talked baby talk per se, she used perfect English, but did it in that baby talk tone that seemed to delight the tiny girl.

His usual approach with Justin was to ask him questions.

He'd pretend ignorance, point to something he knew the boy knew and ask what it was. Justin was thrilled to be able to teach this adult something.

"'S'a bird!" he would trill when Greg pointed at a robin.

The same response came that day on a picnic near the lake with the Krafts when he had pointed at a bald eagle overhead. Greg had felt compelled to add, "A very special bird."

"Why?" Justin demanded.

He remembered that day in particular, because after his explanation to the boy about power and grace and national symbols, he'd looked up to see Briony smiling at him warmly.

And when Justin had run off to play catch—as much as a four-year-old could—with Dad, Wendy had plopped down beside him.

"You forgot to mention they mate for life," she said teasingly.

"Like you and Rick?" Briony had asked.

"Exactly," she'd answered.

And there it was again, grabbing him by the throat until he thought he might pass out from the lack of oxygen.

Because Rick and Wendy had indeed mated for life. A life that had been cut short far too early.

"Unca Greg?" Justin said, snapping him out of the reverie, but not the pain. "Are you sad?"

He didn't want to lie to the boy. He might not know how to deal with this, but he was pretty sure that was not the way to start out.

"I am," he admitted. "But we'll talk about that later, okay?"

"'Kay," the boy said, and went back to his favorite subject, that someday soon they were going to get a dog.

Greg knew Rick had been talking to Sebastian Cross about maybe taking on any pups he got in at Crosswinds Training that looked like they'd be more suited to the family pet job than search-and-rescue, but as far as he knew talk was as far as it had gone.

"You could—" He had to stop, swallow and try again. "You could come see my brother's dog, Pacer, at the ranch."

The boy had been to the ranch before, but it had always been when Malcolm and Pacer had been off working.

"Is that the looking dog?" Justin asked.

It took him a moment. "The search-and-rescue dog, yes."

"He finds lost people," Justin said.

"You got it. He does, along with my brother."

That idea seemed to intrigue the boy, and he began to pepper Greg with questions, interrupted only when Briony came over with Jane in her arms.

"Hi, Aunt Briny," the boy said.

"Jane insisted on saying hello to Uncle Greg."

"Geg," Jane corrected immediately, sounding pretty insistent for a fourteen-month-old.

To his surprise Briony laughed. He could hear the strain in it, though, and realized she was working as hard as he was to put on a united, normal front, until they figured out what to do, how to tell these two innocent, happy, loving souls that their world as they knew it had come to an end.

After a few more minutes of chatter and interaction, they put the kids back down at the table to finish their breakfast. And finally, reluctantly, they drew back into the kitchen to talk to Mrs. Matson.

"It's really true?" she whispered, as if she were still holding out hope.

Greg closed his eyes for a brief moment, opened them again and realized he'd answered her without saying a word.

The tears overflowed, and the kindly woman turned away so the children would not see.

"I've told them nothing," she whispered. "They think they're coming home this morning. But I have to get home soon... You'll stay with them?"

"Of course," Briony said instantly. "Thank you for taking care of them."

Mrs. Matson nodded, then glanced at the table, where Justin was zooming his spoonful of cereal around like an airplane, while Jane started banging her own thankfully empty spoon against the sippy cup. "I just can't believe it. But Rick and Wendy trusted you so completely, I know you'll see to them properly."

"We will," Greg said, his voice still gruff. He would have tried to clear his throat except he knew it wouldn't do any good. He was afraid that lump was going to be there for a while.

After she'd gone Greg and Briony stood there looking at each other. They glanced at the children, then looked back at each other. Greg had never felt so lost. When his mother had abandoned them, he'd felt mostly anger. Maybe because he was the oldest and it fell upon him to help with his younger siblings.

Plus, he'd always known there was something...off with his mother. He had just been too young to realize what it was. He knew from hearing his classmates at school complain about their own mothers that what they'd experienced at home bore little similarity to what he had. He'd had a loving, understanding, patient parent, but it had been Dad.

He felt the sudden urge to call the man, ask for help, but it was a bit too humiliating to do it this soon. There would be enough time when they got some sort of sense of...anything.

But right now, here with Briony, godfather to godmother, he felt like he had to admit it. "I don't have a clue about this."

She drew back slightly, and there was an edge in her voice when she said, "You think I do?"

He knew she meant how she'd grown up. And she was right. At least he'd *had* one loving, involved parent, which was one more than she'd ever had.

"I didn't say that," he pointed out.

"Sorry," she muttered. "A little touchy."

"And exhausted, if you feel anything like I do."

"You have more reason," she said, and her tone had shifted to something much gentler. "You've done nothing but deal with emergencies all night."

He let out a compressed breath. "I have a feeling I should be thankful right now that I'm too tired to…feel much."

"We should both be thankful," she agreed. And yet she had to swipe at her eyes again, indicating she was indeed still feeling. He resisted the urge to reach out and help her wipe the tears away, although he wasn't quite sure why. They were in this together, and they had to handle it together, didn't they? Because he didn't think either one of them could handle it alone.

But he didn't want her to get upset with him again, so he thought about the words before he said, tentatively, "I think we're really going to have to pull together on this. Neither one of us knows much about this, but together, maybe we know enough to get by. At least until things are settled."

"Settled?"

"Meaning we have a chance to get and read the will. Knowing Rick, he spelled out exactly what he and Wendy want to happen."

She nodded, slowly. "I'm sure they did. And just so you

know now, they did ask me to be the financial executor, for the…life insurance for the kids."

He nodded, not in the least surprised. She was not only a trusted friend but an accountant, after all—Wendy had told him that after growing up in chaos Briony liked numbers because they were predictable—so it only made sense, and with her history he could understand that. He was glad she'd told him now. And wondered if Wendy had said anything else to her, about…those kinds of plans. Rick hadn't gone much beyond "I know you'll be there for them." Which was, of course, true. He'd do whatever he could to help.

Briony looked back over at the kids, where Justin was now just about to launch a spoonful of his cereal at his sister. Greg saw it in the same moment and swooped in to stave off the impending mess. Not knowing what else to do he grabbed the spoon from the boy, zoomed it around a bit as Justin had been doing, then popped the bland, too-liquid-for-his-taste cereal into his own mouth. And managed not to grimace at the blandness of it.

"Yum!" Briony said, loudly.

And suddenly both kids were giggling. He found himself grinning at them. Briony got another spoon from the drawer where the kids' smaller utensils were, and handed it to Justin.

"Nicely done," she said, glancing at Greg.

"Crisis number one averted," he said with an eye roll.

He could only imagine how many more there would be before the weekend was over.

He didn't want to imagine what would come after that.

Chapter Eight

"I can officially state I have never been more exhausted in my life," Briony said as she collapsed onto the couch. "And it's only eight o'clock."

"At least they're both in bed," Greg muttered as he dropped down onto the next cushion. She saw him start to put his feet up on the coffee table, then stop.

"They wouldn't mind," she said quietly. "Rick puts his feet up there all the time." It was the first time she'd been able to get the name out without choking up, which she suspected could be attributed more to exhaustion than acceptance.

"It wasn't that," Greg said, sounding almost as weary as she felt. "I'm afraid if I get too comfortable, I'll fall asleep right here."

She appreciated the admission that he was as tired as she was. Although since he was used to a lot more physical labor than she was, it had to be the stress wearing on him as it was her. Plus, she suddenly remembered, he'd been up half the night anyway, helping that mare.

So he's spending his whole weekend—did ranchers even have weekends?—helping babies in trouble...

That didn't surprise her. Rick had always said Greg was the most solid guy he knew. That from age ten, when their

mother had abandoned them, he'd helped his father see to
the younger Coltons, even if he was only two years older
than the next one, his brother Malcolm. He'd been especially good with—and protective of—the littlest, his sister,
Lizzy, who had been a year younger than Justin was now.

She'd always wondered what it must have been like, to
have a big brother who stood with you. Or a father like Buck
Colton, who stepped up and then some when necessary. But
at least she'd had Wendy, and they—

They weren't *they* anymore. It was just her. Alone. Wendy
was gone, forever. The friend, the sister of the heart who had
helped her survive, was gone. She was on her own, from
here on, however long her own life might be.

*And how selfish can you be, worried about that when
Rick and Wendy are dead and their children—your god-
children—are orphans?*

But in that, at least, she wasn't alone. Not completely. The
man sitting a couple of feet away was in this with her, was
her fellow godparent, and as Rick had often said, a friend so
rock solid you could build a fortress on him. She'd known
it was true. It was probably why she'd developed that silly
little crush on him. Well, that and those big warm brown
eyes and that wide flashing smile and the occasional great
laugh. Never mind the rest of him, that tall, strong, powerful rest of him, honed to near perfection by the hard work
of ranching.

But she was past that now. She'd gotten the message
quickly when Greg kept chuckling at Rick and Wendy's efforts to match them up. He wasn't interested, and that was
totally understandable. She was a painfully shy, boring accountant, and he was… Greg Colton.

"I used to think Wendy was joking when she talked about
doing a load of laundry every day." Greg's tone was rather

sour, and when she glanced at him, she saw he was staring at the pile they'd accumulated near the entrance to the hall-way that led to the bedrooms and the laundry room.

"I'm just thankful they aren't using cloth diapers," she said. "That pile would be twice as big."

His eyes widened, as if the thought had never occurred to him. "And three times as smelly."

She let out a short chuckle. "That, too. Although I'm not sure they even still make cloth diapers."

"They do," he answered, and at her surprised look he shrugged. "Dad uses them to polish his car."

That made sense; they were probably perfect for the task. And then, because she couldn't seem to resist asking ques-tions about him when the chance to do so without seem-ing pushy arose, she asked, "But you don't for your truck?"

He looked, surprisingly, a little embarrassed. "I did, when it was new. But it's a work truck, and how it runs is more important than how it looks."

"It looks fine," she hastened to say. "I just wondered when you find the time to keep it as clean as it is, with all you do at the ranch."

"Sometimes I just hose it down to get the big chunks off," he said, in the tone of a rueful admission. "And try to keep the inside decent."

"I noticed."

She had; the cab of the big pickup had had things in it, like a toolbox and a couple of other things she didn't recog-nize, but it also had a small trash holder that held the usual detritus she'd seen strewn about in other vehicles. She re-membered thinking once that it showed that he cared more about what he lived in than what the outside world thought of what he lived in. She'd liked that idea. But back then she'd still been working on that crush...

He got up rather abruptly, and she had the feeling he'd issued himself an order. He headed for the pile of dirty clothes, bibs and towels, swept them up in one motion, and headed into the hallway. By the time she got to her feet she heard the sounds from the laundry room. It was clear he had no problem tackling the job. She was curious about how he went about it so followed him.

Face it, you're curious about everything he does.

You're curious about him.

Which seemed odd, given how long she'd known him. But that was as Rick's best friend, and all their interaction had centered on that. She had, she realized with some surprise, spent very little time alone with him, despite Rick and Wendy's machinations.

Because you're a coward. And you know he doesn't want that anyway, and never has. Stop thinking about it!

And again she felt a horrible upswell of guilt, dwelling on herself at a time like this.

You have to think about yourself, Bri. Nobody else has in your life, ever.

You have!

Because you're my sister.

She teared up again at the remembered exchange, the first time Wendy had used that word to describe them. Sisters. She fought it back, knowing that the best thing she could do for that sister now was to see to her beloved children. She took in a deep breath and spoke as normally as she could.

"Want some help sorting that?"

He turned his head from where he was tossing things into the washing machine. "I gave up on sorting things long ago." He went back to the task, but added, "Except red. If there's something red, I pull it out."

And suddenly she was smiling, and more amazingly,

meaning it. "Spoken like someone who's wound up with pink underwear."

His head snapped around again. Then, slowly, an answering smile curved his mouth. For the briefest moment that dimple flashed, and it made her own smile widen. "Yeah," he said, sounding sheepish. For a long, silent moment, he held her gaze. Then, quietly, he spoke. "We'll get through this, somehow."

She only nodded, afraid that anything she might say would be far too colored by that "we."

Then, suddenly, he moved, and to her shock pulled her into another hug. A supportive hug like the others, she warned herself, even as she thrilled to the feel of his arms around her, his tall, strong body so close.

"We will," he insisted. "We'll do it for them, because… because…"

Words rose unbidden to her lips. "They were a gift to us both."

His arms tightened, and she thought she heard him whisper, "Yes." As if she'd found the words he couldn't.

And that was how this was going to have to work, each of them doing what the other couldn't at that particular moment. And together, they would get it all done.

They had to.

But she still savored the feel of this a bit more personally than she probably should have.

Chapter Nine

"You survived the day, then." His father's voice coming through his earbud didn't sound relieved, but as if he'd only heard what he'd expected.

"So I hear. Not totally convinced, myself." Greg answered his father with an echo of the man's own knack for grim humor. "I don't know how you did it alone, with four of us."

"You can do a lot more than you think you can when there's no choice and there are people you love at stake."

Greg's throat tightened a little. It was becoming a familiar reaction to...well, just about everything. "Thanks, Dad."

"Just a little fatherly advice."

"I wasn't thanking you for the advice. I was thanking you for following it, all those years ago."

There was a moment of silence, which Greg counted as big points scored. It wasn't often his father was left speechless. So before Dad could dissemble or deny, he went on.

"How are things there? How's the new colt?"

"Already poking his nose in everywhere. Perfectly normal. You got it done, Greg. And in time."

He felt that burst of pride and accomplishment only his father's approval could spark in him. But he knew thanking the man again would just get brushed off.

"I'm sorry you're having to pick up the slack."

"Don't worry about it. What you have to do right now is more important. We'll still be here when you get back."

He didn't know how long he'd been standing there after the call ended, staring out the kitchen window at the Krafts' spacious backyard—notable for the various play outlets—when Briony's soft voice from close by almost made him jump.

"Everything all right at home?"

"Yeah," he said. "I was just…thanking my dad. For being there. For always being there."

"Good."

It was all she said, but her tone was utterly sincere. "I'm sorry…that you don't have a dad to thank. Or a mom."

She shrugged. "Given they dumped me in a dark alley at midnight when I was six, I was probably better off."

He stared at her. "They…what?"

She nodded, as casually as if she'd just confirmed her eyes were green. "I don't remember a lot about my time with them, just lots of fights. And when they weren't fighting it was because they were drugged up, although I didn't realize that until I was older."

He swore under his breath. How had he never known this? He'd known Wendy's folks had died in a freak storm when she'd been the same age, because Rick had told him shortly after he'd met her. That she'd come out so amazing was a tribute to her strength, Rick had always said. But while he'd known Wendy and Briony had met in the foster care system, he'd never known how Briony had ended up there beyond that she'd been abandoned.

"Just as well," she said with a shrug. "From what little I know about them, they probably would have sold me to some sex trafficker if they got desperate enough for drug money."

He was gaping at her now. He'd thought he'd had problems as a kid? Dad would have killed anyone who tried to hurt any of his children. And while his mother had apparently gone full cultist with that evil group that had recently been discovered around town, at least she'd never threatened any of them. She'd just…vanished, leaving them with their father. Their loving father, who would protect them unto death.

"How," he asked wonderingly, "do you not begrudge any and everyone who's had even a slightly normal life?"

"And what, exactly, would that accomplish?" she asked with another dismissive shrug. "Besides, normal can turn into abnormal at any moment. You know that firsthand."

He shook his head slowly. "My mother behaved irrationally. But Dad didn't. He was a rock. And still is."

Briony nodded. "I can see that clearly, now that I've met him. You were lucky there."

"Beyond lucky," he agreed, more fervently now than ever. But as he studied her, noticing not for the first time how her hair gleamed redder in the direct light, and how that with her bright green eyes made her look as if she'd be at home in the hills of Ireland, he inwardly chided himself. "How did I not know this about you? We've known each other since…since…"

"Rick and Wendy hooked up, yes." She gave him a wry look. "It's not like I tell everyone. In fact, Wendy's the only one who knows the whole truth."

He heard her tiny, sharp intake of breath. He saw her lips tremble in the moment before she spoke again, and he knew what was coming.

"*Knew* the whole truth. She's the only one who knew…"

She was visibly trembling. And once more, because he could no more turn his back on her in pain like this than he could have let that foal die, he hugged her yet again.

"I'm sorry," she said, brokenly. "I don't mean for you to have to hold me up all the time, it's just—"

"Shh. Don't apologize. The world's upside-down right now. Our world, at least. And…" He hesitated, but then realized she deserved the truth even if it was a bit uncomfortable for him to admit. "It helps me, too. To know I'm not the only one feeling like this."

She didn't respond, but she moved, her arms coming around him to hug him back. Once again. And after a long silence, she finally did speak again, low and clearly heartfelt.

"They'd want this, wouldn't they? Want us to help each other, be there for each other?"

He thought of Rick, the prankster he'd been as a kid—and the trouble it had gotten them into—and Wendy, who would have backed Rick in anything he tried, and suddenly he was smiling.

"Honey," he said, putting on his best exaggerated drawl, "they probably planned it this way."

He felt her go stock-still, and his mind took off, afraid he'd offended her, that it was far too soon to even try to joke, although he hadn't meant it as a joke but only an acknowledgment of who their dearest friends had been, a couple happy and complete in each other, who wanted the same for their best friends.

But then he felt an odd little jerk from her, almost like a twitch. He looked down, past that thick fall of auburn hair that looked like it would be warm to the touch, and realized that twitch had been a short but definite laugh.

"Yes," she said. "Yes, they would have."

And that easily the mood changed; they went from desperate clinging to mutual support. Her trembling had stopped, and his own mind had calmed, as if it were a horse settling into a steady lope after clearing a big fence.

It was several minutes before he noticed he was feeling a different kind of warmth. A physical kind he hadn't felt in a while. Quite a while. When he realized what it was, he almost jerked away. Instead, with an effort, he let go slowly, and took a half step back, leaning against the front of the sink as if that's what he'd intended to do. And he decided from the way she quickly turned to face the window over the sink that she was glad he'd let go. Maybe she'd somehow sensed that little change and wanted away from him before it got embarrassing. After all, she'd made it pretty clear she thought the idea of them...together was a no-go from the get.

She kept staring out the window. He wasn't sure what she was looking at, out in the yard, since it was nearly too dark to see anything. Yet she seemed focused on...something.

"Spot a moose wandering in or something?"

Her head snapped around. "They've never had a moose here. Have they?"

She sounded worried, and he felt bad. "Sorry, trying for a joke. No, they've never had a moose down here. One out on the road once, but not near the houses out here."

"Oh. Okay. Good. Because knowing Justin, he'd be so curious he'd toddle on over to check it out, and that might not go well." He caught the lighter tone, thought maybe she was trying to make up for missing his joke. Or maybe not. But right now a lighter tone was exactly what he needed, so he went with it.

"A thousand pounds of moose and thirty-five pounds of kid? Nah, no problem there."

She smiled, and it seemed once again they'd beaten back the tide of tension and pain. For now.

"Actually," she said, "I was looking at the...structure out there. Playhouse?"

"We called it a fort," he said. "Rick designed all the climbing stuff for Justin, but Wendy made us redo the inside so it could be a playhouse for Jane, too." His mouth quirked as she stared at him. "Or the opposite, if that's the way it worked out."

"You and Rick built that?"

He nodded, puzzled at her reaction. "Last year. Although sometimes I think it was more for us, just to do it, since Jane is way too young and Justin is just now getting big enough to be interested."

She gave a slight shake of her head. "You know if you ever wanted something other than ranch work, you could make a living just doing that for families with little kids."

He laughed. "Kids these days are too glued to their screens. Not everybody's as tough on that as Rick and Wendy are." He realized he'd made the same mistake she'd just made, with the present tense. But he didn't make himself correct it and bring it back up front for both of them again. "But I'll never want something other than ranch work."

"You never get...tired of it?"

"I get tired, often. But not in the way you mean. It's my life, and I wouldn't have it any other way. Because for all the times when I've collapsed in exhaustion after a long hard day, there are other times, other things, like bringing that little colt into the world, that make it worth it."

She was looking at him rather strangely now. But not the way city people often did, boggled at the idea of voluntarily giving up taxis on every corner, in front of the Starbucks on the same corners. After all, she'd lived here in Owl Creek for years, at least since Rick and Wendy had been here, and it was hardly a big city. No, it was more in the way someone looked as they contemplated a life unlike their own, but not...despised.

He wasn't sure why that mattered to him, but it did.

Chapter Ten

Briony came half-awake slowly, not certain why, not even opening her eyes. Nor was she sure why she felt so comfy and warm. Cozy, almost. As if someone were holding her close, protecting her as she never had been in her life. She sleepily wished that were true, and it was too sweet for her to even mind that the first image that floated through her lethargic brain was Greg.

She kept her eyes closed, wanting to drift back into that wonderful sleep, into that dream built on memories of the best times in her life, times like when she and Wendy had sneaked out to see a movie and gotten away with it, to when she had graduated with her accounting degree and Wendy had thrown her a party, and when—

This time she woke up with a start. To reality. Wendy. And Wendy's baby girl, whose cry had been what had awakened her this time.

"I'll get her."

The low, rough voice came from so close it made her almost squeak, "What?"

"You did it the last two times."

And so she found herself suddenly feeling both stunned and abandoned. Because apparently that cozy warmth, that sense of being held, safely, had not only been real, it had really been Greg. Greg, who had just wiggled out from behind her and gotten to his feet—sock-clad feet, she noticed, rather inanely—to head toward Jane's bedroom.

The couch. She was on the couch. And Greg had been behind her, indeed holding her steadfastly in place, and providing that wonderful warmth with the heat of his body.

That lovely, strong, work-toughened body...

The last thing she remembered was them sitting on this couch—on separate cushions—after the third and thankfully successful attempt to get Justin to sleep. Justin, who was starting to realize just how long his mom and dad had been gone. The questions they had managed to stall were beginning, and she knew that soon there would be no stalling, no stopping, that they would have to tell the boy a truth he wasn't even old enough to fully understand. That they were never, ever coming home.

She yawned, stretched and tried not to think of how good it had felt to simply lie here with Greg's arms around her, even though she hadn't consciously realized that's what it was. Had she?

It didn't matter. Nothing mattered except getting through this. There was no room for feeling awkward, as she so often did around him. No time for being flustered, or worrying about what he thought of her. They had to work together to get through this, and that meant setting aside everything else. For the kids' sake. For Rick and Wendy, who had trusted them both enough to make them the godparents of their precious children.

Greg came back into the room, the toddler in his arms. And he was yawning, too. "Didn't they say she was sleeping through the night quite a while ago?"

She got to her feet. "Yes. Months ago. Does she need to be changed?"

He shook his head. "I checked." He'd surprised her with that, not being at all hesitant to deal with such things. But this was the guy who'd played obstetrician to a horse just last night, she reminded herself. She wouldn't be surprised if Greg Colton could handle just about anything.

"She shouldn't be hungry yet," Briony said, her brow furrowing as once more she tried to remember all the baby-raising milestones Wendy had so often excitedly told her about.

"It's quiet back there, and I didn't hear anything that might have woken her up," he said.

"Do you suppose she…somehow she…" she began, then let the words she didn't want to say trail away.

"That she senses something's very wrong? I wouldn't be surprised. She's a clever little widget."

Briony had to blink rapidly yet again as he used Rick's common phrase when referring to his baby girl. Fortunately, Greg was busy trying to calm the unsettled child and didn't see.

Jane quieted a bit as Greg sat down once more, although she was still fussy and, as Rick had always put it, squirmy.

"You suppose she's hungry?" he asked.

"Could be. I seem to remember Wendy saying something about trying to get her to sleep later, with no luck."

"Then maybe—" He broke off at a sound from the direction of the hallway. Then he looked back at her, his expression wearily wry. "Was that the sound of another pair of feet hitting the floor?"

"Afraid so," she said. "You hang on to her—she's calmer now—and I'll go get Justin."

As she tried to settle Justin, telling him his sister was going back to bed, too; it was the middle of the night—well, in child scheduling—she heard Greg's cell phone ringtone.

Moments later he appeared in the doorway, one arm holding Jane, the other hand holding the phone up to his ear.

"Where?" A pause, during which he put the now seemingly resigned Jane back to bed. "Got it. On my way."

On his way? He was leaving?

He ended the call and slid the phone back into his pocket. He nodded toward the door, then looked at Justin. "See you in the morning, buddy."

When they were back in the living room, she turned to face him. "On your way?"

He nodded. "That was Chase." He grimaced. "Late-night calls from him are never good news. My brother Max is already on the way, but he needs more backup."

"Backup?"

"Sorry to leave you with this, but hopefully I'll be back here before they even wake up." She didn't know what to say, so said nothing, just stared at him. "What?" he asked.

"You're just leaving?"

"Briony, he needs help. I'll explain it all when I get back, but right now somebody's in trouble so I've got to go."

And then he was gone, headed for his truck. She walked over to the front window, watching him run down the driveway to where it was parked behind Wendy's car with the car seats. He was obviously in a hurry.

Somebody's in trouble so I've got to go.

She had the feeling she'd just seen the Colton family motto. For the good ones, anyway, and Greg was definitely one of those. Rushing to assist when called.

Rushing, but still taking a moment to pull his rifle she'd noticed earlier from the rack in the truck. And she wondered just what kind of trouble he was heading out to deal with.

And suddenly she had a new thing to worry about. And wondered if it would ever stop.

GREG YAWNED WIDELY as he practically staggered into Rick and Wendy's house. He wanted nothing more than to crash on that couch again—

His thoughts broke off with a jolt as he remembered how he'd crashed on that couch just hours ago. With Briony snuggled up next to him and his arms around her. It had been…unsettlingly comfortable. Warm. Nice. Okay, more than nice. A lot more.

Belatedly he realized she was there on that couch and was now sitting up sleepily.

"Sorry I woke you," he said. "I didn't know you were there."

She stifled a yawn. "I meant to wait up."

Greg blinked. "Why?"

She stared at him. "Why? You have to ask why?"

"I'm not a mind reader, Briony. If there's a problem, say so."

She stood up, slowly. "I watched you leave," she said, over-enunciating every word, "*after* you checked that rifle of yours. What was I supposed to think except that you were headed somewhere you might have to use it? Is that explanation enough?"

To his own surprise, he found himself smiling. Not at what she'd said, but at the fact that she'd stood up to him and said it. If nothing else she was teaching him that shy didn't necessarily mean weak.

"Chase's new lady—" he said the words with no doubt that they were now true "—got herself in a bit of trouble, asking questions about Rick and Wendy's crash. He needed some help getting her out of it."

"Oh." Her expression changed. "Is she all right?"

He nodded. "Chase wasn't about to let her get hurt." He didn't feel it necessary to expand on the fact that he and his cousin had in fact gone in guns blazing, in a firefight that had ended with the man who had grabbed Sloan turning his gun on himself. He didn't understand that mindset and was glad of it.

"Did she…find out anything?" Briony asked.

He hesitated, but she needed to know. To be aware. "They don't think the crash was an accident."

Her eyes widened. "What? You mean somebody might have hit them on purpose?"

"It's a definite probability. He and Sloan found a suspect. She's a tech wiz and found a big money transfer to the driver of a vehicle that matches the evidence."

Briony went paler than he would have thought possible. "Is he…?"

"He was taken into custody." He left it at that for now. She didn't need to know, yet, that the man suspected of running Rick and Wendy off the road had in turn been killed while in a jail cell. Before he could talk. This was enough bad news for one dose. Besides, a lot of this was supposition, and he didn't want to put her through the additional pain if it might not be necessary.

She sat back down on the couch as if her legs wouldn't hold her upright any longer. Her next words, stammered out almost helplessly, solidified his decision. "But why? Why would somebody…want them…want that?"

She looked as if she'd already had more dumped on her than she could bear, so he didn't mention that that money transfer had come from an account associated with the Ever After Church, and thus Rick's father.

"They're still digging into that. I promise, when they have the whole story, you'll know as soon as I do."

She buried her face in her hands and looked so broken sitting there he couldn't stop himself from sitting beside her and putting an arm around her. She moved, and he was afraid he'd made a mistake, but then she leaned into him.

When her head finally came up, he spoke quietly. "Look, I'm really sorry I woke you up. Why don't you go to bed and get some sleep before we have to get up and start again?"

She gave him a long, haunted look, but nodded.

He tried not to think too much about the fact that she'd tried to wait up for him.

And even less about the fact that she'd been worried about him.

Chapter Eleven

Greg stifled a yawn as the bank VP—Owl Creek didn't run to the big-name banks with tons of staff—pulled up the list for the relatively few safe-deposit boxes they had.

"Your ID, please?" he asked as he typed in Rick's name.

He handed him his driver's license. He glanced at it, went back to the screen, then his gaze snapped back to the license, eyes wide now. "Colton?"

"Yes."

Greg wondered why the pointed reaction. It was true, Colton was a very well-known name in town, but it didn't usually elicit a reaction like that. Lately there had been more dodging his gaze, as the truth had trickled out about his family drama. So why here, now, from this person? Had his uncle Robert bought this building along with all the others he'd acquired over the years?

"Related to Mr. Robert Colton?"

"My uncle," he said, guessing now he'd been right and wondering what was coming next. Some comment about Robert's double life, his cheating, his illegitimate children? Greg still hadn't completely wrapped his mind around the fact that he had two new half siblings. Half cousins? Both? He was too tired at the moment to wrestle with that. Besides, right now the most important thing was doing what Rick and Wendy had wanted.

"He was helpful to this bank," was all the man said. Then, with a suddenly warmer, kinder look, he added, "My condolences on the Krafts. They were lovely people."

When he went back to work at his keyboard, Greg felt bad that he'd suspected worse of the guy. "All right, you're here on the list, you have full access. If you'll follow me?"

He started toward the back of the bank, stopped at a rather heavy-looking door, and pressed a finger to the very modern-looking scanner lock. Greg followed him into a room about the size of the foaling stall he'd spent a lot of Friday—had it really only been two days?—night in. A few moments later he was alone in the room, surrounded by walls containing other boxes, with the box he held the key to on the table before him.

He didn't want to do it. Didn't want to open it, because somehow that would cement the reality of all this, a reality he still did not want to face. He'd never thought of himself as a coward, although he knew he wasn't the kind of hero his brother Max was, or even more so his war-scarred cousin Wade. But right now, he felt like the worst kind of coward, shying away like a skittish horse from simply opening a box.

But he had to do it. And soon. Briony was sitting outside with the kids in Wendy's car—they'd had to bring it because it was the only one they had with the proper child seats—and he knew it had to be horrible for her to be sitting in the car she'd ridden in so many times with her best friend. Not to mention that now Jane was so often wailing "Mama" for the woman who would normally be in that car with them, and Justin was asking more and more questions about where his parents were.

But Greg was the one on the access list for the safe-deposit box, so he had to be the one to go inside. And now that he was here, he couldn't even seem to put the damn key in the lock.

He sucked in a deep breath and made himself do it. The key turned easily, with an audible click when the lock was disengaged. It took another deep breath before he could lift the lid.

What are you going to do with it all?

Briony's question, asked as they were on the way here, echoed in his head now.

Run for the attorney?

Something he'd never thought he'd say. But even he had heard the helpless note in his own voice. It had taken him a moment to get a grip before he could look at her and say what he knew needed to be said.

We'll go together. That's how we have to do this, together. As Rick and Wendy wanted us to.

Her eyes had widened slightly, but she nodded. Decisively. And so here they were.

...do this together.

His own words rang in his ears now, and on impulse he grabbed all the papers in the box, plucked out the business card for the attorney and stuffed the rest into the large manila envelope the banker had kindly provided. He closed the box again and pushed it back into the empty slot on the wall of matching boxes. He slid the key back into his pocket—the man had told him the box was paid to the end of the year—and left the little room.

Moments later he was in the driver's seat again. And the irony of the phrase indicating he was in control made him laugh bitterly. The sound seemed to register even with the kids, because they fell silent.

"Is it bad?" Briony asked anxiously.

Greg shook his head ruefully. "Just feeling sorry for my-self."

"You have reason," she said, and the idea that she, too, might be feeling sorry for him stung even more. "I mean, this on top of what's happened with your family already?"

"Right," he said with a grimace.

She was right. In the last six months his powerful and until then respected uncle had died. The respect had been badly damaged by the discovery of his affair with Greg's own mother, producing the two kids she had apparently decided were worth raising herself, unlike him and his own siblings. Then of all things bodies started turning up, serial killings likely connected to some mysterious cult masquerading as a church, and now...did Briony even know the last thing?

He gave her a sideways look that she apparently misinterpreted, because she immediately said, "I'm sorry, it's none of my business, I shouldn't have said—"

She stopped when he held up a hand.

"It's not that. I was just wondering if you'd even heard the latest in my family soap opera."

"The latest?"

He hesitated, but only for a moment. Things had changed. They'd spent the weekend flailing their way through unfamiliar territory for them both. To the point of exhaustion.

To the point of you sleeping with her in your arms, and it feeling so good you didn't want to wake up.

He shoved that unwelcome truth aside, and said flatly, "That my mother, she of the two kids with my uncle, is probably part of the Ever After Church. Cult. Whatever."

She stared at him, lips parted in shock. She hadn't known, then. She let out an audible sound, almost a cough of air.

"Yeah," he said, his tone sour now. "Charming, ain't it all?"

It was a moment before she spoke. "I never in my life thought I might one day be glad not to have a family."

"Family," Justin suddenly said. Both kids had been so quiet—so uncustomarily quiet—it startled Greg. And it also started the Mama wail from Jane, and they were back in the middle of it. "When is Daddy coming?" Justin demanded.

Briony and Greg looked at each other. They knew they could not put it off much longer.

"We'll talk about that soon," Briony said to them in a soothing tone. Then to Greg, "We need to look at this stuff—" she indicated the envelope "—before we go to the lawyer. Sort it, at least."

"Yes, we—"

"Now!" the boy demanded. Jane's wail became louder.

Greg gave Briony an almost desperate look. "Are you above bribing them with evil food? The fast-food place up the block?"

"Not a bit," she said.

It worked well enough that, sitting there in the car as the kids both played with and ate the rare treat of fries and ice cream, they were able to at least sort the papers. Greg set the attorney's business card—she was in Conners, he noted—on the dash as they went through the various IDs and records, the insurance papers, and at last, held together by a binder clip, what appeared to be the will. Greg hesitated, staring at the thing.

Then he looked at Briony. "Should we look now?"

"I wouldn't have a hope of understanding the legalese that's probably in there," she said. "I've never even seen a will."

"I read my dad's. He made me, so I'd know." He grimaced. "Sometimes being the oldest sucks. But maybe we should look, so when we see the lawyer we'll at least have a clue?"

"Good point," she said.

On that, he turned the cover page. To his surprise there was what appeared to be a one-page digest of the pages that followed, signed by the attorney on the card and both Rick and Wendy. Seeing their names there, in Rick's inimitable scrawl and Wendy's tidy, feminine hand, made his eyes blur yet again, and he wondered if it would ever end. He blinked three times, until the typewritten first page cleared enough to read.

He never got past the first paragraph. He read it three times. Then looked up at Briony. He could guess what he must look like by her reaction, wide-eyed and wary.

"What is it?"

He swallowed, because he had to before he could even think about speaking.

"I...we..." He tried again. "They made us their guardians. Legal guardians. Permanently."

He saw her gaze shoot to the back seat, then back to his face. Saw she understood.

Rick and Wendy had left their children, and all legal and financial authority over them, to Greg Colton and Briony Adams.

Chapter Twelve

The woman who had come out from behind the big desk and invited them to sit on the couch in her seating area seemed to be studying them both. Attorney Tanya Carlson wasn't what Briony had expected. She'd formed an image in her mind of a quick, sharp, probably dressed to the nines with spike heels shark-type of lawyer. Instead, they'd found a motherly woman, older, clad in a businesslike dress, clearly expensive but in no way flashy. Her makeup was subtle, and she wore no jewelry except a pair of black pearl earrings and a simple gold wedding ring. Her hair was dark, touched with gray that framed her face.

But she had the eyes of a younger person, sharp, quick and a bright, light blue. Eyes that Briony suspected didn't miss much. And eyes that right now were looking at them with a warmth and sympathy she couldn't doubt was genuine. Although Briony had already guessed that, because the woman had cleared her schedule this morning to see them.

"I'm so very sorry. I quite liked the Krafts and admired their dedication to each other and their children."

"They were that." Greg's voice still held that rough timbre, as if he had as big a lump in his throat as she did. Every step they took on this painful path made it more real, more impossible to deny, that Rick and Wendy were really, truly gone.

For a moment there was silence. It seemed odd to her, and she realized it was the absence of the inevitable kid noise she'd almost gotten used to. The attorney's assistant had taken the kids into an adjoining room.

"She's very good with them. Since I deal a lot with family law, it seemed wise to have someone on hand who had the knack. And the playroom is well stocked with toys to distract all ages," the lawyer had assured them.

That had eased Briony's worry about more than just the kids being occupied. Clearly the woman had thought of all the possibilities, which was probably why Wendy had said she was utterly trustworthy.

The woman held her own copy of the document she'd written up and processed for Rick and Wendy. After confirming they were both dealing with the same version of the will, she leaned back in her chair opposite them as she tapped the cover of the document with her forefinger.

"At the time this was written, Rick was adamantly clear the children had never met his father, and he had never even laid eyes on them. To your knowledge, is that still true?"

"Yes," they said in unison, and both with the same certainty in their voice.

They exchanged glances, and Greg gave her that slightly crooked smile she knew so well. She looked away before the memory of the hours spent sleeping peacefully in his arms glowed in her eyes so brightly even he could see it.

"He never wanted them to meet," she said.

"Rick had nothing to do with him," Greg added, "and didn't want the children to have any contact at all. He made that even more clear in the letter he…left with me."

"He did write the letter?" she asked. "Wendy said he was going to, and I recommended he keep it updated."

Greg nodded as he got out the letter Rick had left him. He hesitated, tapping the edge of the envelope against his palm.

"I know it's very personal," Mrs. Carlson said gently. "But I do need to see it."

Greg took a deep breath, nodded and handed it over. "He said no way in hell was his father to get anywhere near the kids."

"That is what he said to me as well." She scanned the letter, her mouth tightening in a way that told Briony she'd meant what she'd said about being truly sorry. "And that was why they officially appointed you as legal and financial guardians to the children." Looking at Greg, she went on. "They said you and your family would be the perfect safety net—" she shifted her gaze to Briony "—and you would be more than capable of handling the financial end, to see that they had everything they needed. You're an accountant, they said?"

Briony nodded. "I have my own business, back in Owl Creek."

"All right." She folded her hands together and looked at them both. "Whenever someone other than a parent is tasked with guardianship, there has to be a formal appointment. I don't foresee any problem with that—Rick and Wendy made their wishes quite clear in both legal and personal documents. Now I know you must have many concerns, so let's go through them."

"We haven't even told the kids yet," Briony said, sounding as shaky as she felt just now.

"I can give you the name of a specialist here in town who deals in this type of thing. But I can say from my own experience, don't expect them to react the way you have. They won't feel the same emotions as you do, because they don't really get what death means. Or forever."

"My dad said just don't lie to them," Greg put in. "Or try to make it easier by saying stuff like they've gone to a better place. Just give them the truth and lots of time to process it."

The woman smiled. "Your father sounds like a very wise man."

Briony was looking at Greg in that moment and saw his smile at the compliment to his father. She felt an old, tired ache inside that she had never known such a thing. But Justin and Jane would. Greg would be like a father to them, and he'd obviously had a great example in his own.

She looked back to the lawyer, afraid she was going to start crying again. The woman was leaning back in her chair again, considering them both. "Are you two…involved?"

Briony blinked and drew back, uncertain what the woman meant. But apparently Greg wasn't.

"If you mean with each other…no." His mouth quirked. "Not that Rick and Wendy didn't keep trying to make that happen."

"I believe Wendy mentioned at some point her belief that you two were perfect for each other, just too stubborn to see it."

If the lawyer was waiting for a startled reaction, she didn't get it. Because Wendy had said that to their faces, and more than once. And Greg had always laughed it off, as had she. *After you saw Greg laughing. Because deep down, you wanted him not to?*

"Too bad," the attorney said, and that did get her a startled look, from both of them. "I just mean that if you were a couple, preferably married, it would make it that much harder for anyone, such as Rick's father, to contest your guardianship."

Briony's breath caught, and she saw Greg's eyes widen. "He could contest this?" he asked, nodding at the will. "Even when they were so clear he's to have nothing to do with the kids?"

"He is, as far as I know, their only blood relative. That gives him standing. Enough to start a legal action, if he's so inclined. Not saying he'd win, but…"

"I wonder if he even knows," Briony said quietly.

"Fortunately," Mrs. Carlson said, "I'm under no legal obligation to make sure he knows."

"Are we?" Greg asks.

"Do you know how to reach him?"

"No," he answered, then glanced at Briony. She shook her head.

"And you two are the only ones on their emergency contact list?"

"Yes."

"Then I'd say we just proceed. The Krafts made their wishes quite clear, and that should hold up in court if necessary. As far as the police are concerned, they've done their due diligence by notifying you both. But he'll likely hear about it in the news, unless he's a hermit."

"Hardly," Greg said, his tone quite sour. "A hermit can't bilk others out of their money."

She nodded, as if that opinion were no surprise to her. So Rick must have been open with her about his father.

"We'll deal with that if and when it arises. So, I think we're down to one more basic question," the attorney said. She looked from Briony to Greg and back, then addressed them both. "You're willing to take this on? Both of you? Raising two children not your own?"

Briony wondered if Greg had thought about it that way. She honestly hadn't, not about the long term, anyway. She'd been too focused on just getting through the weekend. Opening that door would have left her looking at a long, complicated vista, at a time when it was all she could do to put one foot in front of the other.

Both of you...

That was the one thing that floated to the surface amid the chaos in her mind at the moment. Rick and Wendy had chosen them. Not just her, not just Greg, but both of them together, to raise the children who were the most precious things in their lives. They'd chosen them both, and clearly had expected them to work together to get the job done. And it was Wendy, who had saved her so many times, asking...how could she ever say no? Even if she didn't know the first thing about how a normal kid should be brought up?

But Greg did. Even with his terrible mother, he knew better than she did, because he'd had his father. And siblings. And an aunt he'd told her was more like a mother to him than his own had ever been. It was more than she had ever had. Surely between the two of them they could do this?

And how are you going to feel about all the time together that's going to mean?

She didn't know. She just knew the most important thing right now was that Justin and Jane get her very best, such as it was. It might be hard on her—them—but nothing could match the tragedy those two little ones in the other room were going to have to face, and very soon.

She looked up to find Greg looking at her. As if he were waiting to see what she would say. Did he doubt her, doubt that she'd agree to what her best friend had wanted? Or did he simply doubt she was up to it? She couldn't blame him for that; he knew enough of her history to know she knew very little about parenting, good, bad or otherwise.

She turned her gaze back to the woman in the chair. "I

owe Wendy my life. I will spend it taking care of the children she loved."

Mrs. Carlson nodded, then looked at Greg, who shrugged. "Rick trusted me to do this. I will do it."

Briony felt a little shiver of sensation, because she knew deep down inside that vow, like any other he'd make, was golden. She wasn't alone in this.

She wasn't alone.

Chapter Thirteen

"There are funeral instructions in here."

Greg hit the brakes just before he pulled out onto the street and shot a glance at Briony. "There are?"

She nodded. "It's all…planned. Arrangements made, for back in Owl Creek." She looked up at him. "I had no idea. They were only in their thirties. Who does that in their thirties?"

Greg glanced over his shoulder at the back seat, where Jane appeared to finally be napping and Justin was looking out the side window, seemingly entranced by two people on horseback strolling through town.

"People who have them to think about," he said quietly.

Briony looked at the kids, took in a slow, audible breath and nodded. She slid the papers she'd been looking at back into the envelope and closed her eyes for a moment.

"We need to…get that task we talked about done," he began as he drove Wendy's car out onto the main road.

"The…telling?"

"Yes. I think we should go to the ranch. Dad'll be there to help. And there'll be distractions, like those horses over there."

"And the new arrival?"

He hadn't gotten that far, but nodded. "Yeah. Good idea."

She smiled, although it was a bit wobbly. "I'd like to meet that one myself."

"I'll introduce you," he said, trying to keep his tone light. He didn't want Jane waking up or Justin to start with his questions again. *Where is Mommy? Is Daddy there, too? I want them to come home.*

"So do I," he muttered to himself.

But it wasn't going to happen. He and Briony were on their own, in deep, deep water.

Eventually Justin recognized that they weren't going home. "Where we going, Unca Greg?"

"My house," he answered. "That all right with you?"

The boy perked up instantly. "The ranch?"

"Yep."

"Yay!"

It felt so odd, to hear such a cheerful sound from the boy. The boy whose world they were about to blow up. But he didn't have time to dwell on it because her brother's excited yelp had awakened Jane, who immediately started wailing again. To his surprise Justin tried to calm her, telling her eagerly they were going to see horses and cows soon, and to his even greater surprise it seemed to work. In the rearview mirror Greg could see her staring at her brother but couldn't tell if she was amused or simply puzzled by his excitement.

"Horsey?" Jane said.

"Yes," Justin crowed. "Horseys, an' cows, too."

Jane smiled.

Belatedly Greg realized he should probably let Dad know they were coming, with the kids. He still had his earpiece in and hadn't tried to connect his phone to the car's system, so waited until they were clear of town and pulled over to make the call. He explained quickly but a little vaguely, since Justin was paying attention.

"We'll get them through it, son. Hang in," Dad said. It centered him just to hear his father's steady, calm voice.

As they pulled in through the ranch gate, Justin was almost jumping around—as much as he could in the booster seat he'd recently graduated to—in excitement. Jane was giggling, either at what she was seeing out the window or how her big brother was acting.

When they got to the main house, Dad was outside, waving. And beside him stood a slim woman with short, dark blond hair barely touched with some gray at the temples, dressed in trim-fitting jeans and a blue sweater Greg knew matched her pretty eyes.

"As you can see," Dad said as they pulled to a halt and got out of the car, "I called in the varsity."

"You did indeed," Greg said, pulling his loving aunt into a warm hug before turning to Briony. "This is Jenny Colton, Mama Jen to us, and the only reason any of us are still sane."

"Amen to that," Dad said, heartfelt. Greg looked back at his father, but the man's gaze was fixed on Jen, and he thought how well they seemed to fit together. And not for the first time he had the thought that his father had married the wrong sister. And not just because he'd named his beloved mare after her favorite flower.

As usual, Jen charmed both children within seconds. As a nurse, she had the same knack with patients, inspiring an instinctive—and well-deserved—trust. Justin smiled at her shyly and took her outstretched hand, and Jane allowed her to pick her up and cuddle without complaint.

"While you grown-ups deal with the grown-up stuff, we'll go inside and get some lunch, okay?" she said cheerfully. Justin hesitated, looking back over his shoulder, not at Greg or Briony but at the corral across the way where a couple of horses were looking on curiously.

"We'll go look around in a few minutes, after you eat something," Greg said.

"'Kay," the boy said, looking reassured.

That left him and Briony with his father, who looked at them both consideringly. "Rough morning?" he asked sympathetically.

"You could say that," Greg answered, feeling suddenly weary.

"Where do things stand?" He explained about the funeral plans first, maybe to put off the big hit. "Smart guy," Dad said with a nod. "And responsible. So it all doesn't fall on someone else."

"Yeah." He glanced at Briony, who nodded. He looked back. "Dad?" He saw his father's gaze narrow, and knew he had his complete attention. "They left Briony and me full guardianship of the kids."

If he was shocked, it didn't show. "Not surprising." Dad smiled, and in that smile was all the love he'd always known from this man. "I'd pick you, too."

The protest he'd suppressed broke from him. "But I don't know anything about being a parent!"

"I would say," Briony interjected softly, looking at his father, not him, "you know a lot more than you think you do. You've had a great example."

For one of the very few times in his life, Greg saw his father blush. He could have hugged Briony just for that.

In the end, they took the kids into the barn to see the newborn. Even little Jane was intrigued, watching the colt peeking out from behind his mother as Briony held her up to see.

"Horsey?" she asked, as if puzzled by the newborn's size.

Greg picked up Justin so he could look into the stall, too. "He's little," Justin said.

"Yes. He was just born a couple of days ago," Greg said.

"Do you know what that means?" Briony asked.

"You mean borned like Jane was?" the boy asked.

"Yes," Briony answered. "Not there, and then all of a sudden there."

"I 'member."

Greg was thinking this might be a way into the painful subject, and wondering if that might have been Briony's plan, saying that in the way she had. "Do you remember how she wasn't there, before she was born?" he asked.

The boy looked puzzled. "Before Mommy and Daddy made her?"

Greg couldn't stop himself from glancing at Briony, who looked a bit disconcerted herself. "Yes," he finally answered. "That's what happens before you're born, and…after you die. You're just not there."

The boy's brow furrowed. "Daddy says everybody dies someday, when they're real old, or they get real sick."

So even in this, Rick had laid the groundwork. *Damn, I'm going to miss you, buddy.*

He tried to go on, but his throat was too tight. But Briony stepped in, saying gently, "Yes. Or if they have a really bad accident."

And there it was.

"Oh." The brow furrowed deeper. "Jimmy did that. He lived on our street. He tried to climb on the roof. He fell. He went away and never came back."

"That's what it means to die," Briony said gently. "The never-come-back part."

Greg took in a deep breath, then made the dive. "Your mom and dad had an accident, Justin. A really bad one. That's why they're not here."

"You mean…like Jimmy?"

"Yes, only in their car. It crashed."

"Where are they?"

Don't lie to them. Or try to make it easier by saying stuff like they've gone to a better place. Just give them the truth and lots of time to process it.

His father's wise words echoed in his mind, and he braced himself. "They're dead, Justin. They died in that crash." It was the hardest thing he'd ever had to say, beyond even confirming to his younger siblings that their mother had abandoned them.

"Mommy and Daddy?"

"Yes. I'm so sorry, Justin," Briony said, hugging Jane as she held her, even though what they were talking of clearly didn't register with the fourteen-month-old.

"Oh." The furrowed brow lasted a few moments longer. Then the boy looked back at the newborn colt. "Can I pet him?"

In that disconcerting moment Greg was very glad Tanya Carlson had said what she had, that the children wouldn't feel the same emotions because they don't really understand what death means. Or forever.

But they would learn. Sadly, they would learn.

Chapter Fourteen

"I find singing generally helps calm them down if they get restless during diaper changes," Jen Colton said as she briskly went about that very task.

Briony gave the woman Greg had introduced so lovingly a wry smile. "Not my singing, trust me. I love music, but got the vocal cords of a crow, I'm afraid."

Jen laughed. "Well, make Greg do it then. He has a marvelous voice."

She blinked. "He does?"

The older woman nodded. "We used to think he'd end up a country music star."

Briony knew she was staring but couldn't help it. She'd had no idea the man could sing.

Jen went on cheerfully. "But he had no interest in that whatsoever. He wanted to stay here on the ranch. This is the life he loves."

After learning what had happened with her husband and her own sister, the long affair that had resulted in two children, and the fact that it had taken Robert Colton's death to bring it all to light, Briony thought it more than a little amazing that Jen held it together so well.

Better than I would.

"I…gathered that," she said after a moment. "And he and his father seem very close."

"Buck?" The woman's eyes lit up, and just as she had when she'd first seen them together, Briony suspected Greg wasn't the only family member close to his father. "Yes. He's close to all his children. They love and respect him, because he gives them the same."

Unlike your husband?

She was finding herself unusually fascinated with the dynamics of this big family. She told herself it was because she had no family at all, so naturally she was curious about one this big and complicated.

When Jen was finished with Jane, they put her down for her 3:00 p.m. nap—Wendy had made sure Mrs. Matson had the schedule and she passed it along—in the portable Pack 'n Play they'd found in Wendy's trunk and Greg had quickly figured out. Then they went back into the big living area of the main house, with its open beams and two-story ceiling Briony found uplifting somehow. She remembered Greg mentioning once that his mother hated living in it because it had once been an actual barn, but Briony found it quite charming.

The pool out back was nice, but she found the surrounding garden even more beautiful, and remembered what Greg had told her, that it was all his father's doing. That he liked to try different plants and had a knack for getting things that normally wouldn't thrive here to do just that.

Greg and his father were in an apparently deep conversation, while Justin was playing with what appeared to be a set of toy horses and cowboys on the floor over beside the front window, out of earshot. She thought again of how Rick and Wendy had limited screen time, wondered if the boy was used to toys that required his own imagination in these days of video games seeming to rule playtime. No wonder he seemed so easily engrossed.

"—as Jen," Greg's dad was saying. "I'd trust her judgment more than anyone's on this."

"Careful," Jen said with a smile as they walked over to the pair, "it'll go to my head."

"Not a chance," Buck said, with a warmth that was unmistakable.

Briony sneaked a look at Greg as he watched this exchange, and by his expression she wondered if he'd had the same thought she'd had about these two. If so, it must seem odd, thinking that about his father and his mother's sister. Not that his mother had any place in this, after what she'd done.

Again, it struck Briony that it was strange that she, who once had wanted a mother, any mother, more than anything in the world, would think such a thing. But even though she'd only met him a few hours ago, she'd apparently already decided Buck Colton deserved much better. As did Greg.

"—funeral."

She snapped out of her reflections and tuned back into the conversation. "The funeral?"

Jen gave her an understanding smile. "As their guardians, it will be up to you if they go, of course."

"Not an easy decision, when they're so young," Greg's dad said.

The kids, she realized. They were talking about the kids going to the funeral. Or not going.

She looked at Greg. "Do you think they should?"

He let out an audible breath. "I don't know. I keep going back and forth between thinking it would be horrible for them now, to thinking it would be horrible for them later if they don't."

"You mean when they're old enough to understand, will they be sorry if they weren't there?" Briony asked.

He nodded. "Even if they don't remember much, will knowing they were there be important?" He gave a slight shake of his head, as if to try to clear it. Then he looked at his father and aunt. "Dad? Mama Jen? What do you think?"

Briony noticed that his father deferred easily to the woman beside him. It was easy to see why; the woman radiated compassion. And as a nurse, she'd had a lot more experience than they had dealing with this kind of thing.

"I think Justin at least should be given a choice. Maybe explain to him this is how we say goodbye, and that it's painful and people will probably be very sad and even cry, but it's also how we show how much we loved them. But he could do his own kind of remembrance at home, if he thinks it would be too scary."

"Reality bites at four," Greg muttered.

"Yes," his father said. "But better that than him always waiting for them to come back."

"Yes," Jen agreed. "And be prepared, they'll be asking you for a long time yet when their parents will come home. Don't sugarcoat it, or they'll misinterpret it or put their own spin on it that could be worse for them than the simple truth."

Briony stared at the three people standing there, marveling at what she was seeing. Simple, solid, unwavering support. An odd emotion flooded her, a sort of longing she hadn't felt since childhood, when she had wondered what it must be like to have a real family.

"Briony? You okay?" Greg sounded worried.

"I'm okay. I just…" She couldn't find the words, so simply said, "I admire you all."

Both his father and aunt looked a little startled but smiled. "Here's an idea," Buck said. "Why don't we come to the funeral, and we'll wrangle the kids? Jen, you can handle Jane, and I'll take Justin, and if they get upset or too restless, we can take them away from it all, so they don't disturb anything or go ballistic on you."

Greg's aunt gave his father an absolutely beautiful smile. "That's perfect, Buck. That way they'll have been there, but not traumatized."

To Briony it seemed the perfect solution. And Greg looked so relieved she was certain he felt the same way.

That, however, did not make explaining it as best they could to the kids any easier. Jane's requests for Mama were almost constant now, and Justin, as Jen had warned, asked more than once when his parents were coming back. The stress of each time having to try to explain the concept of never to a four-year-old was taking a toll already.

The only thing that seemed to distract the kids was visiting the barn and seeing the new colt, so they spent a lot of the afternoon there.

"I was thinking," Greg's dad said now, as they relaxed a little as the children watched the newborn, "we'd name him Wick."

Greg gave his father a quizzical look. "You mean like the movie guy?"

"No," he answered.

Briony sucked in a breath as it hit her, and her eyes widened as she stared at this rather incredible man Greg was lucky enough to have as a father. "Wendy and Rick," she whispered. "Wick."

Buck Colton gave her a smile so warm she didn't know

how to feel. And again, that longing for something that could never be, to have grown up with a father like this in her life, flooded her.

"Exactly," he said approvingly.

She looked at Greg, who was smiling now, too. "What I said about him? I understated it."

"Yes," Greg agreed, carefully not looking at the man, "you did. He's even more amazing than you said."

"Okay, it's getting thick in here," his father said, sounding embarrassed.

"Hush," Jen said. "They're right, after all."

For a moment Buck Colton closed his eyes, as if he were afraid of what they'd see there. Or perhaps he was tearing up and didn't want them to notice. Jen reached out, grasped his arm and squeezed. He opened his eyes and looked at her, and for an instant Briony saw the kind of longing she'd once felt for the man's son, before she'd intentionally shut it down, knowing the feeling wasn't returned. But glancing at Jen's face told her that was not the case here. And she wondered what was keeping them apart, other than the chaos that had descended on the family this year.

Buck and Jen were true to their word about helping the children through the funeral a couple of days later, not to mention helping them in between as well. Briony thanked them profusely after the ceremony, knowing none of them would have gotten through it without them. She'd been a little surprised at the number of people who had turned out. There were some who had worked with Rick or Wendy, and even several of the Coltons she'd never met who had shown up simply because Rick had been Greg's best friend. Another example of the kind of family tie she'd never known.

It had been wrenching, heartbreaking, and she'd nearly lost it completely when Greg got up and spoke so clearly from the heart about what his best friend had meant to him. She'd had to fight her own nearly overwhelming shyness to stammer through her declaration of her love for her oldest and best friend, the person who had saved her as a child and been her rock ever since.

Everything after they'd left the small cemetery was a blur to her. And it broke her heart all over again when little Justin ran into the house looking for his parents, even after having just come from their funeral. This was going to be a long, hard haul, and she truly didn't know if she was up to it. But she had to be, for Wendy. She stumbled through the motions, grateful all that was left to do was get the kids down for their afternoon nap, which even Justin, although at the stage of saying he didn't need naps anymore, seemed willing to do today.

When they were settled, Greg came out of Justin's room and dropped down on the couch beside her, although not so close it made her nervous in that way only he did.

"I'm glad that's over," he said with a weary shake of his head.

"Me, too. You spoke beautifully, by the way."

"So did you."

She gave a short laugh. "Hardly. I could barely get five words in a row out."

"It only showed how much you loved Wendy." She managed a smile at that, although it was none too steady. And she was utterly unprepared for his next words. "So, when should we make the move?"

She stifled a yawn before saying, "What?"

"The kids, out to the ranch."

Briony gaped at him. "What?" she repeated, wide-awake now.

"I'll have to rearrange things at my place, but they can

stay in the big house until that's done. Dad'll help, and Mama Jen said she would, too. And—"

"Just hold on a minute," Briony interrupted. "What are you talking about?"

He looked puzzled. "The kids. Dad already said it's okay, and a good idea, and you've said you can work from anywhere, so we just need to—"

"You need," Briony said rather fiercely, "to just be quiet for a minute and explain where you got the idea they were going anywhere."

She realized the contradiction after she'd said it but didn't care. He blinked but didn't point out the impossibility of what she'd asked.

"You saw them there," he said, sounding puzzled. "It's obviously the best place for them to be."

"The best place for them to be is here, in their home. Where everything's familiar. They've had enough upheaval in their lives already."

She was a little surprised at herself and how firmly she'd said those words. But she felt strongly about where the kids belonged, and she had to admit it irked her that he'd apparently made this decision without even asking her.

"But at the ranch, they'd have lots of people around, and the animals as distraction and—"

"No."

She said it so flatly he stopped dead. Then, slowly, almost cautiously, he said, "Wouldn't it be harder for them where they're used to…their parents always being there?"

She had to admit, she hadn't thought of it quite like that. But she wasn't going to shirk her part of seeing to her best friend's children by letting Greg handle everything. Rick and Wendy had chosen and trusted them—both of them—and she took that very, very seriously. She would be in this 24/7, just as Wendy had been.

And there was no way she could live on that ranch, entertaining though it might be. Not among all those strangers, even if they did seem kind and well-intentioned. She just couldn't do it.

"If they stayed on the ranch, it would be like they'd not only lost their parents but been sent away from their home."

Greg looked thoughtful and then, surprisingly, echoed her own earlier thought. "I didn't think about it like that." He grimaced. "Guess I need to remember how confused Lizzy was. She was only three when the mother left."

She didn't miss the intonation. *The* mother. So in truth, he did have a more similar experience, that of having then losing, rather than her own of never really having at all. And she was impressed that he'd thought that way. Rick had always said he'd never been a hardnose.

He had, however, made a heck of an assumption about this. And that was something she had to conquer her shyness to confront. It was that important. Still, it took her a moment to be able to say what she needed to say evenly.

"You might also want to remember that Rick and Wendy left the kids to both of us, before you start making decisions without even consulting me."

He looked startled. "But... I saw you, watching them, when they were having so much fun with the animals, especially Wick—" she saw the flash of combined pain and approval at his father's choice of a name cross his face "—and you were smiling at them, so I guess I assumed you'd want them to have that all the time."

"I was glad they were happy, for the moment. But that doesn't change their reality. And that's the biggest change there could be for them. I don't want them to have to deal with leaving the place where they were happy at the same time."

"So...you're going to move into the house with them?"

She hadn't stated it so concretely even in her mind, but she nodded. "I couldn't live there, on your ranch, anyway."

He blinked. "Why not? You said you could work from anywhere, and there's plenty of room in the big house, if you don't want to stay in mine."

"I couldn't. I won't."

"Speaking of making decisions without consulting the other party…" he muttered.

He did have a point. Was he going to argue with her? Her mind began to race. She wasn't sure she could stand up to a determined Greg Colton, and she couldn't deny there would be advantages for the kids to be at the ranch, but she could not be, and she also knew she was right about too much change at once. Knew firsthand.

And then there was the simple fact that never had the differences between them been so starkly apparent. And she was very glad she'd hidden her response to him, written it off as foolish wishful thinking. Why Rick and Wendy had ever thought they could be together was beyond her. They couldn't even agree on what to do.

But now they had to.

Chapter Fifteen

Greg rammed a hand through his hair, curling his fingers to give it a tug, hoping the small protest from his scalp would be enough to help him focus on what would be best, not what he wanted. He'd been taken aback by Briony's reaction, and her resistance to what seemed to him the obvious solution. It was a good life, ranch life, especially for kids. It had kept him and his siblings going after their mother's desertion.

He was also surprised by Briony's almost fierce stance. Ever since he'd known her, Briony Adams had been a shy, retiring sort who went along to get along. Yet now here she was, standing her ground, glaring at him.

"Look, I can't commute from here to the ranch every day, not and get done what needs to be done."

"You wouldn't be with the kids all day anyway, even if they were there," she pointed out. "You have work to do."

"But I'd be there every morning, and I could check on them during the day, between chores. And you could be there—"

"I couldn't." He thought he saw her tense up, as if she were suppressing a shiver. "I couldn't live there, with all those strangers."

"But they wouldn't be strangers, they'd be my family—"

"They would be strangers to me."

Was this part of that innate shyness Wendy had told him about, or something more? Was she afraid of something about the ranch? Or was the thought of being among people she didn't know that terrifying?

Summoning up the patience he'd learned dealing with recalcitrant or frightened animals, he managed to keep the bite to a minimum.

"So you're going to move in and be here 24/7, while I… what, visit now and then? They chose me as a legal guardian, not a surrogate uncle."

"They chose me, too. And I know in my heart Wendy would want them to stay here, in this home they provided for them."

"How can you be so certain?" he asked.

"I just know how I felt every time I got comfortable in a foster home, only to be pulled out and dumped somewhere else to start all over again."

Greg felt a sudden chill. He'd been so focused on the kids, on Rick and Wendy's death—and the stunning idea that it hadn't been an accident—that he hadn't even thought about the fact that she knew a lot more about being orphaned than he did.

He sagged back on the couch, rubbing at his tired eyes. Life had gotten too damned complicated. Bad enough they'd uncovered an apparent serial killer, that some weird cult that had sprung up was connected—hell, his mother was now connected to that cult—but now Rick and Wendy were dead. Probably murdered by a member of that same cult, or someone hired by them, if what Chase's Sloan, the computer genius, had discovered was true. And because of that, overnight here he was, in essence a father to two very young children.

He'd never thought of his life as carefree, not with his

mother abandoning them all those years ago. He'd always felt like he had to step up and help his younger siblings, on top of the undeniably hard work it took to keep the ranch going, considering what they were trying to produce on a fairly small ranch, compared to the bigger commercial concerns.

But suddenly it seemed that way, when compared to hers. Because he'd ever and always had that rock, his father. And his home. Even with all the work, the ranch had been home. Had been a bastion of stability amid the chaos of the mother's desertion. Had been the center, the core of his life. Even when he'd moved out of the big house, it hadn't been far, only the short distance to the guest house. Briony had never had any of that; she'd been forever adrift by comparison. And now the only stable thing in that life, her dearest friend, was gone.

Like this house was for Justin and Jane.

"Please, Greg." She whispered it, and it sent a little frisson of…something through him. "For now, at least. Later, when they've had time to…adjust, maybe it'll be different."

His eyes snapped open, and he met her gaze. Saw the pleading in it, atop all the hurt and sadness. And suddenly denying her, arguing with her, felt a little too much like kicking one of those frightened animals he'd thought of.

"All right," he finally said. "I won't fight you on this… now. But later, we'll reassess."

She looked so relieved he felt his own tension ease a bit. He tried to get his weary brain to think logistically.

"I'll be here as much as I can. We could trade off on weekends, so the kids always have at least one of us and the other can relax a little."

"Relax? Is that what you do on the weekends at the ranch?"

He drew back slightly, staring at her. "Not exactly, no."

He caught the tiniest twitch at one corner of her mouth—funny, he'd never noticed the perfect shape of it before, natural, real—and realized she was teasing him. That she knew perfectly well relaxing and ranching rarely went together. He felt an odd sense of…something, that she had felt confident enough to do that. Or maybe it was simply because she'd won.

He'd clearly made the right decision for her, agreeing the kids could stay here.

He just wasn't sure it was right for the kids.

But maybe she was correct about how this should all happen. If she moved in here, worked from here, she'd always be easily accessible. She'd be there if the kids needed something, or if something happened. And she was taking this on without hesitation, for Wendy.

He drew in a deep breath. Then, with a slow nod, he said, "Rick and Wendy chose both of us, and I won't break that trust. I meant what I said, that I'll be here as much as I can. And if I'm not here and you need a break or help, you call me and I'll work it out."

She nodded. "We need to do this together. Like they wanted."

Her breath caught again, he guessed on the past tense, since he was having the same problem even in his thoughts. "We will," he agreed. "It'll take some time to work it all out, but we'll do it."

"With the least possible upset for the kids. Their lives have already been shattered."

"So we'll pick up the pieces and put it all back together as best we can. It won't be the same for them, ever, but it'll be a lot better than what you and Wendy had."

She gave him a startled look then, as if she hadn't expected the comparison. *Well, it took you long enough to get there, no wonder...*

"I know I'm...odd. About not wanting to be around strangers, but—"

"I get it. At least, I think I do. I just hadn't put it in context before, how you feel now with how you grew up." And he'd never wondered before if she'd been born shy, or if it had been hammered into her by her life and circumstances.

"Thank you, for understanding."

He studied her for a long, silent moment. Almost decided not to say what he wanted to, but then realized that with the kids and everything else, he might never get the chance.

"How long do they get to win, Briony?"

She frowned. "What? Who?"

"All those people who failed you."

The frown deepened. "What do you mean?"

"Don't you ever wonder if you'd be different, about new people I mean, if you'd had a more...normal childhood?"

She drew back sharply. "Like yours, you mean?"

He gave a half shrug. "Sure, my mother was a bi—was what she was, but Dad was solid, strong and always there for all of us. He taught us not just about life and work and values, but about being true to ourselves. And about not letting his poor choice of a wife determine who we became."

She was staring at him now. He didn't usually vomit things out like this, but it seemed important at this moment, so he kept going.

"If you'd had someone like him in your life, maybe everything would have been different. Maybe you'd even be different. But our job now is to make sure Justin and Jane have that. So you may be right about keeping them here, but I'm right about what else they need."

"I didn't argue with that," she pointed out.

"Just making sure we're on the same page."

"We are. If that page reads 'the kids come first.'"

He studied her for a moment, and it hit him what kind of nerve it had taken for normally quiet, shy, withdrawn Briony to stand up to him as she had over this. And that told him all he needed to know. That she meant exactly what she'd said.

The kids come first.

Chapter Sixteen

Briony could see that Greg was tired. Yet he still showed up at the house every day, as he'd promised. Sometimes it was in the evenings, when she could see how worn out he was after a hard day's work on the ranch. Sometimes, when he had a break, he'd show up earlier. Often, he brought food with him, sometimes a toy for Justin or some bright, color-ful thing to intrigue Jane. And once, in a gesture that nearly brought tears to eyes she'd thought cried out, he'd brought her a bouquet of flowers. Chrysanthemums, she thought. Not that it mattered, just that he'd done it made her feel… something. Or a lot of somethings.

She herself felt exhausted after only a week. She'd known Wendy worked hard taking care of the kids, even though she joked about it and called it a joyous kind of work. But trying to keep up with the kids and her own work seemed impossible. And this morning as she dragged herself out of the fold-out bed in the den—there was no way she was sleeping in the only other open bed in the house, Rick and Wendy's—she began to wonder if she'd made a huge mis-take in insisting they stay here. Began to see the advantage of having other people around as distraction, even if it made her uncomfortable.

Some cold water splashed on her face helped to wake

her up, then she headed for a quick shower. She got out and dried off just in time to hear Jane's first wail of the day. As she threw on her robe—she'd made a trip to her condo and packed a couple of bags the second day, while Greg handled the kids—she braced herself for Justin waking up next. With her luck he'd be full of more questions about his parents. Each time it scraped that already raw and bleeding spot in her heart, and she had to remind herself that was because she knew what death—and never—really meant. The children didn't.

And then there was that hammer blow that had made what she'd thought was the absolute worst even more horrible. That it hadn't been an accident at all.

Her phone chimed an incoming text notification. She rubbed at her eyes before picking it up and trying to read.

Greg. And it was from ten minutes ago, when she'd been in the shower.

On my way with reinforcements.

Reinforcements?

She was too tired to figure out what he meant, and too busy dealing with Jane, who'd decided that it was time she did more than just toddle two steps and then hit the floor for a fast crawl. The girl was trying to walk across the entire room and falling too often for Briony's comfort. Then there was Justin, who insisted on dressing himself and emerged wearing an inside-out T-shirt and shorts. In Idaho. In October.

She'd gotten him changed into long pants at least, and to the table for breakfast. Then she picked up Jane and settled her into the high chair. The first thing the child did was look around for something, anything probably, to drop on the floor. She seemed to have a fascination with watching things fall.

A memory struck, and she found herself smiling despite it all as the image of Jane doing just that, dropping a grape from her seat in the high chair and watching it fall to the floor and bounce.

"Okay, Newton," Greg had said to the child as he'd bent to pick up the small fruit. "Want to drop two now, to see that they both hit at the same time?"

Briony had laughed, the first time in what seemed like forever. "Don't give her any ideas."

She was still smiling at the recollection when there was a knock on the front door. Greg was good about that. Even though he had a key as she did, since she was living here full-time, he always knocked rather than just come barging in.

"Daddy?" Justin yelped as his head turned toward the sound.

"No, Justin," she said wearily. "Daddy's not coming back."

She went to the door and pulled it open to Greg. And his reinforcements. She gaped at the sight of Greg's dad and his aunt, who were holding bags of who knew what, and big smiles.

"I…hello. What…?"

She could tell she sounded as befuddled as she felt as she backed aside to let them in.

"The cavalry is here," Jen said. "And we're armed. Toys, snacks and a picnic lunch for later."

She was sure she was gaping now.

"Enough to keep them out of your hair for a few hours, at least," Greg's father said, with an understanding grin.

"Because you both need some rest," Jen said firmly.

Jane, who had started babbling a string of sounds the moment she saw Jen, was now holding her arms out, asking to be lifted out of the chair.

"I'd better get her," Briony said, "or she'll start drumming on that tray and you won't be able to hear yourself think."

"I'll get her," Jen said. Within a moment she had the tiny girl cooing in her arms.

Greg smiled as he shook his head in wonder. "She's a miracle worker."

"You'll get no argument from me," his father said, before bending to greet Justin, who was looking up at him with the utmost interest.

Briony and Greg exchanged a glance, and she saw that he was thinking what she was, that there was more than just friendship here. Or at least, there could be, if they'd allow it.

"We'll be off. Won't be back until dinnertime," Buck said.

"Which we'll bring with us," Jen added.

"So you two," Buck added almost sternly, "get to bed."

He seemed to realize instantly what that sounded like, and his eyes widened. Jen saved him from further embarrassment by laughing charmingly and saying, "How you choose to follow that order is up to you. Bye!"

And then they were gone, the four of them, leaving her with Greg in a suddenly quiet house. She stole a glance at him. He was looking at the door his father and aunt had just left through, looking bemused.

"They're...quite something," she said, desperate to fend off any jokes about what his father had said.

"Yes. Both of them."

"Apart and...together."

He looked at her then, one corner of his mouth quirking. "Yes. And I kind of like them together."

She smiled at that. "Do you think they...would ever...?"

"I can only hope," he said.

"And your brothers, and sister?"

"Pretty sure they feel the same."

She lowered her gaze. "It must be…interesting. All that family, I mean."

"That's one word for it," he said dryly. Then, in an entirely different tone, he added quietly, "I wish it was something you'd known."

She didn't know what to say, knew he'd meant it kindly, but it was a useless wish. As she knew too well, having wished it for so long herself. She started to turn away, to go back and clean up the breakfast mess. Greg turned at the same moment and they collided. She tensed, intending to immediately pull away, but couldn't seem to move. Memories of the hours on the couch, with his arms surrounding her, holding her safely, flooded her with remembered warmth.

In the moment she wished she had the nerve to hug him, he put his arms around her.

"We're going to make it through this. We have to, for the kids."

She was savoring the feel of this and was a little late to speak. "I know," she finally got out.

…you two get to bed.

She was glad he couldn't see her face. Embarrassed that the reason he couldn't was that it was buried against his chest. Yet he didn't pull away, didn't end the embrace.

And she didn't know how to feel about that.

Or about the fact that, when he finally let go and told her to go get some sleep, she wanted to ask him to take his father's words literally.

Chapter Seventeen

Greg sat for a moment, his head resting on the steering wheel of his truck. It was gut-wrenching, every time. Justin had clearly bonded with him, judging not by the toddler's— was he still a toddler at four and growing fast?—glee whenever he arrived, but by his heartbroken sobs whenever Greg had to leave. But leave he had to, to go back to his other life. The only life he'd ever wanted. Or so he'd thought.

When they were all together under Rick and Wendy's roof, it felt…oddly right. He and Briony had figured out some things, how to deal with the kids' fussing and occasional tantrums, how to distract them, even how to make them laugh. Justin, for instance, was a builder in progress. Or maybe an artist of sorts, given the last thing he'd constructed with his snap-together blocks looked pretty much like a castle. And he'd swear Jane was a budding physicist at least, as she continued to drop things from her high chair and watch intently as they fell to the floor. She seemed to be more intrigued by the things that bounced, which unfortunately included her plastic sippy cup, resulting in more messes to clean up than he could remember just now.

But it was still always tension-inducing, for him at least. He was much more comfortable when he took them back to the ranch, which he was going to do tomorrow because

Briony had a big account she had to finish some work for, and she couldn't afford to be late. He'd wondered if that was why Jane seemed more drawn to Briony, if it wasn't just a female to female thing, but brains that worked alike, with numbers and such.

That thought recurred to him early the next morning, as he was pushing hard to finish the absolutely necessary work so he could get over to the house and pick up the kids. And on impulse he gathered up a few things and stuffed them into his jacket pocket before he left.

He got there in the middle of breakfast, which, to his surprise, Briony had expanded enough to feed him, too. Since it was pancakes, who was he to say no? Justin chattered away delightedly from the moment he arrived, only once veering into the questions that had no answers he could understand.

When they'd finished, he helped Briony clean up while Justin ran to his room to get dressed, but when she went to lift Jane out of the high chair he asked her to wait a minute. He went over to where his jacket hung on the rack by the front door and reached into the big pocket. Then he came back and pulled out one of the chairs so he could sit eye to eye with the girl who had officially, Briony had said, earned the name of toddler now, since she'd gotten to where she could walk several feet before plopping. And Greg had been quick to realize that their reaction to those plops determined whether the landing resulted in tears or laughter.

But now she was looking at him curiously. "Geg," she said, and he rolled his eyes at her. She giggled.

He put the things he'd gathered this morning on the tray. The child's eyes widened as she looked at all the round objects.

"Okay, Newton, go for it," he said.

When Jane looked uncertain, he reached out and took the one that would have the most extreme reaction, the Ping-Pong ball. He held it out to the side, where she always did when she dropped things. He made sure she was looking, leaning to the side, before he dropped it.

She squealed with obvious delight as the ball bounced nearly halfway back up, then shorter bounces as it headed away. He went for the almost perfectly round stone next, which merely hit, bounced once, and stayed. Jane looked perplexed then. Then the golf ball, which bounced maybe half as high as the Ping-Pong ball had and rolled only half as far.

Jane was ahead of him then, grabbing the wooden ball he'd made himself this morning, dropping it and watching intently. It bounced a couple of times, then rolled, but crookedly. Then she was at the marble, which bounced twice, then rolled the farthest of all.

The little girl squealed again, her hands clapping together, then stretching out, reaching toward the floor.

Greg gathered all the round things and put them back on the tray. Immediately Jane began dropping them, one by one, watching them until they stopped moving before she went to the next.

"Wow, she has patience. I figured she'd want to drop them all at once," he said, speaking obviously to Briony but still looking at Jane.

When he got no answer, although Briony was standing right there, he glanced at her. She was staring at him, the oddest expression on her face.

"What?"

"You thought of this?"

"Yeah, this morning. I just grabbed whatever I could think of—well, except the wooden one, I had to sand that down from a wood chunk—because I thought she might think it was fun."

"You were obviously right. She's having more fun with those than any of her fancy toys."

He smiled at that, feeling inordinately pleased. "Small victory, but right now I'll take 'em where I can get 'em."

She looked as if she was about to say something, seemed to think better of it, and said only, "Thank you for taking them today, so I can finish this job."

"You're the one doing most of the grunt work."

"At my own insistence," she said, sounding as if she almost regretted it. "But you're the one having to drive here and back all the time."

He shrugged. "No choice. My work can't be done from anywhere else."

Again, she looked as if she was about to say something, and again stopped. But by then Justin had come back, dressed, Greg noticed, in his little jeans with his shirt buttoned up, albeit off by one button. He'd pulled on lace-up boots, although the laces were untied and flopping on the floor. The boy stuck one foot out, clearly expecting Greg to tie it for him. Glad the boy hadn't stepped on one and taken a header, he quickly tied both laces snugly. The shirt he let be, figuring it wouldn't matter at the ranch.

Even as he thought it Briony bent down to fix the shirt.

"You started one button too low," she said as the boy watched her.

"Oh," Justin said.

He looked up at Greg, who shrugged yet again and said, "I would have mentioned it if we were going somewhere where anybody cared."

Briony froze for an instant, then finished the rebuttoning. When she straightened up her face was flushed.

"I suppose you think I'm being too fussy. Too controlling."

He shrugged once more, this time only one shoulder. "I figure it's just your organizing brain."

"It doesn't...bother you?"

"Why would it?"

"It does some."

She said it in a way that had him thinking it wasn't just some, but many. "Maybe it doesn't bother me because I know how you grew up. It's no wonder you wanted to control what little you could."

She stared at him. "Did Wendy tell you that?"

He looked at her, puzzled. "No. I just guessed. If I'm way off, I—"

"No. You're exactly on. It was the one thing I could control, the only thing. Where and how the few things I owned were placed."

"Makes sense."

"But hard to live with for some people. The whole 'a place for everything and everything in its place' thing."

He grinned at her suddenly, and for some reason her eyes widened. "I should turn you loose on our tack room. It could use some organizing."

It was a moment before she said, "I'd be happy to, except I don't know anything about...tack? That's the horse stuff, right? Saddles, bridles?"

"I'll bet you could learn it in ten minutes, and have it organized in an hour. Rick told me you did the garage." Since she seemed a bit sensitive about it, he made sure his tone was light, teasing. "He told me you interviewed him for twenty minutes, then whipped it into shape perfectly."

She actually blushed. "I needed to know what he used most, and what things were usually used together. Then I went from there."

"See, that's the kind of thing we need. The hands tend to just toss things when they're done and tear the place up when they can't find something."

"Are we goin'?" Justin's rather plaintive question cut off the discussion.

"Right now, buddy," Greg said, picking the boy up easily.

A small scramble ensued as they gathered the things needed for even a short trip with Jane, then the child herself. And soon he was pulling out of the driveway, once more in Wendy's car with the car seats. They'd agreed that's what they'd do for now, whoever had the kids used her car, at least until they figured out what they were going to do long-term.

Long-term.

As in from now on.

He still hadn't quite wrapped his mind around that.

Chapter Eighteen

Once they were gone, the house seemed almost preternaturally quiet. Briony had thought she'd relish a pause in the chaos, but instead she stood in the living room as if at sea. She knew she needed to work, but for a moment all she could do was stand there. Stand there and think about that moment that had momentarily taken her breath away.

That grin of Greg's had lost none of its impact since the first time she'd seen it, when Rick and Wendy had decided it was time their best friends met. They'd prepared a picnic at the lake for them all.

Rick had cracked a joke about something; she'd been too far away to hear what. But that grin had seared across the space between them like some heat-seeking—and dispensing—missile, aimed at her. Their gazes had locked, just for a moment, but that had been enough. She'd stood there, immobilized, long enough that Wendy had noticed.

"Beyond cute, isn't he? And, I happen to know, he's quite unattached at the moment."

It had taken a moment for her friend's point to register. When it had, she'd stared at Wendy in shock. There was no way she would even think about trying to get involved with a guy as good-looking as this one was.

"Hey, come on," Wendy had teased, "you know you have

a weakness for the studly cowboy type, and that's Greg Colton down to the bone."

"Colton? Is he one of…" That would make it even more ridiculous.

"Those Coltons, that own half or more of Owl Creek? Yes, he's related to them, but he's one of the ranching Coltons, so don't hold it against him."

Wendy had seized upon the immediate response Briony hadn't been able to hide, and thus began the efforts to get her and Greg together. Efforts had been ineffective and sometimes even messy, because Briony froze up every time she was near the guy. Even after Rick and Wendy were married, she was still a wreck around Greg, because she really did think him the most appealing man she'd met in a long time. She had developed a bit of a crush on him starting that day at the picnic, but the combination of his looks and the fact that he was a Colton put him way out of her league, and she knew it.

She'd buried her reaction deep and hoped Greg had never noticed. She thought she'd been successful, because more than once she'd heard him refer to her as "Wendy's best friend" to others. And that's what she was to him. Not even really his friend, just a friend of his best friend's wife.

And that was for the best. She had no doubt about that, no matter that occasionally a silly, useless longing would rise in her, needing to be quashed all over again.

That they were now inextricably tied together, for the foreseeable future and beyond, didn't change that. They would do what had to be done for the kids, and they were working hard at getting along to do it, but it would never be any more than that.

No matter that sometimes she wished it could be different.

GREG THOUGHT IT had been a good day overall. Justin seemed to have had a great time, and Jane was still fascinated by Wick. They'd spent a lot of time with the colt, and Greg thought when the kids were a little older, he'd explain about his name. Although he suspected Justin would understand even now.

He got a text from Briony earlier than he'd expected, saying she was done and he could bring them home whenever he wanted. He texted back that they were making cookies with Mama Jen at the moment, and they'd be on their way when those were done. And although she didn't ask, he sent another message saying they'd bring some with them, because those snickerdoodles were unmatched in human history.

She sent back a GIF of a redheaded girl gobbling up a cookie, which made him literally laugh out loud. He sent back the appropriate laughing emoji, and was still smiling as he shoved his phone back into his pocket.

"That's something I haven't heard in a while," Jen had said, sounding pleased as she watched Justin carefully spoon cookie dough onto a baking sheet, while she held Jane up to watch. "And I've missed it."

He realized she was right, it seemed like forever since he'd really, genuinely laughed. He pulled the phone back out and showed her the cookie girl.

She smiled. "She seems really nice, Greg."

"She is."

"You said she and Wendy grew up in similar circumstances?"

He nodded. "They managed to stay friends, even getting bounced around in the foster system."

"That took some genuine effort."

"Yes." He grimaced. "I just wish sometimes she wasn't so…" He tried again. "She takes shy to new levels."

"Yet she stood her ground about keeping these two in their home."

"Yeah. Surprised the he—" he glanced at the kids, just as Jane reached down and stuck her finger in one of the globs of cookie dough on the sheet "—heck out of me."

"Sounds like she can be strong, but has maybe had to hide it?"

He'd never thought about it in quite that way. He turned and hugged her, making Jane giggle.

"You know, I never would have made it without you, Mama Jen."

"I love you. All of you. I feel like you're all mine."

"Trust me, we know. What you did for us, on top of raising your own family…you're amazing. We all wished, repeatedly, that *you* had been our mother, not…"

"My sister?" Jen said quietly.

"Yeah."

It wasn't until the last batch of cookies was in the oven, Jane was plopped within view on the couch and Justin sent off to gather all his things before heading home, that Greg broached a touchy subject.

"She's really connected to that…church," he said, shaking his head in disbelief. He didn't even mention the distinct possibility the so-called Ever After Church was connected to the bodies they'd been finding, and to Rick and Wendy's deaths.

"So it seems." Jen grimaced. "Not that I believe for one second that she's found religion. No, there's money in this somewhere, somehow. That's what she cares about." She sighed. "I shouldn't talk to you that way about your mother."

"Truthfully, you mean?" he asked. "You've got every right. She's your sister. And your twin to boot."

"Only on the outside, I hope."

"Actually, not so much anymore," he said. "I mean, I haven't talked to her, but I saw her when she showed up in town after Uncle Robert's money, and she looks... Well, let's just say her true character shows."

"I'm going to take that as a compliment."

"It was meant as one. But it's also the truth."

They both nearly jumped when a deep, almost rough voice came from behind them. "What she's become has changed her on the outside, and you're still as beautiful as ever, inside and out."

Greg saw color rise in Jen's cheeks as his father came and gave her an enveloping hug. And held it, long enough to have Greg studying them, wondering yet again if maybe...

He was still thinking about that on the drive back to the house. Jane was asleep in her car seat, but Justin was still going strong. The boy had been chattering away, which, given his reticence and near-total silence when things had first caved in on him, Greg took as a good sign. But then he'd lapsed into silence, long enough that Greg looked over to see if he, too, had dozed off after a long, busy day at the ranch.

Finally, in a low, almost tiny voice, the child asked, "Are they mad at me? 'Cuz I got mad at Mommy that time? 'Zat why they don't come home?"

Greg's gut instantly knotted. He was a little shocked at both the fierceness of his reaction and the power of it. He was in a good spot, so he pulled over onto the shoulder, put the car in Park and turned to face the boy.

"Listen to me, Justin. It is not your fault, not in any way. Sometimes bad things happen, and there's no explanation.

It doesn't mean it's anyone's fault. And your parents…"
He hesitated, but remembered the advice they'd gotten and
went ahead. "They're dead, and that means forever, but they
loved you more than anything in the world, and you must
always remember that."

"Then why did they go away?"

He searched desperately for the right words. "They didn't
go away because they wanted to, Justin. A bad person did
something bad or stupid and killed them." His stomach
roiled anew at the probability it had been intentional, that
they'd been targeted. "It wasn't their fault, either. But it especially isn't yours."

"Oh."

The boy seemed to calm a little. Somehow he'd found
the right words.

He thought of all the questions that remained, hanging over them all, and just wished to hell they'd find the
right answers.

Chapter Nineteen

She had to admit it, she was exhausted.

Briony undid what she'd been trying to do—a simple braiding of her hair, which she usually did at night to keep it out of her way while trying to sleep, and from looking like a rat had nested in it in the morning—and rubbed at her eyes. She wondered how she could be so tired after mere days. And tried not to think about the years ahead that were going to be like this, wondering how Wendy had done it so seemingly effortlessly.

I have Rick by my side, and he works as hard as I do with the kids. It makes it easy.

Funny that she should remember those particular words now, while Greg was putting Justin to bed, just down the hall from the bathroom. Because even though he wasn't living here, he did work hard with the kids. Very hard. And he made sure it wasn't always just her, even though she could see in his eyes the weariness he tried to hide, proving that he was as exhausted as she was.

Probably more, if you're honest. He's the one driving back and forth every day. And staying until Justin goes to sleep so they could avoid the burst of tears that always came if he saw Greg leaving.

She brushed her hair once more, thinking of what Greg

had told her, about what Justin had asked him. That the boy thought it could be in any way his fault seemed so awful to her she couldn't imagine dealing with it. But Greg had, and had apparently done it so well the boy's questions had actually eased up for a while.

She wondered how anyone survived being a single parent, with no one to share the job with.

She heard his voice, since she'd left the bathroom door open while she tried to do what was usually simple, although he was speaking so quietly she couldn't make out any words. Almost involuntarily she stepped out into the hallway, as if drawn by an irresistible force.

He wasn't speaking. He was singing.

He has a marvelous voice.

His aunt's words flashed through her mind. And now she knew they were true. Because the low, deep voice she was hearing, singing some sort of cowboy song she guessed was old and traditional, was indeed marvelous. It gave her shivers of a delicious kind she'd never known before.

She listened until he stopped, savoring the sound of him. Then she went back to wrestling with her oddly uncooperative hair even as she thought maybe she should put it off until she was actually ready to go to bed herself. Although as tired as she was, that could well be the moment Greg walked out the door.

Or not, she amended, as a memory shot through her mind.

...you two get to bed.

He had never even commented on his father's words, jokingly or otherwise. It was probably just her silly heart, still harboring vestiges of that long-ago—or so she'd thought—crush she'd had on him, that made it keep going through her mind. Which apparently made her fingers nonfunctional as she had to once more untangle her hair to try again.

"Want me to do that?"

She gave a little start. She'd been so lost in her thoughts—yet again—that she hadn't realized he'd stopped at the open door.

"Do…what?" she managed to get out. Barely.

"Braid it for you."

She just stared at him, not sure if she was more stunned by the offer or the ease with which he'd said it. He must be joking. Surely he was joking.

"You… Braid my hair?" she asked finally when he didn't speak.

He gave that one-shouldered shrug she was coming to know. "I braid horse's manes and tails, can't be that much different."

And so, moments later she found herself standing with Greg so very close behind her, sorting her hair into three long tails with obviously efficiency. She felt pressure growing inside her, rapidly. She should say something. Shouldn't she? She couldn't just stand there and…and…

Enjoy the feel of his fingers in your hair? Her breath caught, and her thoughts veered. *Please, don't let him look up and see me in the mirror, see me blushing like a schoolgirl around the campus hero…*

"You have a wonderful voice," she said abruptly.

Those deft fingers—would they be that good at…other things?—paused. "So I've been told. Never used it on a kid before. Seems to calm the cattle, so I thought it was worth a shot."

She could just picture him riding alongside some big herd, keeping them calm with that voice. If it did to them a fraction of what it had to her, his worry wouldn't be them stampeding away, but more trampling him trying to get closer.

"Do you know where you got the red hair?"

She blinked at the unexpected question. "Not out of a box, if that's what you mean."

He leaned to one side slightly, to meet her eyes in the mirror, and he was clearly confused.

"I just meant if you knew if either of your bio parents had it."

"Oh." And there came the damned blush again.

He went back to work on her hair for a moment before saying, "I didn't mean to embarrass you."

She gestured at her flaming cheeks in disgust. "It comes with the hair. And no, I don't know. I don't know anything about either of them, except they were worthless. If I ever knew anything else, I've erased it from my memory completely."

He'd apparently reached the end, because he reached around to pick up the elastic band she'd laid on the counter next to the sink. It brought him even closer, and his heat warmed her. In more ways than one.

As he worked the band around the end of the braid, he said, "So you got the hair, but not the fiery temper that comes with it, according to all the stereotypes." When she couldn't think of a thing to say to that, he went on in a very soft tone, "Or maybe you just only aim it at yourself?"

She stared in shock at those warm brown eyes in the mirror as he spoke words she'd heard before.

"Yeah," he said, "Wendy told me that once." His mouth quirked. "You didn't think I was Mr. Sensitive and figured it out on my own, did you?"

She felt almost relieved, which in turn almost made her laugh. She did manage to smile back at his reflection.

"She…worried about you," he said. Briony wondered if the hesitation had been because he'd been about to use the present tense, as if her beloved friend were still here. "She said you didn't stand up for yourself enough."

She decided to borrow his one-sided shrug for an answer. And immediately realized why he did it; it made things so much easier than trying to find the words for something she couldn't express.

"But you stood up for what you thought best for the kids."

"That was...different."

"So Wendy was right. You'll do it for others, but not for yourself."

She let out a long, sighing breath as her dear friend's oft-repeated statement made her eyes sting. "Wendy was usually right."

She felt the slight touch as he released her braid—which felt perfect, not too loose, not too tight—and it brushed her back. But then he leaned in closer and put his arms around her, giving her more of that warmth. That sweet warmth. That warmth that was almost enough to ease the ache.

That warmth that was more than enough to cause an entirely different kind of ache.

Every well-trained, self-protective instinct she had screamed at her to pull away. Instead, like the fool she knew she was, she leaned into it, seeking more and more of that luscious heat only he had ever seemed to cause in her.

"Both our lives got turned upside down, didn't they?" he said.

"Yes," she said, trying to make it sound like an answer to his question and not her own inner wish.

"All we can do is what we're doing. See to the kids."

And that quickly—and kindly, she had to admit—he quashed all those urges and longings, reminding her why he was here, and that he was holding her in support, not...

desire. She pulled her emotions back, as she'd had to so many times in her life.

"Yes. And we will," she said, glad to hear her voice sounded calm and steady.

It wasn't until he'd gone, after a final peek into their bedrooms to check on both children, that she thought to go back into the bathroom, grab the hand mirror she'd found in the top drawer of the vanity and look at the braiding he'd done.

It was, of course, perfect.

Chapter Twenty

Greg knew something was bothering Briony within minutes after arriving at the house. And that it was something more than Jane's wailing "Mamamama" over and over again, inconsolably. But every time he tried to ask her what was wrong, something—or a very short someone—would interrupt, until he was feeling as frazzled as she was acting. How did people *do* this?

He'd already had a long, hard day. A big tree had gone down and taken a chunk of the main pasture fence with it. He and a crew of three men needed several hours to get the tree removed and the fence repaired. He'd have liked nothing better than a long, hot shower and an early bedtime. Instead, he took a quick, wake-up-cold shower, dressed again in clean clothes and headed for his truck.

Dad had caught him just before he pulled out.

"Something else go wrong?" he'd asked wearily.

Buck leaned on the driver's door. "No. Just wanted to acknowledge something very right."

"Well, that'll be nice for a change. What?"

"You."

Greg blinked. "Me?"

"I'm very proud of you, son. You're handling this like a man, doing what needs to be done."

He couldn't speak past the tightening of his throat. Barely got out, "Thanks, Dad." He swallowed, then managed to say more steadily, "I had a great example."

He'd thought about that exchange all the way over to the house. That he indeed had always had a great example, the man who had taught him more about life and how to deal with its ups and downs than anyone else could have.

Briony had never had an example like that in her life. Yet she was also rising to the challenge, and proud as he was of his dad's approval, Greg found that much more amazing.

Which was why her current state of obvious worry was nagging at him.

But he still had to wait until, at last, both kids were tucked in and asleep. Jane had apparently exhausted herself from the constant wailing, and Justin had fallen asleep on the couch during the kids' movie he'd insisted he had to watch. Again, Briony had said, adding that he'd seen it three times already this week.

Briony, who was still wearing her hair in the braid he'd impulsively done last night. He wasn't sure how that made him feel, only that it did make him feel…something.

And now here they were, collapsed themselves on the living room couch, the television now muted as the cartoon characters played out their story. Greg tried to think of a tactful way to ask, finally decided he was way too tired to be delicate about it and just asked.

"What's bothering you? You've been on edge all evening."

"That's not enough?" she said wryly, nodding toward the now-quiet children's rooms.

"More than, but…this seems like something else."

She let out an audible breath. "Don't write off that Mr. Sensitive title just yet, then." Then, looking as if it were a tremendous effort, she sat up straight. "It may be nothing, but…"

"What? Tell me."

She drew in a deep breath before saying, still hesitant, "I think someone's watching us."

His brow furrowed. "Watching?"

"I've seen the same black car parked in different spots for the last couple of days. Always with a man sitting in it. And it's never been here before that. And then when I took the kids to the park this morning…it was there, too. With the same man in it."

Greg was upright too, now. All the tension and speculation about how and why Rick and Wendy had died, which he tried to smother around the kids, came roaring back full strength. "I assume you didn't recognize him?"

She shook her head. "No. Or the car."

She leaned far over, stretching to reach the end table, he guessed for the phone that sat there. The action made her shirt ride up and bare some skin above the waist of the knit pants she had on. He'd never really noticed until these past few days that she had a very nice shape, long legs, nice hips, trim waist, and breasts that were nicely rounded and full enough that he couldn't quite believe he hadn't taken note before now.

Of course, she didn't exactly dress to attract. The opposite, Wendy had always said. *The less attention she draws, the happier she is*, she'd said, and she hadn't sounded happy about it. *Even if the right man comes along, she'll never believe it. Or let him get close to her.*

In an odd, incongruous thought, he realized he was close to her. So he guessed that meant he wasn't the right man. But he already knew that. Had always known that. Hadn't he?

She had grabbed her phone now, and straightened back

up. She tapped at the screen a couple of times while she said, "I got a couple of pictures, but not from very close, so you can't really see him."

She held out the phone to him. He took it, telling himself it hadn't been intentional that he'd brushed over her fingers, it had been unavoidable. The tingle it had caused was weird, though.

He focused on the screen.

It was a fairly nondescript black car, not unlike a dozen he could think of owned by people he did know. But even though the image of the man in the driver's seat was distorted a bit by the car's window glass, he was fairly certain he didn't know this guy.

"See? You can't really see him that well, so it was probably a waste of time even trying—"

"Hush, Briony. It was not a waste of time. Not by a long shot."

"You know him?" She sounded utterly startled.

"No."

"But—"

"It wasn't a waste of time, because you got the license number on the car in this second shot."

"Oh."

"Send it to my phone."

She did so, but with a worried look. "But…he hasn't really done anything, except hang around. Hasn't broken any laws, I mean."

Yet.

The warning rang in Greg's head, and no matter how much he told himself he was probably overreacting, it wouldn't go away. Chase telling him Rick and Wendy's crash hadn't been an accident had been seared into his memory as if with acid, and he couldn't just put it out of his mind. And now this guy hanging around Rick and Wendy's house?

"Maybe I'm just being paranoid," Briony said.

"Careful," he corrected, starting to hate her self-doubt. "You're being careful. Just like you're supposed to be."

He grabbed his own phone. Checked that the image had arrived and was clear. Then he called up his cousin Fletcher's number. He knew Chase would have told his brother what was going on, given that Fletch was now a local cop, having transferred to Owl Creek from Boise PD a while back.

"Greg?" Fletcher answered. "We were just talking about you."

That detoured his racing thoughts. "You were?"

Fletch laughed. "Yeah. I'm at the bookstore, and Frannie was saying she needed to call you and let you know that book you wanted came in. By Alexis...detoke something?"

"De Tocqueville. Okay."

"Interesting reading taste you got there, coz."

"Tell her I'll be in to pick it up."

"I will. Now, what's up? I'm assuming you didn't just call to chat."

"I need to send you a photo, and for you to tell me if the guy or the car looks familiar."

His cousin's tone changed instantly, and Greg knew he was now talking to Fletcher Colton the cop. "Send it."

He forwarded the image Briony had sent him.

"Hmm." His cousin's tone was thoughtful, and Greg knew he'd registered something. "Let me call you back in a couple."

He didn't even say goodbye, but Greg knew that was because Fletcher was already on to the next step.

"What?" Briony asked, starting to look a little anxious.

"He's checking on something. He'll call back."

"The car?" Her expression cleared suddenly. "Is he the cousin who's an Owl Creek cop?"

He nodded. "Detective. And he reacted like something was familiar about either the car or the guy."

He saw fear dawning in her eyes and almost wished he hadn't said it. She'd been concerned before, but not afraid until he'd planted the idea this unknown man might be familiar to the local police.

"Maybe it's nothing," he said. "Maybe he's...house hunting or something."

"Do you really think that?"

Greg met her gaze. Odd, before all this had happened, when he happened to think of her, like when Rick or Wendy had mentioned her, he'd thought of her red hair. Now he wondered how he could have thought of anything except these big green eyes.

And looking into them now, he couldn't bring himself to lie. "No."

Less than ten minutes later, he was, to his disquiet, proven right. Fletcher called back, and still in cop mode, didn't waste any time on niceties. The moment Greg heard that inflection in his voice, he put the call on speaker, both so Briony could hear and so he didn't have to tell her after.

"He's a PI from Conners," Fletcher said. "He and the car looked familiar because his photo went around the department here when he got in a scuffle with some guy he was tailing in a divorce case."

"Damn," Greg muttered.

"You're not having some fling with a married woman, are you, coz?"

He assumed that was a joke, since if he had a list of things he'd never do, that was definitely on it. "No," he said flatly.

"Sorry, man," Fletcher said hastily, like a man who'd just remembered there was a personal reason that joke would fall flat. Greg let it pass; after all, Fletcher had been hit by that just as he had. And it didn't matter just now that his mother had had a long affair with Fletcher's father.

"Forget it, man. We all agreed they're irrelevant to us."

"Yeah." Fletcher cleared his throat, then said, "You got a problem I can help with?"

"Not unless you can find out why this guy has been hanging around Rick and Wendy's house. Where the kids are." *And Briony.*

Even as he thought it, she spoke. "Is," she corrected as she stared out the front window. "He's back."

Greg crossed the room in two long strides, looked out the window and quickly spotted the black vehicle across the street.

"He's back," he confirmed to Fletcher. "Across the street and about three houses east."

"I'm close. Why don't I come over there and badge him and see what he says?"

"He hasn't done anything but hang around," Greg warned.

"But my brother says that car crash wasn't an accident."

"No. It wasn't."

"He also said the guy they think caused it was conveniently murdered while in custody."

"Yeah."

"Reason enough," Fletcher said easily. "You stay put, and I'll just stop by and find out what one of Conners's less than finest is up to."

"Thanks, coz."

He ended the call and for a moment just stood there, thinking, turning over possibilities in his mind. Then he realized Briony was staring at him and turned to look at her.

He couldn't even define the expression on her face. Some combination of bemusement and...longing?

"What?" he finally asked.

"That's what it's like?"

He frowned slightly, puzzled. "What what is like?"

"To have family. You just call, and they jump to help?"

He felt a knot tightening in his gut again. "Mine does, mostly. But don't forget, we have a couple of prime ass—" he broke it off, changing mid-sentence "—jerks, too. So maybe you were lucky, in one way. You didn't have any of those to deal with."

"Not sure that outweighs what you were just able to do," she said quietly, and he felt a jab of rueful regret.

"Sorry," he muttered. "I know I don't really get it, but—"

He stopped abruptly when she reached out and put just her fingertips against his chest. He wasn't sure he could have kept talking after that anyway.

"You get it more than I ever would have expected."

He wanted to hug her again, to hold her, reassure her that everything would be all right. Except that would be a lie— he couldn't be sure everything would. And strange things, puzzling things, happened when he hugged her, held her. Things he never would have expected.

So instead, he lifted a hand and put it over hers on his chest, curling his fingers around hers, holding them there against him. That was the only thing that kept him from pacing the floor while they waited. And although they stood that way for a long time, he still felt it was too short when she finally moved, pulling back her hand and looking away from him.

"Do you think it's something to do with the accident?" she asked, sounding anxious again.

"I think speculation at this point is useless," he answered. "We'll know soon. Fletch'll find out why he's here."

Even as he said it his cousin's car pulled up, halting beside the black sedan, carefully blocking it from leaving. Greg thought about grabbing his rifle from his truck and going over there, just in case Fletcher needed some backup, but things seemed calm enough.

Just because you got involved in one shoot-out doesn't make you an expert.

The memory made him grimace, although at least it had turned out well, with Chase's new lady safe and sound. That had made him feel good about what could have ended much worse.

When Fletcher arrived at the door a few minutes later, he didn't look happy. "I can't order him to leave. He's not violating anything. Yet. But I did get him to let slip who he's working for."

Greg sensed he wasn't going to like this. He glanced at Briony, who was clearly still anxious. "Who?" he asked.

Fletcher grimaced before saying flatly, "A Mr. Kraft."

Greg felt it like a punch to the gut. Rick's father.

The one person both Rick and Wendy had trusted them to keep away from the children.

Chapter Twenty-One

Once again Greg's father came through, immediately agreeing to take the kids while they headed to Conners, to the attorney's office.

"I'll call Jen, she'll come help." He'd smiled in a way Briony could only interpret as loving. "She's quite taken with those two. I think she misses having little ones around." A grin flashed, and Briony saw where Greg got his own devastatingly appealing beam. "And much to my surprise, so do I."

"I figured we would have cured you of that," Greg said, managing a smile despite the tension she could feel thrumming just beneath the surface.

"I might have felt that at the time, but it's different now. The responsibility is elsewhere, leaving us just the fun parts."

"You sound like a doting grandparent," Greg said, the smile less forced this time.

His father met his gaze and held it before saying quietly, "Well, they're yours now, aren't they? So I am."

They were in Greg's truck, leaving the car with the car seats at the ranch just in case, and on the road to Conners Briony said, a bit hesitantly, "Your dad is an incredible man."

"He is," Greg agreed. "He's the grandfather the kids need. Not that piece of—"

He cut himself off, and to her surprise Briony found that she liked the fact that he tried not to use rough language, at least around her. She'd already noticed it when he was around the kids and appreciated that he extended it to her. She'd grown up hearing some pretty crude things on a regular basis, and she didn't care for it, and especially didn't want the kids subjected to it as she had been.

"Yes, not that horrible excuse for a father Rick had." She gave him another sideways look. "Maybe you had a better point than I realized, when you talked about me not having had to deal with family like that."

He looked surprised. Whether it was because she'd acknowledged the possible accuracy or that she remembered what he'd said at all, she didn't know.

What she did know was the source of the tension that practically hummed in the truck's cab. The very idea of innocent little Justin and Jane ending up in the hands of the man Rick had so hated was beyond abhorrent to her, and she knew Greg felt the same way. And he, having been Rick's close friend for so long, probably knew even more about the evilness of the man than she did, having gotten her information filtered through Wendy.

When they arrived at the office in Conners, Greg declined the offer of coffee from the receptionist, but Briony accepted, as much to have something to do with her hands as anything. But it ended up untouched when they were ushered into the office right away and Tanya—she'd told them to just use her first name—got right to the point of the information she'd confirmed.

"Can he do that?" Briony knew she'd practically yelped it

at the attorney but couldn't contain her incredulity. "He could try to take custody of two children he's never even met?"

"I'm afraid a blood relative, especially a direct one like a grandfather, would have standing in a case," the woman said regretfully.

Greg, who had never even sat down and was still pacing the lawyer's office, covering the relatively large space quickly with those long-legged, powerful strides of his, stopped and turned to face the woman behind the desk.

"Despite Rick's insistence that his father get nowhere near them? Even though he specifically assigned guardianship to us to keep that from happening?" he demanded.

"He still has standing."

Briony was looking at Greg's face and saw his jaw tighten. "Look, I know who and what Rick's father is. And how much Rick wanted to keep his kids far, far away from him. They even considered moving out of state to get away from him."

"I understand," the lawyer began.

"I'm not sure you do," Greg countered, and Briony could hear the tension vibrating in his voice. "He's a founding member of that cult that calls itself a church."

Tanya drew back slightly. "That... Ever After thing?"

"Yes. The one that may be connected to those bodies they've been finding," Greg answered flatly. He hesitated, but after a moment went ahead. "And it hasn't been proven, but he may have been connected to the non-accident that killed Rick and Wendy."

That took the woman a moment to process, and in that moment Briony's accountant brain woke up. She asked Greg, "Do you think he's after the insurance money? For both kids together, it's not an insignificant amount."

"Oh, I'm sure he is," Greg said, sounding almost glacial

now. "He'll hand it over to the bastard who runs the thing, and the kids to God knows who." His mouth twisted sourly. "Not that God has anything to do with that farce."

Briony felt an odd sense of appreciation for his anger, because she was feeling some of that herself. And she agreed completely with his assessment. She turned back to the attorney.

"What exactly does that mean, standing?" Briony asked.

"Boiled down to the essence, it means most courts would hear his case. Not that he would necessarily win, but—"

Her phone rang, and she held up a finger as she took the call. It was brief, and Briony could see by her expression when it ended that it was not good news.

"He's filed a plea," she said bluntly. "For full custody."

Greg swore, looking as if he wanted to punch something. Or more likely someone. If Winston Kraft were in the room now, she'd be willing to bet he'd be on the floor before he knew what had hit him. And she had to admit she liked the idea of that ranch-hewn power unleashed on the evil man Wendy had so often told her about, fear in her eyes and voice. Her friend knew too well what life would be like for Justin and Jane in the hands of someone like Rick's father. Or worse, simply handed over to that dangerous cult.

"What chance would he have of winning?" she asked.

"To a certain extent it depends on the judge, of course," the lawyer said. "That he's apparently well-off—" she held up a hand as both Greg and Briony started to speak "—I know, it's probably mostly cult money, bilked from unknowing members, but nevertheless, he's got money, and he's married, and that will matter. A married couple always has a better shot."

"He's on his third wife who's half his age," snapped Greg. "But it still counts?"

"All I can say is it would be a factor in his favor. Just as if, say, you two were married it would be a factor. A rather large one, in fact, given that third wife, and that he's so much older and the kids are so young. Plus, there's the fact that the kids are obviously quite familiar and comfortable with you two, while Winston Kraft has never even met them. The connection to the Ever After Church might play into it as well, depending again on the judge."

"You're saying we'd have a better chance of keeping the kids out of his clutches if we were married?" Greg's voice was flat, suddenly unemotional.

"That, plus Rick and Wendy's clearly stated wishes would definitely give you a much better chance." She looked from him to Briony, then back. Then she got to her feet, saying, "Excuse me, I'm going to see if we have a copy of Winston Kraft's filing yet. They were supposed to send it right over."

Briony had the feeling that wasn't the only reason the woman wanted to get out of the room. Greg was still on his feet, while she wasn't sure she'd ever be able to get out of this chair. She lowered her gaze, noticed the ripples in the surface of the full cup of coffee and set it down carefully before she managed to splash it all over.

When he finally sat in the chair beside hers, it was uncharacteristically heavily. His head was down, as if the weight of the world had descended on his shoulders. She understood. Her stomach was churning with growing nausea, and she was flooded with fears and feelings she hadn't had since her own miserable childhood.

It was a long, strained moment before he finally looked up at her and spoke.

"It would be the worst betrayal ever of Rick and Wendy to let that monster get away with this."

"Not to mention how awful it would be for Justin and

Jane." Just the thought of those two precious beings she had loved before but utterly adored now in the hands of the man Wendy had told her about made the churning worse, and she had to fight it down.

"I won't let it happen," Greg said, his voice grimly firm.

"Nor will I. If I have to sell everything I own to pay to fight him, I will."

"There's a better...no, an easier..." His voice trailed off as if he couldn't find the right word. "A more effective way. As she—" he nodded toward the name plaque on the desk "—pointed out."

The ripple of shock that went through her as she realized what he was getting at managed to overwhelm the nausea. She stared at him, unable to put together a coherent sentence even in her mind, as if his struggle for the right word was infectious.

"Did you mean it?" There was a stress, an urgency in his voice that she'd never heard before, would never have expected to hear, not from strong, steady Greg Colton. "That you'd do whatever is necessary to keep them out of Winston Kraft's clutches?"

Knowing she was answering both that question and the one he hadn't yet asked, she took a deep breath, let it out slowly to calm herself and said simply, "Yes."

In the end he didn't ask a question at all. He simply said it.

"Then we have to get married."

Chapter Twenty-Two

Greg knew it wasn't exactly a romantic proposal. But this wasn't a romance. It was a…business deal. No, it was a necessity. This was for Justin and Jane's sake, and if this was what it took to keep them out of the hands of the man Rick had so hated, what it took to keep his best friend's worst nightmare from coming true, then so be it. Besides, it wasn't like there was anyone in his life who was going to feel betrayed. He hadn't even been on a date in…almost a year. Hadn't even thought about it until he'd met Sloan, but his cousin Chase had laid claim, fiercely, before it had gone beyond just a thought. And Briony had said that she wasn't seeing anyone, either.

It would work. It had to. He and Briony had gotten along well enough since they'd pitched in together to see to the kids. Of course, most of the time he at least had been too tired to fight with her, but right now he couldn't remember much he'd felt like fighting about. The initial argument over where the kids should live had been the biggest battle. A battle, he suddenly realized, they were going to have to fight all over again.

Belatedly he realized she hadn't said a word. Maybe he'd made it a little too businesslike, a little too abrupt.

"Look," he said hastily, "I know that wasn't—"

"Yes."

He blinked. Was she acknowledging the coldness of the statement, or…agreeing with it? "Yes?"

"We have to get married."

For some inane reason all Greg could think of was how far removed from any scenario in which he would have expected to hear those words this was. It gave him a clue as to what she might be feeling.

"I know this isn't what either of us want," he began, stopping when she shook her head.

"It has to be done."

For a moment he just looked at her, seeing an unshakable determination in those green eyes that startled him. For all her quietness, all the shyness that generally made her retreat into herself, when the chips were down, Briony Adams didn't run.

"And soon," she added, proving his point.

He nodded. "I'll look into it. We need a judge, I guess."

"And a license." She nodded toward the nameplate on the desk. "She'll probably know what we need to do."

She was so calm it was almost unsettling. He would have expected her to be rattled, upset at the whole idea, or at the very least upset at this turn life had suddenly taken. But the only thing he could hear in her voice or see in her face was a steady determination.

And he wondered if he'd ever really known this woman at all.

Footsteps warned them Tanya was returning. When she was back at her desk, she studied them for a moment, and Greg got the strangest feeling she had guessed what had gone on while she'd been out of the room. Or maybe it wasn't strange. A good lawyer could probably read people well, and he remembered Rick saying she was one of the best lawyers in the state. It was why they'd chosen her. He knew he'd need the best to go up against his father if necessary.

And now it was necessary.

"No copy yet, so they're dragging their feet. Whether that's because they're stalling or don't have confidence in their case, I have no way of knowing." Her mouth twisted slightly. "Or, from what Rick told me, he's possibly just being obstructionist."

"Something he's very good at," Greg agreed sourly. The urgency of the need to protect the kids made him set aside the niceties. "You meant what you said, that we'd have a better chance at keeping the children out of Winston's hands if we were married?"

"It would be a significant factor, I think."

He glanced at Briony. She nodded. He looked back at the attorney. "Then we will."

For a long moment the woman across from them just looked at them consideringly. And, he noticed, without much surprise. "I gathered from Rick and Wendy you two have known each other for some time?"

"Since shortly after they met," Briony said.

"And you both agree this is what you want to do?"

"It's what needs to be done," Greg said flatly.

"The children will need to feel you're truly together in this," she said warningly.

"We'll make it work. For the kids. He can't be allowed to get his hands on them."

"We're hoping you can tell us how to go about this," Briony said. "I'm guessing the sooner the better?"

"The more time you've been established before this goes to family court the better, yes." She tapped the pen she'd picked up on her desk a couple of times, then spoke quickly.

"You'll need to apply for a license at the county recorder's office, over by the courthouse. There's no waiting period in Idaho, but you'll need someone with the legal ability to officiate." She thought for a moment, then went on. "I happen to know a retired judge who could handle that. You let me know when, and I'll give him a call."

Greg looked at Briony, searching her face, her eyes, for any sign of doubt or that she might be changing her mind now that they were talking details. Any sign that the reality of what she'd agreed to had struck and she wanted to back out. She seemed to realize what he was doing and held his gaze steadily. Then she looked back at the attorney.

"How about today?" she said.

He felt a little jolt. Today? Suddenly he was the one dealing with the reality of the decision they'd reached. But maybe it was a good thing. The less time they had to think about it, the less time the insanity of it all had to register.

"The kids are already safe with your dad, let's get it done," Briony said.

"I...yes. Sure." He shook off the remnants of his own shock—when had shy little Briony become so steadfast and determined?—and looked across the desk. "Can we do that?"

"I'll make the call to the judge. And hopefully the recorder's office won't be jammed. You have the necessary ID? Driver's licenses will do."

They both nodded.

Ten minutes later they were back in Greg's truck, the county offices their destination. Briony was staring out the side window, as if she didn't want him to be able to see her face.

"Second thoughts?" he asked as he started the engine, his voice sounding as rough as his gut was feeling.

"No." She said it firmly, but she still wouldn't look at him.

He opened his mouth to speak and realized he had no idea what to say, so shut it again. In this case, he had the feeling the less said the better.

It wasn't until they were on the main road headed south that something else hit him. "I'd better warn Dad."

"Which will shock him more, that you're getting married, or married to me?"

There was an almost bitter undertone to her voice that jabbed at him. "Actually," he said coolly, "I wanted to warn him about the PI hanging around."

She had the grace to sound embarrassed. "Oh. Sorry. That was self-centered of me."

He glanced at her, then went back to the road ahead. And nearly groaned aloud at the phrase his mind had chosen. "This isn't about us. It's about Justin and Jane, and keeping them safe."

"I know. I just…"

His mouth twisted wryly. "Not how you ever thought about getting married, huh?"

"Actually, I never thought much about getting married at all."

He blinked. Glanced at her. "I thought…" His voice trailed off, his at the moment chaotic mind warning him he could be stepping into quicksand.

"That all women spent half their time dreaming about it?" she asked sweetly. Too sweetly, telling him it was good that he'd stopped when he did. "I didn't. I didn't think I'd ever trust anyone enough."

Given her history, he could understand that. He waited while the car in front of them, a compact, trendy thing driven by a guy who looked terrified by the bigger utilitarian vehicles around him, decided what to do about the semi rig they'd just caught up to, then when they were finally clear of the backup the guy had caused, thought maybe he knew what to say.

"I'd never do anything to hurt you."

"I know that."

That surprised him, and he shot her another sideways glance. "You do?"

She shrugged and said, "Rick always said you were a straight arrow. He told me if I ever needed anything, and he or Wendy weren't around, I could go to you. That you'd help however you could because that's who you are."

And that quickly the harsh, bitter ache was back, tightening his gut and his throat and making his eyes sting.

"He was the best friend anyone could have," he said, not even caring that every bit of that blast of emotion echoed in his voice.

"As Wendy was for me."

"So we'll do this for them. And we'll keep their children safe." He said it in the tone of a vow more real than any other he'd make today.

"We will," Briony said, and her voice held the same certainty his own had.

They would make other vows today, but none were more important than that one.

Chapter Twenty-Three

She was married.

Briony felt a little numb as she sat in the truck staring at the paper in her hand. She hadn't lied to Greg when she'd said she hadn't thought about it much. And just about the only times she had were when Wendy had brought it up, insisting that there were trustworthy men out there.

That Wendy's usual example, after her own beloved Rick, had been Greg seemed the highest of ironies now.

Look at Greg. He's not just honest and trustworthy, he's kind, hardworking, loyal, not to mention superhot...

Wendy had said it with utter sincerity. She hadn't been able to argue any of that, then or now. It was why back after they'd first met, she'd had to spend so much energy stifling that stupid yearning she felt every time she saw him. But she'd done it because she had to. Because it would never work out, and the very last thing she wanted was some silly crush of hers to affect the dearest thing in her life, her oldest and closest friendship, the only thing that had enabled her to survive her chaotic childhood. If Wendy, who even as a kid had been more outgoing, tough and self-admittedly stubborn than she, hadn't essentially taken her under her wing, Briony wasn't sure she would have made it at all.

And now, after maybe five minutes in a little alcove off the judge's office, she was where Wendy had always wanted her. Married to Greg.

Married.

The word rang in her head until she wanted to put her hands over her ears to see if it would muffle it a little.

"This is a business arrangement, right?" she said, not looking at him.

"What?"

"We're clear on what it is, and isn't, what it will and won't be, right? Do we need to lay it out in so many words?"

There was a moment of silence before Greg answered, in a brusque, almost sharp tone. "Focus on the kids, not us. This isn't an accounting job."

She felt her cheeks flush with embarrassment and was glad she was turned away from him. "You're right," she said, her voice barely above a whisper. "Sorry."

There was another pause, but his voice had changed completely, become something soothing when he said, "You don't need to protect yourself in this, Briony. We both want the same thing, and we can work with that."

How did he know her so well, know that the hard-learned urge to self-protect had risen up in her anew? Or was she just that readable?

And it has nothing to do with the simple fact that you could so easily fall for him like a ton of bricks.

She sat in silence, not even seeing the buildings they were driving past. And a couple of blocks later, she was barely aware that he'd pulled over to the curb and parked along the main street of Conners.

"You coming in, or not?" Greg's voice cut through the buzz.

"What?" she asked.

He nodded toward the store they were in front of. She

looked. Blinked. A jewelry store. She turned her gaze back to him. Couldn't think of a thing to say.

"You heard what he said. If we want to present the right image, you need a ring."

Had she heard that? She vaguely remembered the retired judge, who had obviously been apprised of the situation—and had a strong personal opinion of the Ever After Church—had said something about the custody case, but she had been so dazed at the reality of the fact that she had just pledged herself to this man forever she hadn't really processed the details.

"What about you?" It was the only thing she could think of to say.

He grimaced. "A ring would only get in my way on the ranch."

For some reason she didn't stop to analyze that jabbed her into saying, a bit snappishly, "So I'm the only one who's supposed to declare myself to the world?"

"I didn't mean—"

"I thought the whole idea was a united front?"

"I know that, I—"

"Or at least the image of one?"

For a long moment he just stared at her. Then, with the slightest twitch of his mouth, he asked, "Who are you, and what have you done with quiet, shy, retiring Briony Adams?"

She realized he wasn't, as she'd expected, angry. He was amused. In fact, he sounded almost…pleased? She wasn't sure that didn't jab at her more. With an effort, she kept her voice cool.

"It's Briony Colton now, isn't it?"

This time he blinked. And she knew he hadn't processed that any more than she'd processed what the judge had said.

"I...yeah, it is." He lowered his gaze, but it almost instantly shot back to her face. "That is, if you want it to be."

"That united front, remember?"

He nodded slowly. "Okay." He took in and let out an audible breath. "Okay, two rings. As long as you understand that there are times I'll have to take it off."

"As long as it stays on until the kids are officially ours."

He nodded. And Briony was just thinking that Wendy had been right, he really was kind, and loyal and all the rest, when he blew up her train of thought completely by adding three words.

"Agreed, Mrs. Colton."

"You did what?"

Greg saw the shock in his father's face and felt an inward twinge. No, more than a twinge. If there was ever a person in his life he didn't want to disappoint, it was this one.

They'd found him in the big barn, scrubbing his hands after doing some cleanup. Greg didn't find the various scents of the barn, from fresh hay to manure, at all distasteful, but he was used to it. Briony was another matter, and he'd been a little wary. But she'd only watched for a moment and asked if that's what he'd been talking about. It had taken him a moment to realize she meant his comment about the ring getting in the way. When he'd nodded, she'd nodded in turn, as if she understood now. And the tension of those moments seemed to fade away, even as he found himself yet again running his thumb over the simple gold band that now graced his left ring finger. The band that matched hers, and that he'd seen her doing the same with, that frequent testing of something you're not used to.

But now he was facing an even bigger tension, as his father stared at him. "The lawyer and the judge agreed, it betters our chances of keeping the kids out of the hands of Rick's father," he explained. "Especially now that we know Rick's father is coming after them."

Buck looked from him to Briony. "And you're…okay with it?"

"I'm okay with anything that will help those children. They need us, and I… I need them."

Such wonder echoed in her voice that Greg felt a pang of longing as if he were feeling the emotions that were so clear in her voice and expression. In the distance he heard a child's laughter and recognized it as Justin's. He looked past Dad and saw Mama Jen at the far end of the barn, walking toward the foaling stall with Jane in her arms and Justin happily trotting alongside her.

"We'll win," he said firmly. "He won't get them."

His father, who had looked about to say something, now flickered a glance from him to Briony, then turned an ear toward the sound of the children. When he looked back at Greg, he said firmly, "Whatever you and the kids need."

It was only later, when Briony and Mama Jen were dealing with dinner and getting the kids ready, that Dad took him back outside on the front porch. Greg knew what was coming, had expected it, but that didn't mean he was looking forward to it.

"You really did this," Dad said, glancing at his left hand.

"Yes." He explained everything the lawyer and the judge had said.

His father listened, as he always did. Then, quietly, he said, "I know you have the kids' best interests at heart, but I have yours. So take it from someone who got married…in haste. It can hurt." Greg didn't know what to say to that. And Buck quickly added, "It was worth it, because it brought me you, but it wasn't for the right… I didn't…"

He stopped, ramming a hand through still-dark brown hair that was gray only at the temples. His father, usually quick to smile and tell a corny joke, was rarely flustered, but clearly he was now. And the sight of this man who, Greg knew, loved his children more than his own life in such straits made him bring up something he'd known for years but they'd never talked about.

"I know you only married her because she got pregnant with me."

His father went very still. "You do?"

"I figured out she was already pregnant as soon as I put my birthday together with when you got married." He managed a slightly crooked smile. "Of course, that wasn't until Lizzy was born, so by then I figured it didn't matter." He grimaced then. "Boy was I wrong."

Because three years later the mother was gone. From them, anyway. And on her way to an affair with his father's own brother, resulting in the two half siblings they'd never known about until that brother had died.

"Greg, listen, I—"

"It's okay, Dad. It really doesn't matter, to me, anymore. I got the best out of that deal. Just think, what if she'd taken me with her?" He gave an exaggerated shudder. When he saw the slight smile curve his father's mouth, he went on. "And this is different, really, Dad. I mean, it's similar, we didn't get married because we're madly in love or anything, but it was the right thing to do."

Madly in love with Briony Adams. Now, there was a wild thought.

Briony Colton.

Even the silent mental correction rattled him. He wasn't nearly as calm on the inside as he was trying to appear on the outside. And his father was studying him so intently it was adding to his nerves.

"Tell me, son," he said, very quietly, "how do you feel now about being the reason your mother and I got married?"

"Like I said, I got the best end of that deal. I feel bad for you, all those years when you could have been with…the right sister."

Now he'd done it. His father gave him a startled look, glanced toward the house as if Mama Jen could have heard him, then looked out toward the barn with a totally disconcerted expression on his face. Did he really think nobody had noticed the way he looked at her? The way he changed around her, smiled more, laughed more?

"We're not talking about me," Dad said gruffly. "We're talking about you."

"We're talking mostly about those two little children in there," Greg corrected gently. "And we're going to see that they have the best life they can have, under the circumstances. Just as you did with us, building a loving home for us here on the ranch." He took a deep breath before continuing. "Which brings me to the biggest favor I have to ask."

"I told you, whatever you need. I meant it."

"Even having us all live here, on the ranch?"

To his surprise, his father lit up. "Especially that. It would be great to have you all here, and easier on you, too. Lots of people to help out."

"Including Mama Jen?" he asked, just to see his reaction.

"Don't poke that bear, Gregory," Dad warned.

He threw up his hands in surrender. "Okay, okay. I'll butt out. But just so you know, I'm all for it."

And he dropped it there before his astute father could point out that a guy who just got married not out of love but out of pure responsibility was in no position to opine on someone else who'd done the same thing.

Chapter Twenty-Four

"Move in here?"

Briony was feeling suddenly exhausted, emotionally if not physically, and was in no mood to have this fight again.

"My place only has two bedrooms," Greg said, "but the kids can have one, you the other, and I can bunk in the main room. We can leave them here with Dad while we go back and get whatever you and they need from the house."

She summoned up what little reserve energy and resolve she had left to say firmly, "We resolved this, and you agreed it's best for the children to stay in the home they're used to."

He stared at her as if she'd made that up. "Briony," he said, almost gently, "they can't stay there now. He wants the kids—the money that comes with them, anyway—and he already knows where the house is, thanks to that PI."

She felt a sudden chill that she hadn't realized that. She'd been so swept up in everything else—getting married, among other things—that she hadn't really put together that the PI who had been outside the house had likely already reported to Rick's father where it was.

She felt a fierce ache as all her old uncertainties rose anew, telling her she wasn't smart enough, wasn't good enough to handle this, to see to the safety of Wendy's precious children, not if she couldn't even figure out something this obvious.

"They'll be safer here," Greg went on, "with my family. My brother Malcolm has his search dog who's also a good watchdog, my cousin Wade who works with us a lot is former Special Forces, and while my brother Max is with his new lady now more than he's here, he's still former FBI. And Dad will be fierce about protecting them, just like he was with us. Plus, the hands will help look out for them, and watch for trouble all over the ranch."

"I didn't… I should have realized…" She sounded as shaky as she felt. She must have looked it, too, because he reached out and grasped her shoulders. Strangely, it steadied her, not just on the outside, but the inside, too.

"Look," Greg said, "it's been hectic. A lot's happened, most of it ugly. Cut yourself some slack."

She let out a harsh little laugh. And her voice was shaking when she said, "I've worked so hard to…have control over my life, and now I see all I've done is make myself unable to handle change."

Only when he pulled her closer for another of his wonderful hugs did she realize how much she'd wanted it, wanted him to do it. And when he spoke, she could actually feel the rumble of that lovely deep voice as her ear was pressed against his chest.

"Hey," he said, "that's not true. You've changed your entire life for the kids, and you've done a great job of it. But now you're going to have help, lots of it. Just because they…" Her heart wrenched a little as he stumbled on the word, if only because it was proof it was still as painful to him as it was to her. He tried again, as she somehow knew Greg always would. "Just because they left them to us doesn't mean they expected us to do it alone. After all, they had us to help them. So now we've got Dad and my brothers and sister to help us."

It made so much sense when he put it that way. But she had to fight the innate shyness that rose up to protest the idea of being around so many people, all the time. "I don't handle lots of people well, I pull away. They'll think I don't like them."

He was silent for a moment, as if he were considering what to say. She'd always liked that about him, that he seemed to think before he spoke, rather than blurt out whatever popped into his head first.

"They'll think you're overwhelmed. Because they know I have been, since…that night."

That startled her. She pulled back and looked up at him, albeit carefully, since she didn't want him to pull away. "You? Overwhelmed?"

"Between the kids and the ranch, it's felt like I've been underwater, never getting close enough to the surface to breathe."

She felt a little stunned, not only at the admission, but that he'd made it. And to her. "I…but you're always so strong."

"As my Dad would say, that's not strong, that's stubborn. But sometimes stubborn's the only thing that gets you through."

That made her smile, at least as much as she could manage just now. "I like your Dad."

"He's the best," Greg said simply. "And I'm sorry you never had somebody like him to be there for you."

I've got that now…

It was a silly thought; he was here for the kids, not her. She knew that, but at the same time she had the feeling that if she truly needed help, he would be there. Hadn't he proven that already?

Before she said something irretrievably foolish, she dived back to the original subject. "Your father... He's okay with this? With the kids, and me, moving in?"

She was sorry she had when he did let go of her, but not before he'd given her a last reassuring squeeze.

"My father," he said with a grin, that devastating Greg grin, "is delighted."

"What about—" she held up her left hand, with the gold band that felt startlingly heavy on her finger "—this?"

The grin faded, and he shrugged. "That, he's not so sure about. But he has his own reasons for being wary that don't have anything to do with...us."

Us. Her and him. Together. They really were an us now. An official us. And Briony didn't quite know how to deal with the feeling that gave her. The kids had kept her too busy and often too tired to worry about anything except what came next. And now all of a sudden here she was, looking at her life upended, her future completely changed, and with no idea how it all made her really feel.

But somewhere, buried down deep, there was a tiny part of her that was saying, "You're not alone anymore." And she couldn't deny she liked the sound of it.

But neither could she deny the knowledge that were it not for Rick and Wendy and their love for them, they wouldn't be here like this at all.

She guessed that meant the inveterate matchmakers had won in the end.

"Do I want to know what you just thought?"

Greg's quiet question snapped her out of the swirl in her mind. She looked up at him, one corner of her mouth lifting in a wry half smile. "Just that... Wendy and Rick would be laughing if they were here."

He blinked. "Laughing?"

"They finally got their way."

It took him a split second. But then she saw him rubbing his thumb on the ring, much as she often did. And his mouth quirked. "I guess they did."

WHEN DAD CALLED in the troops, he really called in the troops. The main area around the house was awash with people—siblings, cousins—and several dogs. And they'd all come prepared to get the job done, be it moving boxes or distracting the kids. The kids who were clearly enamored of Malcolm's search dog, Pacer, who was doing a beautiful job of keeping them entertained.

In the end, they had presented it to the kids as just staying here for a while, since at the moment that was true. Once the court case was decided, then they'd have more decisions to make, but for now, they made it sound like a vacation. Justin was thrilled with the idea, while Jane was more wary, although she was obviously quite taken with Mama Jen. But then, most kids were. Still, the little girl was fascinated with the animals and seemed quite willing to stay, with no wailing to go home. Yet, anyway.

They'd decided they would bring enough of the kids' things over to make it feel familiar, which required some things that had been occupying the space to be moved out to the barn for now. But there were a lot of strong Colton hands available, and it got done in short order. And eventually Greg found himself collapsed in one of the lawn chairs his brother Max had built, with Justin in his lap. The boy had unhesitatingly climbed up on his own, which he took as a good thing. That feeling was confirmed when he looked up to see his Mama Jen smiling at them both and nodding.

"We really gonna stay here, Unca Greg?"

"For a while. You okay with that?"

The boy nodded, looking around. "I like it."

"I think you just like the animals," he teased, and the boy grinned.

Greg supposed it was the total change of scene, perhaps letting the boy forget for a little while just how long it had been since his mother or father had held him, kissed him or tucked him in at night. He hadn't missed his own mother much at all, but that was different. Very, very different from having a loving, giving mother like Wendy had been.

After a dinner prepared to thank them, the helpful and no longer hungry crew departed. Greg did the cleanup, since Dad, Mama Jen and Briony had done most of the cooking. It was nearly dark, and he came out of the kitchen to find Jane asleep in Mama Jen's arms and Justin asleep in Dad's. He felt an upswell of emotion that nearly cut off his breath.

"I took a picture of them," Briony whispered beside him. He'd been so enraptured by what he was looking at he hadn't even heard her approach. "It's just so sweet."

"I…thank you," he managed to get out. Then, turning his head to meet her gaze, he added, "For the picture, and for reminding me how lucky I've been."

Something warm and yet slightly unsettling came into her eyes then. "I wish I'd been that lucky."

"Well, you are now," Greg said.

"Because I'm married to you?"

Greg pulled back with a start. "I didn't mean—"

"Relax, silly. I was just ribbing you."

He relaxed a little. Was glad she was able to joke, and his mouth twisted in a half smile, a little rueful. "This is a whole different kind of 'had to get married,' isn't it?"

"Every day a new adventure." She quoted Rick's oft-repeated saying with the same intonation he'd always used. And Greg couldn't help himself—he laughed. But as he did, he felt the sting of moisture in his eyes yet again.

And wondered if it would ever stop.

Chapter Twenty-Five

She'd teased him. She'd actually teased him. She'd never done that before, unless they'd been with Rick and Wendy and the joking had been going all around, usually at a picnic or barbecue at the lake. Only with the armor of her dear friends had she felt strong enough to join in the friendly mockery.

Briony felt that now familiar tightness in her chest, the fierce ache of missing that convivial connection, and the agony of knowing it would never, ever happen again.

They were on their way back to the house, and she was mentally going through what to bring now that there was much more empty space. Fortunately, Greg had had the presence of mind to ask the kids what toys they wanted, so she had a list. She was surprised at how short it was but guessed that Justin at least was so focused on the novelty of the ranch he wasn't thinking about other things. And Jane was simply unhappy at the moment, which Briony certainly understood.

Greg spent some time taking Jane's crib apart, but she was a little amazed at how quickly he got it done.

"I helped Rick put it together," he said when she made a comment about it. And the undertone in his voice told her he was feeling none too happy about this, undoing what he and his best friend had done.

She felt the same qualms as they gathered everything and got ready to leave the home Rick and Wendy had made for their family. But she couldn't argue the facts as Greg had presented them, and still felt a bit naive for not having re-alized them herself.

"Don't worry about it if you forget something," Greg said when at last they had everything they could think of. "I can come back if necessary."

She noticed he said *I*, not *we*. Just as he'd at first said to give him a list of what she'd wanted from the house, and he'd go get it. The idea of him pawing through her under-wear and other things she'd moved to the house had made her uncomfortable enough that she'd insisted on coming along. Only—once again—later did it hit her that he might have been thinking of her safety, with that PI on the loose and Rick's conniving, unscrupulous father's intentions now declared.

But only on the way back to the ranch did it strike her that the man she'd been worried about going through her under-wear, even just to pack it, was…her husband. She laughed at herself and nearly let it slip out as they drove through town.

When they reached the gate to the ranch, it really hit that, for now at least, this would be her home. This vast, expansive place was the kind of place she'd always wanted to live. The problem was, when she'd imagined it, it was so she could live with lots of room, away from other people. And now she was going to be in a guest house with three other people, more in the big house just yards away, and even more who worked here, coming and going.

As if to prove her point, three ranch workers crossed the driveway in front of them, all waving cheerfully. Another was washing down a piece of equipment she didn't recognize, and also waved as they passed.

"Not exactly your solitary life, is it?"

Greg's quiet comment startled her out of her reverie.

Why'd you become an accountant?

Because it's solitary. I wanted to work by myself, without a lot of people around.

They'd had that exchange about the third time Rick and Wendy had finagled a joint evening together. But it had been so long ago she was beyond stunned that he'd remembered it after all this time.

"No. No, it's not. But it's for the kids, so I'll adapt." *I hope.*

He pulled his truck to a stop in front of his place, turned it off, but didn't make a move to get out. She saw his jaw tighten slightly as he stared through the windshield at the tidy place that had become his home.

The home she and the kids were about to invade.

"It's not exactly your life anymore either, is it?" she said quietly. "Not your personal space, either."

"It's not that," he said, barely loud enough for her to hear. "It's just… I miss him. Them."

"He was your best friend just as Wendy was mine. The hole in both our lives is…immeasurable."

He turned his head to look at her then, and she knew she hadn't mistaken the sheen in his eyes. And it warmed her more than she ever would have thought to know she wasn't alone in this pain.

"Then we have to fill it with their children," he said, and she caught an undertone of determination in his deep voice.

She held his gaze steadily as she agreed. "They're the only thing that can do it."

For a moment neither of them said anything more. As

if everything that needed to be said had been. But then Greg reached out and took her hand, clasping it firmly, part handshake, part reassurance and part understanding. They were in this together because it was the only way it would get done.

And it had to be done.

With that, Briony and Greg Colton got out and went to get the children.

"JANE!"

Briony's startled exclamation kicked up Greg's adrenaline. It took him a moment to spot the child in the big room of the main house, but when he did, he let out a short laugh. "Well, doesn't that just figure."

He watched for a moment as the child toddled across the entire length of the great room, aided by hanging on to his brother's dog. Pacer walked carefully, slowly, as if he completely understood what his job was here, just as he did on a search-and-rescue mission. Jane was giggling with every step, any sign of the shyness around strangers he'd noticed before vanished now. She looked like a delighted little cherub, with her bright blond hair, big blue eyes and rosy cheeks. And Pacer was the perfect height to help her keep her balance as she moved into this new adventure.

He looked over at Malcolm. "Teaching Pacer another new skill, bro?"

His brother laughed. "Not me. They did this on their own. I just kept an eye on them."

Briony looked a little rattled, and Greg wasn't sure why. But then Jane looked up at her, smiled widely and crowed, "Bri, doggy!"

Briony's expression changed completely. He'd heard the phrase about someone melting, but he'd never thought about it much. He did now, because that's exactly what she looked like, as if she'd melted inside. He couldn't remember if Jane had ever really tried to use Briony's name before. By-By was as close as he'd ever heard her get.

"Unca Greg!"

He turned in time to see Justin headed for him at a run, arms upstretched, something clutched in his right hand. He turned, braced, because he'd learned what came next, a flying leap in his direction, leaving him the responsibility of catching the four-year-old. He managed it fairly neatly this time, unlike the first time when it had been like grabbing an unruly calf who had squirming refined down to an escape technique.

"Look!" he exclaimed excitedly. "Look what Mr. Buck made. Just for me!"

The child held out a small wood carving of a long-legged foal. Dad had a knack with a knife and wood, always had. In fact, he had a carving very similar to this on a shelf at home.

"It's Wick," the boy explained, his eyes gleaming with excitement as if the gift had been the latest, coolest video game or something.

"I can see that."

"Do you know where that name came from, Justin?" Briony asked as she reached out to put a gentle hand on the boy's arm.

Justin nodded. "My mommy and daddy. Mr. Buck told me."

"That makes this even more special, then, doesn't it?" she said softly.

The boy nodded. "I'm glad we came here," he said. "I like it."

"Good," Greg said. "Now get all your stuff that's here at the big house, okay? We brought the things you asked for, so now we have to decide where to put it at my house."

The child's brow furrowed. "Your house is the one over there?" he asked, pointing in the right general direction.

"Yep."

"Good. It's close," he said, the furrow vanishing. "'Cuz Mr. Buck said I could come over anytime."

Still clutching the wooden horse as Greg put him down, the boy quickly started to do as asked, and gather up the few things that were here, including his jacket and a toy truck that looked as if it had lost out to the hand-carved horse.

"Your father is really something," Briony said, looking at Greg.

"He is," Greg said.

"And then some," Malcolm agreed from very close by.

Briony looked down quickly, and Greg saw that Pacer had gently nudged her knee. Beside the big shepherd mix, Jane stood holding her arms up to Briony. She bent and picked the little girl up.

"Okay, buddy," Malcolm said with a grin at his dog, "looks like you're off duty for the moment."

"Thank you for watching out for her with the dog," Briony said.

Malcolm blinked. "She's family now. And so are you."

Greg felt a little jolt. So that answered that. Dad had told him. He was glad; he didn't want to have to explain over and over again.

"By the way," Malcolm said, "Mama Jen's coming back over tomorrow afternoon and we're going to have a big barbecue, so everybody can meet Briony and the kids. Dad wanted a sit-down dinner, but Mama Jen thought it would be easier on you guys if we did a barbecue outside."

Greg noticed his brother's gaze flicker to Briony, who had tensed immediately at his first words, but eased a bit as he finished. He wondered if Jen had singled her out as the reason for that. He'd told his aunt she was really shy, and a barbecue would give her more chance to escape, at least now and then. It would be like her to think of something like that.

"Probably a good idea," he said, picking his words carefully. "If we're asking them to keep watch, they should at least meet everyone."

He felt Briony relax. Which was weird, because he wasn't touching her or anything. He could just feel her tension fade away. He'd be willing to bet it was because he'd presented a logical, realistic and necessary reason for the gathering. Just as she had when he'd pointed out why they should stay here, she put the welfare of the kids ahead of her own nervousness.

But the main thing he was thinking as they gathered everything up and headed for his place was that as…interesting and sometimes unpleasant as his life had been, it couldn't have been anywhere close to hers.

Chapter Twenty-Six

"He asked it again," Briony said wearily as she quietly closed the bedroom door on the sleeping children. Then she had a second thought and reopened it a little, thinking if they woke up in a strange place and were scared, it would be easier to hear them.

Greg looked at her from where he was, a little to her surprise, tidying up the debris from unpacking the kids' things to get to their pajamas while he'd put Jane's crib back together. Stuff had ended up a little strewn about, and she'd already had it in mind that she'd pick up everything before she even sat down, because she had the feeling once she did sit it would take a bulldozer to get her moving again. She was exhausted, and not just physically.

"When they're coming back?" Greg asked.

She nodded and saw a muscle jump at the side of that strong jaw. Funny how she noticed—and almost treasured—every sign that she wasn't alone in this quagmire. It was almost like she was…glad he was hurting, too, and that seemed perverse of her, or at the least cold.

Misery truly does love company.

"I kept to the script," she said when he didn't say anything.

"Good." He seemed to hesitate, then added, "I know it's hard."

"It is, but we have to think about how kids who have no idea about…death…might interpret platitudes," she said.

"Yeah." He grimaced. "You tell them they're in a better place, then they're liable to go looking for it."

Despite everything, she smiled a little at that. She'd always liked his sense of humor, and that had never changed.

A long moment of silence spun out between them before Greg, stretching in a way that seemed to emphasize the breadth of his shoulders, his chest, asked, "Are you as exhausted as I am?"

She had to fight down an unwanted reaction to the way he moved before she could say, fairly evenly, "If I sit down, I'll be asleep in thirty seconds."

"Sounds about right," he agreed, his tone wry.

"Much as I would like to, we have to talk first, don't we?"

He looked suddenly wary. "Talk? Like one of those capital *T* talks?"

She studied him for a moment. She really didn't know that much about his relationship history, other than a couple of times when Rick had teased him about a woman named Jill. Greg's reaction had been an eye roll and a promise to put Rick on the floor if he didn't drop it. But that had been spoken like a man who'd had too many of the kind of talks she knew he meant, those deep, emotional ones. The kind she knew people had—Wendy had assured her of that—but she'd never experienced because the few relationships she'd had never got that deep or lasted long enough.

Wendy had told her more than once that was her own fault, that she shied away from deep connections because she didn't trust them. Didn't trust other people. And she couldn't really deny that.

I know it's true, because I felt the same way, until I met

Rick. But he wouldn't budge, and eventually I realized he was for real.

Wendy had tried so hard to convince her there were people she could trust. How brutally cockeyed was it that it took Rick and Wendy dying to prove that to her? Because if nothing else, she knew she could trust Greg Colton when it came to the kids. He would do what was right. And she was pretty sure his father and his aunt fell into the same category. Judging by what she'd seen today, probably his siblings, too. They'd already been so much help—

"So, talk," Greg said, making her realize she'd been once more lost in her thoughts. When you were generally wary of people, that happened a lot.

"I just meant about how this is going to work. Logistically, I mean."

"Oh." She almost smiled at the sound of relief in his voice. Then, in a very businesslike tone, he said, "Well, there's only the one bathroom, so we'll have to figure that out. Are you a morning or evening shower person?"

"Morning, usually."

"Good. I'm evening, because working on the ranch all day can make a guy pretty grubby."

A sudden realization flashed through her mind, all those days when he'd come to the house from the ranch, and she'd noticed his hair was damp. He'd showered after his workday at the ranch and before heading to another few hours of working with the kids and giving her a break. Then, unexpectedly, an image of being here while he did just that, of standing maybe right here at the kitchen counter, listening to the water run in the bathroom just off the hallway entrance, imagining it running over that tall, strong body... that tall, strong, naked body...

She sucked in a long breath, trying to steady herself. She

thought she had buried this kind of reaction to him long ago, back when Greg had laughed at Rick and Wendy for trying to set them up together, telling them that just because they were the only two single people they knew that didn't mean they were a match. Because back then, even when she was agreeing with what he said, she was regretting the truth of it.

"—try to be quiet when I roll out in the morning," he was saying, and she tuned back in hastily.

"I don't want to kick you out of your bedroom. I can sleep out here. You're too tall to sleep on this couch."

To her surprise, he chuckled. "You're not exactly vertically challenged, lady. What are you, five nine or ten?"

"Nine," she said, surprised he'd gotten so close.

"So I've got three inches on you. Big deal. And that couch is almost eight feet long. I'll survive. At least until things settle down and we get Winston Kraft out of the kids' lives. Then we can reassess."

He was so…reasonable. And generous. And kind. And… trustworthy?

She gave in because she couldn't really counter anything he'd said. But after they'd both finally surrendered to that weariness, she wished she'd fought harder. He'd come in with her to grab some things, including clothes and a book from the nightstand—one of his many cousins ran the bookstore in town, she remembered—and had pointed out a couple of empty drawers in the chest beside the closet, where he also shoved his own things on hangers to one side, leaving her a nice empty spot that would more than accommodate what she had with her.

She tried not to think about whose space she was invading as she got into her preferred knit sleep pants and shirt. A moment later there was no way she couldn't think that she should have taken him up on the offer to change the sheets on the bed. But he'd said he'd only slept on them once since they'd been washed, so she'd said not to bother.

And now she was lying in a swath of cloth that smelled like him. Not that she couldn't smell the clean of the laundry soap, but there was more. Not just the scent of the bar of soap she'd seen in the shower, or the aftershave she'd seen in the bathroom cabinet, but that indefinable something that had said "Greg" to her from the first time she'd sat next to him at a table, on Rick and Wendy's first effort to get them together.

She tried to focus on the fact that she was finally going to get to sleep, and that she'd better do it before Jane woke up in the night and her wailing for her momma woke Justin, and they'd be in chaos again. That was more important than the fact that she was at last sleeping in Greg's bed.

Without Greg.

When she finally fell asleep, she dreamed about that pitiful wail. Stirred restlessly, not knowing what to do to comfort the distraught child. On some level her brain thought it was real, and she felt as if she were underwater and fighting to reach the surface. But by the time she did and opened her eyes, it was silent. So it had been just a dream.

When she woke again, the sky was slightly less dark, and she knew dawn was approaching. She felt a little more rested, despite the worrisome dreams. That in mind, she tiptoed quietly down the hall to peek into the room to check on the kids. She opened the door a couple of inches and peered in.

Jane was gone.

Jolted fully awake, Briony smothered a gasp and went through the doorway, thinking she had to just not be seeing right in the dim light. But there was no denying the crib was empty.

She whirled around to look at the twin bed against the opposite wall. Justin was there, sleeping apparently peacefully after his long, active day. She turned again, heading for the door, her heart hammering in her chest. Where was Jane? Had something happened to that poor baby? God, she had to wake Greg, tell him. Had Kraft somehow gotten to her? Found out they were here, gotten past all the barriers and broken in to steal her? But then why not Justin? Unless he was afraid the older child might make too much noise, might tip off—

She came to a halt three steps into the main room. And as the scene before her registered, she thought her heart physically jumped. Greg was there all right, stretched out on his back on the couch.

And a sleeping Jane was cradled carefully on his broad chest.

She had heard that wail; it had been real. His eyes opened, telling her he'd only been dozing, probably out of concern the baby might slip or fall to the floor if he went fully to sleep.

For a moment she just stood there, her gaze locked with his. Greg had done what Greg would always do, the right thing. Tears stung her eyes and then overflowed. And for the first time it wasn't for Rick and Wendy. It was because they couldn't have picked anyone better as guardian for their children than this man.

This man who was now her husband.

Chapter Twenty-Seven

Greg wanted to jump to his feet and go to Briony, but he couldn't without waking Jane. So he just looked at her. She seemed so…something. She seemed smaller somehow, dressed in a short T-shirt–style top and loose sleep pants. She was crying, as she had often since that awful night, and to be honest he'd had his own bouts with fighting back the flood of emotion that still battered at him at the thought of never seeing his best friend again.

But this seemed different somehow. And it wasn't just that she looked oddly relieved as she stared at him. Belatedly it struck him. She'd probably checked the other bedroom first and found Jane wasn't there.

Even as he thought it, she whispered, "I looked and she was gone. I was afraid…"

Her voice trailed away without completing the thought, but he could imagine what she was afraid of, what she probably imagined when she saw that empty crib. That somehow Kraft had gotten in here and grabbed the tiny girl now sleeping so soundly on his chest.

"Sorry," he whispered back. The child didn't seem to be stirring at their quiet exchange, so he went on. "I heard her and remembered Rick saying he used to do this until she went to sleep. I was about to get up and put her back."

She shook her head. "Don't apologize. You're both… beautiful."

He blinked. Felt an odd rush of heat. It took him a moment to realize he was both embarrassed and pleased by her words. And had no words of his own to answer that clearly heartfelt declaration.

Gingerly, he shifted on the couch, holding Jane close while swinging his legs down to get his feet on the floor. Once he was upright, he stopped, waiting, to be sure the tiny girl hadn't awakened. He carried her back to the bedroom and laid her gently down in the crib, Rick's laughing explanation of all the things he'd had to learn about babies running through his head. He tried to focus on that, but his mind wanted to dwell on the look in Briony's eyes when she'd called them beautiful. He knew she probably meant the moment, probably the sight of Jane sleeping so peacefully, but she'd said…both.

When she was settled, thankfully still sound asleep, he straightened and turned to look at Briony. There was a gleam in her lovely green eyes he'd never seen before.

Lovely green eyes?

They were lovely. Especially when they were focused on him like they were now. As if he was the only thing that mattered to her right now. And not just because of the kids.

He shied away from the fact that the idea pleased him. As if he liked the idea that he mattered to her beyond the situation they found themselves in. Which was…silly.

He'd wondered on occasion, after Wendy had told him that, how differently she might have turned out had her life been different. Would she have been the lively, vivacious woman her hair and eyes suggested? Or was that just his imagination, sparked by the occasional flashes of spirit he saw?

Like when she faced you down over where the kids should be?

He smiled inwardly at that thought. Because for all her shyness, when it came down to what she thought was the best for the kids, she'd gotten past her reticence and stood her ground. And he had a gut-deep kind of feeling that she always would. Which was a side of her he'd never seen or known even existed before.

Even as he thought it, he realized how unobservant he'd been. You didn't survive the kind of life she'd had and come out steady enough to build your own life and business as she had without having a pretty solid core. And who was he to criticize how she protected herself in her life? After all, as his father had once told him, his tactic of pretending he wasn't hurting inside didn't make it go away. At the time he'd thought it was just typical fatherly advice. Only later, when he'd grown up a bit more and understood what his mother had done, did he realize Dad had been speaking from firsthand experience.

All of this ran through his mind and somehow, he ended up saying, very gently, "It's still early. Why don't you try to get some more sleep?"

As if the suggestion had triggered it, she yawned. She quickly put her hand up to cover her mouth. The movement of her arm made her shirt ride up a little, and he got a glimpse of smooth, pale skin and the beginning of the curve of one hip. When the arm came down it shifted a breast just slightly. A nicely curved, full breast.

Whoa. Back off, Colton.

"I think I will," she said, "and you should, too."

Still reeling a bit at his unexpected reaction, he couldn't

find any words to say. And as she turned to go back to the bedroom, he found himself noticing her nicely curved backside, too. And it was like another kick to the gut.

She was almost to the hallway when she stopped and looked back. Caught him dead to rights, staring at her. But she didn't seem to notice. *Or care, more likely.*

"They knew what they were doing when they picked you," she said quietly.

Again, words failed him. And then she was gone. He had to fight the urge to go after her, to figure out what had just happened here. What had suddenly awakened him to the fact that she wasn't just Rick and Wendy's friend, she was someone he'd like to know better. That he was curious about what was going on behind those green eyes when she silently studied something. Or someone. Like him. Wanted to know what she was thinking, what made her so sure he was the right guy for the job of raising Justin and Jane.

Then of course there was that other pesky little detail. That after all this time he'd realized that while she might be quiet and shy, she was also a knockout. After all this time, his body had suddenly realized it and kicked to life so fiercely it had almost taken his breath away.

Great, Colton. Complicate things even more, why don't you?

Trying to shove it all out of his mind, he went back to the couch, hoping to grab a little more sleep before the long day ahead began. But when his head hit the pillow, he knew it was futile. Because all he could think about was that that pillow was from his bed. His bed, that Briony was now in, in those loose-knit pajamas that somehow made that slight reveal of skin and shape sexier than any blatant lacy nightwear.

He stared up at the ceiling, wondering how, in the space

of just a few minutes, he'd gone from the slight and oddly gratifying pressure of baby Jane on his chest to the greater and very different pressure of Briony on his mind.

It wasn't until later, when he shifted position yet again, trying to find that elusive sleep, that it hit him that the woman he couldn't get out of his head was his wife.

And he groaned aloud at the ridiculous morass his life had become.

Chapter Twenty-Eight

Briony didn't think she would ever get that image of Greg and little Jane out of her mind. The big, strong man so gently cradling the tiny girl on his broad chest, and the baby—she knew Jane was a toddler age-wise, but in that moment, that image, she had looked so small she couldn't call her anything but a baby—sleeping so soundly, trusting utterly in the man who held her. As if she somehow knew she was safe there.

Anyone would be safe there.

Rick had always told her she could trust his best friend. And she'd believed it, or at least believed that Rick believed it. She'd just never expected to have to rely on that assessment.

But here she was, curled up in his bed while he slept, certainly less comfortably, on the couch a few yards away. There was only a closed door between them, but she knew it might as well be a steel barricade, because he would never take advantage of it. Even if it was his own house, his own bedroom, his own bed she'd taken over.

Her husband's bed.

She buried her face in the pillow to stifle the faint moan that escaped her. But the pillow still had that faint, clean scent of that soap in the bathroom, which made sense if he always showered in the evening. But that sent her mind careening into other areas, like again imagining him in that shower, imagining water sluicing down over that masculine body, sliding over the taut muscles of his chest, the tight curve of his backside, and…other parts.

This time there was nothing faint about her moan. Her attraction to the man broke free of the compartment she'd so carefully kept it in for years, billowing out like an erupting volcano's smoke.

The man she had just married. Tied herself to for life. That was the vow she'd made, even as she knew—as they both knew—this was more a business arrangement for the sake of the kids than anything.

They hadn't yet talked about what would come after. After they'd won the case and been given full custody of Justin and Jane. She wouldn't let herself think it would come out any other way, because the thought of those two innocents going to the likes of Rick's father was too horrific to even consider. They had to win. They would win. And she would do whatever she could, whatever she had to, to make that happen.

Including baring her soul and letting what she'd always felt show to the world. Or at least, the judge who would decide the case. She would look at Greg as if it were all true, as if she truly were his wife in more than just name. She would look at him with everything he'd made her feel last night showing. Given how powerful it had been, that ought to do it.

And if it made things more awkward between them afterward, once the kids were safely theirs, so be it.

In the meantime, she had this big gathering to get through tonight. She'd never been comfortable at large parties, and that's what it seemed this was going to be. At least it would be casual dress, and outside where everybody wouldn't be crammed into one room. Maybe she could even escape for a breather now and then. Surely nobody would miss her—this was for the kids after all, so everyone would know who they were protecting. They just needed to be able to recognize her, and over the years she'd found her hair alone was usually enough to accomplish that.

When the time finally came, even outside she was a little stunned at how many people there were. She'd known the Coltons were a big family, but she hadn't quite realized how big until she was confronted with most of them. And it hit her anew when she was introduced as not just the children's co-guardian, but as Greg's wife. She understood their shock, since there had been no lead-up to it, probably never even a mention of her.

They had to know Greg had married her only for the sake of the children, and they were probably feeling sorry for him. Yet there was no sign of that in any of them. Some were brusquer than others, some friendlier and more welcoming, but no one shunned her or looked at her as if they didn't want her here. Especially welcoming was his sister, Lizzy, a slim, pretty strawberry blonde who smilingly said she was glad to have another redhead in the family.

But most importantly, they were all wonderful with the kids. Particularly Greg's cousin Hannah, who had brought her precocious five-year-old daughter, Lucy, who immediately joined up with Justin and Jane to keep everyone entertained.

Greg's dad fired up the big grill and had everyone lined up for some of his amazing ribs and chicken. Mama Jen added her plethora of savory side dishes including garlic mashed potatoes—this was Idaho, after all—and, to Briony's surprise, her effort at a pumpkin custard pie with a whipped topping vanished quickly and earned her more than one accolade.

It was the kind of thing she'd never experienced in her life, and sometimes throughout the afternoon she had to remind herself that all these people, save the ranch hands who stopped in for their share of the fun and food, were related. She had so little experience with this kind of family, in both size and strong connection, she was a little bewildered by it. But they were all kind to her, and she got through it, only retreating for a breather twice during the three-hour affair.

And the next day, Sunday, was the peaceful, restful antidote she needed. The children were quiet, probably having shouted and whooped themselves out yesterday, and while it had become clear to her that the ranch workers never took a day off, even they were less harried than during the rest of the week. They spent time watching Wick frolic in the small corral next to the barn, and she would have sworn the little colt recognized the kids by the way he trotted over to the fence on those long, gangly legs to greet them.

And looking at the animal who already seemed to be growing reminded her of the story Buck had told her of the night he was born, including what Greg had left out, that he had likely saved the little guy's life by doing what was necessary at that dangerous moment.

"I have a feeling," she'd said, "that's what he always does."

Buck had given her an approving nod, which warmed her more than it should have coming from a man she'd only just recently met. "Then you know my son," he'd said, and the pride in the older man's voice nearly brought tears to her eyes.

After that, the time at the ranch both flew by and dragged, depending on what was happening. The slow part was having to wait, impatiently, for the custody hearing date. The attorney had promised to let them know the moment they had a date, and she jumped every time her phone rang, but it was always a client. Or Greg, checking in on her and the kids when he was out in some far corner of the ranch.

The time when she wasn't obsessing about the hearing seemed to pass in a rush. The kids were kept so busy, so occupied with this fascinating place and its various human and animal occupants, that they were tired enough to sleep soundly most nights. And Briony found the relief of no longer being the only one to look out for them amazing. Greg's aunt was so caring and generous with her time, and his father almost beyond belief with his patience and wise suggestions. Beyond her belief, anyway. She'd never known a man like Buck Colton before.

Except Greg. He had learned well from his father.

She almost felt guilty about how much easier her life was here, with all this help, especially when she watched how hard Greg worked both doing his ranch work and then coming home after a long day and expending even more effort with the kids. At least he wasn't having to drive to the other house every day. If she'd had any idea how truly hard he worked she would have given that more weight.

And it was clear he was always thinking about the children, because one day he'd take Justin with him when he was going someplace he knew the boy would like—he had a fascination with the forest and its creatures, and occasionally a calf would stray—and the next would take Jane with him, carefully held in a sling she never would have imagined him using, when he had to head toward a marshy area where the song sparrows that so fascinated her tended to gather and sing their chirping, trilling songs.

He was so kind, so loving and gentle with them…and

yet he was the man who'd gone racing toward a gunfight when his cousin Chase had needed him. She'd never known a man like that in her life. Until now, hadn't been fully convinced they existed.

And so she caught herself in the quiet evenings she relished, usually when they were ensconced on the couch, her checking figures on her laptop, him reading whatever book he had going—he clearly preferred print books, but beyond that seemed to have a bit of everything on the shelves on the far wall—glancing over at him. Often. And loving the image that seemed to imprint on her brain, that matched her earlier fanciful imaginings, his chiseled profile, his concentration, and the way his brow sometimes furrowed, or he smiled as if something on the page had amused him. Once she asked him what had made him smile, and he said only, "Nice turn of phrase."

So much for the stereotype of dumb cowboys...

She'd felt as if she wasn't doing her share, since the kids were so enraptured by the ranch and all its doings, even little Jane who had decided that playing in a big pile of clean straw was the greatest thing ever. So, at the risk of falling into a stereotype herself—and because he usually cooked more than she did—she took to the kitchen. She did a little investigation first, checking with the ever-helpful Buck, on what Greg's favorite foods were. For a moment he looked at her a little oddly, but then quickly gave her a helpful answer of "Beef's his favorite, other than that anything but brussels sprouts."

She wrinkled her nose at the very thought, making Buck laugh. It was only later that she realized that perhaps he'd been surprised that she didn't already know what Greg did and didn't like to eat. But when she put a savory beef stew that had turned out even better than she'd hoped on the table and called Greg to eat, and he'd raved over it between hefty spoonfuls, she suddenly understood the gratification you could get from cooking for someone who did so much for you. Someone special.

Your husband.

It still jolted her every time she thought it. But the jolt was overwhelmed by the warm feeling she got watching him eat what she'd made. That he didn't expect her to do it all only sweetened the feeling.

It was Monday evening when the phone call came. Greg put his book down to answer. She could tell by the way he went utterly still, his expression intense, that it was important. When he finished with "We'll be there," her heart took a little leap.

He put the phone down and looked at her. And Greg-like, he didn't make her wait. "That was Tanya. Some other case reached an agreement out of court, and the judge agreed to give us the spot on the calendar. Wednesday morning. So now we're in a rush and we need to be in her office tomorrow for prep."

For a long moment they just looked at each other. It was finally here, the moment when the rest of their lives, the kids' lives, would be decided. She'd been so anxious for it to be settled she'd thought she'd feel a blast of relief when they had a court date. Instead, she was suddenly trembling.

"Greg," she said urgently, "what if…what if we lose?"

"We won't," he said, sounding rock-solid determined.

"But if we did, the kids…if he gets them…" She couldn't get past the horror of the idea to finish the sentence.

"He won't," he said this time.

"You can't know that. He could buy off the judge, or—"

"He will not get his hands on them. Even if I have to take them and run to keep them safe, he will not."

Briony stared at him, stunned by his words. That he would do that, leave this place he loved, his home, his amazing family, give up his entire life to fulfill the vow his best friend had asked of him… She knew, now that she'd been here and seen his life here, what a sacrifice that would be. And yet he was clearly decided, determined. He would do it, for the children. He would do it for his best friend. He would do it because he'd promised. Because he was the kind of man she'd never known in her life, the kind who kept promises, who helped others, who didn't always put himself first but also stood his ground, the kind of man who would never, ever intentionally hurt anyone—unless it was to protect someone he'd made one of those vows to.

He made a vow to you.

Sure, it had been more of a legal agreement than a wedding, but still Briony knew that he would take it as seriously as any other vow he made.

And in that moment, as she sat staring at his man unlike any other she had ever known, Briony admitted the truth she had buried so deeply she'd hoped it would never surface. But it burst free now, and she was left to deal with the simple fact. She may have just had a crush all these years, but now she knew the man, the real man. Knew who and what he was. Which, she supposed, made this inevitable. Even though they'd never so much as kissed.

She had utterly fallen for Greg Colton.

Chapter Twenty-Nine

Something about the way Briony was looking at him made Greg…uneasy? Uncomfortable? Unsettled?

Maybe all of those.

Because she was looking at him as if he'd done something wonderful, something amazing, even though all he'd done was voice his determination to do exactly what she was doing, devoting everything to keeping Justin and Jane safe and as happy as possible under the circumstances. He didn't know why she was so…whatever she was.

What he did know was that he was suddenly flooded with the need to live up to that look in her eyes. To have earned it. To deserve it. And he didn't quite know when or how her approval had become so damned important to him.

Or why he'd been obsessing about the feel of her in his arms, when all he'd meant to do was offer some comfort, some support in this monumental job they'd been tasked with.

In a way, it had started the night she'd made that amazing beef stew. Other than Dad, and Mama Jen if she was here, he pretty much saw to his own meals, and admittedly they weren't always great. Too often he went with whatever was quickest and easiest because he was too tired after a long day to think about anything else. And that beef stew, with whatever combination of spices and flavorings she'd used, had been a wonder.

So you're some old-fashioned male, charmed by a woman cooking for you? Some chauvinist who likes his woman barefoot, pregnant and in the kitchen as the old saying—

He felt as if he'd been hit by a wrecking ball. Because he'd suddenly—and ridiculously—remembered she wasn't his woman.

She was his wife.

His wife, and he'd never done anything more than hug her.

"And if it comes to that," she said now, very softly yet somehow defiantly, "if the judge rules the wrong way… I'll be right there with you."

She'd go on the run with the kids, with him? The thought that if worse came to worst, he wouldn't be alone made his stomach do an odd little flip.

He told himself she'd only do it for the children, but…she was still looking at him, steadily, with that warming glow in her eyes. As he stared back at her, her lips suddenly parted, as if she'd needed to take a deeper breath. He knew the feeling. He was feeling it himself. And suddenly he wanted to do more than just hold her.

He wanted to kiss that mouth, to see if those lips were as soft and sweet as they looked. And that kick-in-the-gut feeling suddenly dropped lower, and his body woke up in a rush.

"Don't look at me like that," he said thickly.

Her head tilted slightly. "Like what?"

"Like you want—" He cut himself off sharply. "I think I'd better go for a walk."

She blinked. "Why?"

"Because right now I want to kiss you."

Her breath caught audibly, and bright color rose in her cheeks. "And that's…a problem?"

His own breath jammed up in his throat. "You saying it's not?"

"Maybe I'm just saying… I'm curious, too."

"You know what they say about curiosity."

"I am not," she said slowly, "a cat."

"And I," he said slowly, replacing the bookmark and closing his book slowly, methodically, as if concentrating on that would divert everything else that was rocketing through his brain and body, "need that walk."

He stood up. Something changed in her then; she seemed to collapse into herself. And it unexpectedly hit him what courage it had taken shy, quiet, unassuming Briony to be as…forward as she'd just been.

"Briony," he began, then stopped, not knowing what to say.

"Never mind." It was almost a whisper. "I'm too much of a coward for you anyway."

Coward. The woman who had done what she'd done, who had faced him down more than once, who had taken on a load she'd never expected to carry and done it without hesitation or complaint, and who had just now offered to give up what life of her own she had left to go on the run from Winston Kraft, a coward?

He sat back down, this time right next to her. "You are many things, Briony. A coward isn't one of them."

She looked up at him then, those lovely—really, how had he not noticed how gorgeous they were?—green eyes glistening. That urge he thought he'd quashed rose up again, more fiercely this time. Almost undeniable.

Her lips parted and she lowered her eyes, making him

wonder what those long, thick lashes would feel like against his skin.

And then it was undeniable. He was moving before he even realized it, leaning in, lifting her chin with a gentle finger, giving her every chance to retreat but hoping she would not.

She didn't.

Her lips were softer, warmer, more enticing than he could have imagined. He caught the scent he only now realized he'd always associated with her, a light, clean, almost sage-like fragrance. Instinctively he moved closer, cupped her face with his hands to deepen the kiss. He felt the drag of his own work-roughened skin against the silk of hers, and half expected her to pull away at the harshness of it. Instead, she lifted her arms to his shoulders, as if hanging on. As if she needed the contact.

As if her senses were swirling as wildly as his own were.

When he finally broke away, only because he had to breathe, he stared at her in something resembling both wonder and shock. Never, ever would he have expected that kissing quiet, shy Briony would send every nerve in his body into overdrive. And she was staring back at him with an expression he couldn't quite put a name to. Almost… resignation?

And then, so low he had to strain to hear it, she whispered, "I knew it."

"Knew what?"

"That it would be…like that."

His brain was still spinning enough that it took him a moment to come to the conclusion that this meant she'd thought about it. Before. Maybe even before just now? Rick had once hinted that he thought Briony had a bit of a crush on him, but he'd thought it was just part of their matchmaking scheme.

Now he wasn't so sure.

Nor did he have any idea how he could have missed the potential chemistry between them. Had Rick and Wendy's machinations made him blind to it? Or at the least, resistant to the idea? He didn't know. All he knew for sure was…he wanted more.

Lots more.

"Don't worry," she said, and his gaze snapped back to her in time to see the look that was now definitely resignation on her face.

"What?"

"I know that it's just…circumstances. That we've been forced together, that it's…convenient, that we're married in name only."

"Briony," he began, but stopped when she shook her head.

"I said don't worry. I won't cross that boundary again."

"As I recall," he said wryly, "I'm the one who started that kiss."

"Only after I practically begged you."

He raised a brow at her. "I missed that part."

"Greg, please…"

Sudden doubt assailed him. "Look, if it wasn't…if you don't want…all you have to say is no and it'll never happen again."

She stared at him, wide-eyed. "How could you ever think I wouldn't want…more? I thought you wouldn't. You've never been in the least interested, all those times when Wendy and Rick tried to set us up."

"I know. Maybe I was just being…stubborn."

For the first time since the kiss, he saw a glint in her eye that had become familiar by now. Usually seen right before she launched a volley at him. Which had surprised him no end, coming from she who was usually so quiet and almost withdrawn. Wendy had always said Briony had more spirit than she'd ever shown in front of him, and he knew now that was true.

And he knew he was right now when she said, in that light, teasing tone, "You mean you resisted being pushed? I don't believe it, not you."

"Yeah, yeah," he muttered, but couldn't stop his mouth from quirking upward at one corner. And he realized with a little shock that he liked it—a lot—when she teased him like this. That he saw it as progress, that she'd either developed the nerve or was comfortable enough now to let it show.

Progress toward what, exactly, he didn't know. Or wouldn't admit, even to himself. But somehow, telling himself it was likely just the situation—and that they were married, even if only for the kids—wasn't working as well as it once had.

He took himself off for that walk, if for no other reason than to cool himself down in the chill October air.

Chapter Thirty

Briony tossed the blouse she'd been holding down on the bed. She needed to stop by her condo after the meeting with the attorney today, after she'd had a chance to ask her advice on what she should wear to the court hearing tomorrow. She was thinking what she called her "meet the client" suit, the most expensive outfit she owned. But maybe that would be too much. Too…showy, or something. Maybe she should stick to—

The whoop from the living area cut off her thoughts. She heard energetic running footsteps that she recognized as Justin's, and the delighted giggle of his sister, and wondered what miracle Greg had wrought this morning to have them laughing and happy already.

The same kind of miracle he worked on you last night?

A little shiver went through her as she remembered that kiss. Every hot, sweet moment of it, but most especially when he'd reached up to cup her face, as if he wanted to be sure she didn't pull away. As if there'd been the slightest chance she would have wanted that impossible pleasure to stop. Ever.

And that he, the ever assured and confident Greg Colton, had felt even a moment of uncertainty in a strange way warmed her, had given her the courage to tease him, in that way he surprisingly seemed to like.

When they were finally on their way to Conners, Greg at the wheel, she turned her focus to keeping the kids in the happy mood Greg had put them in. Since they were to be assessed today by the court's chosen juvenile bereavement counselor, who would then submit a report to the judge, she supposed happy was a good place for them to be.

Even as she thought it Greg spoke. "I talked to my cousin Fletcher this morning."

She immediately thought of the tall, broad-shouldered man who had helped them with the PI, and had brought his charming girlfriend, Kiki, to the barbecue. The memory was quickly shattered by a spike of worry.

"Did he hear something? About the PI or Winston?"

"No," Greg assured her quickly. "I just called him to ask about Judge Thompson. He said the guy's by the book, but fair. And off the record, he doesn't have a high opinion of the Ever After Church."

"So smart, too," she said, relieved.

Greg flashed her a grin. That devastating grin. "Fletch said he overheard him say once, off the record, that calling Ever After a church gave churches a bad name."

A little to her own amazement, Briony laughed. She tried hard to hang on to the mood as they walked toward the lawyer's office, but Jane was fussing and she couldn't help thinking that wasn't a good sign, and what if she wouldn't settle down in front of the counselor? But then Greg lifted the little girl up in the air, making the whooshing sound she seemed to adore, and the fussing became a delighted giggle. Justin only asked if this was the place with the room with all the toys, and Briony said in a loud, mock whisper that yes, it was, and there were rumors there would be cookies. Justin brightened, while Jane piped in, "Cookie?"

As they neared the door to the office, Briony saw there was a woman standing there, watching them. It wasn't the woman who'd taken the kids into the playroom before, at the first meeting, so she wasn't sure why she was so intent on them, unless…unless she was the counselor. She supposed that made sense, for her to watch them unaware, see how they interacted with the children before settling into a more formal process. But it still made her nervous. She hadn't really thought about the possibility that the counselor could turn in a negative report, that maybe she—

"Hope she's not an Ever After fan," Greg muttered as they got closer.

"I was just thinking that," Briony said, her eyes fastened on the woman even as she took heart that they'd both had the same thought. She managed a smile as the woman opened the door for them, introducing herself as, indeed, the counselor.

Although she tried to pay close attention to the attorney's preparation and instructions for tomorrow, one part of her mind was solidly planted in that room next door. It was only when Greg reached out and took her hand that she was able to focus completely on what the lawyer was saying.

Tanya noticed the move immediately.

"So, how's the marriage of necessity working out?"

Briony felt her cheeks heat and couldn't have spoken even if she could find the words.

"We're good," Greg said, his voice holding that little note of roughness that made her nerves twitch.

But his fingers tightened slightly around hers, and that was all it took for her to be able to meet the lawyer's eyes and say evenly, "Yes, we are. And so are the children."

"And you're really, truly prepared to keep going? To commit yourselves to this?"

She glanced at Greg. He met her gaze and held it, warm, steady... Greg-like. She looked back at Tanya. "We already have," she said firmly.

The woman seemed to consider that for a moment, then nodded. Then the preparation began as she laid out what would likely happen tomorrow.

"We've done our disclosure to Kraft's attorney, slime though he may be. I suspect he's withholding on our discovery requests, which I can turn on him. Mr. Kraft himself has left me two voice mails that are outside the realm of civility, and I'll be using those. But the most crucial factor is what we all already know—that he had no interest in even meeting his grandchildren until the possibility of a significant amount of money entered the picture."

"Bastard," Greg muttered, then quickly looked at the lawyer. "Sorry."

She smiled and shrugged. "When the shoe fits... Now, since they filed the motion, they get to present first. This is not necessarily bad."

She went on to break down the entire process for them, added a little plan of her own that made them both smile, agreed with Briony's choice of attire, suggested the same for Greg, then focused on him.

"You carry a well-known name in Owl Creek," she said.

"Blessing or curse?" Greg asked, sounding a bit sour.

"Both, given that your family's...shall we say strife is fairly well-known, and will probably be used against you if possible. However, it's also well-known that your father is a solid, stable and upstanding citizen, so if he could be here—"

"He will be. I'll call in the whole darn family if it'll help."

She smiled. "I'd say the owner of the Colton Ranch and the CEO of Colton Properties would suffice."

Greg smiled back, steady now. "Good. Chase owes me one anyway."

"After you helped him rescue Sloan and take down a kidnapper, I should hope so," Briony said.

Tanya's brows rose. "Well, well, more arrows for my quiver. I'll need some details on that."

They spent some time going over things, then repeating it all. Then, finally, the attorney leaned back in her chair and asked simply, "In your minds, what is the best possible outcome?"

"That Rick's father never breathes the same air as those kids," Greg said flatly.

"Agree," Briony said instantly.

"You two seemed to have reached complete accord."

"We have," Briony said. *Well, as far as the kids are concerned.*

There was a split second of silence before Greg agreed, that rough note back in his voice. "Yes. We have."

The memory of that kiss flooded her, sending heat rippling through her all the way to her cheeks, and hardly for the first time in her life she rued the pale complexion that went along with her hair.

"I see," the attorney said, and by the way she was smiling Briony thought she probably did. "All the better. Speaking case-wise, of course."

Briony had never been happier for the interruption of the children coming out of the playroom. Justin ran, as usual, and the counselor was carrying Jane, who was fiddling with the necklace the woman wore, looking at both sides intently.

"Doggy," the child said, as if she thought an explanation was required.

Briony looked at the necklace and saw it was an intricately carved head of what she suspected was a wolf rather than a dog, but that didn't matter beside the child's recognition it was something doglike.

"Close enough, sweetie," she said, leaning in to give Jane a kiss on the forehead before she took her from the counselor's arms. The woman looked at Tanya and nodded, adding, "You'll have my report in a couple of hours."

"Good. I need to get it to the judge. He's being understanding with the timeline because of the rush, but I want it there ASAP anyway."

"You'll have it."

They watched her leave. "So we won't know until tomorrow...what she'll say?" Briony asked, feeling anxious.

The lawyer smiled. "I already know. If there was a problem, she would have asked for a private consultation. Now, that's not to say they won't try to rebut her, but she's well established in this jurisdiction, and has the respect of the court and most attorneys."

"Most? As in not Kraft's?" Greg asked.

"He," Tanya said flatly, "has respect for nothing and no one. And that will help us win this."

Briony drew in a deep breath. Then, quietly, she said, "Rick and Wendy chose their attorney wisely."

That got her a wide smile, and there was a glint in the woman's eyes when she said, "Tell me that again tomorrow afternoon."

Chapter Thirty-One

If there was any resemblance between Winston Kraft and his son, Greg couldn't find it. Short, skinny, with a rather pinched face, there was nothing of Rick's height and strength in the man. He'd already known there was no resemblance in mind and heart, or in strength of character, but now he knew it was physical as well. Rick had always said he took after his mother, thankfully. It was obviously true.

But Rick had learned right and wrong from the man, although not in the way nature intended. Rick had always joked he'd known the right thing to do by watching his father and doing the opposite. Never had Greg felt the truth of that more than right now.

Tanya had assured them they didn't need to subject themselves to this after their already long morning testifying and being battered by Winston Kraft's self-aggrandizing lawyer. It would be quick, she'd said. He could only hope she was right. He reminded himself Rick had trusted the woman completely, and Rick was no fool. After all, he'd seen through his own father.

He watched the two men disappear into the judge's chambers along with Tanya.

"He's a repulsive little worm, isn't he?" Briony whispered

as the door closed behind them. She glanced at a woman sitting in the gallery of the room. "And she isn't helping."

He had to stifle a laugh, inappropriate in a courtroom setting even if the judge wasn't present at this moment. But the woman who had come in beside Kraft definitely was not helping Kraft's case. She was clearly the much younger third wife, a flashy platinum blonde who had on even flashier jewelry, including a massive diamond on her ring finger, and eye makeup that he'd swear sparkled on its own. She was wearing a dress that looked more suitable for a party than a custody hearing. This was the kind of woman the phrase *gold digger* was invented for. Greg had known the moment he'd seen Judge Thompson give her a studying look this was not going to be the influence Kraft had probably hoped for, perhaps showing how rich he was. Not to take care of the kids, but maybe to make the judge believe he didn't really want all that insurance money.

Briony, on the other hand, looked wonderful. Smooth, professional and competent in her business-style navy blue suit, with only a pair of gold earrings as jewelry.

And her wedding ring.

Sometimes he still had to remind himself.

And he knew he would always treasure the look and the quiet, "My, but you clean up nicely, Mr. Colton," she'd given him when she'd first seen him in the—coincidentally, or fated?—navy blue suit and blue-and-white subtly striped tie Mama Jen had given him for the occasion. She'd suggested some other shoes, but that he'd declined, sticking with his dress cowboy boots.

"I am who and what I am," he'd said, and Briony had given him a smile and nod that had him feeling oddly proud.

Now Briony turned to glance over her shoulder, where a large chunk of his family was seated, siblings and cousins alike. And most importantly his father, sitting directly behind them. Briony was smiling that same kind of smile when she turned back. Her fingers tightened around his, and suddenly he felt calmer, despite the fact that he would have sworn half an hour had passed only to glance at the clock on the courtroom wall and see that it had been barely ten minutes.

When it finally happened, when they emerged after just short of an hour, it was over in a rush. He took heart from the fact that Rick's father did not look happy as he stalked out. At all. And that Tanya gave them a wink and a nod as she retook her seat.

He'd never been much on legalese, and all the quoting of Idaho's Title 15, Uniform Probate Code, was worse than Greek to him—he at least knew a little of that, from a ranch hand they'd once had—but the part that needed to be clear was. He and Briony were appointed permanent guardians to Justin and Jane Kraft, with the determination that they shall work together cooperatively to serve the best interests of the minor children.

They'd won. The kids were theirs. He almost enjoyed watching Kraft and his hotshot attorney storming out in anger.

"Well, that should convince the judge he's right, if he had any lingering doubts." Buck Colton's voice came from behind them, and Greg turned to see both his father and aunt smiling widely. They'd had their own time under questioning and had been a strong cornerstone of their case.

"He already knows he's right," Tanya said. "Not only did they hold back some requested information, a clear violation of discovery rules, they tried to bombard the court with motions, and that's a hot button with any judge." She grinned then. "And then there's the glamour-girl third wife."

They all laughed at that. "She was a bit…over-the-top," Jen said.

"And it says a lot about Kraft's judgment that he thought she would be helpful, showing up like that," Dad said.

"Indeed," the attorney said with a smile. "But the deciding factor, if I know Judge Thompson, and I do, was one simple thing." They all went quiet, waiting. "Winston Kraft couldn't pick either of his grandchildren out of a photo lineup, and he had to admit to the judge he'd never met either of them in person. Which he lied about in the filing papers. Even his attorney was angry at him."

As he watched the brisk, professional woman, after a promise to forward the final papers as soon as they arrived, leave the courtroom, Greg felt a little numb now that it was over. They'd won. They had legal custody of the kids. They'd kept their vow to Rick and Wendy, and their precious children would never have to deal with his con man, grifter father.

When they got outside, he sucked in a deep breath of pure, crisp October-in-Idaho air. It felt cleansing, as if the last of the miasma that clung to Winston Kraft had been vanquished.

"Come on," his dad said. "We've got some celebrating to do. I reserved the patio at the Tides."

Greg stared at his father. The Tides was a high-end restaurant on the lakefront, Owl Creek's fanciest establishment. "You what, assumed we'd win?"

"I did," he said firmly. "Idaho still holds up what's right."

It wasn't until they were walking out to their respective vehicles—it had taken a small fleet to get all the Coltons who offered to come to Conners—that his dad took him to one side and said quietly, "Kraft was pretty mad. I'll put the word out on the ranch to be extra watchful."

"Thanks, Dad," Greg said, meaning it more than ever. "And I don't mean just for this. I mean for everything, ever."

His dad blinked. And Greg was sure that, at least for a moment, he'd seen a little extra sheen in Buck Colton's eyes.

"I…"

Words apparently failed him, and Greg counted that a win. And with the thought of credit where it was due, he added, "I've always felt that way, but Briony said I should make sure and tell you. Often."

"She's a good woman, son," Buck said. "You could do a lot, lot worse for a life partner." His mouth twisted wryly. "Take that from someone who did."

He hated that his mother could still make Dad react like that. "She doesn't matter anymore, Dad. Sure, the family's got to deal with her to some extent, but she doesn't matter beyond that."

It was only when they were headed back to Owl Creek that the phrase his father had used really hit home. A life partner. Briony, a partner for life. And he couldn't come up with any words to describe the feeling that gave him. But he couldn't get it out of his head as they drove the road back home.

"The Tides is that fancy place in town, right?"

Briony's question snapped him out of his musings. "Yeah. You've never been there?"

She shook her head. "Rick and Wendy used to celebrate their anniversary there. I would watch the kids sometimes."

He glanced at her. "I know. I'd watch them the other times."

His gaze was back on the road when he heard her let out a sad little laugh. "Do you think they were…training us? Just in case?"

"I wouldn't put it past Wendy," he answered quietly. "She was always thinking ahead, planning for the worst."

"We had to," Briony said simply, and in that simple exchange he got the best sense he'd ever had of just how bad their childhoods had been.

"It's amazing you both turned out as warm and as caring as you did," he said.

"I do care," she said, very softly.

And suddenly that kiss, the kiss he'd never planned, never expected, was crackling in the air between them. And this time it wasn't that he couldn't come up with any words, it was that he didn't dare say them. Didn't dare say that he wanted to try that again. And again after that.

And maybe even more. A lot more.

So he kept quiet until they hit town, and smothered the thought that he'd actually rather go straight home and indulge in those thoughts as they pulled up at the Tides.

The sparkly strings of lights that marked the patio were on, even though it wasn't even starting to get dark yet. Which was a good thing, since it was barely over sixty degrees now, and once the sun set it would start the dive to about twenty degrees less. But everybody here was dressed accordingly, telling him they'd known this was happening.

A buffet table was already set up, with an array of the foods the place was known for, and Greg spotted a tray of champagne glasses near an at-the-moment-unmanned bar.

"Your dad really did all this?" Briony asked as she stared through the windshield, sounding more than a little awed.

"He arranged it," Greg agreed. "But I sense Mama Jen's fine hand here."

She started to speak, but then hesitated. That life partner thing went through his head again, and it made him say gently, "Say it, Briony. You don't have to hold back anymore."

"I was just wondering…how would you feel if she and your dad got married now?"

He met her gaze as she voiced the secret wish he'd been lugging around for a while now. "Like we had the mom we should have had," he answered honestly.

She smiled at that, and it was amazing how good that made him feel.

It turned out the celebration was more fun than he'd expected. And he welcomed the chance to thank all the family who had turned out in support. He guessed the presence of the CEO of Colton Properties, an FBI agent and a couple of cops, among others, hadn't hurt their cause any. The food was good, and the champagne a rare treat.

Sunset had begun and the patio lights seemed brighter as the sky dimmed. The lake was glowing now as the light that remained hit the angle that made the reflection off the water seem even brighter. Greg was enjoying—he wasn't quite sure why, except maybe it would make life easier— watching Briony across the patio talking with his sister, as she'd earlier been talking with his cousin Frannie, who had arrived with her rather intimidating boyfriend, Dante. During that conversation they'd glanced over at him more than once, which had him wondering just what that conversation had been about.

Soon he saw Briony standing alone on the edge of the patio, looking out over the lake, a very slight slump to her posture, and it struck him that she might have hit her limit on socializing in a large group. Or if she'd slept as badly as he had last night, maybe she was just exhausted.

He walked over to her and asked quietly, "Had enough socializing?"

She gave him a startled glance. "I… Is it obvious?" she asked, sounding worried.

He smiled. "No."

She seemed relieved, which oddly pleased him. The other inference there, that he'd learned to notice even the nonobvious with her, surprised him a little. Yes, he'd spent a lot of time with her, but he'd thought he'd been too focused on the kids to absorb anything else. Apparently not.

She looked back out at the lake. "It's so beautiful here."

"It is. I just hope it's a while longer before the entire outside world discovers that."

"And ruins it forever?"

"Something like that, yeah. My uncle Robert started it, trying to turn us into a tourist destination, and it's already happened more than I like."

"Progress," she said, and he liked the ironic tone she put in it.

"To some people."

They looked out over the peaceful water again, until his father came up behind them.

"Why don't you two take off? It's been a long day for both of you. Jen and I have got the kids. We'll get them home and see to them until morning. Take my truck and give me the keys to the car with the car seats."

Greg turned to stare at his father. There had been…something in his voice, something under the lighthearted words, that made him think he was up to something. He had to be, arranging for them to have a big chunk of alone time. See to the kids until morning? Leaving them a night alone… together?

Whatever Dad was up to, Greg couldn't deny the idea of having some peace and quiet was appealing, and he knew it would be to Briony. When he'd gone, Greg looked at her.

"Want to take them up on that? Escape?"

"Yes," she said instantly. "It's not that everybody hasn't

been wonderful," she added hastily, "and it was wonderful of them to turn out for the kids today, but—"

She stopped when he held up a hand. "I get it. It's wearing. Even I'm tired. Let's go."

He pulled out the car keys and gave a whistle that made his dad turn his head. He tossed him the keys. His father grinned, pulled out his own keys and tossed them back along the same arc. He smiled back, a little embarrassed, before they turned and walked toward where Dad's ranch truck was parked.

When they got there Briony looked at him for a moment, and he saw that glint of spirit her rough life had never been able to fully destroy. "I'll drive, shall I? I stopped at half a glass of champagne."

"And I had three glasses," he admitted, and fished out the keys and handed them to her without complaint. It was apparently the right move, judging by the smile she gave him then.

And as they got into the truck, he couldn't help wondering—hoping—that it was just the first of his right moves for the night.

Chapter Thirty-Two

Briony didn't complain when Greg opened the passenger-side window to let in some of the air that had chilled rapidly after the sun had set. She had the heater blowing on her feet, and she had to admit the brisk, clean air was invigorating. Something she needed as well, considering how little she'd slept in the last couple of days. She wasn't all that used to driving a big truck, and the last thing she wanted to do was to ding up Greg's father's.

She suspected Greg was in the same tired boat. Knowing their entire future had depended on what happened today made for some long, sleepless hours.

Their future.

She'd been so consumed by thoughts of what could go wrong—because in her life, they so often had—and what they would do if they lost, she hadn't spent a lot of time thinking about what would happen if they won. She had no doubt Greg would never hand the kids over to Wendy's evil father-in-law, just as she had no doubts she would be right beside him on that. For the kids' sake. Even if it did mean they had to grab them and run.

That he had felt as she did, willing to give up everything to carry out Rick and Wendy's wishes, told her everything she needed to know about Gregory Colton. He was who he appeared to be.

I am who and what I am.

She could count the number of people she knew that fit that description on the fingers of one hand. And now Greg was one of them.

Ironically perhaps, one of the others was Rick's father, in a very negative way. Because he absolutely was who and what he was, an evil, malicious, immoral con man who wrapped his cons in pseudo-religion and sold it to gullible people who couldn't see who and what he was. That could not make her think any less of him, since she already thought the worst.

But that Greg was who and what he was...that was a new certainty that made her feel a tempest of emotions. She glanced over at him as she stopped the truck and waited for two oncoming vehicles to pass before making the turn on the road that led to the ranch gate.

"You really would have done it, if we'd lost," she said, and it wasn't a question.

He turned his head and gave her a steady look. Steady, that was Greg. "Run with them, rather than let him get his filthy hands on them? Absolutely." Then, after a brief moment, he asked quietly, "Would you really have gone with us if I did, if we'd lost?"

"I would." She said it instantly, and with all the certainty she could put into her voice. "I'd be with you every step of the way."

Something changed in his expression then; something glinted in his eyes that she could see even in the dim light of the truck's cab. Something that made her pulse kick up and wonder exactly why his father had done this.

She drove on, the mood that had seized her growing

with every heartbeat. When they reached the ranch gate Greg got out without a word to open it. She pulled the truck through, then stopped as he ran—ran!—to get back in. Her ricocheting brain seized on that simple fact, and no matter how she tried to put it down to just wanting to get home, she couldn't stop herself from wondering if he'd been eager to get back to her.

She drove toward the main house, then up to the spot where she'd noticed his dad always parked. She double-checked the unfamiliar gear shift to be sure it was in Park, then took her foot off the brake and turned off the engine.

Finally, she turned in the seat to look at him.

"Leave the keys in it. Dad always does in case someone needs it."

The words were prosaic, but there was an undertone to his voice that matched the glint she'd seen in his eyes. He didn't say another word as they got out and walked to their house.

Their house. She was even thinking of the place that way. Their future, their house, and now…their kids. She had a husband and two children. Children she loved.

A husband she could too easily love.

She'd never had an overactive imagination, and what imagination she did have usually ran to envisioning the worst that could possibly happen. She'd never spent much time picturing the good things that could happen, because except for Wendy, in her life they never had.

Until now.

Now she had Greg and the kids. And the kids deserved a life where they could be happy. Where they could remember Rick and Wendy with love, but not spend every day gutted by the loss.

And what did she deserve? Certainly not a man the likes of Greg, but…she had him. And now that she was certain of who and what he was, she knew he would never walk away from the responsibility he'd taken on.

They were safely inside—interesting, that that was the word that popped into her mind, safe—before he turned to her, grasped her shoulders, met her gaze head on and asked quietly, "What's wrong?"

"Nothing," she said, aware of the shakiness in her voice but unable to stop it. "Absolutely nothing."

She saw understanding dawn in his expression. "And that's what scares you, isn't it? That's what you've never had before."

"There's always been something that just went wrong or is about to sometime soon."

There was a long, silent moment before he spoke again, but he never let go of her. "I had it easier. Mom just walked out, Dad stepped up, and it was over." He grimaced. "Well, it was until her other life came to light." The grimace became a smile. "But we got two pretty great half siblings out of that, so I'm not complaining."

She managed a shaky smile in turn. "Maybe there's no such thing as a life where…nothing's wrong."

The look he gave her then was steady, reassuring and very, very Greg. "If nothing's gone wrong in your entire life, then you haven't really lived it."

She stared at him. "When did you become a philosopher?"

His mouth twisted. "About the time I became responsible for two kids whose lives were just torn apart."

She couldn't stop herself. She reached up to cup his cheek. He looked startled but didn't pull away. In fact, he leaned into her touch.

"Our lives, too," she said.

"I know," he said, more softly than she would have

thought a tough, rugged cowboy his size could ever speak. "But maybe…maybe it's not all bad. Or maybe at least we can make something good out of it."

She couldn't speak; she could only look at him. And she saw what he was asking in the depths of those warm brown eyes. She tried to summon up all the reasons it would be a mistake. But they didn't seem to stack up against all the reasons she wanted this. Had wanted this, if she was honest, for a long time. A very long time.

"Bri?" he asked, his voice barely a whisper as he used the nickname he never had before, that only Wendy had ever used, the only person she'd ever allowed to use it.

Until now. Because in Greg's rough whisper, it was the most beautiful name ever. The most beautiful name in the world.

"Yes," she whispered back.

And then he was kissing her, and impossibly, it was even more incredible than she remembered from before. And for the first time in her life, she threw caution to the wind, because in this moment she wanted nothing more than for this to go on and on. She thought of all the times he'd been there for the kids, and for her, rock solid and unshakable, unlike anyone she'd ever had in her life. Even Wendy, sometimes caught up in her own troubles, hadn't always been able to be there.

Greg had never missed a beat. For any of them, even her when Rick or Wendy had asked, since she never would herself.

But she asked him now. Because she would rather have this memory be of this moment, when they'd won, when they were happy, when things were right, than if they turned to each other in shared misery.

He broke the kiss, but only to shed his jacket. When she

reached to tug at his shirt, her fingers already tingling at the thought of what running them over those taut abs would feel like, he put a gentle hand over hers.

"Do you mean what it seems like you mean?" His voice was oddly shaky, and she realized he sounded like she felt.

"I'm tired of being curious," she said, hearkening back to that first kiss.

"So am I," he said, and it came out half relieved, half stirring in a way she'd never heard from him before.

What had begun slowly, tentatively, suddenly became a whirlwind. He couldn't move fast enough for her; she couldn't move fast enough for herself. She wanted to touch every inch of him almost as much as she wanted him to touch every inch of her. When her clothes were tossed aside, she was still unzipping his jeans, and when he reached to cup her breasts, rubbing his thumbs over her nipples, she cried out at the sensation that ripped through her.

"My hands are rough," he said apologetically against her ear as he bent to tease it with his tongue.

"Don't apologize," she said. "They're the hands of a working man." Then, in a burst of nerve that had to be brought on by pure, raging need, she added teasingly, "So put them to work."

He laughed, a low, rough-edged but delighted laugh. And that she could draw that sound from him made her feel more than a little delighted herself.

And then he followed her bantering order, and put those rough, strong, yet impossibly gentle hands to work. And before she could process how it had happened, he had swept her up into his arms and they were in the bedroom. His bedroom, although now hers, too. And his bed, which he'd shared with her, if not physically.

Until now.

Now he was naked and beside her, his body declaring to her like nothing else could that this was real, that he wanted this. And if it was just a reaction to the opportunity for sex, she didn't care. Right now, she didn't care about anything except that she wanted him more than she'd ever wanted anyone or anything in her life. She reached down to caress surging male flesh and reveled in the sound of his groan of pleasure.

She urged him on, although she did feel a jolt when he turned to reach into the nightstand drawer she'd never opened, dug into the back and pulled out a condom.

"Dad, ever hopeful," he muttered when he saw her gaze follow the movement. She couldn't help her wide smile.

He fumbled with it, as if he hadn't done it for a long time. She offered to help, but he gave her a sideways look that was somehow incredibly hot as he said, "You touch me in the way that would take, and this is going to be over fast."

And then, at last, she was in his arms again. His hands were touching, caressing, stroking, leaving fiery paths along her skin everywhere they went. She heard the noises she was making, sounds that had never been wrung from her before, capped by a cry of his name as he finally, finally slid into her.

It had been so long, and with the way he stretched her, it should have been difficult. The ease of it now only told her what she'd already known—she was hungrier for this man than she'd ever been for anything or anyone in her life. The controlled strength and power of him as he thrust into her again and again made her heart race even faster, and unlike the two other times in her life when she'd tried to find this with a man, with Greg she was able to let go completely, because she knew down to the marrow of her bones that he would never, ever hurt her.

And with that her body unleashed, every nerve coming to life, her hands savoring the feel of him, her mouth the taste of him, and her ears the sounds he made when he drove deep. She hit the kind of peak she'd never really believed in before and she cried out his name as he drove deep one last time and her body clenched fiercely as a wave of sensation swamped her. She felt him shudder in her arms, heard him say her name as if it had been wrenched out of him.

She clung to him as it slowly ebbed, feeling as if she'd been granted every wish she'd ever had.

Chapter Thirty-Three

Greg felt as if he'd never move again. Felt blasted on so many fronts he couldn't even sort them out, maybe because she'd fried every circuit in his brain as well as his body. In ways he'd never, ever expected.

Briony. Shy, quiet Briony had just taught him a universe of new lessons in only a few minutes. Minutes that he wanted an immediate repeat of, except for the slight problem that, utterly drained, he couldn't even muster the strength to roll off her.

Oddly, she didn't seem to mind, in fact was holding on to him as if she was afraid he'd leave her and she didn't want him to. As if she wanted him right where he was, his body pressed into hers.

He marveled at the fact that even the idea of that began to stoke that fire again. And the feel of it, the feel of her hands on his backside, holding him against her, felt so unreservedly, totally right.

He told himself no one would have expected this beneath Briony's quiet, reticent exterior. But if he was being honest—and he always tried to be, although sometimes it was harder with himself than others—he wouldn't have expected this kind of explosive combustion from himself, either.

Not that he hadn't had normal urges and needs, and not

that satisfying them hadn't been pleasurable, but he'd never felt anything like this. Never known it was even possible. And somehow, he didn't think it was merely because it had been a while since his last casual hookup. Right now, he couldn't even remember when that was, let alone what it had been like.

All he knew for sure was, it had been nothing—*nothing*—like this.

Briony. Of all people, of all women, Briony.

"Greg?"

The slight tinge of her old uncertainty in her voice was enough to snap him out of his floating, blissful thoughts. His head came up, and he saw that same touch of uncertainty in those beautiful green eyes. He hated the sight of it. Hated that she'd had the kind of life that instilled those doubts in her. That she could feel them at all, but especially that she could feel them now.

And he felt a familiar determination building in him, the kind he felt when he had a big task before him but knew it had to be done. A determination that if it was the last thing he did, he'd erase those doubts forever.

But right now, he wanted that look in her eyes gone. He wanted a smile out of her. He wanted to know this had been as amazing for her as it had been for him. So he propped himself up on his elbows, lifting his head so he could look straight into those eyes, and gave her a crooked half grin.

"Son of a gun," he said. "They were right."

She blinked, and puzzlement replaced the doubt. He welcomed it. Besides, puzzlement was a cousin to curiosity, and wasn't that what had landed them here to begin with?

He let the grin loose, holding nothing back. "Rick and Wendy. They were right all along. How the heck did they know we'd combust like this?"

Her eyes widened, and slowly, so he was able to savor every moment of the change, she smiled. It was like the sun rising over the lake, brightening everything around with an inimitable sparkle.

"Maybe," she said, and that glint he was coming to love lit the green of her eyes, "because together they did and they recognized it?"

"Maybe. Maybe they did. Makes me feel pretty stupid for resisting all this time."

"Not stupid, cautious," she said. "I'm sure a guy like you has to be."

He raised a brow at her. "A guy like me?"

"You know. Someone whose word is gold. Someone who's always ready to help a friend. Who always does the right thing, even when it's hard. The kind of man people mean when they say honorable and principled and…trust-worthy."

He understood on some gut level the pause before that last word. Understood that of all things, trust was the hardest for her to give.

Understood that she was giving it to him now.

The knowledge tightened something deep inside him, and he wasn't sure exactly what the feeling was. He only knew he'd never felt anything quite like it before. Like so many things with her. That she would choose those things over the more typical compliments to his looks or his eyes or the prosperous ranch was so… Bri.

He went for a joke to stall until he figured it out. "And here I thought you were going to compliment my backside," he said, tensing the muscles still under her hands.

To his surprise she squeezed back, and the glint was even more obvious when she said, "I thought I already had."

Because he didn't know what else to do, he kissed her

again. And again. And before he'd even left her completely his body hardened again, and he set about discovering if it had been a fluke, this conflagration he'd felt, even though he thought he already knew the answer. It hadn't been a fluke.

A few minutes later, as he nearly shouted her name under the force of the climax that hit him, he had his proof.

Rick and Wendy had indeed been right all along.

It was later, as they held each other in the darkness, that Briony whispered, "Do you feel…guilty?"

He'd been about to doze off, but even his sated brain realized this was not something to brush off with a platitude. He dug the fingernail on his index finger into his thumb, a trick he used when he had to wake up in a hurry. The little pain did its job, and the sleepiness retreated, at least for now.

"About what?" he asked carefully.

"Us…being like this. It being so…good, when Rick and Wendy are…gone."

Despite the pleasure of hearing her say how good it had been, a warning went off in his head, telling him that how he answered this was important. He'd come to know a bit about this woman, about the uncertainties that were the source of those moments of doubt, of insecurity. He ached inside for the life she'd had, so much worse than his own, no matter what people thought of his mother and her actions.

In that moment he wished for some of his father's wisdom, and the knack he had for putting his answers and advice in just the right way. Hoping he'd learned enough by just listening, he gave it a try.

"I miss them, every day, more than I've ever missed anyone. But I don't feel guilty. Because this is what they wanted. All these years, this is what they apparently saw and tried to make happen."

He heard her let out a long, slow breath, felt the brush

of it over the skin of his chest as she snuggled against him. "I'm glad," she whispered. "We're a little late, but… I think of it as a final thank-you to them both."

He shifted one arm to pull her even closer. "I'm glad, too." He hesitated, then figured he'd done okay so far and plunged ahead. "Can we build on this, Bri? Can we build a family, not just for Justin and Jane, but for us?"

She turned her head, and in the faint light of his—no, their—bedroom, he could see her eyes looking into his. "I should be asking you. You're the one who knows about family. Can we?"

"We can."

"Then we will. Because a promise from Greg Colton is golden."

The warmth that flooded him then had nothing to do with arousal or sex, and everything to do with something much bigger. And for the first time he thought they might just be able to build something else between them.

Love.

Chapter Thirty-Four

Greg had never really looked forward to the Fall Fest. He'd already been pretty much beyond the kind of games and prizes it offered back when it had first started. And as an adult, sometimes he'd been so hard at work on the ranch that he didn't even realize it was happening until he tried to go into town for something and found it swamped with people.

But today he found himself preparing for it cheerfully, almost with gleeful anticipation, because the kids were going to love it. They were already excited, Justin because of the games and prizes, and the presence of the vendor for his favorite treat, a fried doughnut hole concoction Greg secretly enjoyed himself. Jane, he suspected, was just excited because everyone else was.

He'd overheard Briony chatting to the little girl as she got her ready this morning, telling her all about the festival and what would be there. Jane probably comprehended more than he realized, but all that really mattered to him was that the little girl was happy and giggling back at Bri when she slipped into that high-pitched, teasing voice she used with her.

As opposed to the low, husky teasing voice she used with him at night.

With an inward grin, he thought he was going to either

need to stop remembering those luscious hours or step out into the fall chill to cool off. It had dropped below freezing last night, and even with the fortuitously sunny day ahead, it was going to take a while to warm up. Which meant layers for the kids, shirts, sweaters, jackets, heavy socks and warm boots.

He gave a slightly amazed shake of his head as he found himself thinking in those terms before anything else. The kids really did come first, and it felt as natural as breathing.

"Unca Greg, Unca Greg!"

As if conjured by his realization, Justin came running toward him, carrying the insulated boots that would indeed be warm, but were a bit hard for the little one to get on. He had a sudden vision of the days to come, when maybe someday it'd be this little guy helping him pull on his boots, when he was old and gray. He swept the boy up in that way that never failed to make him laugh and plopped him down on the couch before kneeling down to help with the stubborn footwear.

The boy slid off the couch and stamped his feet as if to settle them in the boots. "We going now?"

"Yeah," he said, "as soon as your sister's ready."

The little boy made a grimace that made Greg laugh in spite of the depths of emotion the kid had tossed him into just moments ago. He heard footsteps behind them and turned to see Briony approaching with Jane in her arms. And something about the image that met his eyes made his throat knot up, as if he were seeing something of such incredible beauty there were no words to describe it.

When she looked up and met his gaze, he knew there was no "as if" about it.

The little one was dressed in layers just like her brother, so that except for the heavier outer jacket, they were ready.

Not to mention that Briony looked amazing in a simple pair of black jeans and boots topped with a soft green sweater that made her eyes seem to glow, and that slid over her, clinging in all the right places.

Places he'd been kissing and caressing not so very long ago.

And if he didn't stop this, he was going to be unable to walk.

"Will Pacer be there?"

He looked back down at Justin, who was clutching the stuffed dog that had been one of the few toys he'd wanted from the house.

"Yes," Greg answered, knowing from his brother Malcolm that the local and state SAR agencies were doing some PR at the festival. "And some more search dogs, too. There will be a special booth where you can meet them."

"Cool," Justin said. He looked at Briony, who was holding his sister. "Can we go now?"

He nearly laughed at the boy's impatient tone and the look he gave his sister, as if she was the reason they weren't already there.

Just wait, kiddo. Someday you'll be waiting for a woman and happy to do it.

That he'd never expected to be that guy himself only made his smile wider.

Briony, as she always did, noticed. "Looking forward to this?"

"Actually," he said, his voice a little rough, "I was more looking back."

He saw color rise in her cheeks and knew she'd gotten his point. Last night had been particularly spectacular, until he'd been afraid they'd wake the kids. What they had done was fall asleep, exhausted, until Justin had walked in on them this morning. It was the first time the kids had found them together in bed and judging by the boy's reaction—or lack thereof—he found it perfectly normal. He'd just been anxious to get going to the "big party" as he called it, and they were delaying him.

Greg was a little surprised at the boy's eagerness, but sadly understood when, in the car on the way, Briony teased him a little about being so excited and the boy said, "Mommy and Daddy will be there. They always go."

"Mama? Dada?" Jane chimed in, sounding hopeful.

Every time it happened it was a punch to the gut. He glanced at Briony and saw the sheen in her eyes, knew it had hit her just as hard. But they had to handle it as they always tried to, with consistency.

Briony turned to look at the children in the back seat. "They won't be there, honey," she said softly, and the pain in her voice made Greg's worse. "They can't ever be any-where again."

"Oh."

Justin's brow furrowed as he wrestled with concepts he was too young to understand. Greg was almost grateful for that, although it made it harder on him and Briony to have to hear the question and answer it, over and over, every time reawakening the pain that their newly hectic lives managed to mute somewhat.

Only the knowledge that they were doing what Rick and Wendy had wanted, that their beloved children were safe with them, made it bearable at all.

When Justin had gone back to peering out the window, Greg reached out and took Briony's hand in his, squeez-ing gently.

Will it ever get easier?

I think it'll get easier than it is now, but it will never, ever be easy.

He'd asked that just yesterday, when it had been Jane wailing, and it had taken him a trek out to the barn to see Wick to calm her down. Her quiet response had reminded him she had more experience with loss and heartbreak than he'd had, even with Jessie's—he'd started to correct himself to saying that rather than Mother's—more and more unhinged behavior. And he couldn't honestly say he missed his uncle Robert either, despite what had been a powerful presence. Not after they'd learned how he'd cheated on Mama Jen for years with her own sister.

"Remember the morning after the hearing," Briony said quietly, giving his hand a squeeze in turn.

He knew what she meant, and it made him smile. Justin, with his usual energy, had been up and ready to go and further explore the ranch, and Briony had had to herd him back for some breakfast first. And in the middle of his bowl of oatmeal he'd announced with all the officiousness a four-year-old could muster, "I like it here. We should stay."

That moment gave him such hope, that they could do this, that they could build the life they wanted for the children—and themselves.

When they got to town, it was already bustling. The Fall Fest got a little bigger every year, until it was drawing people from all over southwest Idaho. He knew most of his family would be here at one time or another, and before they'd even gotten to the center of the park area where most of the kids' games were, including the bounce house Justin had his eye on, they'd encountered three cousins and his sister, Lizzy, who fussed happily over both kids, getting them both to laugh. And then Dad and Mama Jen appeared, eliciting squeals of delight from Jane and Justin both.

Lizzy took off to wander the festival just as he spotted Malcolm and Pacer at the booth set up to promote the search-and-rescue teams that served the area. He was talking to a tall Black man with close-cropped hair, who held the leash of another dog, a yellow Labrador who looked as fit and energetic as Pacer. Both men wore similar rugged clothing and what looked like communications gear, as if ready to go into action at any moment. He supposed they had to be.

Justin had already spotted the dogs and was off that way at a run. Pacer's tail was already wagging, and he gave a happy bark as his new, playful companion approached. The dog might be all business on the job, but he could romp with the best of them when off duty.

"He's kind of working here," Malcolm explained to the boy, "so he can't really play right now."

"Working?" the boy asked. "Is someone lost?"

Malcolm laughed. "No, but he has to show people what he can do, so they keep wanting him around."

Justin's brow furrowed. "I always want him around."

"I know," Malcolm said solemnly. "And so does he."

As a visitor to the festival stopped to ask about the dogs, Malcolm began to explain how Pacer was a trailing dog, who followed scents both in the air and on things, rather than a tracking dog who followed actual tracks.

"You mean like on TV when they give the dog something of the lost person's to sniff, and then they start off looking for them?" the visitor asked.

"Exactly like that," Malcolm said, sounding justly proud of his clever, dedicated dog.

"He finds stuff I hide, too," Justin exclaimed, sounding nearly as proud, and the visitor smiled.

With a promise that they'd come back to visit the dogs

again while they were here, Greg and Briony convinced the kids to explore the rest of the festival. As they continued to walk around, Greg watched Briony, savoring the look of enjoyment on her face. He wondered if she'd ever been part of a gathering like this before, a cheerful, happy event where people just enjoyed being in this place at this time. He doubted it. Or if she had, she probably hadn't let it seep into her, not through that protective shell her hard life had given her. Seeing her now, smiling, looking around in somewhat bemused wonder, did his heart good.

They ended up at the enclosure of a small petting zoo that had both Justin and Jane excited. They'd really bonded with many of the animals on the ranch, but these were creatures new to them—a couple of baby goats and lambs, a surprisingly cute little pig, a big pen of rabbits, a smaller one of what looked like hamsters or guinea pigs, a rather sizable tortoise, and a couple of ponies Justin zeroed in on—so Greg wasn't really surprised when they both demanded to go in.

One of the trained attendants offered to go with Jane in case her newly acquired walking skills failed her, so off they both went while Greg and Briony waited at the fence. He wanted to ask her how she was doing, but people kept stopping by to say hello, many saying how nice it was to see him here, and he began to get the feeling Briony wasn't the only one who needed to get used to doing things like this. And not just for the kids' sake.

"Your family really is the backbone of this town," Briony said, sounding bemused.

"Yeah, if you could take a couple of them out of the equation," he said wryly. But then, in a much softer tone and with a smile he added, "They're your family, too, now."

For an instant she looked startled, but then an expression of such happiness and warmth spread across her face that his stomach knotted, but in a good way. So much had changed in the last month; there had been so much pain and upheaval. But there had been good, too. Especially the joy and pleasure they'd found in each other, and that gave him such hope for the future.

They would build that life they'd talked about. He knew that now. And he knew something else, as he stood there watching Briony interact with Lizzy, who had just arrived.

It would be a good life.

A sudden commotion across the enclosure drew his attention. A boy about twice Justin's size had apparently tried to ride the tortoise. Attendants rushed over to wrestle the protesting kid off the poor creature. He didn't envy the parents of that one, judging by his reaction to being told tortoises weren't for riding. And judging by the look on the face of the woman who came to round the kid up, this wasn't new territory.

"Poor woman," Briony said.

"She's got her hands full," Greg agreed.

He was just wondering what he'd do if Justin had tried something like that when Briony grabbed his arm.

"Greg!" At her suddenly sharp tone, his head snapped around to stare at her. "Where are they?"

She was looking around almost frantically, and he put his hand over hers soothingly as he scanned the enclosure. Then he scanned it again, slower. Then, his pulse racing now, a third time. Then the area nearby. Then a three-sixty turn to look all around them.

As he muttered a curse, he heard Briony almost whimper.

Justin and Jane were gone.

Chapter Thirty-Five

Briony had never felt panic like this, even in the worst days of her early life when she'd questioned her own survival. This was worse. Different, and worse. The thought of Justin and Jane lost, out there somewhere, terribly scared, pierced her to her soul. If she'd needed any further proof of how important those kids had become to her, she had it now. Because she knew she wouldn't stop, wouldn't rest until they were back, safe and sound.

She could feel the same sort of tension in Greg, although once they were certain the kids were nowhere in sight, he'd responded more usefully than her own frantic running about rechecking. He'd gone right to his brother and Pacer. Malcolm in turn had called in the other SAR dog and his handler, Ajay Wright, and the whimsically named yellow Lab, Pumpkin. The two men and their dogs immediately began an organized and obviously professional search.

"We'll call in other teams if necessary," Malcolm assured his brother. "In the meantime, use your phone to keep in touch. I'll be live with Ajay via radio, so I can relay anything."

Word spread fast that two little children were missing, and it wasn't long before every Colton and many others at the festival were searching the grounds and beyond. This eased her panic a little, and she was almost able to breathe normally again. Almost.

"We'll find them," Greg promised her, his strong arm coming around her shoulders, dispelling a bit of the chill that had come over her.

"And him, if he's behind this," said Greg's cousin Fletcher, who had just finished a search of the game booths area with no results.

His words stopped her breath, and Briony looked at the man. She told herself that as a police detective it was only natural for him to suspect the worst. But until he'd said it, she hadn't allowed herself to consider the possibility that Justin and Jane hadn't just wandered off. Hadn't allowed it because it would change everything. Change from two small children who'd wandered off from the crowd and gotten lost to a much more horrible possibility.

They had been taken.

And there was only one likely suspect for that.

She turned back to Greg. "Do you think— Would he— Could he?" she stammered.

"From what Rick told me over the years, I wouldn't put it past him for a moment," Greg said grimly.

"I'll make the call," Fletcher said, and pulled out his phone and hit a single button she guessed was to his colleagues at the police department. Somehow that simple action made the possibility they'd been kidnapped very real to Briony, and it was all she could do not to shatter right here in front of everyone. Only the strength she'd had to develop as a kid in the system enabled her to keep from flying into a million pieces.

As if he'd sensed it, Greg pulled her into an embrace. "We'll find them, Bri. We'll find them."

She felt both helpless and useless as the search expanded.

Malcolm called in more SAR teams, Fletcher had what had to be most of the Owl Creek Police Department out searching, and Greg's father had additional plans for searching on horseback to cover the surrounding forested areas that couldn't be easily reached by vehicle.

Then there was the cousin she'd heard about but only now met, even though he worked on the ranch. Greg had told her of Wade's background as a Special Forces operator, and the explosion that had scarred him and cost him an eye, but seeing the eye patch he still wore drove it home to her like nothing else.

She supposed her silly reaction explained why he was scarce around the ranch. He probably didn't like dealing with people who reacted by staring at him like she had. She felt bad and resolved to find him and apologize when this was over, and Justin and Jane were safely back home.

But when he faded off into the trees to do his own search, she almost hoped that, if it were truly Rick's father who had taken the kids, that this guy be the one to find them. She had the feeling he would not go easy on the man. And unlike law enforcement, he might not feel compelled to hold back.

More time passed, and then more, with no luck or leads. Briony had always thought of Owl Creek as a small town, but suddenly it seemed vast and overwhelming. She felt even more useless after Greg mounted up with his father and expanded the search, but she was ridiculously unprepared for this kind of thing. Only when Greg's aunt took her to the Colton Properties building up on Main Street and sat her down at a desk with a phone and a list of numbers to call did she feel as if she were doing anything.

"Thank you," she said to the woman, almost fiercely.

"We'll call every person in town if we have to, and the searchers will not quit," Jen promised, giving her the kind of warm, motherly hug she'd rarely had in her misbegotten life. "We'll bring your kids home."

Briony liked the way she put that. *Your kids.* Hers and Greg's. She dived into the phone calls, quickly learning that identifying herself as Briony Colton usually got her quick cooperation. She had the feeling she was only starting to understand what it meant to carry that name around here.

But her newfound energy faded as hours passed, darkness fell and they were still nowhere. She had gleaned one tiny bit of information that was further evidence against Rick's father but didn't help to find the children now at all.

She sat in the building that had once housed the hardware store that had begun the Colton success story here in Owl Creek, rubbing at eyes that were dry and stinging. As was her nature, she'd taken to keeping a record of everything that had been checked on, people and places. Word had gone out, so her phone rang every time a searcher finished an area or neighborhood, and she made notes. If nothing else, it might save time by keeping others from duplicating her effort. Time that could be put into actual, physical searching.

It was nearly four in the morning when the front door swung open and Greg came in. She immediately got up, looking at him with concern. He was rubbing at his eyes much as she had been, and she knew he probably had to be even more exhausted than she. At least he'd been out physically looking. And she could tell by his uncharacteristically sapped posture that, just like her, he had no good news to share.

But she would never, ever give up on finding Justin and Jane, and she knew Greg wouldn't, either.

"I've called half the people on this list, and I think your aunt called the other half," she said wearily. "Nobody has seen them or knows anything about where the kids might be. Although," she added, feeling she owed it, "most of them were very kind and concerned and many offered to join in the search." That Colton name again, she supposed. "I did find one thing, not that it helps now."

"What?"

He pulled out the earpiece he was wearing, the one he usually wore around the ranch to avoid startling any livestock with the sound of the phone. He rubbed at his ear as he sat on the edge of the desk she'd been using as she paced, trying to shed some of the edginess she was feeling.

"One of my calls turned out to be the insurance agent that sold Rick and Wendy their policy. He recognized the names immediately and was one of the ones who volunteered to go out and search." She stopped her pacing, halting in front of where Greg was leaning on her borrowed desk. "He mentioned that Rick's father had come to him as a client also. And that the policies for the kids were mentioned, although he swore he gave no specific numbers or amounts."

Greg was zeroed in now. "What did he give him?"

"That the kids would never have to worry about money in their lives."

Greg let out a smothered oath. "All it would take to set Kraft on the hunt."

"Yes," she agreed. "And no surprise, it happened right before he filed for custody."

"Figures." He rubbed at his eyes again. "Malcolm and I—and Pacer—just got back from Conners."

That surprised her for a moment. "Conners?" And then it hit her, that that was where the so-called church was. "You went looking for Kraft."

He nodded. "We went to their…compound, I guess you'd call it. Malcolm said Pacer would alert if he caught any trace of the kids having been there recently. He didn't. And," he added with a grimace, "we overheard one of the…cult members—and now that I've seen it, there's no doubt in my mind that's what it is. Those people are living like poor refugees, while Acker, Kraft and the rest of the leaders— probably including my mother—" the words had a bitter tone "—live like royalty."

She wished she could think of something comforting to say, but couldn't, so resumed her pacing as Greg went on.

"While we were there, we overheard one of them saying Kraft didn't show up for last night's services. And that Markus Acker was none too happy about it. Implication being he doesn't know where he is, either."

Her breath caught in her throat. She stopped her pacing again and turned to face him, her fingers curling into her palms, nails digging hard, as if the pain could change the obvious.

"So we were right, Kraft grabbed them," she said, tears starting to sting anew. "And has them…somewhere."

He nodded. "And apparently somewhere other than the compound."

She tried to think, to figure out what this would accomplish in Kraft's mind. Her accountant brain said *nothing*. "How does he think kidnapping them is going to get him access to that money?"

"People don't successfully build cults like Ever After by being timid or uncertain," Greg said sourly. "I'm sure he thinks he's smarter than all of us put together and will figure out a way. Rick always said he looked down on other people, called them stupid and gullible."

"And set out to prove it, apparently," Briony said, unable to stop a touch of bitterness creeping into her own voice. "Thinking if he can help bilk hundreds of people out of their life savings, he can surely get his hands on that insurance money."

"Probably," Greg said, rubbing at his unshaven jaw. "Or maybe…"

His voice trailed away, and she sensed he'd thought better of what he'd been about to say. "Maybe what?"

"Nothing."

"Greg, there's nothing you can say that's going to make this worse."

He let out a long, audible breath. "Don't be too sure of that."

"What?" she demanded.

He hesitated again, then finally said it. "Fletcher was wondering if he was one of those guys who just can't lose. Will do anything to avoid it and gets into that self-centric mode of…if I can't have them, nobody can."

Nausea hit her in a rush, and she wished she hadn't pushed him to say it. Because she'd had secondhand experience with a case like that, where a drug-addict mother had stolen her three children from the foster family who had been granted temporary custody. The foster family she and Wendy had been with at the time.

She'd murdered all three.

Chapter Thirty-Six

He wished he hadn't said it. She looked as if the words had broken her. It took him a while to coax the story out of her, that horrific tale of three innocent children, one even younger than Jane, who had met an ugly end at the hands of a parent with just that mindset.

And when he had the story, he didn't know what else to do except hold her. Tight.

"Now what do we do?" she asked, sounding as if she were trying very hard not to let that old helpless, hopeless feeling rise in her.

"We expand the search. So far we've stayed in the general vicinity of where they were, but we've pretty much covered all of town. So now we're heading for the outskirts. Malcolm and I will be starting on the eastern outskirts as soon as Pacer has a chance to rest and eat."

"What about you?" she asked. "You need some sleep."

"I'll sleep when they're home safe." He met her gaze steadily. "About the same time you will."

She hugged him. His arms went around her immediately, and they stood there for several long, silent moments, and Greg felt oddly as if, somehow, they were giving each other a strength neither had alone.

And he vowed they would build that life they'd talked

about. As soon as Justin and Jane were home safe. But now, the search had to go on.

TIME TICKED BY, and Briony could swear she heard every click of the clock on the wall as her desperation grew. She dialed and dialed and dialed. Some people were gruff or even angry, but most were kind and concerned, many even offering to join in the search. Because it was the way her brain worked, she found herself calculating how long it would take to talk to every permanent resident in Owl Creek. Each call took three to five minutes, sometimes more, times the population divided by households, say an average of two to four people per, except places like the ranch where there were many more, which threw her figures into disarray—

Stop it! It's going to take two days to call everyone, so you've got a day to go, just keep dialing!

When she woke up with a start and realized she'd fallen asleep at the desk, she felt both guilty for sleeping and shocked when she realized it was dark outside. Night was here, and still no word.

"I'm glad you slept a little," said a kind voice from behind her. Greg's aunt, back to be helpful again.

"You should have woken me up," Briony said, getting to her feet.

"I was here if any calls came in."

"They're still searching, aren't they?"

"Of course. Even if everyone else quits, the Coltons will never give up, and there's a fair number of us."

Briony shook her head in wonder. "But so many of them barely know the kids, or me."

"But they know Greg, and Coltons stick together." She frowned. "Not to mention none of us are fond of that cult they call a church, for various reasons."

"You've been…wonderful, when you have your own… complications to deal with."

The frown became a grimace. "My charming sister, you mean. Yes, she's one I would not include in that loyal group."

Briony almost asked about Robert Colton, Jen's late, adulterous husband who had a years-long affair and two children by that sister, but decided it wasn't the time or the place, and none of her business to boot.

The little bit of sleep she'd gotten—last she remembered looking at the clock had been two hours ago—seemed to have helped. She was able to think a little, at least. She picked up her phone and texted Greg.

Your aunt's here. She says everyone's still searching?

It was a moment before he answered, and she wondered where he was.

Yes. We're rotating now, so people can get some rest, but still searching.

Where are you? She would have asked about him getting some rest himself, but she knew he'd meant what he'd said about resting when the children were home safe.

Just finishing a grid search of the woods at the south end of the lake. Malcolm's taking a break to rest Pacer, then we're heading back out in a couple of hours.

Jen, who had come over to check on the status, said quietly, "I can handle the calls here for a bit. Why don't you both get some rest? Neither of you will do the kids any good if you're so exhausted you miss something."

"I wish he would, but he won't go home until the children are found."

Jen gave her a sideways look. "You still have a place here in town, don't you?"

Briony practically gaped at her. That told her more than anything could how tired she was—she'd never even thought of her little condo just a mile or so away.

Or it tells you how much you've come to think of the ranch as home.

That surprised her even more. Because it was true, she did think of it as home, despite her misgivings about living around so many people. She just hadn't had any experience with living around so many kind, helpful people. One of the kindest was standing beside her now, with yet another solution to a problem.

"Thank you, that's a great idea," she said, and started to type out a response.

"Take my advice," Jen said with a wry smile, "just tell him to meet you there, not why. No one more stubborn than a Colton man on a mission."

"I think I will always take your advice," Briony said, meaning it. And when she saw the pleased look on Greg's aunt's face, she was glad she'd said it.

She did take that advice. She'd get him inside, make him sit down while she did…something, and hope what had happened to her here at the desk would happen to him and he'd sleep a little despite himself. Maybe it would be easier because the children had never been there, so it wouldn't seem quite so…empty.

She was close enough and the coffee shop was open so she stopped and bought some things, knowing her kitchen at the condo was bare. When she got there and let herself in, it felt…strange. She'd lived here for nearly three years, been proud of her first real estate purchase, and yet she'd barely thought of it in the last three weeks. Hadn't even thought much about what she was going to do with it, because the kids sapped all her spare time and energy.

And oh, she wanted them back doing that again, wanted their noise, their needs, their silliness. And she wanted those moments with Greg when they both looked at them and then each other, exchanging in a glance the weary delight of parents everywhere.

Greg had only been here once, to help her pick up what she needed for the move to the ranch, but she had no doubt he'd find it again easily. And just ten minutes after she'd arrived, he was there. He greeted her with concern, clearly wondering why here, and she regretted adding to his worries when he looked so utterly dead on his feet. But she got him inside and sat him on the couch while she brought over a delicious-smelling pastry and a cup of thick, rich hot chocolate—the caffeine-laden coffee could come later—and he ate it quickly, his body probably demanding the nourishment while his brain was still busy elsewhere.

"I just thought we needed a few minutes of quiet, to think," she said as she sat beside him. "Especially you. You've been running at full speed for nearly twenty-four hours now."

"And you've called nearly the entire town," he said after he swallowed the last bite of fruit-filled decadence.

"With little results," she said wearily.

"You found more proof that it's likely Kraft," he pointed out. "Now we just have to figure out where he'd take them."

"I would have thought the compound."

"Me, too. But Acker was angry enough at him for vanishing that he let us in, and Pacer would have let Malcolm know if there was any trace of them anywhere."

"Then he could have taken them anywhere," she said, fear bubbling up anew.

What if he'd left the area, maybe even the state? How would they ever find them? The kids must be terrified by now. First, they lose their loving parents, then they have to move out of their home in a rush, they just get settled in at the ranch and now this, all in the space of three weeks? How could they possibly deal with that?

She tried to focus on the goal of coming here in the first place. She excused herself to use the bathroom. When she was done, she splashed cold water on her face, grimaced at her tired, bloodshot eyes, then ignored them because his were worse. She grabbed a towel to dry her face and hands and took her time about it. She tried to divert her mind by thinking about what to do with the place. Sell it, rent it out?

Finally, she tiptoed quietly back to the living room and found, to her relief, that it had worked. Greg was still sitting upright, but his head was back against the couch cushion and he was asleep. She watched him for a long time, feeling such a tangle of emotions she couldn't sort them out. Emotions she'd never expected to feel, rising out of things she'd never expected to have.

A husband and two children she loved with all her heart.

Chapter Thirty-Seven

Greg was stunned to realize he'd actually slept. And when he took the cup of very black coffee Briony held out to him, and got a good look at her face, he knew.

"You planned this, didn't you?" he said before taking the first sip, which had quite a kick.

"I accidentally slept a couple of hours back at the desk, and it made a world of difference. And I knew you had to be even more tired than I was, out there trekking around all over."

"And I need to get back at it." He felt guilty just having taken this couple of hours, when the kids were out there somewhere, no doubt scared, and maybe worse.

"I know," Briony said quietly.

He downed the caffeinated brew, hoping it hit hard and fast. He stood up, acknowledging he did feel a little better. Or at least ready to start again. He looked at the woman who'd thought to do this because she was worried about him.

He put down the now-empty cup and pulled her into his arms. Just a few seconds, he told himself. Just a few seconds and then he'd get moving. He held her close, and feeling the way she hugged him back made him feel like he could go on forever.

When his cell phone buzzed, had it been in any other circumstances, he would have delayed answering it to savor her closeness a little longer. It was strange; he'd never felt as if he had a big hole in his life until she had filled it. Only then had he realized how much he'd needed this.

Needed her.

The phone signaled again. He was still reluctant, but when he pulled it out and looked at the screen, the decision was made.

"Malcolm," he said. "He'd just text if it wasn't important."

Briony went still. He swiped to answer the call.

"Bro, I've got something." Malcolm's words came quickly, and he could sense the tension in his brother's voice. "East side, up at the end of the gravel road past the bank. Remember that old mobile home that's been parked up there forever?"

"Yeah?"

"We were out in the trees above it when Pacer went nuts. Breeze was coming up from there, so I stopped and watched. Didn't see anything, no movement, lights on, or anything, but he never settled. He's totally zeroed in on that place, and you know what that means."

Greg did indeed know what that meant. He had as much trust and faith in that dog as his brother did, because he'd seen all the times it had been Pacer who'd found the quarry, from injured hikers in the mountains to children lost in the woods. If Pacer signaled he'd found something, he had.

"You alone up there?"

"At the moment, yes. I called it in, but if you're still at the headquarters in town, you're the closest."

"On my way."

"Armed and ready?" his brother asked.

"Damned straight," Greg said, thinking there was nothing

he'd like better than to take out the person who'd grabbed the two kids who were now his own in all but blood.

He ended the call and looked at Briony, trying to decide how much to tell her. He didn't want to get her hopes up, only to have them dashed if the kids were no longer there.

"Malcolm's dog found something up in the hills above town. I'm going to help him check it out."

"Found what?"

"We don't know for sure yet, he just signaled on a place."

"I'm coming with you."

"Briony, just wait here. I'll let you know as soon as I do, I swear."

She shook her head. "I'm coming with you," she repeated.

"It may be nothing," Greg said, antsy to get moving.

"You're saying that dog would ever make a mistake?"

Pacer had, in fact, never made a mistake when it came to finding things connected to a scent he had cataloged in his brain. Greg remembered once when a hiker he'd found came to thank them, and Pacer had instantly reacted to the familiar scent of the woman.

But it wasn't Pacer he was worried about right now.

"Don't get your hopes up," he cautioned.

"Greg Colton, do you really think I don't know how to handle disappointment? I'm going, so quit wasting time."

He knew she was right. There was no more time to waste.

"We have to take my truck," he said, heading out at a run. Briony was on his heels. He passed on his usual chivalrous opening of the passenger door for her, since she was already there anyway.

"Where are they?" she asked as she slammed the truck door shut.

"Up behind the bank on Main and Cedar," he said as he started the truck and they began to move.

"But didn't the searchers already check all around there?"

"He's a lot farther up the hill than they'd reached yet. That's why Malcolm was up there."

He hesitated. Briony reached out and put a hand on his arm. "I can't tell you what it means to me that you want to protect me from whatever pain we might find. No one, except Wendy, has ever done that for me in my life. But for Wendy, I have to do this. Tell me the rest."

He took one hand off the wheel and put it over hers for a moment. Everything they'd become to each other since that awful night was in that touch. And he knew she was right. He went back to driving and answered her.

"There's a gravel road that's really overgrown, and it ends way up top where there's an old mobile home parked. That's where Pacer went wild on him."

"A mobile home?" Her voice went up a notch. "So they could be inside?"

"He hasn't seen any movement or signs it's occupied," he cautioned.

"It's practically the middle of the night—there wouldn't be, would there?"

"Maybe," he agreed cautiously. "Bri, if this is something, you have to stay here in the truck until we know it's safe."

"If the kids are there—"

"I mean it, Briony. If it is Kraft and he has them there, who knows what he might do. This could get dangerous, and I can't focus on getting the kids away from him—" he glanced at her again "—if I'm worried about you getting hurt."

When he said those last words, something flashed in her green eyes for a moment. But she only said, in a determined voice he'd come to know, "I'll stay out of the way, unless I can help. Or there's a chance to get the kids, one or both, out of there. There's two of them—there should be two of us."

He found he could not argue with that. But he still wasn't happy about the idea of her being in a possible line of fire.

"He could be armed," he said warningly as he turned his attention back to driving, silently glad there was virtually no traffic at this predawn hour.

"He probably is," she agreed, much more easily than he would have expected. Then she gave him a slightly crooked but definite smile. "Do you really think I didn't figure out why we had to take this rather than the car with the car seats?"

He gave her a sideways glance. "I told you, it's a rough road."

"So this has nothing to do with it?" She reached up to touch the stock of his rifle in the rack above their heads.

He looked back at the road, not sure how to answer. "That bother you?"

"Not if that's what it takes to get the children back safely."

"Good."

"Not saying I hope you have to shoot him to end this."

"But end it I will."

"I know."

There was something in her voice he hadn't heard before. They were nearing the turn now and he couldn't look at her, so he just spoke her name. The nickname she'd told him only Wendy had ever been allowed to use, before him.

"Bri?"

And then, in the darkness of his truck's cab, she said what neither of them had spoken aloud yet.

"I love you."

He felt as if his chest had taken a lot of blows today, but this was different from any of them. For a moment he simply couldn't breathe. The street was deserted so he risked a glance at her. She was staring down at her hands in her lap, a look half wondering, half scared on her face as she rubbed at her wedding ring.

And he somehow knew she'd never said that to a man in her entire life. He couldn't begin to tell her what that meant to him. Not now, anyway, because they were almost there. They'd reached the start of that gravel road, and for just a moment he stopped the truck. She looked up at him, and he reached out to cup her cheek. And admitted what he'd known for days now.

"I love you, too, Bri."

Her eyes widened, as if she truly hadn't expected him to say it. He saw in her expression a trace of the courage it had taken her to be the one to say it first, and regretted that he hadn't done it, to make it easier on her. He wanted to make her entire life easier from here on out. And as soon as Justin and Jane were back safely with them, he would set about doing that.

"Be careful, Greg. Please, please, be careful."

He heard what she wasn't really saying. That she wasn't worried only about him having to shoot Kraft, she was worried about him maybe getting hurt in the process.

And that gave him a feeling he would carry with him up this hill as if it were armor.

Chapter Thirty-Eight

She didn't regret telling him, and that surprised her. She'd expected to soon be wishing she'd never said those words, never admitted to him how deeply she'd fallen.

She had never expected him to say them back. Especially when she had to stack that up against her certain knowledge that Greg Colton did not lie.

He meant it. He really meant it. It wasn't just a reflex answer; she knew that by the way he'd taken a few seconds of their precious time and stopped, touched her cheek as he'd said it.

He loved her.

She felt a chill go through her when he stopped the truck, parking it across the gravel road, and realized he was doing it to block Kraft—she was ever more certain they were dealing with Rick's twisted, evil father—from escaping in a vehicle. She felt another chill when he reached for the rifle, apparently checking to be sure it was loaded, although she wondered why he had to, given it was his. But she also knew she knew nothing about weapons, so let it go.

He took out his phone, and a moment later was talking to his brother. He'd put his earbud back in, so she could only hear his side, but it told her enough.

"Blocked the road," he said, confirming her guess. "Any

change?" A moment of silence for her as he listened to Malcolm. "Got it. I'm going to move in closer from below." Another pause. "Yeah, slow and quiet from here on."

The call ended, and he looked at her as he spoke in a whisper. "No movement yet. But he got a call back from Fletcher. He's on his way, but also had some info. That place is owned by a member of Ever After."

She sucked in a quick gulp of air. "It's him," she said, her voice even quieter.

Greg nodded as he reached back and grabbed his cowboy hat. "Agreed. Question is, is he alone?"

She hadn't even thought of that. Another shiver went through her. "There's only one car parked up there," she said, "but that's not proof."

"Doesn't matter. We're getting them back, right now." Greg settled the hat on his head, and at her look said, "So Malcolm will know it's me from a distance."

"Oh." That made sense, even as it made her shiver even harder at the reason that was necessary.

She looked up the hill to where she could see the large, rectangular shape of the mobile home. Even in the faint light it looked worn and tired, with moss or water stains leaving darker patches against the lighter structure. It was a stark contrast to the expensive-looking car parked near the front end of the battered house trailer. The car without any license plates that she could see, at least from here. Maybe it was brand-new. That would fit.

"I can't imagine the father Rick and Wendy talked about in a place like that," she said. "Comfort and flash—like that car—were always his first priorities. Not necessarily in that order."

"I know," Greg said, and his tone was grim now. "If it's a sign of how off the rails he is…"

He didn't finish the thought as he opened the driver's door. He didn't need to. They were dealing with a grifter and a swindler, a kidnapper and…maybe a murderer. And that *maybe* was getting fainter and fainter as certainty began to replace it.

She wobbled a little as her feet hit the ground beside the truck. She met him in front, the heat from the motor radiating from the grille in the chilly air.

"He could really have been behind Rick and Wendy's crash," she whispered.

Greg only nodded. Then he looked at her. "Want to take back that hope?"

She knew he meant her hope that he didn't have to kill the man. "No. I don't want you to have to do it, but if it happens, I won't be sorry."

He leaned over and kissed her, quick, light, but full of promise. But then he went straight to instructions. "Stay right behind me. When we get closer, you stay behind the tree line while I move in. If you see any movement in the trailer, freeze, and text me."

Her brow furrowed. "Will you have time to look and see it's me?"

He gave her a crooked smile then. "I'll know." For an instant she wondered what it was, but then his gaze narrowed intently as he added, "And if I yell run, you run. And don't stop until you're down in town again. Then call my dad."

She blinked, but before she could react, he'd slung the rifle over his shoulder and they were moving, slowly, off to one side but definitely uphill. She kept close, but remained aware of staying behind and out of his way. She knew her job now was to be there just in case, for the kids, nothing more. This might not be Greg's bailiwick either, but he was

a lot more capable than she was of dealing with a dangerous man like Kraft.

But when he crept into the small clearing where the trailer
sat, she felt useless. Worse than useless. But she did her assigned task: she watched the mobile home, scanning it front
to back. From this closer vantage point, she could see just
how worn-out the thing was, that there were dents, dings,
taped-over broken windows, missing siding—

Broken windows. Including a big one on the end closest to her. The entire space appeared to be covered with a
sheet of heavy plastic duct-taped in place. She edged a little closer, mindful of Greg's words and staying among the
trees. Trees, she now noticed, that grew close enough to that
end with the missing window that branches were brushing
against the trailer.

She crept closer, with a slow care that she'd swear was
more tiring than running. The big cedar tree closest to
the mobile home was her target—the branches were thick
enough and low to the ground enough to easily hide in.
When she got there, she crouched down to slip under the
lowest branches that brushed the ground. It was a healthy
tree, with a lot of growth, so it was a little tricky, but she
made herself a spot that was barely a yard away from the
corner, and maybe four feet from that missing window. The
smell of the evergreen filled her nostrils, and she took a
deep breath just because the fresh, clean scent seemed to
clear her mind.

She waited, crouched down in her little space. And
waited, staring at that back window space, watching for
any kind of change in either light or shadow. And waited,
hearing only the rustle of the branches above in the very
slight breeze. Or was that Greg, moving quietly closer?

She didn't know how long she'd been there, but long

enough for her to want to change position. She didn't, not willing to risk even the tiny noise that might make. She stayed, crouched, barely breathing so she could hear— She smothered a gasp as a tiny sound came from the direction of that taped-over window.

A sound she recognized.

If you see any movement in the trailer, freeze, and text me.

Hearing counted, too, didn't it? She grabbed her phone and tapped out a message to Greg.

I heard Jane cry! Near the back. Big window broken.

She held her breath as she waited for an answer. Suddenly realized what would happen when he did and quickly muted all sound on her phone.

The wait was only about fifteen seconds but felt like fifteen minutes.

On my way.

Relief flooded her. Greg was on his way. To her, to them, and everything would be okay. And it didn't even bother her that she'd never had that kind of faith in a man in her life. Because she knew, down to her bones, that it was not misplaced. Not with this man.

She didn't hear him until he was only three feet away, and along with the little jump her heart gave—which seemed to happen often with him—she marveled at how such a big man moved so quietly. He put a finger to his lips to indicate not to speak, then edged closer to the plastic-sealed window. As he went, he pulled off the hat and dropped it on the ground so he could get closer, but he slid the sling of the rifle off his shoulder and held it across his chest. He stood with his back against the wall, his head turned slightly, clearly listening.

He stood there for a couple of minutes before he nodded back at her. She felt a rush of relief—she'd been right; he must have heard it as well. He edged back to her, moving with a slow care that told how he'd been so silent. He leaned in close to whisper to her, "I'm going in through that window. I'll hand them out to you. You take them and run, no matter what happens. All right?"

She knew he meant if Winston Kraft discovered him. The thought chilled her, but the kids... Justin and Jane had to take priority here. And their parents—for that's what they now were—would do whatever it took. Both of them. She reached up to touch Greg's cheek as she nodded yes.

He pulled his phone out and started tapping out a text message, a longer one. He held it out so she could see it, as if, she thought with no small amount of wonder, for her approval before he sent it.

They're here. Need a distraction at the front end of the trailer, near the car. Pacer howl on command?

She nodded, feeling a little breathless. He sent the text. The answer came back quickly.

Just listen for him. We're close. When?

Two minutes.

Copy. From now.

Briony stayed close behind him as he edged his way to the back of the mobile home. When they were up against the corner of the structure, he set down the rifle and slid the knife he always carried out of the sheath on his belt. She felt a jolt of fear. Was he going to take on Kraft with a knife? They didn't know for sure if Rick's father was armed, but it didn't seem safe to her to assume he wasn't. Then she saw him slide the blade up to the edge of the plastic, test it with a little cut, and realized it was to slice his way in.

Once more time seemed to have slowed, and no matter how she tried to calm herself, her pulse was racing. *If only the seconds would tick off as quickly.*

She quashed the old fears that tried to rise, that it would go wrong, she'd make a mistake, something bad would happen. It wouldn't. Her life had changed; she had two incredible children and this amazing, wonderful man had her back now. Determination flooded back, and she could almost feel her spine stiffen. They would do this, and when they did, she would never let those old fears sneak in again. She would be the woman Greg deserved to have, and—

The howls that broke the night's silence made her jump and sent a chill through her. They were close enough she heard a harsh, muttered oath from inside, then the sound of hurrying footsteps. Greg was already moving, slicing through the heavy plastic as if it were paper. He caught the lower frame and hoisted himself up in one smooth, powerful motion. Despite his size he made it through so quickly it amazed her, and how quietly he did it amazed her even more. He landed on the inside as if he were wearing sneakers instead of cowboy boots.

Pacer was still at it, punctuating the howls with chains of sharp, loud barking, sounding ferocious instead of like the sweet, caring rescue dog she knew he was. But beneath it all, she would almost swear she heard Justin cry out, "Unca Greg!"

The next thing she knew a wailing Jane was in her arms. She wanted to hold the little girl, to cuddle her and assure her she was safe, but then Justin was there, his little booted feet waving in the air as Greg got him clear of his make-shift prison.

"Briny!"

He reached out to her, and she pulled him against her with her right arm. She'd never tried carrying them both at once, but she'd do it now no matter what. She backed away from the trailer to give Greg plenty of room to jump out. Pacer kept up the racket, but suddenly there was a sound that topped even that.

A shot.

Greg's rifle was leaning against the wall below the window.

You take them and run, no matter what happens.

Briony was caught in a position she'd never been in, never expected to be in. She knew what she had to do, she'd given her word to the man she loved, but that man even now could be hurt, even die inside that run-down hulk. All the bad things she'd been through in her life dwindled to nothing beside the biggest fear she'd ever felt, that the precious, sweet life she'd finally found was going to vanish like everything else had—

No! She was not going there. She started downhill, keeping her word, holding on to the only two who could make her do it. But she couldn't stop the tears the fear for Greg drove out of her, nor could she focus on Justin's jabbering about what had happened or Jane's crying.

And then she heard the shout.

"Bri!"

She spun around, awkwardly off-balance with the weight of the two safe, unharmed children as she saw the man who had seen to that safety running toward them. Running, with those long, strong legs, so fast that he was there throwing his arms around them all before she could catch enough breath to even say his name.

"You're okay?"

They asked it simultaneously, and then echoed each other's relieved laugh that the answer was yes for both.

"Unca Greg punched him, that bad man!" Justin crowed.

"I heard a shot," Briony said, still a little breathless, as if there simply wasn't enough air.

"Along with everything else he sucks at, he's a lousy shot," Greg said, and suddenly the air was there.

She looked back toward the mobile home. "Is he—"

"Fletcher got here. He's in handcuffs now, where he belongs."

She stared at him. "And you still came out that window?"

He cupped her cheek, and she saw everything she could ever have wanted to see in his expression. "It was closer to you."

Then he leaned down to kiss both children on the forehead, assuring them they were safe now. And now Briony saw the other car parked behind his truck on the gravel road, and two more coming up behind them. The troops were here.

It was over.

Epilogue

"Don't thank me," Malcolm said. "I taught him to signal when he found something, but it was Seb Cross at Crosswinds who taught him to raise hell on command. I never would have thought of it."

Greg watched Justin and Jane playing with a delighted Pacer, and tilted his beer can toward his brother in grateful salute.

"You got all your people notified we have them back?"

Malcolm nodded. "I finally reached Ajay—that's Pumpkin's handler—and his group, so that's all the search teams."

Greg took a long sip of the cold brew. He didn't indulge that often, but this sure seemed like the day to do it. The kids were home safe, Briony was beside him and holding his other hand like she would never let go, and he was happier than he'd ever been.

They were gathered on the patio by the pool. Even Wade had appeared, albeit briefly since he was working today. Mama Jen had invited everybody who'd been on the search to come out to the ranch, to thank them all for their help, but that would be later.

Greg looked up when his father came out of the house. "Just got off the phone with Fletcher. He says Winston—" he used the name unfamiliar to the kids, who were within earshot "—has been booked for the kidnapping, and they think they have a link between him and the crash. They're investigating that, but he said with luck the guy will never get out."

"Is he talking?" Greg asked.

"Nope. Not about this, not about that so-called church or his connection to Acker. At least, not yet."

Greg had his doubts the man would ever crumble. In those moments in the mobile home, he'd looked into those dark, soulless eyes and known the man was everything Rick had ever said he was and worse.

But they would get to the bottom of this. Of all of it— what happened to Rick and Wendy, and the evil that was the cult Rick's father helped build. They would get to the truth because Coltons never quit.

His dad went over and, of course, sat next to Mama Jen. She reached out and squeezed his hand, and his father got that look on his face he only got around her. Someday, maybe, his secret wish would come true. After all, the wish for himself he'd never even dared voice had, hadn't it?

He turned to look at his wife, wondered if he looked as smitten as his father had. Didn't care, because it was true. And when Bri smiled back at him, a smile full of love, prom- ise and the future, he sent a silent toast to the friends he would never forget, along with a reaffirmation of his vow to see to their children.

"I think," Dad said, "we need to look into expanding that house of yours. You need at least another bedroom and bathroom. Maybe a playroom, too, for wintertime. And a fenced yard area."

"Been thinking about that," Greg admitted. "Maybe two more bathrooms." He had in mind a new main bath, with a big shower and a tub big enough for two. He'd suggested it to Briony, and just the look she gave him put the seal on that plan.

"Hey, we could build a fort out back," Malcolm put in cheerfully.

"That, too," he agreed.

Greg heard the sound of his father's phone and looked that way. Dad gave Mama Jen's hand a squeeze and got up, walking a few feet away on the patio. Greg looked back at Briony as she carefully watched Justin, who had developed an interest in the pool despite that it was a bit chilly for swimming.

"Going to need a fence, since there's open access from our place," Greg remarked. "We had one when we were little but haven't had any little ones around in so long I didn't think of it."

Briony smiled in a way that had him thinking she'd perhaps already had the thought but had been hesitant to say anything.

"Don't do that," he said gently. "Whatever it is, whatever it's about, you can say it, ask it, or if necessary, demand it."

The look she gave him then had him thinking about a quiet night to come and just how they might spend it.

His father turned around to face them. His expression had Greg on his feet in an instant.

"Dad. What is it?"

"Nobody can find Lizzy. And she's not answering her phone."

Jen got up swiftly. "She was searching for the children, too, wasn't she?"

Malcolm, also on his feet now, nodded. "I saw her right after we knew what had happened. She was all in."

Greg was glad he'd only taken a swallow of that beer. Because the Coltons were back on alert.

He looked at Briony, who met his gaze levelly, then looked at her father-in-law. "Where do we start?" she asked.

And despite the newly hatched worry about his sister, Greg knew that his wife was now and from now on thoroughly a Colton.

* * * * *

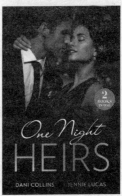

COMING SOON!

We really hope you enjoyed reading this book.
If you're looking for more romance
be sure to head to the shops when
new books are available on

Thursday 4th
July

To see which titles are coming soon, please visit
millsandboon.co.uk/nextmonth

MILLS & BOON

LET'S TALK

Romance

For exclusive extracts, competitions and special offers, find us online:

f MillsandBoon

𝕏 @MillsandBoon

⬡ @MillsandBoonUK

♪ @MillsandBoonUK

Get in touch on 01413 063 232

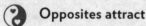

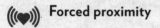

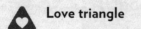